GRIP is the first novel by Michael Wills, MP, who writes under the name David McKeowen. A former diplomat, TV producer and director, Michael Wills has been MP for Swindon North since 1997.

GRIP

DAVID McKEOWEN

HODDER

Copyright © 2005 Michael Wills

First published in Great Britain in 2005 by Hodder and Stoughton
A division of Hodder Headline

The right of Michael Wills to be identified as the Author
of the Work has been asserted by him in accordance with the
Copyright, Designs and Patents Act 1988.

A Hodder Paperback

I

A CIP catalogue record for this title is available from the British Library

ISBN 0 340 75233 5

Typeset in Plantin Light by Palimpsest Book Production Limited,
Polmont, Stirlingshire

Printed and bound by Clays Ltd, St Ives plc

Hodder Headline's policy is to use papers that are natural,
renewable and recyclable products and made from wood grown in
sustainable forests. The logging and manufacturing processes are expected
to conform to the environmental regulations of the country of origin.

Hodder and Stoughton Ltd
A division of Hodder Headline
338 Euston Road
London NW1 3BH

for Jill

ACKNOWLEDGEMENTS

This book would never have been written without the steadfast faith and support of my agents Ann Evans and Jonathan Clowes. They know how much that means to me and I hope they think it was worth all the effort. I was undeservedly fortunate in my publisher Nick Sayers who transformed the manuscript with his patient, deft and imaginative editing. I am greatly in his debt. I am also grateful to Sara Walsh, Mary Loring and Louise Bloor, who all brought a keen, creative eye to bear on the text and improved it greatly. And my thanks also go to Judith Auld who put it all together so diligently. My children, Thomas, Joe, Sarah, Nicholas and Katherine, are owed an apology for my protracted absences from the family holidays during which so much of this book was written. The dedication is for the person to whom they and I owe most of all.

eight months earlier . . .

one

february 2000
The light was already failing in the early afternoon but there was just a suggestion of spring in the unseasonably warm, damp weather. A few crocuses were dotted around the muddy lawns and the mourners, mindful of their newly polished shoes, were careful to stay on the path as they made their way to the chapel.

Inside, the body lay in its mahogany, brass-handled casket, lined with maroon velvet. No-one had been able to agree on the music so there was none, and the short obsequies were spoken into a stiff, cold silence. From somewhere, a scent of geranium and lime-flowers drifted on the dank air.

Never again. A river running bright with possibilities now suddenly dry.

Then, as the bones and flesh burned behind the curtains, mourners filed out into the pale afternoon. The ceremony over, the formal procession eased into sociable circulation as they came through the doorway. A young man laughed as he gestured to three other men standing around him and the girl on his arm. Two older men, grey-haired, hands thrust in their overcoats, conferred earnestly while their wives stood

I

slightly apart and chatted amiably together. Shortly afterwards, a woman emerged from the chapel on her own and paused by the doorway to brush away a tear, and the trace of wetness was a transfer of grief on her cheek.

The little congregation began to break up and move off towards their cars. As they did so, a man appeared in the doorway to usher a new group of mourners into the chapel. The furnace was once again ready behind the curtains. It had finished with the mahogany casket and its contents and the ashes were now waiting to be collected round the back.

two

tuesday 6.30 a.m.

At half past six on the morning of his birthday, James was woken by voices in the kitchen. Sushila and Mark were arguing about something in the newspaper as they got ready for work. The Vengaboys were on the radio. 'Boom, boom, boom, boom,' they went as Mark did up his tie and Sushila polished her shoes. James still found it unsettling to see them in suits. A year ago, he thought drowsily, none of them had got up until the afternoon and now Sushila was putting on the jacket of her little black suit as the sun rose. It was disconcerting. A year ago, she had not worn knickers. 'Boom, boom, boom, boom,' sang the Vengaboys on the radio. He was twenty-three today.

Twenty-three. How had their ocean of possibilities crystallised down to these jobs and this shrinking ambition and this daily struggle? Now Sushila and Mark had a common language with a vocabulary of offices and prospects and rivalries and salaries. Miranda, with whom he shared a room at Prendergast's, would have been at home round this breakfast table. But James was not. Whenever he heard them talking like this, he was chilled by foreboding. He went back to bed.

When he woke again, it was seven thirty. Sushila and Mark had left for work and the flat was quiet but someone was shouting in the street outside. They sounded cross. A car horn blared. There was more shouting.

James opened his eyes and stared at the ceiling. The curtains stirred in the early morning breeze.

Chris would be here soon.

three

Virginia carefully positioned the twenty-third candle in the cake. There. Twenty-three years of her baby's life in strawberry pink. She hoped James would not think the cake was meant seriously.

'Julie,' she called. 'Could you put those flowers in the sink in a vase and bring them here.'

There were going to be twenty-three items at his birthday dinner, one for each year of his life, and the project had stretched her ingenuity for weeks as she combed through old photograph albums for inspiration. But finally Virginia reached twenty-three and now the table was crowded with allusion and resonance – satsumas from every Christmas stocking, Smarties he had picked off his fifth birthday cake, quiche he had refused to eat when he was nine, and Rice Krispies from the breakfast in bed she had served for him and that blonde girl, the first time he had had someone stay the night. And then there was the Liebfraumilch that had made him sick when he was thirteen.

'Here you go,' Julie said. 'Where do you want them?'

As she came into the living room, there was a

7

sudden resemblance between the two women. The warmth of the early morning sun caught the high cheekbones and dancing eyes they shared and they could almost have been sisters.

'If you are going to steal chocolate,' Virginia said, 'you shouldn't leave the evidence all round your mouth.'

Julie laughed and wiped her mouth with the back of her hand. Tiny and with her blonde hair in an elfin bob, she looked as if she had just left school. Only the fine lines round her eyes suggested otherwise. 'Now, where do you want them?' she said.

'Over there,' Virginia said. 'What do you think?' As she spoke she looked quickly at her watch. There was just time to salt the almonds and submerse the chicken in its apricot marinade before she had to leave for school.

'Lovely,' Julie said. 'I can't believe he's twenty-three. They grow up so quick.'

'But you never stop worrying about them,' Virginia said.

Julie looked at her sympathetically. 'It's hard, isn't it,' she said, 'when it's your only one. And they are so unpredictable. Two is different. You know where you are with two. The older one is always trying to please you and the younger one will never do anything you say.'

'Rubbish,' Virginia said. 'Everyone's different.'

'No, it's true,' Julie said. 'Look at Courtney and Nicole.'

'Come on, Julie.'

'What do you mean "come on"? They are just like that.'

'I mean firstly they are three years old.'

'Nearly four.'

'And secondly, Courtney is twenty minutes older than Nicole. What does that prove?'

'You can see it. Nicole is going to be a rebel.' Julie opened her arms for emphasis. 'You can just see it.' As she punctuated the point with her hands, she caught a photograph on the table. 'Whoops,' she said. 'Sorry.'

Virginia bent to pick it up and placed it carefully back on the table. James was turning into a handsome young man. He was beginning to look like Francis.

'Your girls are lovely,' Virginia said. 'And so is my James. They are all our babies. Always.' She hoped James was going to enjoy this evening. He was so polite when they were all together it was often hard to work out what was really going on in his head.

'I'm off now,' Julie said. 'I've got to take the girls to school.'

'Where's Lisa?'

'In bed. The lazy cow.'

'You spoil that daughter of yours.'

'That's what mothers are for. Anyway, I love taking them. I pretend they're mine.'

'They are.'

'Not the same. But it's lovely being a grandma. No worries.'

Virginia put the champagne in the fridge. She

hoped Francis might unbend enough to drink. At least she had made sure Alex was not going to be there. He would only have complicated the evening. 'Can you come back later and give it all a good hoover?' Virginia said. She scooped up some of the marinade with her little finger and licked it. They ought to enjoy themselves. It was delicious.

'Virginia,' Julie said. 'I hope you don't mind me asking, but can you pay me the four weeks you owe?'

'OK. I'll leave it in an envelope for you on Thursday.'

Julie looked at the floor. 'Would it be all right if you paid me now?'

'Are you in trouble?'

'Me?' Julie laughed. 'I am always in trouble. No, it's the twins' birthday on Saturday and I promised Lisa I'd get them a Barbie dress each. They're on offer at Woolworths and I'm worried if I don't get them today they will all go.'

'Why are you wasting your money on that rubbish?' Virginia said.

'It's what they want,' Julie said. 'And I need the money. It's forty-five pounds for the two and I don't get my benefit until next week. Please, Virginia.'

'OK,' Virginia relented. 'I'll go to the cash-machine on the way home. Come by tonight to pick it up. Before eight. Now, how do I look?'

'Lovely. Francis will see what he's missing. And Rachel will be jealous. Perfect.'

'Thank you. You will give it a good going-over, won't you?'

'Don't worry,' Julie said as she went, closing the door behind her.

Virginia inspected the table. It glowed with love. Surely James would feel that. Everything on it was a memory. And every one was precious. Virginia could still feel James in her arms, five minutes old, warm and soft in the delivery room.

four

tuesday 8.15 a.m.
The baby nestled in her arms, the tiny perfect hand clasping itself instinctively round Francis's little finger. She lay in a pethidine daze feeling the warmth of her child. The tearing pain had faded, the infant's first seconds of screaming had given way to peaceful sleep and there was an exhausted joyous calm in the delivery room. Through her drowsiness, Rachel could feel Francis gently stroking her hair. The miracle of birth had awed the room into hushed reverence.

New life.

If only.

A hundred and forty-seven loving, diligent, careful acts of sexual congress and not one out of eighty billion sperm conscientiously ejaculated by Francis had managed to wriggle its way up to fertilise one of Rachel's eggs. Not one.

Which was why she now waited fretfully in the polished calm of Harley Street, in the immaculate waiting room, with its expensive wallpaper and huge centrepiece of lilies on the table, and a longcase clock ticking gravely in the corner.

Sometimes longing came rolling over her like the

Atlantic. A baby. Oh how she wanted Francis's baby. And sometimes she could see, in the brilliant colours of a dream, another life. With Francis. And their baby. And no-one else. Rachel paced up and down beside the window and thought about escape.

Once Virginia had taken them and James out for supper. And when James had gone to the bathroom, Virginia had asked Francis for more money so James could go on holiday to Los Angeles. And Francis had felt for Rachel's hand under the table and stroked it gently with his thumb as he spoke to Virginia, showing her he understood how Virginia and her demands made Rachel feel. And Rachel knew, she just knew, there was a life where they could escape from all of that and be happy.

But the months passed and she had still not found how to get them away.

And now here she was in this Harley Street waiting room. And this was still her life. Worry and struggle. With Virginia and her grip on Francis. And James and his constant demands. And no baby.

Dark, small, smoothed into her neat black suit, Rachel checked her watch again. The man was now twenty minutes late. Why did doctors always think they were the only ones whose time was precious? It was bad enough that a stranger was going to trawl through the precious intimacy of her life with Francis, but his lateness was now giving her time to remind herself just how difficult she was going to find it.

And where was Francis? His breakfast meeting

should have finished half an hour ago. She needed him here.

Rachel opened the door of the waiting room and walked over to the receptionist, sitting behind another smaller bowl of white lilies, in a lilac suit, writing carefully in a ledger.

'Excuse me,' Rachel said. 'My appointment was for eight o'clock.'

The receptionist looked up.

'Weren't we expecting Mr Carroll as well?' she asked.

'He was meant to be here at eight o'clock,' Rachel replied. 'Like the doctor.'

She had told her managing partner she had a doctor's appointment this morning but she knew too many hours out of the office would count against her, no matter how good the reason. They were going to make three new partners at Rother & Fenwick in September and she deserved to be one of them – her work was first class, Brendan had said so at her last work review. But she also knew that the partners needed to feel they could rely on her.

'The doctor is here, Mrs Carroll,' said the receptionist, 'but he is busy. He will be with you as soon as possible.'

'And when might that be?' asked Rachel.

The woman in the lilac suit stared at her. 'As soon as possible, Mrs Carroll. He is just tied up at the moment.'

'Please could you un-tie him. I am afraid I cannot wait all day. The appointment was for eight o'clock.'

'If you would just take a seat in the waiting room, Mrs Carroll. The doctor will be with you as soon as possible. Would you like to wait for Mr Carroll?'

Rachel looked at her. Good point. Where on earth was Mr Carroll? Did she want to wait for him?

'No, I would not,' she said to the receptionist. 'It's up to Mr Carroll whether he wants to turn up or not. But I would like to see the doctor. As soon as possible. Please.'

Rachel walked over to the window to see if Francis was coming up the street. No sign of him. Outside, the traffic crawled by but double glazing kept the waiting room in sepulchral silence, punctuated only by the ticking of the clock in the corner. She really had to get back to the office.

And she really needed Francis here, now, holding her hand, stroking it gently while she waited. She needed him to soothe away these tense, tangled feelings of anxiety and embarrassment.

Where was he? She rang his number on her mobile phone. And went straight through to his voicemail. 'Where are you, Francis?' she said. 'It's nearly half past eight.'

Where was he?

five

Francis was having difficulty with his breakfast. The bean curd, smothered in a film of dark brown sauce, would not stay within the chopsticks. If he held it delicately to preserve the tremulous shape, it slithered between them. But if he gripped it more tightly, the chopsticks sliced through it and were left holding nothing.

Philippe was not paying any attention to Francis's problems. He carted rice into his mouth with lascivious gusto while he talked about his flight from New York. 'She was gorgeous,' he said. 'And I got her number. And I am going to call her this afternoon.' He looked up from his bowl and grinned goatishly at Francis. His English was fluent and barely accented. He spooned some more sea-spice prawns onto his bowl of rice. 'This is good,' Philippe said. 'Just what I wanted.'

As the great city around it began to stir, the Chinese restaurant, tucked away at the end of the alleyway, was alive with conversation and the clatter of plates. Open twenty-four hours a day, it was currently offering last suppers and breakfast to the unearthly

16

inhabitants of the early morning. Outside, the mechanised sweepers brushed Soho clean of the night's detritus and the first light of the sun softened the empty streets with a pale golden glow.

'I tell you, Francis, she was really gorgeous,' Philippe said again. He sat hunched over his bowl, with his jacket draped over the back of his chair, the top button of his shirt undone and his tie loosened so it dangled down over his prosperous belly. He felt good. He had just showered at the hotel after a swift run in from the airport. And he was refreshed and hungry and the food was good. And it was a glorious new day in London, a city he always liked. Philippe was suffused with well-being. He wanted to share it with Francis. 'You know what they are like when they are nineteen. They bloom,' Philippe said and then he shovelled more rice into his mouth.

From the back of the room came staccato clicks and clacks as Chinatown waiters played dominoes, drinking tea, getting ready for the day shift. At the big round table in the centre, Francis thought he recognised a man in a cream linen suit from a film he had seen with Rachel. He was holding pharmaceutically wired court with two other young men, and five slender women with huge eyes and shimmering dresses, still high from the departing night. A dumpy middle-aged Chinese woman in spectacles and a grubby brocaded tunic stomped between the tables, pouring tea and depositing steaming plates of food.

Francis looked surreptitiously at his watch. This breakfast was growing into a problem. He was now going to be seriously late for Rachel. He hated upsetting her and she would be fretful about where he was. Her hands would be clasped together in that way she had. He could see it. The hands tightly clasped together while the thumbs circled each other, round and round. To a casual observer she would appear poised and calm. But he knew where to look. At those sweet chubby thumbs. How would he be able to make it up to her?

'You know, Francis, sometimes it's just the time and place. It's just a shared moment which you know will never work again in the same way. It's just special for that time, that place.' Philippe looked at him, inviting him, as another experienced player in the game of love, to participate in this colloquium. In the smoky early morning light his features had the demure bloom of soft fruit and the sexual allure of bean curd. As he remembered the girl on the plane, he leant forward towards Francis and his hands emphasised his words as if weighing up two luscious cantaloupes. 'It was a spark, Francis,' he said. 'It was a real spark.'

As Francis listened to him, he realised with an awful sense of inevitability that the number this girl had given Philippe, if indeed there was such a girl and such a number, was probably invented and passed across to halt Philippe's persistent and unwelcome wooing. Why else would a young and beautiful girl give her number to him?

'She sounds great,' he said sympathetically. 'I hope it works out.' He really had to leave and meet Rachel. He had better do it now.

six

The packet sat on the kitchen table. They looked at it.

'There it is,' Chris said.

It was oblong, about the size of a dictionary, wrapped in purple paper with a label displaying a neon-blue sign, rather like a distorted bishop's mitre superimposed on a background of dark, starry night.

'Thirty grand,' Chris said. 'Please.'

James stared at it.

'Why don't you take a look?' said Chris.

James warily unfolded the purple paper. Sitting neatly inside were fifty small polythene packets each with a tiny version of the starry-night label and its neon-blue logo. He could see the white crystalline powder glittering behind the polythene. This was what thirty grand looked like.

'Go on,' Chris said and smiled at him. 'Don't you want to check it out?'

'It's OK,' James said. 'I trust you.'

'Don't you think you should check it?' Chris smiled at him again. 'Just to be sure?' James felt uneasily that Chris might be mocking him.

The doorbell rang. The noise tore through the still air of the small flat.

'Who's that?' Chris said. It was time for him to go. He had done his job.

'I don't know.'

The bell rang again.

'Are you expecting anyone?' Chris was whispering now.

'No,' James whispered back.

Again the bell rang. And again.

'Are you sure?' Chris hissed. He did not need this. He had done his job.

James looked at him. Was he sure? 'I think so,' he said. He could smell something unusual. What was it? Geraniums. And lime.

The bell rang again.

'What's going on?' James said.

'Fuck,' Chris said. 'It's the police.' He had delivered. It was now down to this chicken-scratcher. Whatever happened now, he owed the thirty grand. It was time to go.

'Why should it be the police?'

'How the fuck should I know?' Chris definitely did not need this. 'I'm out of here.'

'But what should I do?' James whispered.

And then someone started hammering on the door.

Fuck it. 'Get a knife,' Chris said. He could not get out now they were outside the door.

'What for?'

'What do you mean "what for"?' Chris hissed at him.

'You're not going to use it, are you?' James said.

Chris looked at him. Was he mad? 'Yes, I am going to use it,' he said. 'Get the fucking knife.'

'What are you going to do?' James said. Was he mad?

Chris looked at him. Who was this schoolboy? 'We have got to get rid of it,' he said. 'Can't risk it. Now get the fucking knife. And where's the toilet?'

James pointed to the bathroom.

'Get the knife,' Chris said. 'Now.'

The hammering started again.

'Now,' Chris said.

James sliced and Chris emptied. And a small pile of scrunched-up polythene grew rapidly at their feet in the bathroom as James opened the tiny packets with his kitchen knife and Chris sprinkled them into the bowl. Outside, in the hallway of the small flat, they could hear the bell again.

'That's enough. Flush it,' Chris said. 'That's half of it. Get rid of it. Now. Go on. Now. We'll flush the packets last. There's only traces on them.'

They stopped to watch the white powder swirl around the bowl and disappear.

This time someone kept their finger on the bell.

'Come on,' Chris said. 'Keep cutting.'

The white powder covered the surface of the water in the bowl once more. James could see it beginning to congeal into lumpy white paste.

'Come on,' Chris said. 'Just open the fucking bags.'

The banging started again.

'Flush it quick,' Chris said. 'Now. Now.'

And then they heard a voice. 'James,' it called. 'James. Open the door, will you.'

'Who the fuck is that?' Chris hissed.

It was Sushila. 'James, I know you're there. Open the door,' she called.

'It's my flatmate,' James said. Chris looked at him. Then they both stared at the bowl. Neither of them said anything. A small lump of white powder had survived the flush and swirled disconsolately round in the bowl.

'I'd better open the door,' James said finally.

Chris said nothing, unable to take his eyes away from the small lump of white powder in the bowl.

As James opened the door, Sushila brushed past him into the room.

'Forgot my keys,' she said as she went into her bedroom.

'Why didn't you answer the door?' she said as she came back into the living room. 'If that guy downstairs had not let me in I would have still been stuck outside.' She glanced towards the bathroom. The door was ajar and Chris could be glimpsed inside. He did not appear to have moved. 'Who's that?'

'Just a friend,' James mumbled.

'OK. I've got to rush. I'm going to be so late – thanks to you.' She looked at herself in the mirror and adjusted her hair. 'Bye-bye,' she said. Over her shoulder, James could see Chris still immobile in the bathroom.

'Oh, I nearly forgot,' she called as she shut the door behind her. 'Happy birthday.'

'That's thirty grand you owe me,' Chris said, coming out of the bathroom. 'By Friday.' He looked at James. 'Is it your birthday?' he asked.

seven

tuesday 8.25 a.m.

Other people fuck things up. That was the considered opinion of Roger Oates. Based on long experience. Things fuck up and it is other people who fuck them up. There was never any good reason why they did this, as far as Roger could see. They just did it. And, even more remarkable to Roger's way of thinking, this was not an unfortunate accident. These people chose to do it. Even when they were presented with a cornucopia of choices and they could choose any one they liked – *any one* – it was remarkable how often other people would pick the one, the only one, that fucked things up.

Roger Oates inspected his cuticles, stretching out his fingers. First the left hand. Then the right hand. He picked at a loose piece of skin on his little finger. It was not turning into a good day. Of course, he recognised this part of the job was unavoidable – he had to share the responsibility for maintaining the integrity of the brand. But he never enjoyed it very much and today he had a lot of other things to do as well and this was the other side of London and anyway, this part of the job was mainly down to his partners.

But he was expected to be supportive. And so, irritatingly, he had to be here, dealing with the consequences of Jason choosing to fuck things up. Jason did not have to have done what he did. He just chose to do it. And now he was taking up a good part of Roger's morning.

Jason was tied to a chair, a wad of fabric stuffed into his mouth and held in place by strong adhesive tape wound round his head. His arms and legs were strapped to the chair. There was a sour smell in the small, windowless room. The young man had been unable to control his terror. He could not have been more than eighteen, the same age as Samantha's boyfriend. To Roger's way of thinking, that was the bad thing about daughters. You bring them up like princesses. Then one day they bring home a toerag like this. Or Samantha's boyfriend.

Roger did not know two of the men. They looked like brothers or cousins, bodybuilders who spent most of the day in the gym, with broad, muscular shoulders straining against expensive suits. Neither of them spoke. They had strapped the young man to the chair and gagged him. The third man was Phil Crask. Roger had done business with him for years. Phil was in charge here. This is what happened to thieves. It had to be done. Otherwise you could not stay credible. This is what had to happen.

'You've been a bad boy, Jason. You know that, don't you?' Phil Crask looked at the terrified young man strapped to the chair. An answer was clearly expected.

The boy nodded.

'You were told when you started work the one thing you do not do – not once, not ever – is steal. Not *once*, not *ever*.' He repeated the words slowly. He had a strong South London accent.

Roger would have preferred not to be there, he had other things to do. But he knew it was expected of him. It was business. And it had to be done.

'You can lose things. We understand that. Everyone loses things sometimes.' Phil quietened his voice. It was more menacing. He enjoyed the performance. 'But the one thing you don't ever do is *steal*. You do not take the product. That's not careless. That's wrong.' Phil was a couple of years younger than Roger and the middle one of the five Crask brothers. He nodded towards Roger. 'If you thought you could rip him off because he wasn't one of us, that was a mistake, Jason. If you thought that what I said didn't apply to him, that was a bad mistake, Jason. It was worse than a mistake, Jason. It was wrong.'

The young man's eyes pleaded with Roger as if Roger was different. Roger watched the eyes begging him. He saw Jason thinking that if Roger had got him brought to this room, he could get him out again, stop it all happening, that somehow Roger was different enough not to want it to happen.

Roger looked at him blankly as his mind turned it over. Jason had not done this on his own. He was not bright enough. Chris was involved in some way. He would have to find a way to deal with him as well. But in the meantime this might send a message.

'He's our friend,' Phil said, nodding back towards

26

Roger but keeping his eyes on the young man in the chair. 'He deserves respect. Anyone who does business with us gets our guarantee. They don't get ripped off. You were told.'

Phil moved closer to the young man and put his face very near to his. 'I think the Arabs have got the right idea, don't you, Jason? They chop it off.' Phil smiled with his mouth. 'Get up.'

The two other men moved forward. One of them took out a knife.

'Don't worry,' Phil Crask said. 'It's not going to be your prick, Jason. Not this time.'

The man with the knife cut the straps that held Jason's arms behind the chair and then bent down to cut the straps around his ankles.

'Get up,' Phil said. Jason did not move. He stared terrified at Phil Crask. 'Get up now,' Phil said.

Jason stood up unsteadily.

'Back up against the wall,' said Phil Crask.

Jason took two steps backwards until he was standing against the wall.

'Tools,' Phil said.

One of the men opened a black leather briefcase and took out a hammer and two very long thin nails. He handed them to Phil Crask.

Jason made a noise through the gag. It sounded as if he was pleading. He was still looking at Roger. Roger looked back at him.

Phil stepped forward. He took Jason's left ear and held it out at right angles to his head. Then he took a nail, and with one smooth movement hammered it through Jason's ear into the wall. Then he repeated the action with Jason's right ear. Then he handed the hammer and nails back to one of the men who put them back into the briefcase.

Jason had obviously been too shocked to make any noise as the nails went in. Now he began to whimper and tears began to run down his cheeks.

'I would stand very still, if I were you,' Phil Crask said to Jason. 'It will hurt less.'

Jason seemed to shrink against the wall.

'We will be back for you in two days,' Phil said to Jason. 'I hope you spend the time usefully. Think about the wrong you done. And think about how you are never, ever, going to do it again. Because next time, it won't be your ears that get nailed to the wall . . .' Phil Crask stared at Jason '. . . it will be your fucking balls. Understand?'

Phil clearly expected an answer. Jason looked as if he was about to nod. Then he remembered. He moved his eyes.

'I will take that as "yes",' Phil Crask said to Jason. 'Tie him up.' One of the men stepped forward and put the straps round Jason's ankles again, and then tied his hands together in front of him.

'And just in case you think it might be worth tearing your ears off the wall,' Phil said to Jason, 'the door will be locked and there will be someone upstairs. So I would not even think about it. If I were you.'

Jason stared at him soundlessly, petrified.

'It will get worse as the hours go by,' Phil Crask said to Jason in a kindly tone. 'You will want to move.

More and more you will want to move. You will be desperate. Everyone says you get really desperate. But then you will ask yourself: do I really want to tear my ears off? And you will probably decide that you do not. Probably. Not everyone comes to that conclusion at the time. They usually do later. But it's up to you, Jason. And so the time will pass. But – a word of advice – it will be much easier for you if you spend the time not thinking about how badly you want to move but about what a bad mistake you made and how you are never ever going to make that mistake again. I would take that advice if I were you, Jason. But it's up to you. We will be back in two days.'

Phil Crask looked at Roger. 'I don't think he will rip you off again,' he said.

eight

'How am I going to find thirty thousand pounds?'

'Not my problem.'

'But I don't have thirty thousand pounds.'

'You'd better find it. By Friday.'

'But you told me to get rid of it. You threw it all away. Why do I have to pay for it?'

Chris looked at him. Was this chicken-scratcher mad?

'Listen up my brother.' Chris spoke very clearly and distinctly so James could understand. 'You took delivery. You owe me thirty grand. By Friday.'

'But I was going to get the money by selling it. How am I going to get it now?'

James's mind skittered. Chris had made it clear he was going to have to find the money. But how? Could he possibly ask his father for thirty thousand pounds? For this?

'That is your problem, man.'

Perhaps he could ask him tonight. But it was quite a lot of money for a birthday present.

'And you better get that thirty grand by Friday. Roger likes prompt payers.'

'Who's Roger?'

'Don't find out.'

What could he say if his father asked him why he needed so much money? But at least his father would have the money. Unlike him. James might have to find a way to persuade his father to part with it, but at least he would have the cash.

'By Friday,' Chris repeated.

nine

'Have you thought any more about the proposition?' Francis asked.

'Yes, yes, the proposition,' Philippe said. 'InterTrust. Great name, Francis. How's it going?'

'Making progress. We're close to tying up Jones & Oliver.'

'Good, good. Here, have some of this. It is really delicious.' Philippe pushed a bowl of prawns towards Francis.

How could Philippe think he was still hungry? He was going to be so late for Rachel. On the way over to Harley Street he would get her something to say sorry.

Francis looked at the deep purple orchid in a small glass in the middle of the table. It was beautiful. It would do.

'Go on, Francis,' Philippe said. 'Try it.'

Five vigorous generations of entrepreneurs had created this round, amorous, world traveller, one generation after the other reinforcing the driving gene for accumulation, ranging out from the gentle wooded hills of eastern France to build ironworks and textile mills and portfolios of railway stocks and South African bonds and then a private bank and holdings in software developers, supermarkets and oil.

And now, the genetic raw material buffed and finished by Harvard Business School, Philippe sat on the board of the investment trust which minded the family money. And invested in entrepreneurs like Francis and start-ups like InterTrust.

And so no matter how tiring Francis found the early morning rendezvous, no matter how tedious the maundering chatter about women, no matter how galling the patronising assumption he would always be free whenever Philippe flew in, Francis always made himself available. Now and whenever Philippe called.

'Go on,' Philippe said again.

'No thank you,' Francis said as calmly as he could.

Philippe pulled the bowl back towards him. 'Well, if you are sure,' he said. 'But I will have some more. It is so good.' And he scooped up some more rice on his chopsticks.

Francis breathed in the herbal fumes of the tea. The sun was beginning to filter into the room. It was going to be a lovely day.

It was all worked out. InterTrust needed five million to get through the next year and into the flotation. The cash-flow projections and the start-up costs sat stacked up in the spreadsheet waiting to be called into action. And all it needed to be brought springing into life was five million. From Philippe. Who was still eating. And keeping him waiting. And making Rachel's thumbs revolve round and round each other.

Francis looked at the little glass bowl and the orchid. It was beautiful. He reached out and inched it towards him. It was such an intense purple. Rachel would love it.

Philippe shovelled another prawn into his mouth.

Francis gently stroked the orchid between his forefinger and thumb.

It was plastic.

Where was he going to find something for Rachel at this time of the morning?

'Have you thought any more about coming in with us?' he asked.

Philippe looked up from his bowl and fixed Francis in the eye. It was obviously something they taught at Harvard. 'How much are you putting in yourself?' he asked.

'Two hundred and fifty thousand,' Francis said. Philippe did not react. He looked at Francis for a moment, considering. Then he looked back at his bowl. He said nothing. Francis could not tell whether Philippe thought two hundred and fifty thousand was enough. Or not.

It might not sound very much to Philippe but Francis had remortgaged the house to get that money. And, on top of the mortgage he had already taken out to buy the house, it had cleaned him out. There was nothing left. Not even for a holiday this year unless Rachel became a partner. And if he lost that money, he lost his house. Everything. Investors expected him to put in enough to care about losing it. And he would. He really would.

'More rice,' Philippe called to the matron in the brocade tunic who continued doggedly clearing the table next to them.

Philippe had to come in now. In four months Francis would be the age his father had been when he lost his job. And sold their house. The day they had moved out, his father had gone to Manchester for a job interview. Looking back, Francis wondered if it had just been an excuse so his father could avoid the humiliation. Fourteen-year-old Francis had helped the removal men carry the crates out to the van while his mother made them tea. And as he walked back again and again into the empty, desolate house that had once been his home, all he wanted to do was curl up on his bare bed and sob. But he knew he had to be strong and support his mother. So he just went on helping the removal men carry the crates out to the van. Back and forth while his fourteen-year-old heart was breaking. Francis was not going to end up like his father.

'More rice. Over here,' Philippe called, waving his hand.

Francis sipped his tea and looked at Philippe. He was going to be really late for Rachel. Come on, Philippe. Everything is in place and waiting to go. It just needs five million from you. Now.

The phone had rung at half past ten last night when they had already gone to bed. 'Don't answer it,' Rachel said. But Francis answered every call. You never knew who it would be.

It had been Philippe.

'Francis,' he'd said, 'I'm just leaving JFK. I'll be at Heathrow at five thirty your time. Meet me at the Jade Dragon at six thirty. You know the one. Be there.'

'He's jerking you around,' Rachel said.

She was probably right. But she still had time to get it wrong. Francis did not. She was thirty-one, and he was forty-five. If one thing did not work for her, something else would. Sooner or later. It was not like that when you were forty-five. He could not take the risk.

Philippe patted his mouth with a paper napkin. 'Remind me of the turnover projections for years one and two,' he said. And Philippe nodded sagely as Francis ran through the figures again for him. And at the round table, the film star in the linen suit, his arm draped around the most beautiful of the young women, was laughing. There was a large mirror at the back of the room and Francis could see them reflected in it, an image of unthinking, confident youth.

'Interesting,' Philippe said. 'Interesting.' It was what he always said. The bean curd sat congealing in a dark brown mound on the plate in front of Francis.

InterTrust was more than interesting. It was part of the revolution. The Internet was creating a new economy, new ways of doing things, weightless wealth. And as it laid waste to the old world, new opportunities were rising from the ashes. And Francis had spotted one. InterTrust. A great idea. Everyone said so. And the more he thought about it, the better it became. And this was the time to go with it. All around him, he saw real money gushing from other Internet businesses. As fast as the Internet had come from nowhere, so too were the fortunes being made instantaneously. All around him. Other people's fortunes, based on other companies coming to market. Now.

'Remind me, Francis. What do you still need?'

'Five million,' Francis said. 'I emailed you the break-down last month.' As you know, he thought. As you know only too well. One day, he thought, I will be done with all this. InterTrust will have floated and I will have my fuck-you money. And then fuck you, Philippe, and your dawn meetings in Chinese restau-rants and your sexual fantasies and your rich-boy questions. Which you ask over and over again, just to jerk me around. Then it will be goodbye, Philippe. But first, just give me the money.

'I am thinking of putting in three or four.' Philippe sipped his tea. 'I have talked to my directors. They are happy in principle but they need reassurance, just a little bit more. This technology, it's a little bit of a problem for some of them. They do not understand it.' He wiped his mouth with the back of his hand. 'That was good,' he said. 'Really good.'

The waitress was stomping towards the table. Francis put his hand up and waggled it to indicate he wanted the bill.

'I'll get this,' he said to Philippe.

The waitress ignored Francis and stomped past their table over to the film star.

'No, no,' Philippe said, 'I insist. I'll get it. And

anyway, we've not finished yet. We can't leave such delicious food here.'

Francis watched the waitress painstakingly carrying away the plates from the film-star's table towards the kitchen. How was he going to make this up to Rachel?

'I tell them this is iron and steel in the eighteenth century,' Philippe said. 'Railways in the nineteenth century and the motorcar in the twentieth century,' he said. 'But you know what the difference is? Speed. Those technologies took generations to take hold. But this one? Five years ago, who had heard of the Internet? Now look at it. You have got to move. You know that. I know that. But these old men need convincing. I tell them you've got to seize the moment. Look at Microsoft. First-mover advantage. They've got to understand that. First-mover advantage. You can't be second. They have got to understand that. Winner takes all.' He smiled contentedly at Francis. 'They need to get hold of the idea that a younger generation is taking over. The old ways of doing things are gone. They have got to understand that if you don't move fast, you are dead. Dead.'

Francis understood that. Sometimes it was palpable the way he could feel the seconds draining away through his fingers. Since he had had the idea for InterTrust, he had watched Modern Media Inc. shoot up 181 per cent by the end of the first day's trading and VerticalNet up 183 per cent. Fortunes built in hours. Since he had got the first funding in place, he had seen GeoCities.com more than double in the first day's trading and TheGlobe.com up by 605 per cent.

Financial empires established in a day. And he was still not ready to move.

And all the time he was getting ready, his funding was burning up. The City office. Burning it up. The back office in Bangalore. Burning it up. Golden hellos for the technical brains. Burning it up. Fat salaries for marketing and plump fees for the bankers and lawyers and accountants and consultants. And stock options for all of them. All burning it up. And soon it would be burning up the paltry two hundred and fifty thousand he had scraped together. And then a few weeks later it would all be gone. Burned up. And still he was not ready to move. He watched fortunes being made and not one of them was his. But he was not going to end up like his father. He was not.

And still Philippe was talking. And talking. And Rachel was waiting.

'Get in first. Dominate. Clean up,' Philippe said. 'I know that. You know that. But how are we going to convince these old men?' Philippe smiled complicitly at Francis.

The film star got up. The most beautiful of the girls was holding his hand. At the back of the room, no-one looked up from their dominoes as the elegant group began to make their way out into the pale golden morning. But Francis remembered what it had felt like to have a fresh day ahead blossoming untroubled and full of promise.

Philippe loosened his tie and sighed a happy little sigh. 'I tell you, Francis, she was gorgeous,' he said again.

Francis looked at him, the man with the round face in the Charvet shirt, manufacturing an intimacy he did not want, making him late for Rachel, this man who could turn his idea into his legacy. InterTrust. His Big Idea.

'What do you think?' he asked, seizing the moment as Philippe paused to sip his tea. 'Ready to come in for the float?' The film star and his friends passed their table and one of the girls glanced at him with a reflex flicker of interest. But even at this distance Francis knew she could see the deepening creases around his eyes. 'The clock is ticking, Philippe,' he said. 'The funding will all be in place soon. If you want in, you will have to make up your mind.' Rachel was right. He had to resolve this. 'I am afraid I need to get going now.'

'OK, Francis. Let me think about it.' He always said this. 'I need to go over what you said.' He always said this too. 'I think we are nearly there. I would love to work with you on this. It's really exciting. Don't worry about the bill. I'll get it.'

Francis got up and extended his hand for Philippe to shake. Another wasted meeting. Rachel had been right. He wanted to take the younger man's soft hand and crush it and keep on crushing it until he whimpered. He could kill him.

As he turned to leave, Francis caught a glimpse of himself in the mirror. He looked more and more like the photographs of his father at Francis's wedding to Virginia, with the handsome looks worn and furrowed by age and defeat. The reflection could have been unsettling but his exasperation with Philippe was still boiling. Inheriting his father's looks did not mean he was going to end up like him. *Good, but not quite good enough* had been his father's balance sheet. It was not going to be his. Fuck Philippe.

As the door closed on the smoke and noise of the restaurant behind him and Francis walked out into the early morning, he saw a black cat prowling delicately down the other side of the deserted street. It stopped by some dark grey rubbish bags and then daintily picked its way around them, moving on with enigmatic feline intent. Francis loved this time when the morning was still unformed and soft, like the warm, intimate smell of milk on a baby, and everything was still possible.

He had a plan and it was just a matter of keeping a grip and sticking to it. Francis buttoned his jacket. He felt better.

Starting a business was like gardening. You had to prepare the ground. And for a long time, above the surface it looked as if nothing was happening. But, unseen in the loamy earth, the seeds were germinating until suddenly one day they burst forth in blooms of riotous colour.

ten

tuesday 8.35 a.m.

Three fucking problems in half an hour was above the national average. It was even out of line for London. It was not acceptable.

Roger sat in his car and inhaled the scent of his cologne, trying to calm himself.

First problem, that little prick Jason. Second problem, he was now stuck in a traffic jam. In a Ford Mondeo, with air-conditioning that did not work. And now, third problem, Chris had just rung with some problem about a possible late payer. Meaning: grief.

It was turning into a bad day. And it had started so well with the South Seas in his bathroom.

Good days usually started with him thinking about them and their promise of the future. Like the warm air of the dryer across his hair, South Sea maidens would one day purr over him. Like the power shower upon his tingling scalp, the surf would, one day soon, break upon the shore in front of him. And the scent of the colognes he bought for cash in Jermyn Street was a bouquet of Hawaii and the soft, spiced fragrance of tropical women. Oh how those South Sea maidens would sprawl on white sands as the surf rolled in off the ocean, one day very soon. Those tickets for Honolulu were in the safe.

Come on. Roger put the heel of his hand on the horn. What did these people think they were doing? *Come on. Move.* The traffic edged forward three feet and stopped again.

Roger had created his large marble bathroom, where he contemplated Hawaii, when he first started making money. Chocolate marble from floor to ceiling, half a wall covered by mirror, smoky gold mirror-tiles on the ceiling, floor-to-ceiling Roger. Everywhere Roger looked he could see muddy blond Rogers reflected back at him. The bathroom was his one visible, traceable indulgence, but he reckoned that if they came working out how much his bathroom had cost, the game was up anyway. And, meanwhile, surrounded by marble, Roger dreamed his dreams of South Sea islands.

But right now, marooned in his car, Roger thought about Chris. He knew he was involved somehow in the scam. Jason was a lightweight and he would never have done it on his own. And Chris was wild. At nineteen his blood was still crazed with hormones.

And now, on top of that, he had brought him this problem with a possible late payer. A thirty-grand problem. But was it real? Was there really a risk that this punter would be a late payer or was this another scam by Chris?

Roger put his hand on the horn again. For fuck's sake, what was wrong with these people?

Not long now and he would be in Honolulu and

43

all this would be history. But first he would have to sort this out.

He picked up the carphone. 'Chris,' he said. 'Me again. I want to see you. Tomorrow. Usual place. One fifteen.' He put the phone down and sounded his horn again.

As well as seeing Chris, he had better check out the late payer himself. And see if there was a real risk of default here. And then he could work out how to get the thirty grand.

Roger had always done business with sensible people: students, academics. They did not have uncontrollable habits, just bad personal hygiene. They nearly always paid, and when they did not, it was not hard to persuade them to change their minds.

But sometimes, when they were difficult, pressure had to be applied to the parents. And now he had to find out whether pressure was going to be necessary in this case.

eleven

tuesday 8.45 a.m.

'Are you OK?' Rachel asked.

Francis knew what she meant. 'I am sorry I'm so late,' he said.

'Where have you been?'

'I am really sorry, darling. Philippe just talked and talked.'

'And?'

'Progress, I think.'

'How much?'

'Quite a lot, I think.'

'I mean how much is he going to invest?'

'Oh,' said Francis. 'We did not quite get to that stage.'

Rachel looked at him.

'I know,' he said. 'You were right. And I am really sorry I'm so late. But I do think I made some progress with him. Is the doctor ready?'

'Fortunately for you, he is even later than you. And he cares even less. And his receptionist cares least of all.'

Francis heard her tone soften as her wrath found a new target. 'I am really sorry,' he said again. And

45

he was. Although he could not really see the purpose of the appointment himself as they had only been trying for six months, it was important to her. Francis watched her as she paced up and down, neat in her little black suit. Rachel always exuded confidence that she would get what she wanted. He picked up a magazine in case she caught him watching her.

Rachel stared out of the window and fretted. It was her mother's fault.

Rachel had always known she would be a lawyer. And she was. And a firm like Rother & Fenwick would be the place she would work. And she did. And one day she would fall in love. And then she met Francis. And then she would get married. And now she was wife to Francis Carroll, the next step was to become a partner at Rother & Fenwick. Simple steps along the road. And none of them involved children.

And then her mother had done it. Her irritating hints after the wedding had driven Rachel mad, but, worse, they planted the idea. Rachel should have a baby. And the more she thought about it the more right it seemed.

A family of three.

Francis was, even now, raw with the pain of leaving Virginia and losing his son. And he did not seem to know how to get over it. And until he did, their marriage cowered under Virginia's shadow. Which was where Virginia wanted it. Rachel knew, she just knew, that Virginia was one of those women who had to own, for ever, every man they had slept with.

But a bonny new baby would heal her darling

husband, binding them even closer together and pushing Virginia and James into a gypsy existence along the periphery of their lives.

And the more she thought about it the more she wanted it. And the more she wanted it, the more she worried about it. She worried that she was not pregnant yet. She worried that Francis was not as keen as her to have a baby. She worried he was only coming here today to humour her. And she worried and worried that she should have conceived by now. She had had enough of these whirling, shapeless worries. And so she made this appointment. Getting a grip, she called it to herself. She did the research and this doctor was the best. He would find the answer and then everything would be back under control, and they could get on with their lives.

Rachel watched Francis as he leafed through the magazine. She concentrated on making him look up to catch her watching him. And then he would smile, crinkling his eyes, showing her that he loved her. And as she watched him, she felt a familiar longing. She wanted to stroke his handsome, lovely face and feel his arms around her, his hands firm on her back. She wanted his touch on her. She longed for him to look up.

But Francis just went on leafing through his magazine.

'Mr Carroll?' The receptionist in the lilac suit appeared in the doorway. 'There's a taxi here for you,' she said.

Rachel stared at him. He had only just arrived.

Forty-five minutes late. And now he was leaving again. What was he thinking of?

'I'll be straight out,' he said to the receptionist.

The words jammed up in Rachel's mouth. She could not speak. How could he?

'Francis,' she managed to say, but he had already gone through the door.

What did he think he was doing? Rachel sat down and exhaled slowly through her nostrils as her yoga teacher had taught her. This morning was turning out to be even worse than she had ever imagined it could be.

The door opened and Francis came rustling back into the waiting room behind a huge bouquet of flowers swathed in cellophane. Rachel saw stocks and lilies and roses. 'I am really sorry,' he said.

Rachel felt the tension seep away and tears start in her eyes. What had she been thinking of? 'Oh Francis,' she said. 'They are gorgeous.' She put her hands softly on his cheeks, feeling the stippled ghost of his beard under her fingertips, and kissed him on the lips. 'Thank you,' she said. 'Thank you.'

'I got the taxi to go and get them while I came in. I didn't think I should be any later.' He smiled. She kissed him again.

'Thank you.' She loved it when he was so pleased with himself.

'Mr and Mrs Carroll.' A nurse in the whitest, crispest tunic Rachel had ever seen opened the door. 'This way please.'

Rachel took the bouquet and put it on the

receptionist's desk as they passed. 'Please could you look after these until we have finished with the doctor,' she said.

They went down a short corridor, carpeted in deep, soft pink pile. The nurse knocked at a door. 'Come in,' said a deep male voice.

Dr Gray was a small man, surprisingly small for such a deep voice, Rachel thought, and in his late thirties. He wore rectangular glasses in a black wire frame and a fine wool charcoal suit with a deep purple tie. Plum, Rachel thought. He finished writing something before he looked up.

'Mr and Mrs Carroll,' he said. 'How can I help you?' He smiled sympathetically.

Rachel thought an apology for being an hour late would be a start. But she explained why they had come.

'Six months?' Dr Gray asked.

'Yes,' she said.

'No previous problems down there?'

'No,' Rachel said.

'What about you, Mr Carroll – any history there?'

'No,' Rachel said.

'I can't help you,' Dr Gray said. 'Six months is too soon to be able to make judgements about this. We define infertility as an inability to conceive after a year of unprotected sexual intercourse.'

Rachel waited for Francis to speak. They were paying this patronising little man to sit there and pontificate about their life, and he just sat there saying nothing.

'Let me explain,' said Dr Gray.

'Please do.' In a courtroom, witnesses would have crumbled under her tone, but the doctor did not appear to have noticed.

'There are physiological reasons for infertility and physical ones,' he continued. 'Sometimes the sperm is not up to scratch in some way, sometimes the woman has hormonal problems, sometimes the fallopian tubes are defective in some way and sometimes the vagina is unfriendly towards the sperm.' He smiled at Rachel: 'Chemically speaking, that is.'

He paused for her to smile in response. Rachel stared at him coldly. 'And your point is?' she said.

'We can usually identify these problems, and often we can do something about them.'

He looked sympathetically at her. Why didn't he look at Francis? It was as if the two men were colluding in humouring her because she was just a woman, with neurotic concerns that only women felt.

'But sometimes, around ten per cent of the time, there are more mysterious reasons for infertility. Things of the mind, probably, but in any event we just do not know what they are. And medicine can do little about this. Quite simply, sometimes, especially nowadays, I suspect, people get so tense that in some way it becomes hostile to conception. And the more you worry, the more likely you are to make conception more difficult. Six months is really not very long.'

'But you don't *know* this is the problem, do you? Not for a fact, do you?' Rachel said.

'As I am trying to explain, Mrs Carroll, if you start

this process – which can be highly stressful – too soon, you may achieve the opposite of what you want.'

'But that isn't inevitable, is it?' Rachel had locked in on him now. 'Sometimes, I accept, there may be psychological reasons,' she said. 'You say so and I am sure you are right. But sometimes, from what you have just said, there are physiological reasons. And you cannot know – can you – which is which until you have examined us.'

Francis was dismayed by her use of the plural.

'And the longer you wait to examine us, the longer we will have to wait to have a baby. And we do not want to wait. We want a baby now. That is why we have come to you.'

'Yes, I know,' Dr Gray said. 'But I wouldn't recommend it. You'll create extra anxiety for yourselves. And what for? It is really far too soon to be able to say whether or not you have a real problem with conception.'

Furious with herself, Rachel felt as if she was going to cry. She had steeled herself to come here and that waiting room had been purgatory for her, while Francis had been so unforgivably late. And then he had kept sneaking looks at his watch. And now this man, in his plum neckwear, was telling her there was nothing he could do. And nothing she said was changing his mind.

Dr Gray seemed to sense surrender as he leant forward and said: 'Six months is really too soon. If you have not had any luck in another six months, please come back and see me. And I shall be delighted to do whatever I can to help you then.' He smiled sympathetically at her again, ignoring Francis. The consultation had obviously ended. 'Any questions?' he asked.

All doctors were taught to ask that nowadays, she thought. She shook her head. 'No. Thank you.' Francis also shook his head and put his arm protectively round Rachel as they got up to go.

They feel sorry for me, she thought, infuriated – both of them. And they do not understand. I am not upset. I do not care about this doctor. If he will not help us, I will find some other way.

'Perhaps you could settle the bill with the nurse on the way out,' Dr Gray said as he stood up and opened the door for them.

One hundred and fifty pounds? Rachel thought as she stepped into the bright Harley Street sunshine with her bunch of flowers. Just to be told to come back in six months? I could have told myself that.

A young woman with blonde hair and sunglasses was sitting in a convertible BMW parked outside the consulting rooms, roof down, radio on. 'Boom, boom, boom, boom,' it went. It was the Vengaboys. As Rachel came out with Francis holding his arm around her, the music stopped and a perfunctory news-bulletin began. Skirmishes in Kosovo and new moves to break the impasse over weapons-decommissioning in Northern Ireland. Something about the Millennium Dome. And other things. And more other things crackling on and out into the roar of the traffic.

And what if she really could not get pregnant? How long would Francis stay with her then? It was so unfair. All over the world, millions of women were able to do this every day. Why couldn't she? The only fruit from Francis's seed was James. How unfair was that?

Rachel felt her life narrowing and narrowing until it focused on this: somewhere in Francis was the one sperm among all those billions that could make it to meet the one egg inside her, which sat unknowingly waiting for it to arrive. Just as she had waited unknowingly all her life for Francis to arrive. And he had. So why hadn't this?

Francis looked anxiously up and down the street for a cab. He had back-to-back meetings all day. He had to get on.

He hailed a taxi. 'Do you mind if I take this?' he said.

Rachel looked at him. 'Of course not,' she said. 'Your meeting is obviously more important than mine.'

'Don't be like that, darling,' Francis said, and kissed her. 'I'll see you this evening,' he called as he got into the cab. 'Don't forget. Virginia is expecting us at seven.'

Rachel raised the flowers to her face, submerging herself in the heady scent of the stocks. She had known for some time that choice is an illusion of youth. However much you plan, however carefully you plot the map of your future, things still just happen. Rother & Fenwick happened. Francis happened. Lives collide. And, when Francis thought they should buy for the future, a big empty house in Surrey happened.

But some things were so important you had to make them happen. No matter what else could be left to chance, this was going to happen, and nothing – not a smug, complacent consultant, not lazy sperm, not sluggish eggs, none of it, nothing, no-one – was going to be allowed to stop her having Francis's baby. Nothing, no-one.

Rachel said this to herself as she waited for a taxi in the bright Harley Street sunshine. Nothing. No-one.

twelve

tuesday 11.15 a.m.

It had taken Roger two hours to get back to his office from Sydenham and the bright morning had clouded over. Outside the window, the cars on the westbound A40 were stuck, again, in a jam that Roger could see stretched for miles.

He drew on his cigar and the comforting luxury of the aromatic smoke filled the office while he sat looking out at the cars and ruminating. Both his problems today were down to Chris. First: cash-flow. It was king – poor cash-flow could kill a business – and late payment could never be tolerated. And second: staff treachery. This was a fact of business life, but it too could not be tolerated. And now, thanks to Chris, perfidy and late payment were both on Tuesday's agenda.

The plaque behind the reception desk in the entrance said 'University Books'. It was a legitimate business and that was a source of pride for Roger. He was the UK agent for university publishers all over the world. Not the big ones everyone had heard of, but obscure presses that earnestly turned out arcane works on nineteenth-century Canadian philosophers and Malaysian chemistry-textbooks.

Roger sat back in his black leather chair. At just this second, somewhere in Japan or Latin America or the Mid-West or Austria or Egypt, some academic, scraping along for a year on what Roger spent on his summer holiday, was tapping away at a keyboard memorialising a lifetime's knowledge that nobody wanted to read. He did not know why they did it. But, he thought, it is good that they do. It was perfect cover.

He visited every college with his Mondeo full of samples, and he was proud of the fact that every year for the last six years, University Books had declared a profit. He took £40,000 a year in salary and a dividend of £10,000. Anyone who looked through the books could see how he could afford the semi-detached house in Southgate and the annual holiday in Majorca for his wife and two daughters. The books were straight. Roger was proud of that.

All the real money, from the real business, supplying drugs to the studious middle-classes, went into the Swiss account in cash. All the real spending – the clothes, the expensive meals – was done in cash. And the money for Honolulu was stacking up in Geneva, steadily accumulating under the prudent and discreet husbandry of a Swiss private bank.

Roger puffed thoughtfully on his cigar. It had been a clever little business he had built, he thought. His niche market had money and the appetite to spend it. And he kept a grip on it all by doing most of the work himself. And he had always been a good payer. Cash in advance. He took the risk. And he knew it was appreciated. Salim, the Crasks, Mario – they all liked doing business with him. No problems. He knew his business and respected theirs. He never took risks. When you did business with Roger Oates you knew he would never do anything stupid to get the law interested.

It had been a good business but you had to know when to get out. It wasn't good luck that made the business work, that was hard graft and vision, but bad luck could fuck you up. No matter how clever you were, no matter how hard you worked, bad luck could fuck you up.

And Roger knew the longer you went without getting fucked over by bad luck the more likely it was to get you. Every day it got more and more likely. If you took the square root of the days you had worked and divided them by a hundred, that was the percentage chance you had each day of bad luck fucking you over. That was the law. Roger's law. A percentage which grew like a coral reef, imperceptibly but inexorably day by day, a percentage growing according to the immutable laws of arithmetic, stalking you to fuck you up.

Light summer rain began to streak the window.

Roger remembered the Mexican he once met with Jon Crask. Good-looking. Pale blond hair and a soft tan. Ramirez. Important in Oaxaca, Jon said. He was not more than thirty. Cream silk suit, beige cotton T-shirt, one thick gold band on his wedding finger. He had insisted on going to the Ritz, drinking two bottles of Dom Perignon, making Roger uncomfortable, talking in low confiding tones throughout the meal. He talked about women, about a deal in Palm Beach, about his Ferraris and about his plans.

'The thing about Yanquis,' he said confidently, 'they make a lot of noise but they never kill you.'

'Yes,' Roger thought, 'but they get you one way or another.' And they had. The Mexican disappeared and his body was never found. Salim told Roger it had been fed to pigs. Phil told Roger it was under a Louisiana freeway. They both said the Medellin cartel had been told about his plans and had not liked them. 'They always get you,' thought Roger. 'Best they don't get to know you.'

And best to get out before the bad luck creeps down from the crossroads at midnight to get you, summoned when the percentages decided it was time.

Another twelve months was all he needed to get out. By then he would have enough put by and he and Maggie would be off to Hawaii. Just him and Maggie. The girls were old enough to look after themselves now. It was South Seas but civilised. American. The long surf rolling in on the white sand, fringed with low-hanging palms, fresh pineapples for breakfast, barbecues in the soft subtropical evenings, contraband Cuban cigars. That would be it.

Roger inhaled. But for now he had to screw his thirty grand out of the late payer or those who loved him. And then he would deal with Chris. Only twelve months more of this aggravation and then he would be gone: American Airlines direct to Honolulu, him and Maggie, gone.

In Sydenham, Jason was keeping very still.

thirteen

tuesday 7.15 p.m.

'There you go.' Virginia counted the money. 'A hundred.'

In Battersea, Virginia was ready to celebrate the birthday of her only child. There was a chicken in the pot and Liebfraumilch in the fridge. But first she and Julie stood by the French windows opening on to Battersea Park in the gentle summer evening. Scents of cut grass and traffic drifted into the room.

'Can you keep fifty for me?'

'I thought you wanted it now?'

'I only need forty-five for the dresses. If you keep fifty then you can save it for me. If I take it now I'll only spend it.'

'That's what it's for.'

'No. You'd better keep it. In case something comes up.' Julie folded the notes carefully and put the little wad in her purse. 'Thank you,' she said.

The bell went. It was Francis and Rachel.

'Hello, Frankie,' Julie said as they came in. 'Don't worry, I'm not staying for dinner. With your son. Remember him?'

Why did she dislike him so much? Francis

wondered. He had always done his best for James. And Francis was not sure she was good for Virginia. She seemed to encourage the outlaw in her.

'You are declaring it, aren't you, Virginia, if she is still working here?' Francis said.

'Do I look stupid?' Julie said.

'I'm sorry, Julie, I didn't mean to imply anything.' There was no point in antagonising her further. 'It's just that it's important these things are done properly. Virginia, please tell me she's not claiming benefit.'

'None of your business,' Julie said.

'No, no, of course not,' Francis said quickly. 'It's just that you do need to be careful. Anyway, don't they make you get a job if you claim benefit nowadays?'

'So they say,' Julie said. 'But they still let you choose what you want to do. It's not Nazi Germany. And I tell them I want to be a silversmith.'

Virginia laughed.

'What?'

'Nothing. It's a good idea,' Virginia said.

'Well, I think it is a good idea. I like silver. All my jewellery is silver. And I was one of the best in my class at DT.'

'So why aren't you working? As a silversmith?' Francis said.

'Because I'm not ready yet. I've got to help Lisa out till the twins are bigger. It's hard being a single mother. Isn't it, Virginia?'

'But don't they make you get a job?'

'Don't worry, Frankie, they do try. They do their

60

best to look after all those taxes you pay. But I tell them I need training and I have got to find a course that fits in with my childcare commitments. That always puts it off for another few months. Silversmith courses are hard to find.'

'A modern problem,' Virginia said.

'That's how I see it too,' Julie said. 'So don't worry, Frankie. Got to go. Thanks for the money, Virginia. Have a nice evening everyone.' As she turned to open the door with her left hand, she put her right hand behind her and squeezed Francis's buttock. 'Bye, Frankie,' she said and turned to wink at Virginia over his shoulder.

'Why are you still employing her?' Francis said as the door closed behind her.

'I like her,' Virginia said.

'She is very lively,' Rachel said.

'She doesn't like me,' Francis said.

The bell went again. It was James.

'Hello darling,' said Virginia and kissed him on the cheek. 'Happy birthday, darling,' she said.

'Happy birthday, James,' Francis and Rachel said.

'How's work?' Francis said.

'Fine,' James said.

'My son the lawyer,' Virginia said and stroked his cheek.

'What sort of work are they giving you to do?' Francis persevered.

'This and that.'

'How much longer have you got to go with your articles?' Rachel asked.

'Nine months,' James mumbled.

Francis wondered whether it would have been different if he had stayed. Was it inevitable that their conversations would be awkward now James had grown up and left home, or would it all have been more relaxed if he had always been around? Or was it just him? Virginia, a graceful hostess, was at ease – but then she always was. And Rachel seemed determined to be comfortable with this family she had taken on with her marriage. Perhaps it was just him.

'Are they giving you interesting work?' he asked James. He glanced at Virginia. She was watching him as he struggled to keep up his conversation with James. He could not decipher her expression. For a moment he thought it might be affection. For James? Or him? More likely it was wry amusement at his incompetent attempts at bonding. These things had always been so easy for her. She was what Human Resources professionals called emotionally intelligent. It was one of the things he had loved about her.

'It's OK,' James said. As usual his father was trying hard. They were so different, his Mum and Dad. She could be embarrassing but somehow it was OK. Dad would never do anything to make people look twice at him but somehow he could never connect. Somehow it was never quite OK. How could he ask this man, his father, for thirty thousand pounds?

'Come on, let's sit down,' Virginia said.

Rachel watched her move as she put her arm round James and went to the table with him. She hoped she would look as lithe and good as that in ten years' time. Virginia was special, there was no doubt about that. 'Is Alex not coming?' she asked.

Francis picked up the bottle of Liebfraumilch and inspected the label.

'No,' Virginia said. 'He's working tonight.'

'How is he?' Rachel said.

Francis was still scrutinising the Liebfraumilch label.

'Fine,' Virginia said. 'Fine. How's work?' she asked Rachel.

'Busy. It's coming up to partnership season so everyone is very busy – and very keen to seem very busy.' She looked at James who was eating crisps. 'Is it like that at Prendergast's?'

'I suppose so,' he said. 'I don't know really. It's a bit above my pay-grade.'

Virginia brought the chicken to the table, steaming on its bed of couscous.

'That looks great,' Rachel said.

'Yes,' said Francis, 'it does.' Virginia had always been an effortlessly good cook. He noticed she had painted her nails purple with little gold stars on them. Only Virginia would do that, he thought. Her long, slender fingers pushed the hair away from her face. He remembered those fingers.

'So how is it going, darling?' Virginia said to her son.

James spotted an opening. 'It's OK, but I'm thinking of going back to college if I can get the money together.' He watched Francis closely as he said it. 'It

63

might be quite expensive.' Like, a thirty-thousand deposit. Like, tomorrow.

'Don't do that,' Francis said. This was an area where he could help James. Emotionally unintelligent he may have been, but he did know something about the job market. 'At least finish your articles first,' he said. 'Get the qualification. It was hard enough to get this far. Don't give up just when you can see the finishing line.'

Not promising, James thought. The door was definitely closing again.

'I know what you feel like,' Rachel said helpfully. 'It feels like you are never going to finish and get some interesting work to do. But it's worth the wait.'

That was the door shut. James gloomily forked some couscous into his mouth. Thirty grand. There was no hope here. Where was he going to get thirty grand?

As the evening faded and the noise of laughter and music from the park died away, they worked their way through the twenty-three mementoes of James's life. They even drank the milk and ate the Smarties cake.

'What about this, darling?' Virginia said as she poured the Liebfraumilch. 'Do you remember this? Do you want some?' she asked Rachel. 'It made James sick when he was thirteen.'

Rachel laughed. 'I wouldn't have thought he would want to be reminded of that,' she said.

'But that's just the point,' Virginia said. 'It's not just

the good times we should celebrate – it's all our special moments – that's what makes us who we are.'

'Never mind, James,' Rachel said. 'We've all been there.'

'I haven't.' Francis spoke before he could stop himself. How could he be so pompous? It was if being in the same room as Virginia flicked a switch in him that drove him to conform to her image of him. He was sure he was never like this at work or when he was alone with Rachel.

James looked at his father. How could he ever have thought of asking him for thirty thousand pounds?

'Of course you wouldn't have, Francis,' Virginia said. She couldn't help herself. He had been trying so hard all evening, but he was so earnest. She had always hoped he would learn how not to be quite so literal about everything.

She saw his handsome face tighten as she spoke. She'd never understood how someone so handsome could be so anxious about everything. And he was still a good-looking man. He had loved her teasing him when they were married but now she knew it was different. She should not do it. It was not fair when he had been trying so hard. She relented. 'Not everyone has to make the same stupid mistakes,' she said, smiling at him. 'No offence, darling,' she added, ruffling James's hair.

Francis saw she was trying. 'I have made enough stupid mistakes of my own,' he said, smiling back. And then he realised this might be misinterpreted by Virginia.

And then he realised this might be misinterpreted by Rachel.

'Anyway, we had better go,' he continued rapidly. 'I started at six this morning and I have got another early start tomorrow. Happy birthday, James.'

'Yes,' Rachel said as she leant over and kissed James on both cheeks. 'Happy birthday.'

'Thank you, Virginia,' Francis said.

'Yes,' Rachel said as she went over to Virginia and kissed her on both cheeks. 'Thank you for a lovely evening.'

'Are you going too, darling?' Virginia asked James.

'No,' he said. 'I'll hang around for a bit.'

They stood by the French windows and watched as Francis and Rachel got into their car and drove off.

'There's something I need to ask you,' James said.

fourteen

wednesday 10.45 a.m.

Francis was worried about James. Virginia had just called, asking to see him urgently. He assumed it was something to do with James and he wondered why she had not mentioned it last night. What now? James was so unfocused and Virginia was such an erratic mother. How would James have turned out if he had stayed? Francis knew he sometimes came across in the wrong way but he had done his best for James. He had really done his best. But was it still his fault?

Virginia was also worried about James: her hand-some, darling boy, pain festering under that sham-bling charm. Was it her fault he had turned out like this? If Francis had stayed with them, would James have been different?

And Rachel was worried about James as well. Every time she saw him, she worried. He was only eight years younger than her but he lived in a dream. He was rubbish at life. Virginia spoilt him, and every time James – or Virginia – had a problem, Francis had to sort it out for them. Was it always going to be like this? Was James baggage they would have to lug around with them for the rest of their lives?

James was wondering if Sushila would shag him. For old times' sake. He felt like he needed a shag. He was looking out of the window from his seat on the top deck of the bus. Ten forty-five. He had decided to go into work after all. 'Boom, boom, boom, boom.' The sound of the Vengaboys went round and round in his head. 'Going to Ibiza.' That was another of their songs. He wished he was going to Ibiza.

He had decided he should take the day off to sort out the problem with Chris. He had not wanted to go to Mum about it but James realised he had no choice. And, as it turned out, she had been great about it. He should have known. 'I'll sort it out,' she had said, and he knew she would but she had not done it yet. And Chris would be getting impatient. James needed to call him.

And he could not face phoning him from the office, ducking in and out to make surreptitious calls on his mobile. It was all too much.

But then, at ten o'clock, he'd realised this would be the seventh time he had called in sick since Easter and he would have to be careful how many more times he did this before he went on holiday. So he decided to go in and say he had been to the doctor. That way, he thought, he would escape censure for being late and gain credit for staggering into work when he was ill. He could call Chris tomorrow. He was sure Chris would be cool about it.

He hoped Mum had the money herself. Otherwise she would have to ask Dad. And his father always got that stiff, distant expression before he paid up. James hated that. His father never actually complained when he was asked anything like that. He just looked pained.

James liked the bus. He had come to believe he might have an aptitude for making documentaries and he got some of his best ideas on the top deck, looking at people and the world going by. Lighthouse-keepers, the Fifty Worst Ways to Get Dumped, Celebrity Gardens and A Personal History of the Morris Minor: they had all come to him on top of the bus. But James recognised that he would need to go to film school to develop his talent. And that was expensive, and that was a problem. He had heard they were pretty tough about grants nowadays and his father probably wouldn't cough up. And anyway, he didn't even want to ask his father. He hated that pained expression of his. He really hated it. So he was going to find the money his own way. And it had all been going so well until yesterday.

'Boom, boom, boom, boom.' He could not get the Vengaboys out of his head. A short, round woman in a purple coat sat down beside him exuding sweat. 'Boom, boom, boom, boom.' What did she do? She looked as if she had just been released into the care of the community. Too obvious. There had been lots of documentaries about that.

What about honey? Where did that come from? Was honey-collection all automated nowadays? Or even synthetic? Or was it all still collected by armies of pottering beekeepers, gently inserting their swaddled arms into the furiously buzzing hives to stock the shelves in Tesco and Sainsbury's? There would have to be thousands and thousands of them to produce all that honey. What would fifty-thousand massed beekeepers look like? That could be interesting.

James was suffused with a glow of achievement. Recently he had noticed that his ideas sounded more and more convincing. He could imagine people would really be interested in his programmes on Channel Four. Or BBC2. Not Channel Five, though.

The round, purple woman got up and moved to another seat at the front of the bus, muttering to herself. Did she smell less pungent in winter? If so, would it be because she wore more clothes to mask the smell or because she sweated less? An interesting conundrum. James sat in an amiable reverie until the bus pulled up outside Prendergast, Markby and Matthews.

In the lift, James looked at himself mournfully in the mirror. He certainly did not look well.

'Hello,' he said plaintively to Katie the receptionist.

She grinned at him. 'Late night?' she asked. He thought she might like him.

'I'm not well,' he said.

She grinned again. 'Obviously a late night,' she said. 'Drink lots of water.'

'I'm really not well,' he said. 'I've been to the doctor.'

He suspected she did not believe him but he moved on past her.

He shared an office with Miranda Evans, a paragon. James knew she had little interest in him. She did not even disapprove of him. He was too irrelevant even for that. Early on, she had worked out he was no threat.

'Hello,' he said as he walked in.

Miranda was staring intently at the screen on her desk. 'Good afternoon,' she muttered without looking up.

'Busy?' he asked.

'Yes.'

'I'm not very well,' James told her. 'That's why I'm late.'

'Sorry to hear that,' she replied politely, eyes still fixed on the screen. 'I hope you feel better soon.'

What would she say if he really was ill? James wondered. Was she so dismissive because she guessed he was faking it? Or did she really not care? He sat down at his desk and felt sorry for himself. No-one would care if he really was ill. Not Katie. Not Miranda.

'Have you seen Evans the Partner?' he asked. It was his joke. To distinguish their boss from Miranda. Not that it was difficult to distinguish them. The joke had not caught on. Miranda ignored it every time. But its familiarity comforted James.

'No,' she said.

James gave up and went down the corridor to make his excuses.

'Ah, James,' Colin Evans said as he knocked on the

door. 'I was just coming to look for you. I've got something you could do that would actually be useful.' There was a neat pile of legal files on his desk. Professionally posed photographs of his family sat on a shelf behind his head. 'Sit down,' he said. 'Look at this,' he said, handing James a thin file.

James opened it carefully. In his experience, when somebody handed you a file, it was the start of a journey into boredom; days of tedium reading up the references, hours in conference, absently taking notes and calculating how much each minute cost the client. He supposed the clock ran even when the clients were talking and the lawyers sipped tea. He calculated that they were paid jointly during an average meeting around fifty pounds to drink tea. Was it another twenty pounds to ask how the family were? Where did all the money come from to pay all the lawyers in the world?

He looked at Colin Evans – was he supposed to read it now?

'Have a look at it,' Colin Evans repeated.

The file had one letter in it, from someone called Chivers about his father's will, complaining he had not been left as much money as he thought he should have been.

'This isn't something we would normally take on,' said Colin. 'As you know, we don't do wills or personal trusts.'

James felt his mind beginning to congeal. If even this firm didn't do this stuff, it threatened to plumb new depths of boredom.

'But Raymond Chivers is a partner in Taylor

Marks.' Colin Evans mentioned a firm of accountants with whom the firm did a lot of business. 'It's a favour for him. Personal business. You might find it interesting. He's coming in tomorrow. You might want to look out Goodchild v. Goodchild beforehand.' He took another file from the neat pile.

The meeting was over. Time was money. At least he hadn't noticed James was late. James considered mentioning his trip to the doctor to get credit for coming in but he decided it might be better not to draw further attention to himself. He got up to leave.

'Any reason why you were in so late?' Evans asked, without looking up from his new file.

'I had to go to the doctor,' James mumbled.

Evans the Partner grunted and continued reading. James couldn't decide whether the grunt meant Evans could not care less or that he was not convinced by the lie. Either way, it was probably best to leave.

Miranda Evans was typing furiously when James returned to his office. 'What have you got there?' she asked, without looking up from the screen.

'Something to do with a will.' James put the papers on his desk and sat down.

'Oh,' said Miranda, losing interest, relaxing, still typing.

James started to read the papers. And his mind began to wander. Dennis and Joan Goodchild executed identical wills in favour of son Gary. Joan died. Dennis left it all to his new wife. What would happen if his father died? Had he left it all to Rachel?

73

Would she give anything to him? They were very different. She was at Rother & Fenwick and obviously loved it there. He wondered why his father had married her. She was so different from his Mum. Perhaps that was why? He didn't seem to know what he was doing a lot of the time, his Dad.

His phone went. It was Katie. 'You've got a client,' she said. He could hear a suppressed giggle in her voice.

'What do you mean?' he asked suspiciously.

'You've got a client,' she said again. 'He's waiting for you in reception.' Again he could hear the amusement in her voice.

'If this is a wind-up,' he said, 'don't think there won't be retaliation.'

'Would I do that to you, particularly when you are in such a fragile condition?'

'Yes.'

'I promise you,' she said. 'You have got a client. He specifically asked for you. Your first real client.'

He could not work out what she found so funny. Why shouldn't he have a client? 'I'm coming to see you,' he said ominously.

'We're waiting for you,' she said. 'Me and your client.'

James hung up and shut the file, grateful for the distraction, and walked into the reception area.

Katie grinned at him. 'Your client is in the waiting room,' she said. 'Now, are you going to say sorry? Would I wind you up?'

He looked at her. 'We'll see,' he said. Why shouldn't

he have a client? He could not imagine who it could be, though.

He opened the door of the waiting room. 'Hello,' he said, and put out his hand. 'James Carroll.'

The man did not get up. 'I know who you are,' he said. 'Is this private here?'

There was nothing in his tone at all, just a soft South London accent. James began to get an idea of who he might be. 'I'll get a room,' he said, and went back to the reception desk.

'A conference room?' Katie asked. 'For a conference? With your client?'

He was no longer in the mood for this. 'Have you got one or not?' he said.

'OK, OK. Barnet is free.' A previous senior partner had named the conference rooms after London suburbs.

James showed his client to the table in the window-less room. 'Would you like some coffee? Or tea?' he asked, still trying to preserve the idea that this softly spoken man in a grey suit really was a client.

The man did not answer him. 'Sit down,' he said, 'and make sure that door is closed. Now, for the purpose of this conversation you are my lawyer and that means client confidentiality applies. You have learnt about that, have you?'

James nodded.

'Now listen you little prick,' the man said to his new lawyer. 'No-one should ever be late paying me. Do you understand what I am saying to you?'

James had now definitely worked out who he was.

This must be Roger. He spoke so softly that James had to strain to understand him but he still felt himself cowering in case anyone could hear. He had checked the door was shut and he knew these rooms were soundproofed but it would be a total disaster if anyone heard this. How had this man found him here? He was almost sure he had never told Chris where he worked.

'I'm sorry,' James said. 'Really sorry. I am getting the money together. It was an accident.'

The shock of his two lives colliding like this was making everything happen very slowly. He was used to Chris and he was getting used to Prendergast's. He was not used to being in both worlds at the same time. Nor owing thirty thousand pounds. He had never even seen so much money. And it had only ever been a one-time deal.

'I don't want an apology,' Roger Oates said. 'I want my money. Now.' His tone never varied and his voice never rose. James could feel panic lurching up in him. God, he hoped his mother had got the money together.

'It was an accident,' he said. His stomach churned. Chris had only mentioned a boss yesterday when things went wrong. It had been so easy to deal with Chris. This Roger was different. He would have been frightening enough anywhere but somehow it was so much more chilling to be menaced in the sedate tedium of Prendergast, Markby and Matthews. 'I am sorry,' he said again.

It was as if the comforting mediocrity of the

windowless conference rooms named after London suburbs and the forty-three partners and their supporting staff – decent, well-meaning professional people, going home every evening to comfortable houses in well-tended streets, contributing every day in their professional and well-meaning way to upholding the great and deep-rooted authority of the law which supported this nation of fifty-five million people – were all no more than a thin layer of crust over a seething stew of violence and evil that had just bubbled through into the Barnet conference room, terrifyingly, unstoppably.

'I just said I don't want an apology,' Roger repeated patiently. 'I want my money. Now. Am I going to get it?'

'Yes,' James said. 'Honestly.' The man was petrifying.

'When?'

'As soon as possible, honestly.'

'Honestly is honestly not good enough. This is my money. And I want it. Now,' Roger said, 'have you actually got the money?'

'I'm still getting it together.'

'I suggest you finish getting it together very quickly, Mr Carroll. I won't ask so politely next time. Honestly. I would get it together very quickly if I were you.'

This had been a useful visit. It had helped him clarify the situation. This was not a scam by Chris and this little prick was not holding out on him. He was terrified but he was not trying to lie or be smart. He obviously just did not have the money. Still, it had been worth a try. He would have to go to the next stage now.

'Thank you for the conference, Mr Carroll,' Roger said as James took him to the lift. 'We'll be in touch.'

'That wasn't very long,' Katie called as the lift doors closed behind Roger Oates. 'Taking his business elsewhere, is he?'

Christ, I hope so, thought James as he went back to his office. Christ, I hope Mum has got the money together. Now.

fifteen

wednesday 12.15 p.m.

Francis looked at his list of things to do. Speak to the lawyers about the prospectus. Change the menu for the breakfasts with analysts. Sort out an argument between the accountants and the bankers over earning projections. And find the finance. That was on every list, prompting him to follow up this new contact, lunch with those former colleagues, flatter these fund managers and hunt down money wherever he could find it. A lot done and a lot still to do, but when he looked at his list Francis felt good. It was all under control.

He buzzed Joanne on the intercom. 'Please can you find ten minutes for Marion after four o'clock,' he said.

'Of course, Francis,' she replied.

He had only started making these daily lists after his divorce from Virginia. The mechanical cataloguing of his tasks seemed to hold back the feelings of futility and failure. But even when he had healed enough to know he did not need to do it any more, he still compiled his lists. Twice a day. They had become familiar barriers against the panic and disorder which had once threatened to overwhelm him. As the Roman Empire once built walls against barbarians, so Francis made his daily lists.

He buzzed again. 'Oh and can you check Lloyd is still on for two o'clock.'

'Of course, Francis,' Joanne said.

In his office, in a tall glass tower faced with pink marble, the air-conditioning purred, insulating him from the heat and grime outside. Silvergate House was engineered to be agreeable and the disruptive was designed out. Francis looked out of the window at his expensive view. Sometimes that four-hundred-pound-a-day vista infused him with confidence that his fledgling vision for InterTrust would soon soar over the City. It told him that, soon, as he liberated the buccaneer within himself, he would be floating on life-evolving oceans of cash.

And yet there were still the other times, when, driving home in a grey twilight, he glimpsed a cold warning flitting between the wastelands of filling stations and fast-food joints, flickering a message that he was never going to turn heads in New York restaurants. And then he would lose it all. First the two hundred and fifty thousand. And then the house. Like his father.

To silence such malevolent murmurings he would pull up the projections for 2000–01 and survey the calm columns of figures marching majestically across and down the screen, promising Francis he would not end up like his father. He just needed to get the flotation away successfully and he would be set.

There was a knock on the door. 'Mrs Carroll is here to see you, Mr Carroll,' Francis's secretary said. That Mrs Carroll, Joanne's tone suggested.

Francis looked at his watch. Twelve twenty. Virginia had a gift for upset and it was typical she should ring up out of the blue and summon him to lunch on such a busy day, and then, on top of it all, arrive early. She had said it was urgent but then she usually said that. It was probably something to do with James. Probably yet another request for money. He wondered again why she had not said anything last night.

Francis wished he could have asked her to wait, but there was a right way to do things and a wrong way. And it would have been churlish for him to have refused to see his ex-wife when she arrived.

'Please show her in,' he said.

He got up and came round the desk as Virginia walked in. He held out his hand to indicate where she should sit but she came up to him and kissed him on the cheek. Her scent wafted around him, discomfortingly, intimately familiar. He was conscious of Joanne shutting the door discreetly behind her as she left.

'Hello, Virginia,' he said, stepping away. 'You're early.'

'Only ten minutes,' she responded. 'And anyway, I can remember when you would have been thrilled to have that extra time with me. Enjoy it, Francis.'

'I'm busy,' Francis said.

'No you're not,' Virginia pointed out. 'You are seeing me. You could just carry on over lunch.'

'I will be ready at half past twelve, as we agreed. I have to finish what I'm doing here first,' Francis said, doggedly. He opened the door and said to his secretary: 'Please show Ms Carroll to the waiting area and confirm the table at Zampone.'

He returned to his desk and scrolled through the financial projections on the screen for what he estimated was long enough to signal his irritation to Virginia.

The developers of Silvergate House had installed a modern Italian restaurant in the basement for the convenience of their tenants. 'This is nice,' Virginia said as she settled back against a banquette. The restaurant was already filling up with men and women in suits, talking in the crisp, urgent tones of money. The windowless room was parchment white, with sharp directed lighting picking out the soft grey leather seating and linen tablecloths and the tiny crystal vase with a sprig of freesia in the centre of every table. Waiters bustled discreetly, bringing menus, pouring wine, bearing plates of fish and meat and pasta, easing the flow of commerce around the room.

'This is nice,' Virginia said again, in the satisfied tones of an anthropologist lighting upon a tribal Eden.

'Have you decided what you want to eat?' Francis asked.

Virginia looked at him. 'Can I have something off the main menu or should I stick to the special lunch?'

'Have whatever you like,' he said, and then felt graceless.

'On reflection,' she said. 'I think I will stick to the special lunch menu. It looks delicious.'

Francis looked at her. There were thin lines etched round her mouth and laughter crinkles round her eyes, but her hair was still as lustrous as when they had got married. She had kept her cheekbones, he thought uncomfortably.

'Yes it does, doesn't it,' he said, trying to soften his voice. 'I will join you.'

The restaurant was full now with the hunter-gatherers hard at work, snouting out deals and snuffling up the fodder presented before them.

Virginia asked about Rachel. Francis asked about school.

'Francis,' Virginia said finally, 'I need to ask you for something – for James.'

So it was money. As usual.

'If that's what you wanted, you could have asked last night,' Francis said. 'Or you could have rung. It would have saved you the fare. You didn't need to see me.'

She looked at him. 'Oh Francis,' she said ruefully. She forked a scallop into her mouth. 'I wanted to talk about James with you. Something important. The phone is not the right way of doing that.'

Francis pushed his plate back. He said nothing.

'Is everything all right?' asked a waiter, appearing solicitously at the table.

'Fine,' said Francis shortly.

'Oh, yes,' said Virginia, 'delicious.' She smiled up at the waiter. Francis saw interest spark in his eye. She still had that effect on men.

Words surfaced from the babbling room around them. 'Fifteen per cent', 'Y2K', 'back end', 'front end'. 'Million.' 'Billion.' 'Morgan Stanley.' Money talking.

Virginia looked at the familiar tight look on his face. He was not meeting her eye. 'Francis,' she said softly. 'It is important we talk – really talk – about this. It is important for James.'

Francis remembered that low smoky timbre and something stirred which he knew should have been buried long ago. And then he felt a prick of anger. How could she use that tone, which belonged to their most precious private times together, to ask for money?

'And?' he said. He hated how she could push him into being the cold and defensive man he did not want to be.

'It would be nice if you took a little more interest in James,' she said. 'None of this is his fault. It was your choice – remember?'

'Virginia, I will give you whatever it is you want. Just tell me and I will do it.'

He had been so happy, in those faraway sunlit days, besotted with Virginia and doting on their baby boy. At the weekends he'd done the household accounts with James sitting on his lap, punching the calculator keys with one hand, James sucking the little finger of his other hand. He'd adored him. A chain of Carrolls had stretched out behind and before him – back through his father and and grandfather then down through James and then eventually through James's children and their children and grandchildren, a pulsating link between past and future.

Those humdrum tasks had once stitched them together, but the last ten years had unravelled all that. He observed at intervals how the peachy boy had stretched into an awkward, lanky teenager and was now thickening out into a handsome man. Francis marked the milestones but he was not with him on the journey. He wished he could have been. He wished he could explain this to Virginia – and to James.

The smiling, friendly waiter was back. 'Would you like dessert? Or coffee?' Francis ignored him and looked at Virginia.

'Coffee,' she said.

'Two coffees please,' said Francis. The waiter disappeared. 'How much do you want?' Francis said.

'"How much do I want"?' Is that what it all comes down to?' Virginia said. 'Thirteen years and you leave us and this is what it comes down to?'

'I provide you with everything you and James need,' he said stiffly. 'Thank you,' he added as the waiter put the coffees on the table.

'Not everything,' Virginia said, ignoring the waiter.

Francis looked at his coffee miserably. It always ended up with Virginia making him feel mean-spirited. 'He's twenty-three, not three,' he said defensively. Francis never understood why he should be made to feel like this. He had always behaved decently and responsibly.

Virginia took a sip of her coffee. She knew she always ended up saying the same things to Francis whenever they met like this. It never made any difference. But she could not let go. She felt the hurt in

James every time he returned from seeing Francis. He never said anything but she knew. Why could Francis not see it?

'How much do you want?' Francis asked again.

Virginia looked at him. 'What's the point,' she thought. 'Thirty thousand pounds,' she said.

'I'll pay it into your account,' Francis said. He signalled to the waiter to bring him the bill. It had been money after all. That was all. It was wearingly inevitable. All this drama and urgency, so typical of Virginia, and it had just been another request for more money.

Then he registered what she had just said. 'Thirty thousand pounds? Why do you need as much as that?' he asked. Every spare penny he had was assigned to InterTrust. He had expected her to demand a few hundred. Not thirty thousand. What on earth could James want all that money for? And where was he going to find it?

'James needs it,' she said. 'It's complicated.' She had dreaded the question. She could see no way of wrapping up the answer.

'I'm sure I can find a way to understand,' Francis said drily.

'He needs it to pay a dealer.'

'What do you mean?' said Francis, and then 'thank you' as the waiter placed the bill on the table by him.

'He owes the money to a man for drugs,' Virginia said patiently.

'Dealing drugs?' Francis asked incredulously. 'James has been dealing drugs?' This did not belong in his life.

'Listen to me, you stupid man,' Virginia said. 'He has been buying drugs and there was an accident and he needs to reimburse the dealer. I did not say he had been dealing himself.'

'How much does thirty thousand pounds "buy" you? Wake up, Virginia. How much can the boy stuff up his own nose? I'd be grateful if you could explain the difference between buying thirty thousand pounds' worth of drugs and dealing.' This really could not belong in his life.

'If you want to know, don't interrupt me.'

'I'm listening.'

'He was buying some cocaine for some friends, for a party or something . . .'

'And that's not dealing?' This did not belong in his life of Rachel and Surrey and lists of things to do for InterTrust. It could not belong in his life.

'Do you want to know or not?'

Francis waited in furious silence. It was typical of Virginia to do this to him now.

'It was only for his own use – he swears – and his friends. They all do it. But the dealer had a lot with him to deliver on his rounds.'

'Is this how you have brought him up?' Her matter-of-fact tone incensed him.

'Do you want to listen or not?' she said. 'Someone knocked on the door. It's not completely clear to me what happened next but it seems that they panicked. And they seem to have flushed the lot down the lavatory. And now the dealer wants him to pay for all of it.'

'Why shouldn't the dealer pay? He was responsible for it,' Francis said, realising finally that this was now unmistakably and unavoidably in his life.

'It's not one of your contracts you get your lawyers to sort out.' Virginia tried to keep the exasperation out of her voice. 'These are bad people, Francis.'

'More coffee?' The smiling, friendly waiter was back again to collect Francis's credit card.

'No,' said Francis.

'No thank you,' said Virginia.

'He needs us,' she continued. 'I know he's been stupid, but he's young. He'll make his mistakes. And we need to be there for him when he does.' Virginia looked at Francis, trying to make him look at her.

Francis looked at the table. 'Mistakes?' She called this a mistake? Francis had made mistakes. He knew what a mistake was. This was not a mistake. It was a disaster. What sort of mother was she?

'Francis,' Virginia said. 'Please don't look so sour. He has made a mistake. He knows it. But it's happened. There's no going back. Whatever you feel about it, it has happened. We can't make it un-happen.'

He remembered this language from before.

'Don't be negative,' she said, 'We must focus on what should happen now. We should focus on what we have to do now.'

Francis did what he was told. He focused on telling Rachel he had just given thirty thousand pounds to Virginia to buy cocaine for James. Even if she became a partner there would be no holiday this year. Or next. She would go mad. And he could hardly blame her.

'It's easy for you,' he said. 'We don't all have your free-floating morality.'

'Oh Francis,' she said. 'This is James. He needs help. What are you going to do about it? Haven't you got the money?'

'Of course I have got it.' Francis was stung, as he knew she meant him to be. 'That's not the point. How have you let him grow up like this? Thirty thousand pounds of drugs? This isn't a "mistake", Virginia. It's a crime. And now you are asking me to pay for those drugs, Virginia. That's a crime too. And then you expect me to smile and sign the cheque? How could you have let this happen?'

'Don't be so melodramatic,' she said. 'This sort of thing happens all the time nowadays. They all do drugs. This could happen to anyone.'

'It's not happening to anyone,' he said. 'It's happening to me.'

Virginia looked at him. Nothing changed. He had always glowed with bad temper. And he still did. And he still just did not get it.

'You don't get it, Francis,' she said.

'Get what?' he interrupted. 'What don't I get? What exactly don't I get? I get it that you want thirty thousand pounds from me. I get it that it's for drugs. Cocaine. Thirty thousand pounds for cocaine. I get that. And I get it that it's a criminal offence to buy drugs. And an even worse one to fund drug-dealing. I get that. And I get it that you want me to commit that criminal offence. I get that too. So what exactly is it that I don't get?'

'You are still fixing on negatives,' Virginia explained.

'Don't give me that hippie nonsense.'

'What's the point in raging against him for being stupid? Or me for being such a bad mother? That's the point, Francis: what is the point? It's negative. The point is to do something about it. Don't stare at the problem – look for the answer.'

'And the answer in this case is what? Paying thirty thousand pounds?'

'What other option is there?' Virginia asked.

'Go to the police. This is against the law. Let them deal with it.'

'And what do you think would happen to James if the police "deal with it"? Do you want him to go to jail? Do you?'

'And what do you think will happen to James if he's allowed to think that he can behave like this and there will never be any consequences from his actions? His stupid, criminal actions. Do you want your son to grow up without any sense of responsibility, unable to stand on his own two feet and take the consequences of his actions – like a man?' But as Francis spoke he realised how pompous he must sound and how little weight James's moral development would carry over the darling boy going to jail.

Virginia looked at him, flushed with temper. 'Francis, James is in trouble. It happens. Being a parent is not a deal you can opt out of when you feel like it. What do you do when your son crosses a drug baron? You help him. That's what you do.'

'What do you mean "a drug baron"? Why do you have to talk like that?'

'All right, Francis, don't give me the money. I just thought I would ask. I hope you don't mind me asking.' Virginia finished her coffee and pushed her chair back. 'I would have thought you might have wanted to support your son when he needed it. But don't worry, I'll find some way to do it myself. Thank you for lunch.'

She always did this. She always made him feel bad about himself when he had done nothing wrong. 'I didn't say I wouldn't help him,' he said. 'I will think about it.'

Virginia was always coming back for something else. It made Rachel furious. And he could understand why. It must be hard enough marrying someone so much older and even harder when a first wife and son still lurked in the background. And it must be intolerable when the first wife was as demanding as Virginia. And now she was asking for thirty thousand pounds.

'I'll think about it,' he repeated. He needed to get back to the office. He should not have to cope with this now, not when he had so much else to do. Why could Virginia not handle this on her own – for once? He felt a vein beginning to throb in his temple.

'James doesn't have time to think about it,' Virginia said. 'Are you going to give him the money or not?'

'I'll think about it,' Francis said again. 'I will call you tomorrow.' He held out his hand to Virginia. He did not feel like kissing her goodbye.

'Goodbye, Francis,' Virginia said, ignoring his hand.

He watched her as she turned and walked out of the restaurant, graceful and elegant. And he felt sick.

Where was he going to get the money? He had set aside everything he had for InterTrust. If he took thirty thousand pounds from that, what would it mean for his baby company? What if a deal depended on him investing the full two hundred and fifty thousand he had already told investors he was ready to put in? Would they regard the sudden disappearance of thirty thousand as an act of bad faith and then not come in at all?

But if he did not pay, what would that mean for James? Telling the police and James going to jail. Or what? As Virginia had pointed out, these were bad people. They tended to drive their bad debts into the woods and blow their heads off with sawn-off shotguns.

What choice did he have?

He would have to pay up.

But why should Virginia always, always assume she could get whatever she wanted just by asking for it? She could wait until he had seen Charles and discussed the implications for InterTrust. What difference would a couple of days really make? It would do her good to wait for a bit for once.

And these people were hardly likely to do anything to James while they still thought they were going to get the money, were they?

Were they?

As he waited for the lift to take him back to his

office, Francis thought about James. And his mind was a wasteland prowled by worry and fear. What was going to happen to him?

Once, shopping, Francis had lost James for ten minutes. He had been sorting through frozen vegetables in the freezer compartment when he suddenly became aware that James was no longer beside him. He was so careful. He always made the five-year-old boy hold his hand wherever they went. But just for a moment he had let him go as he assessed the carrots. And then James was gone.

Francis looked up one aisle and down another. 'James,' he called. People looked at him curiously and edged away.

'James,' he yelled, running faster and faster through the vast fluorescent shed. 'James.'

But James was nowhere to be seen. Finally, Francis stopped running and went to the helpdesk. And there they put a call out and it soon emerged that a helpful assistant manager had scooped him up and taken him away to await collection. 'It's always happening,' she said to Francis, trying to reassure the distraught father. But Francis would never forget how he felt when he'd realised James had gone.

And now, in Silvergate House, a familiar gust of panic scurried through him. And he felt the ground fall suddenly away beneath him.

sixteen

wednesday 2.00 p.m.
Mumtaz was not in any of the guidebooks. Entered
through a narrow doorway on a busy stretch of
Kilburn High Road, it was an evening restaurant. Its
regular customers came after work and the passing
trade lurched in after the pubs closed, as the hot,
sour smells of vinegar and chilli beckoned enticingly
from the door. But at lunchtime the odours of
oil and spice appeared to be less attractive and
Mumtaz rarely had more than a handful of its tables
occupied and they only needed one waiter to look
after them, a slight, middle-aged Bengali who moved
with ponderous solicitousness. Roger liked it for
lunch.

That Wednesday afternoon, he sat waiting for Chris.
The restaurant was empty apart from a man in his
thirties with thinning fair hair, who sat with his back
to the room reading the *Daily Mail*. In front of him
was a belly spreading with the disappointments of
early middle age, a pint of lager, a plate of poppadoms,
a heaped bowl of rice, and three metal platters swimming in brown gravy. There were colour posters of
the Taj Mahal and Goa on the cinnamon-coloured

walls and, in the corner by the door to the kitchen, a fan circulated the sweaty air.

Roger sipped a tepid Coca-Cola. He liked to hold his meetings in Mumtaz. Not because of the food – he hardly ever ate anything – but because it was so improbable. He would never bump into anyone he knew here. Roger insisted Chris never met him at the office. Just in case. If it ever came to it, he did not want anyone to tie him up with Chris or Jason. And the game really would be up if anyone ever found him doing business here.

Without taking his eyes off the newspaper, the man at the other table placed a brimming spoonful of curry in his mouth. Roger looked at his watch. Chris was late. Forty-five minutes late. The Bengali waiter sat at the back near the fan and stared into space. Roger took another sip of the Coca-Cola. These boys were becoming a complication. Jason would probably stay in line now but he had never been the real problem. Roger knew that. It was Chris who was the difficult one. And he could infect others. And he had probably done so already.

The solitary diner put a final spoonful of curry into his mouth and pushed the plate away. Roger looked at his watch again.

He had suspected they were cutting the cocaine. Roger prided himself on the quality of his product. It was packaged up for delivery with a label he had designed himself – 'Scotty', with a picture of the character from *Star Trek* – that was run off at the print shop round the corner from the office. It was a quality brand. His customers relied on that. But on some of the rounds business had been falling off. When that happened, Roger had learnt that unreliability was often the reason. And it had not taken much to get Jason to confess. But Jason had not given up anyone else. It had just been him, he had insisted.

Roger did not believe him. He was too stupid to do it on his own. But Jason refused to say anything about Chris. Even in the basement with Phil Crask when he had been clearly terrified. It made Roger wary. Either Chris really had nothing to do with it or Jason was even more frightened of Chris than he was of Phil Crask. So there was a fifty-fifty chance that Chris was a problem. A serious problem: Phil Crask was a frightening man.

The Bengali waiter reappeared and sat back down on his chair. It was not a good sign that Chris was so late. It was something other than the carelessness of youth. Roger looked through the menu again. It passed the time. He already knew what he would have. He always had it: chicken tikka and a cup of tea.

The door opened, letting in the noise of the traffic outside. The solitary diner looked up briefly and then returned to his newspaper. Chris was tall and well-built in a way that indicated regular visits to the gym, with what the Bombay papers' matrimonial columns referred to as a 'wheaten' complexion. He was dressed in silver jogging pants and a white T-shirt with the designer's logo in a large silver semi-circle on the back. He walked with an unselfconscious coiled energy. His black hair had been shaved close to the skull. He sat down opposite Roger with a smile. 'Sorry I'm late,' he said politely. A scent of flowers wafted round him. Roger waited for the excuse. None came.

Chris picked up the menu and looked through it. Roger watched him carefully, waiting to see if his stare would trigger some response. Chris seemed oblivious. 'What are you having?' he asked.

'Chicken tikka,' Roger said. He raised his hand to call over the waiter. 'We'll order. What are you having?'

'A beer,' said Chris.

'What are you having to eat?' Roger asked coldly.

'Nothing,' said Chris. 'I'm not hungry.'

Roger said to the waiter: 'Chicken tikka, five poppadoms, a plate of rice, a cup of tea. And a beer for him.' The waiter stood by the table and painstakingly wrote this down. Chris ran his hand over his shaved head and looked around the restaurant. The man was still carefully reading the *Daily Mail*. Roger said nothing. Through the window he could see a shiny blue BMW convertible parked on the double yellow lines right outside the restaurant. The little prick was doing well out of him.

The waiter disappeared into the kitchen. As if in honour of Chris's arrival, an ancient sound-system was switched on and a plaintive Bollywood lament swirled through the room. Neither of them spoke. Roger could still smell those flowers. It reminded him of something.

'What's that funny smell?' he said.

'What smell?'

'That smell you brought in with you.'

'Geranium and lime. My favourite flowers. I have the cologne made up specially.'

Roger stared at him. Who did the little prick think he was?

The waiter returned with a beer that he placed carefully in the middle of the table. Chris reached for it and raised the glass. 'Cheers,' he said pleasantly.

Roger looked at him but said nothing.

The solitary diner turned round. 'Oi,' he said, raising his hand towards the waiter, 'the bill.' The waiter inclined his head in an ancestral gesture of assent and disappeared back into the kitchen. He returned with a scrap of paper. The man took out a wad from his pocket, peeled off two ten-pound notes and put them on the table. 'Keep it,' he said. 'Thanks.' He got up and lumbered out.

'Great music,' said Chris, smiling at Roger. Roger looked at him but did not say anything. Chris took another swig of his beer. The waiter returned, miraculously balancing a platter of chicken tikka, a plate of poppadoms, a bowl of rice, a cup of tea and an empty white plate. He placed the food on the table and took a grimy white napkin from over his arm and, courteously, carefully polished the empty plate before laying it in front of Roger.

Roger spooned the chicken tikka and rice onto his plate and took a mouthful. He chewed it, looking at Chris expressionlessly. Chris looked back at him with the start of a smile. Roger said nothing. He took a mouthful of tea. Chris continued to look at him. The music continued to swirl aimlessly around the deserted room.

Finally, Roger spoke. 'We've got a problem,' he said.

Chris waited.

'It's a serious problem,' Roger said and then he waited.

'What's that?' Chris asked affably. Roger looked at him sharply. This boy was a serious problem, he thought.

'It starts with Jason,' he said. 'You heard what happened to Jason?' It was a direct question and he knew Chris would not be able to avoid responding.

'Yes. It's a shame,' said Chris. Roger waited. Chris looked sad for Jason but he did not say anything more.

'Shame?' said Roger. 'I think Jason thought it was a bit more than a shame, don't you?'

'These things happen.' Chris shrugged.

Roger never lost control. He prided himself on that. This was a business and you had to approach it in a business-like way. But Chris was an irritating little prick.

'These things don't just "happen", you little prick,' he hissed. 'They happen because something else happens. There is a reason for everything. Nothing just happens. And you know what happened there?'

Chris looked at Roger with a half-smile but said nothing.

'He was ripping me off.' Roger was staring at Chris as he spoke, looking for something in his eyes, some recognition. Chris looked back, the amiable half-smile unfaltering.

'I know you know,' Roger said. He knew he sounded more like Phil Crask than Roger Oates but there was something about Chris that irritated him. 'I know you know,' he repeated, 'and you should know what happens when something happens like this. It's not going to happen again.'

Chris sat looking at him with the unwavering half-smile. It was infuriating. Who did this little prick think he was?

'If this happens again, then something is going to happen. Someone is going to get hurt. *Really* hurt.' Roger spoke quietly but as emphatically as he could, slowly, stressing the adverb. But the expression on Chris's face did not change. It was as if he could not care less what Roger said.

'Do you understand what I am saying?' Roger said.

Chris sipped his lager and swilled it once round his mouth before swallowing, savouring it.

'Do you understand what I am saying?' Roger repeated.

Chris took another mouthful of lager and nodded. 'Yes,' he said. 'I understand what you are saying. But I do not understand why you are saying it.' Chris had a soft, pleasant voice and he looked cordially at Roger as he spoke.

At the back of Roger's neck, the muscles began to tense and throb, distracting him. He cocked his head from one side to the other to ease the strain. Chris watched him curiously. As he moved his head, Roger felt he was getting back his sense of control. This little prick was too smart for his own well-being.

'There have been complaints,' he lied. 'Scotty is being cut. My customers don't expect that from Scotty. They are upset.' He paused momentarily to add weight to the next words. '*I* am upset,' he continued. He stared at Chris as he spoke. He did not expect him to give it up as Jason had given it up but he wanted him to know he was on to him. 'The Crasks are upset,' he added for good measure.

'Are you accusing me?' Chris still spoke low and pleasantly but an edge had entered his voice. Roger relaxed. At last they were onto it: familiar ground.

'Look at it from my point of view, Chris,' he said. 'The way I see it I have a quality product – known quality. Scotty is *known* as a *quality* product. And then some little prick thinks they will make a bit on the side and so they cut it. And then it's not a quality product any more. They're ripping off the customer and they're ripping me off. Put yourself in my place, Chris. How would you feel?'

He looked at Chris paternally, as if he was teaching him something he needed to know. He was back in control now.

'I would kill you,' Chris said. There was no half-smile now. He was completely serious. Roger felt his words had been snatched away. He looked at Chris, this time because he could not think what to say next. He wanted to tear his head off his neck. This little prick had a serious attitude-problem. Serious.

'So I should kill you?' he said eventually.

'I did not say that,' Chris said evenly. 'I said I would kill anyone who ripped me off. And I would.'

Roger believed him. That was the problem. The little prick was fearless. 'When I was your age,' he said, 'I was not frightened of anything. I thought bad things only happened to other people. Now I am older, I know that bad things can happen to anyone: to Jason –' he paused slightly '– even to you.'

Chris smiled, a full, warm grin. 'You're not very frightening, Mr Oates,' he said. 'You try hard, and it might work with Jason. But it doesn't work with me. Look at you: you can't even ask me straight out: am I ripping you off? Am I ripping you off?' He paused briefly. 'You're scared to ask, aren't you?'

For the second time, Roger felt the words disappear. The little prick. The fury was choking him. The little prick. That was all that came into his mind. Over and over again. Very quickly, the words tumbling over each other. The little prick. The little prick.

Chris sat back and looked at him, still smiling.

Gradually, Roger got the rage back under control. 'Listen to me, Chris,' he said, leaning forward, half-whispering. 'I can't prove you've been ripping me off but I don't need to. A guess will do. And I guess you've been stealing from me. Jason owned up. And he's too stupid to do it on his own. So that puts you right there. In the frame. And that's good enough for me. So now it's up to you. You've been warned. You won't be warned again. Take it or leave it. You choose.'

Roger sat back. His heart was thudding. He was still struggling with his fury. 'Who's scared?' he asked, almost to himself.

Chris had stopped smiling but he did not look

scared. 'It's your choice, Mr Oates,' he said. 'You think someone is ripping you off and that's a problem? That's not a problem. That's easy. Get the Crasks to do over Jason.' His soft voice displayed no sympathy for his friend. 'That's not a problem. Your business is shit. That's a problem.'

How old was this little prick? Roger wondered. He talked as if he went to Harvard Business School. Where did he learn this stuff?

'I don't care what you think about my business, Chris. You just do what you're paid to do, Chris. And don't steal.' Roger was now speaking as softly and deliberately as Chris. It was helping him keep his voice under control. 'Or you will be sorry.'

The Bengali waiter came out from the kitchen but, apparently sensing that something was wrong, he disappeared again. The fan clattered away in the corner and the music seemed to be on an endless loop of frustrated passion.

Chris nodded dismissively. 'Yeah, yeah,' he said. 'I'm sure I will be. And so will you. Why don't you ask yourself why some little prick like Jason steals from you.'

'Because you tell him to,' Roger said.

Chris ignored him. 'Because he's got no respect,' he said. 'And why has he got no respect? Because your business is shit, that's why,' he said. 'That's the problem,' he added helpfully.

'My business is shit?' Roger repeated incredulously. 'Who are you to tell me my business is shit? Who do you think you are?'

'It's obvious,' Chris continued calmly. 'You're not doing any high-margin products. If you did crack, you could double the turnover.' Roger wondered where Chris had learnt to speak like this. 'And you let the punters take liberties. You're soft. If they don't pay on the nail, twenty per cent interest. And if they don't pay that, don't give them credit. Whack them.'

It occurred to Roger that Chris was bidding for a partnership. He smiled at him. You're not as smart as you think, he thought. That was the trouble with being young. They could not understand. They did not have the experience. This little prick thought he was hard, but what did he know about pressure? How could he understand how smart this business really was? How important it was to keep out of trouble? Avoid heat? How could he understand there was no point in making fat margins for six months and spending the next fifteen years in jail. Or ending up under a motorway. Like that Mexican.

Now that was a sweet thought. This little prick propping up the M40, for ever entombed in his designer sportswear, gleaming mouth filled and little half-smile fixed for ever with concrete.

'Be careful you don't make a mistake,' Roger said.

Chris smiled again. 'OK,' he said. He swigged his beer. 'Enjoy it while you can, Mr Oates,' he said. 'Your people have had their day.'

'What the fuck do you mean – "had our day"?'

'I mean there are three billion of us – and how many of you? And where does the stuff come from? It doesn't grow in Kilburn, does it? It grows in our countries, in the fields of our fathers: in Pakistan, in Colombia, in Burma and Laos and Peru. Cochabamba doesn't sound much like Kilburn to me, Mr Oates. Who does the work? We do. Who takes the risks? We do. Who makes the money? You do. That's wrong, Mr Oates, that's imperialism. You take our crops and you take the profit. The Empire is finished, Roger old chap – time to take back what is ours. End racist capitalist expropriation. The future is bright, Roger, the future is brown.'

What was he talking about? Why was he talking like a Mongolian-politics textbook?

'What the fuck do you mean – "three billion"? You and Jason, that's two, you thick fuck, not three billion.'

'Three billion brown people, Mr Oates. My people. Indians, Chinese. The future. You lot are finished. Twentieth century. The future is brown.'

'What the fuck are you talking about, you fucking little prick? They are not the same, Indians and Chinese. They're different. And they're not your people. You're from Kilburn, you demented dickhead, not Cokistan. And it's just you and Jason – that's your people. Two of you. Not three billion. And I don't give a fuck whether you are brown or pink or fucking tangerine. Just don't fuck with my business. Do not fuck it up.'

'OK,' Chris said, starting to get up. 'Nice to see you again, Mr Oates.'

Roger thought he would have to be very careful. Chris was mad. Not just a little prick, but an insane little prick. He could be trouble. Roger did not want to go back to the Crasks so soon after Jason. It might look like he was losing his grip. He might have to do this himself. He smiled menacingly at Chris.

'Let me get this,' Chris said, and put a fifty-pound note on the table. He smiled at Roger. 'Nice to see you, Mr Oates,' he said again as he left.

Roger watched him get into the BMW. The little prick had not even got a ticket. He would have to deal with this idea that he was soft and that punters were getting away with it. Before anyone else believed it. He would have to show everyone that he was keeping a grip on it all. A tight grip. He had better get that thirty grand before Chris started spreading the wrong idea about how soft he was. He had better go and see Davey.

seventeen

wednesday 2.05 p.m.

As Francis came into his office, he saw Virginia had made him late. The three men due at two o'clock were sitting patiently, sleek and bronzed, in the reception area. These men were coming to see him because they wanted to invest in InterTrust. And he was late. And you never kept money waiting. He forced a smile.

'This is a nice set-up, Francis,' Lloyd Fredricksen said.

Trim, silver-haired Lloyd, with a photograph of his boat in his wallet, had sacked Francis eight years ago. But money is no more sentimental than it is patient and nowadays Lloyd ran a new £200 million venture-capital fund. Francis had asked him to invest and here he was, once again, coming to weigh Francis on the scales.

That had been a bad time for Francis. Finally, absolutely, divorced from Virginia, adrift in his mid-thirties, earning well but going nowhere much and then Lloyd had sacked him. And Francis would never forgive him for that hammer blow. But money is practical even more than it is unsentimental and impatient and Francis needed five million to keep InterTrust going until the flotation cashed in. And Lloyd had two hundred million pounds to invest.

'How much is it costing you?' Matt Barker asked. Matt and Lloyd had worked together for years. Francis didn't know the third man, Dan Cornell, as well.

'Enough,' Francis replied, with a confident laugh. He knew it looked good. He wanted them to be impressed. Knocked out. He wanted to show Lloyd what he had let go.

A wide, confident corridor led off the reception area to an open-plan office, twenty people burning up money with keyboard symphonies of taps and clicks. Francis's personal assistant sat in a large room to the side. The walls were the golden yellow of cream-crust, but that was only the framing for the monitors that covered them from ceiling to knee height – silver screens showing the flickering, thrilling dance of equities and bonds in Taipei and Toronto, Sydney, Rome, Buenos Aires and London. The room rippled and shimmied as the nerves of a hundred markets twitched and shivered in trepidation and exultation.

The jittery ballet of the markets had been broken up with screens showing carefully constructed montages – besides the live feeds from all the twenty-four-hour news stations there were timeless images of water – waves and waterfalls – and mountains, avalanches in slow motion.

It was all mute. It was as if the rich, soft carpet had soaked up the noise that should have accompanied the frenetic movements on the screens. Only the occasional vibration of the telephones and the matching modulated tones of the personal assistant, subliminally audible, indicated that this was not a fifty-thousand-pound art installation from Hoxton.

This was all Francis thought he needed in here. The backroom operation was in Bangalore. Even if it had not been cheaper, his investors would have expected it to be.

He led Lloyd and his colleagues down the corridor to his office.

His office looked like a million-dollar-banker's office. Sometimes Francis worried that he had played too safe – solid enough for a million-dollar office but not quirky enough for a billion-dollar one. But mostly he was happy with it. The rich yellow, the light woods, the vista from the great thick glass windows.

In a corner, a flat-screen monitor charted the blue rise and and the red fall of shares that had caught the momentary interest of a dyspeptic broker in Milwaukee or sparked the disdain of a business-studies graduate in Manchester. Red and blue. The constant intoxicating excitement of not knowing what fate those millions of capricious investors would deal out today. Blue and red.

The three investors arranged themselves around the table. Joanne brought in the coffee. Francis started the show. He had polished it so often it now shone and gleamed. 'We are living in revolutionary times,' he began. 'Five years ago, who had heard of the Internet?'

Usually, the performance against the setting of his perfect million-dollar office invested him with confidence. In his office, Francis could feel the swelling majesty of the money that would flow through it, rolling over the maple conference table, out through the windows, to mingle with the Mississippi floods of capital washing through the City of London to Europe and New York and Asia and beyond to all of the known universe, building the factories and the malls, creating the jobs and the personal trainers, buying cars and computers and Mediterranean villas and clapboard cottages in the Hamptons and commissioning string quartets and video installations and making possible second careers and third wives, opening shops and flying planes, worlds fecund with choice and opportunity.

But now, after his lunch with Virginia, as he intoned the friendly figures for disposable income and savings ratios in households with Internet access, there was no infusion of confidence. Instead he just kept thinking about James.

'That's the opportunity – fifty per cent of households with disposable incomes of at least eighty thousand dollars a year spending at least two hours a week on the Internet,' he said.

He thought: How do you spend thirty thousand pounds on drugs? What was James thinking of? What has happened to him?

Lloyd asked a question about the software.

Francis said: 'I can arrange a demonstration for you if you want to follow up. I've got a team producing an upgrade now in Bangalore. Ashok Sen is leading the team. Eight years with Oracle. I am lucky to have him.'

'You should talk to the boy,' Virginia had said in the restaurant. 'He's mortified. It's only money. You can afford it. Six months from now you won't even notice it's gone.'

The hurt had propagated like a virus. Him. Virginia. James. Or had it been the other way round? Virginia. Him. James. Wherever it had started, it had ended up with James.

In the corner, the monitor flickered: a wave of blue swept down it. Then an avalanche of red.

Matt asked about the burn rate. Obviously, they had worked out a routine before they came: Matt would do the money, Lloyd the technical stuff and Dan would ask about the people. He hoped this mechanical preparation did not mean they were just seeing him out of politeness. He gave the figures to Matt, angling the laptop so the three men could follow the spreadsheet.

'Daddy,' James had said when Francis left. Nothing else. It was not even a question. Just a statement without expression. Flat. That was all he heard then. The flatness. Now when it echoed round his head he heard the desperation of a boy who could think of nothing else to say, nothing to make his world turn around, nothing to make things different, nothing to make them stay the same, nothing to make it the way he so desperately wanted it to be. Nothing. Not a thing.

Matt was asking more questions, about rates of return, security. Francis heard himself answering, fluent, articulate, the figures persuasive. Did he sound as detached as he felt? Perhaps that was why the meeting was going so well. Begging never worked, he thought. Particularly not with Lloyd.

'Are you able to get the talent?' Dan asked. 'It's hard at the moment. Demand for Y2K work is going through the roof.'

'I am having to pay for it but the costs are all factored into the figures,' Francis said. 'And I can assure you that we are getting the best. Everyone wants to come in on something like this. They can see a future in it. It's not like the Millennium Bug. By March next year, that will all be over. But InterTrust will just be beginning.'

Thirty thousand pounds. Why should she think he would just have that amount of cash instantly available?

'Remind me how much you are putting in,' Lloyd said.

Francis felt his stomach hollowing. Why were they all asking this question? 'Two hundred and fifty thousand,' he said.

Lloyd pursed his lips. 'Hmm,' he said.

'What?' Francis said. 'It's five per cent of what I am asking you to put in.'

'Exactly,' Lloyd said. 'You are looking to us to take ninety-five per cent of the risk.'

'And ninety-five per cent of the reward,' Francis responded. 'And the difference is that it's not your personal money. This is my house we are talking about here.'

'What about stock options for the staff?' Dan asked

quickly. Francis took him through the position, explaining the implications for the flotation. He had done it so often now, it flowed. Rachel would have been proud of him.

Matt worried away at the figures, going through catechisms of 'what if'.

And in the corner, the monitor blinked implacably: red and blue, blue and red, fermenting money.

'Look at the figures another way,' Matt said. 'What if you don't get the customer base up to a hundred thousand by next Christmas, you have then got two scenarios, haven't you?'

There were two scenarios that could account for why Matt was doing this. Either they were serious about coming in and for so much they wanted to be completely sure. Or Matt was making a point about why they were not going to come in at all.

Sudden doubt churned in Francis's gut. Matt had never liked him. Was it always going to be like this, he thought, never quite getting there? Like his father. First Philippe yesterday morning. Now this. He felt again the same sick feeling he had felt when his mother had told him that his father had lost his job and they were going to have to move house. Rage flushed through him. This was not going to happen to him. He was not going to let someone like Matt Barker do him in. He was not going to let Lloyd do him over again. He was not going to become his father.

In photographs he looked like him. Good-looking. 'So neat,' Virginia's mother said when they met at the wedding. It had been a revelation to see his father through the eyes of Virginia's family. They saw groomed good-looks, self-possession, business vocabulary and comfortable affluence. But Francis grew up with the tense evening silences the day a colleague was promoted, triple Scotches before dinner, serious golf with board directors taking him away at weekends, absent-minded affection. The defeats had rooted in his father like cancer. He said nothing but Francis saw the hurt eating him, as a carelessly optimistic and handsome and promising twenty-five-year-old became a punctilious reserved man of fifty and the spark went out of his eye. Crushed dreams powdered Francis's adolescence. He was not going to be his father. The game was not over. He was still playing.

'It's not quite so simple, Matt,' he said pleasantly. He explained it again, politely reminding Matt of the core assumptions. He could feel his confidence flowing surely back as he spoke. The comfort of the facts, the strength of the figures, the boldness of his vision, all flooding out the acid doubt that Matt had created.

He felt the men leaning towards him.

Lloyd said: 'Thank you, Francis. This is an interesting proposition.' He had always been pompous and patronising. What sort of man carries a photograph of his boat in his wallet? But Francis knew they were going to come in. 'I think we could be interested.'

Francis thought, it's working. The heady scent of greed was irresistible. How could they let this opportunity pass? When TheGlobe.com had been up over six hundred per cent on the first day's trading. When

GeoCities had sold for $3.6 billion. When even Exchange.com had sold for $200 million. Irresistible.

'But there is a problem,' Matt said. 'We like your proposition. It's different. We think it could fly.' Francis hated his level, sincere tone. He used it himself. He knew what it meant. 'We like you,' Matt continued. 'We think you could make it work.'

Lloyd and Dan sat patiently, watching Francis.

'But dotcoms may have peaked,' Matt went on. 'We've had three IPOs pulled in the last week. It's an overreaction. We still feel the long-term is good. But short-term, there is a problem.'

Francis sensed Lloyd watching him for a reaction. He said nothing.

'We are not sure we could get an IPO away in the current climate,' Matt finished. 'And you know we have got to see an exit before we commit. And you are asking a lot of money from us.'

Francis waited. He felt time stop in the still room. 'Could be interested' did not, after all, mean 'would be interested'. Was he going to have to scale down. Or shut down? He might need every penny of that thirty thousand pounds for InterTrust now. And even if he didn't, Rachel would still go mad that he could even contemplate putting their home at risk. And for this. How could Virginia have let it happen?

'You are a talented man, Francis,' Lloyd said. 'We want to get behind you.' Francis hated him, this patronising, condescending silver-haired man with a photograph of his boat in his wallet and five million pounds that Francis needed.

'The clock is ticking, Lloyd,' Francis said. It was the sort of thing Lloyd would say. Francis hoped he recognised it.

Lloyd smiled a wintry smile and said nothing.

Virginia had looked so English in the wedding photographs, with her wiry blonde sensuality, holding his hand and smiling wickedly at him, deliberately subverting the formality of the occasion. His mother could not understand why Virginia wanted to mock everything and why her serious, handsome son, who could have had anyone, should have brought home this strife when life would provide him with so much else to worry about.

'We will want to run through some figures,' Lloyd said. 'But we should get back to you next week.' Matt and Dan smiled at Francis. At least they had not said anything more about the two hundred and fifty thousand. It was not a 'no' but it certainly was not a 'go' either.

How was he going to tell Rachel? Perhaps he did not need to tell her? Surely sometimes it was best not to shine a searchlight into every corner of a relationship?

'Good,' Francis said. 'Thank you for coming.' He shook hands with each of them as they left the room, as if it were all much the same to him whether they got back to him or not.

If he just paid up but did not tell Rachel, it would not require him to lie to her, just not to tell her. And after all, he did not always tell her everything about everything. How could he?

And then he felt ashamed. How he could he not tell her? 'Trust is a glue,' he said to investors, 'it holds cyberspace together.' He should have realised that it was true not just for investors but for Rachel too. He had to tell her and he would do it tonight. He would see Charles on his way home and then talk it over with Rachel. She would understand. Then he would give Virginia her answer. But in due course. It would do her good to wait a bit.

eighteen

'Listen to this, man, the two of them are sitting at the breakfast table, rapping, blah, blah, blah, eating their Cornflakes, and then bang, the door opens, and then bang bang, they're dead. Just like that. One minute it's like the weather and Tony Blair and Cornflakes and the next minute they're dead.'

Davey Boswell sat in the all-white lobby of the hotel and poured himself green tea from the dark metal pot, a replica of Mongolian tribal teaware. A Mesopotamian water-clock in the corner showed the time. Ten to three.

'Anyway, this chick is making their toast in the kitchen. She's just put the Cornflakes on the table and they're alive, these two big Jamaicans, and then she's gone back to the kitchen and the next minute bang, bang, brains all over the wall. Two dead Jamaicans. It's like the Harlesden Breakfast Bloodbath. Heckler & Koch MP5K by the sound of it.'

The brand name was said precisely and affectionately.

'And the chick doesn't see nothing. But she hears it. And it's like nothing happens in her head. She's in the kitchen, she hears the noise and it's like so quick she doesn't stop to think like man this is bad shit I'd better keep my head down. It's reflex. She turns round to see what's going down and there's brains all over the wall and nobody there, just two dead Jamaicans. Who'd been sitting there eating Cornflakes the last time she turned around.'

At the other end of the lobby, a young, beautiful receptionist, dressed all in black, stood motionless behind a desk, contemplating the middle distance. Roger always met Davey here as he blended in so well. Now in his mid-forties, Davey had long hair streaked with grey, tied in a ponytail, and a drawn, angular face. He wore a black linen suit and a black T-shirt. He was indistinguishable from the middle-aged rock stars who used the hotel on their swings through London. He was enjoying the story he was telling Roger.

'Anyway, so the next thing, the neighbour's banging on the door and he comes in and sees these two Jamaican dudes at the table, faces blown away, brains everywhere – and this chick, it's amazing, man, she's like in the kitchen still making the toast. She turns around, sees the brains all over the wall and she just turns back around and goes on making the toast.'

Davey looked at Roger as if he still couldn't quite believe it.

'Can you dig it, man, she's still making their fucking toast. And the neighbour looks at her and thinks maybe she's like deaf and blind, you know, one of those mutes, because how could anyone go on making toast when these two dudes have got their brains all over the wall next door. I mean she's not even, like, crying. She's just making the toast.'

Roger nodded politely. Davey always had some story like this. Blah blah blah as he put it. It was never very interesting and none of it made him any more money. But Davey was useful so he always listened politely to his interminable stories. Davey obviously now sensed Roger's disengagement.

'Anyway, it's going to mean trouble, man, because these two dudes were like a major connection for the Crasks. Yardies, you know. Major, major source. And big-time crackheads on their own account. They like kept Harlesden supplied. This is war, man.'

Roger nodded again. These things happened from time to time and he always kept away. Too much grief, too much risk, too much uncertainty. You never knew when you were going to be eating your Cornflakes and someone would walk in through the door and blow your brains out. Better, to Roger's way of thinking, to keep away from all that. That was the beauty of his business and something those little pricks like Chris never understood.

But Davey was useful. Roger left most of the physical work to the Crasks. Much of the other stuff he did himself. But every so often there were things he needed someone else to do, and someone reliable. And that was Davey.

Roger had known him since Davey got out of prison. Once upon a time he had obviously been a happy little hippie drifting around the festivals peddling penny packets of grass and helping out as an occasional roadie for rock bands that never quite made it. Something had gone wrong and he had ended up in jail and emerged two years later, still talking like a hippie but with a hardness that kept people careful around him.

Davey had done his time in full because he put a man in prison hospital for six weeks, knocking him out with a saucepan and continuing to batter him until his nose was pulp. Davey was probably not a psychopath. It was more likely that the drugs had just corroded the connection in his brain between event and significance. It wasn't that he especially enjoyed pulping noses and killing people, it was just another thing that had to be done when it had to be done. It was all the same to him. Life for Davey was lived on an even keel of small pleasures and everyday tasks: good dope, Jack Daniels, bacon sandwiches, Jimi Hendrix, preferably all together, eased him through the week – and if he had to take time out to do a job, like whack someone, well then he took time out to do it. It was all much the same to Davey. He rubbed along.

Davey's temperament was debated among his acquaintances. Some thought it was steady. Others thought he was a gill short of a pint. Some said the drugs had bombed his brains out. But it was universally acknowledged that his work was characterised by bleak implacability. Even the Crasks were disconcerted by how he took out an accountant who was skimming a syndicate in which Davey was involved. He had rung the front doorbell, shot the man's wife when she opened the door, kept moving, walked into the kitchen where the man was eating his dinner, shot him, kept moving, marched upstairs when he heard the children screaming and shot them too. The baby was eighteen months and the little boy was three years old.

Everyone understood the need to be careful, but even the Crasks thought that Davey had gone too far. The baby was in her cot and these children were hardly going to be witnesses. Davey had been lucky to get away with it. Because of the little children there had been massive publicity and the police had poured resources into trying to find the killer.

Davey somehow escaped. But he noticed how much attention it got on television and he was more careful after that. He learned the lesson. But no-one forgot what he had done. Even the Crasks were careful around him. Even the Crasks never knew quite where they were with someone who was so obviously out of his skull.

'More tea?' Roger asked. Roger liked Davey. He was his own man but Roger never had any trouble from him.

'No, I'm cool, man. What's up?'

'Two jobs. First, watch that little prick Chris. I want to know what he's doing, who he's seeing. Be careful, I don't want him to know. Report back tomorrow.'

'Cool.' Roger knew Davey would be careful. He didn't really need to say it. Davey would just hang out, amiably chatting to everyone he met, squirrelling away the information.

'And I need you to start keeping an eye on someone else,' Roger said. 'You might need to move on them next week.' He passed a piece of paper across with three names and addresses on it. 'This man has got the money but he might respond quickest if something happened to one of the others. You work out the best way of doing it.'

Davey nodded.

'But don't move till I say so. They will get a warning first. But if they don't want to listen, you will need to get going quickly. I don't need any delays in getting the money.'

'Cool,' Davey said.

Roger had a system for dealing with payment. It was carefully calibrated to extract money from even the most recalcitrant debtors, while avoiding unnecessary cost and trouble. There were not many bad payers, but, occasionally, customers were too out of it or too stupid – to Roger's way of thinking they let anyone into university nowadays – and then, in a final attempt to secure pain-free payment, Roger would try to deal with the parents. He did not like doing this as something could always go wrong with these middle-class professionals, used to arguing and getting their own way and getting paid for being smart.

And sometimes the parents resisted. But when they pointed out that no court would enforce such a debt or told him they would have turned him over to the police if they had not wanted to protect their child, Roger just smiled a wry smile, almost to himself, and nodded but said nothing. Then he got them mugged.

Not badly hurt. Just shaken up and robbed of their watch to remind them every time they looked at their wrist how much easier it would be to pay up than risk this violent world erupting again into their ordered lives.

It rarely failed. These people were used to making calculations. Every day at work they balanced risks and made judgements. They were intelligent people and, in the end, it was easier just to pay up. The lawyers and the doctors and the businessmen and the account-ants and the journalists, they were mostly all the same in the end. Mostly, they all paid up in the end.

Every now and then it did not work. And then Roger had to call in help. Usually the money then arrived, plus interest, minus the fee to the Crasks or Salim. Roger never asked what had persuaded them to pay up. He did not need to know.

Once or twice, the money never arrived. He never asked why not. He knew the Crasks – or Salim – would have done their best and it had just not worked. He knew sometimes people persuaded themselves they were heroes. Then there was a risk they would go to the police. And once you got the faintest suspicion that might happen, you had to move fast. Reading them accurately was an essential skill. You could never allow them to bring in the police. That really would be more trouble than it was worth. Easier to get them whacked. That way you had a good chance – not a guarantee, mind, but a good chance – of escaping grief. And it happened from time to time.

He did not need to know how. There were three

and a half thousand deaths on the roads every year. Middle-aged men died of heart-attacks all the time. Every so often a mid-life crisis caused middle-aged men to run off and never be heard of again. Their families never knew what had happened to them. But Roger had a good idea. He did not need to know in detail how the Crasks retained their credibility – he just knew they would have done.

But Roger did not want to go to the Crasks again so soon after asking them for help with Jason. He would have to do this one himself. He would have to show he had a grip on the business.

'You may have to get a move on,' he said again. 'I don't want anyone thinking they can take liberties.'

'Cool.'

Roger knew he could rely on Davey. And in the white calm of the hotel he felt that, one way and another, it was all, as Davey would say, cool. This was how he earned his money: deploying his resources, doing the business. In control. Something those little pricks could never understand. Any fuckwitted pimple could make money for a few months. But it took skill to spot the risks before they became a problem and deal with them before they dealt with you. This was how to go on getting the money in, not just for one mad, careering three-month binge before you were extinguished like some demented butterfly, but month after month, nice and safe and easy, month after month.

This is how he did it. And only one more year, getting the money in, month after month, and he was gone: American Airlines direct to Honolulu, him and Maggie, gone. 'Keep in touch,' he said.

'Cool, man,' Davey said.

Roger knew Davey was already mulling over how to get the money out of the banker: how he was going to calibrate the pain and where he was going to inflict it.

nineteen

wednesday 5.30 p.m.
Virginia felt exhausted. At her desk, at the end of the parents' evening, tiredness seeped through every part of her as she sat and thought. She took a strand of her hair and trailed it under her nose. It had been a dreadful day. A fragrance lingered of distilled flowers, a private scent – hers – among the public ones of polish and ink and the damp anoraks of young children. Specks of dust were caught in the soft light of the empty classroom.

What on earth was she going to do about James? Francis, obviously, was not going to help. So she was going to have to do something.

She loved her son but she sometimes wondered if she had been too indulgent. They had always been close – as anyone would have expected a single mother and an only son to be – and Virginia loved that, but he did seem just a little slow in learning to cope for himself.

The light was turning downy in the summer evening. The children's voices from the playground were fading, as one by one they were removed to go home. Her life. The jaded room which needed painting and a new floor, walls covered with the bright energy of the children's colouring and dreams. Her desk, tidy, with a new laptop, incongruous on the scratched wood.

She was not upset by the fact that James had been doing drugs. It was not something she liked to think about but if she had asked herself the question she would have admitted she assumed he was. They all did. She had. But it was typical of James that he had ended up in such a mess. Everyone else's children might snort cocaine but it would be James who had to end up owing thirty thousand pounds to a drug baron. It was typical of his shambling incompetence.

And it was typical of him that it would all happen now, at the busiest time of her year, just when she was ready to collapse into her desperately needed summer break.

The parents' evening always put a seal on the school year. For Virginia it signalled the imminent departure of twenty-eight infants to rampage somewhere else for a while and the promise of a long summer of adult pleasures, uninterrupted by work. She loved the feeling of another school year done, another class started out on learning and life and the exhilarating sense of impending liberty, the summer stretching ahead with all the time in the world for the blood to flow slow and golden through her veins like honey.

But before then there was always a purgatory of paperwork: twenty-eight reports, forms for the free school meals next term, forms asking for stationery and floppy disks for September, forms requesting noncontact time for computer training, a personal reply she had to write to Mr and Mrs Court responding to their complaint that she had misunderstood Patsy's talents in English and Art, and a shorter reply to Ms Brocklehurst thanking her for her letter thanking her for the care she had taken with Suzie. And she had to do it all by the end of the week. And clear up after the school play – another landmark performance of 'Bugsy Malone' – which she had co-produced with Melanie.

And then, in the middle of all of this, James and his problem. At least he felt he could still turn to her for help. That was some comfort. But how was she going to get him out of this mess?

There were now only a few books on the right-hand pile: epitaphs for children whose parents had not turned up. The left-hand pile towered untidily, a term's achievement. The throng of parents had thinned and then dwindled away.

She had not expected Francis to be quite so awkward. The lunch with him had unsettled her. Of course, he was always difficult and she could never stop herself going too far when she met him. He was so punctiliously polite and reserved that he provoked her to prod and push until he reacted. And, of course, she had expected him to react badly to the news about James. She had expected him to complain and lecture her about the drugs. But, in the end, she had still expected him to pay up, as he always did.

She could hear the caretaker sweeping outside in the corridor, humming something to himself as he swept. Zygmunt. The children called him Ziggy. So did everyone else. He was Polish.

She never liked asking Francis for money. It was difficult for him, and in his stiff, tortured face she could see his conscience wrestling with his instinct to turn away. It made her uneasy. She could see why he might think it unreasonable for him to have to still go on paying. But he had the money and what he paid her for James was nothing to him. Small change. Not much for all the years, happy years, they had spent together.

She had not expected him to ask for time to consider the request, as if she were an irresponsible girl asking for an overdraft to buy a Renault Clio. If he did not want to pay, he could just say no rather than patronise her with his deliberations. It used to irritate him when she teased him by calling him a bank manager. I am a banker, he would say stiffly, not a bank manager, they are quite different things. Well, who had been right after all? As it turned out, she had been right. He really had become a bank manager.

Outside the door, the sweeping stopped and she heard Ziggy picking up paper from the floor. They said he had been a pilot in the war. Now he was hunched and old and wore, summer and winter, an old, rust tweed jacket. She never saw him wear anything else. He would want to lock up soon.

'Sweet dreams,' Francis used to say to her as, moist and warm, they drifted off to sleep after sex. To others it may have sounded banal, but not to them. Those two words stood for their passion. She knew what he meant by it: not a simple synonym for 'goodnight' that a parent might say to a child at bedtime, but rather that he could not bear to be parted from her even by sleep, but if that had to happen then at least he wanted her to have the consolation of sweet dreams. It was part of their history. He bought her the Emmylou Harris version of the old Patsy Cline song for their second Christmas together. Sweet, sentimental Francis.

What had happened? What had that lovely, secretly emotional young man become? How could he now be so pious about something so important? James may have been stupid but he was in real trouble and yet Francis would rather preach and prattle instead of just helping them sort it out.

Ziggy tapped on the door and put his head round it. 'Are you going to be very long, Mrs Carroll?'

'No, it's all right, Ziggy,' she said. 'I'll be going soon.'

Hadn't Francis realised how difficult it was for her to see him in the middle of the day? She had to beg Melanie to cover her last class in the morning so she could get away before lunch, and then she had had to spend fifteen pounds on a taxi to get back in time for the afternoon. Why did he think she would have gone to all that trouble if it had not been really important? What had gone wrong with Francis?

But what was she going to do if he did not pay up? If Francis was not going to help, she would have to find a way to sort it out herself.

But she could not find thirty thousand pounds. She just did not have it. She supposed she could mortgage the flat. That should raise it. But it would take weeks. And James did not have weeks. So she would just have to work it out some other way.

twenty

wednesday 5.40 p.m.
Davey sat in his car, watching.

It was a black Saab 9000, styled by Giugiaro and capable of doing nought to sixty in 6.7 seconds. Davey liked it because it was the car Cozy Powell died in. He realised that most people only remembered Cozy for his 1973 hit 'Dance with the Devil', but Davey knew he was one of the greatest-ever heavy-metal drummers, powering classic albums by Black Sabbath and Whitesnake, not to mention Rainbow, the Brian May Band, and Emerson, Lake & Powell.

Davey sat, watching. There was no-one about. It was a good time of the day. He listened, motionless, staring out of the window, to the thundering rhythms of 'Headless Cross' on the Saab's CD player. He could feel the beats in his head. He did not need to move.

Cozy had been talking to his girlfriend Sharon Reeve as he drove at 104 mph along the M4 in his Saab 9000. No-one can be certain exactly what went wrong but he seems to have lost his grip on the steering wheel. 'Oh shit,' Sharon heard him say on the mobile. And the rest was silence. 'The good die young,' as it said on his website.

Davey thought of the car as his tribute to a rock legend. He sat staring out of the window as Cozy thumped his way through the album.

Then he saw her. Nice-looking chick, Davey thought. Foxy movement. She'd got legs – she knew how to use them. She walked to Cozy's rhythms. She was older. Maybe Cozy's generation. She could even have been one of Cozy's old ladies. She had that kind of look about her.

Davey watched from the Saab across the street as Virginia walked across the playground to the car park and got into her car. Davey watched as she slowed down to go through the gates and then accelerated down the road. Then he reached into the glove box, took out a notepad and a pen, and slowly, painstakingly wrote down the number. And then he took out the piece of paper Roger had given him and started leafing through the *A–Z*.

twenty-one

wednesday 5.45 p.m.
Rachel loved her job. And she loved her office in the
brand-new steel-and-glass building that Rother &
Fenwick had taken over, every floor of it with its own
marble-floored reception area, large abstract canvases
on the walls and every room flooded with natural light,
with the high corner-rooms possessing spectacular
views over the City.

She loved the way every expensive contemporary
painting was by a name you could read about in the
newspapers, and she loved the maple tables and Eames
chairs and the sixty-inch plasma screen set out in
every conference room.

She loved it that Rother & Fenwick were indispensable advisers to governments and great transnational
corporations, not two-dimensional lawyers dealing
with the mundane complexities of commercial law but
a partnership of brilliant professionals operating at the
cutting edge of global commerce, easing the great
flows of money and business around the world with
creative solutions to unclog the arteries of trade and
industry.

And she particularly loved it that Rother & Fenwick

sponsored an international multimedia festival and a lecture series on the social challenges of the human genome project, and made pro bono secondments to an environmental lobby group and a law centre in Tower Hamlets, and the way it all murmured softly and confidently that Rother & Fenwick were rounded individuals, decently sensitive to their responsibilities to the community. It made her proud to be part of Rother & Fenwick.

But now Rachel sat in her soft leather chair in her steel-and-glass office in Rother & Fenwick and trawled the Internet to get pregnant. If doctors would not help her, she would have to do it for herself. If Francis could not shake off his past on his own, then Rachel would have to do it for him. She would get pregnant. For every problem there was a solution. All you had to do was find it. And now she was on the case. This was going to happen. She was going to get pregnant.

The search engine was now offering her 374,000 pages to trawl through. There were websites on Islam and infertility and how the Torah could help tackle childlessness. There were infertility associations in Canada and Australia and clinics in Mexico and Chicago. There were websites exploring holistic approaches to fertility and horrifyingly detailed descriptions of the environmental causes of infertility. Coffee, alcohol, cigarettes, pesticides and food additives all appeared to be responsible for Rachel's inability to become pregnant. There were medical centres selling expensive technological solutions and witches offering ancient wisdom.

It was just as well that Marie was on holiday and she had the office to herself. Rachel had already been logged on for nearly an hour and there were still more than 373,000 sites to explore. It would have been impossible if pretty, clever, inquisitive Marie had been there. But now she could get on with it. Rachel had not raised her eyes from the screen since she had logged on and her head was beginning to hurt. She leant back in her chair and looked out of the window. She could not go on like this. She would be menopausal before she finished going through all these websites. She had to focus.

She liked the sound of the Wise Women solutions. Holistic, natural alternatives. Women's alternatives. As far as could possibly be imagined from smug, complacent, plum-tied, male Doctor Gray. It conjured up soothing images of comfortable women with long, grey hair roaming autumnal woods in New England, searching out the herbs and roots which from the dawn of time had brought relief for the pain women had to bear. Rachel liked the thought of that. Natural remedies. It sounded just what she needed.

There was a knock and the door opened. No-one ever waited for a reply to a knock on the door in Rother & Fenwick. Penny Warrender, one of the most senior women partners, came in. 'Hello, Rachel,' she said.

Rachel started and hurriedly logged off.

'Are you busy?' Penny asked.

She could not possibly have seen what she was doing, thought Rachel. Not possibly. 'No. Yes. But I can always make time for anything you want me to do,' she said. She made herself sick. Penny could not possibly have seen what she was doing, could she?

'Good. Would you be able to take a look at the Ramsden case for me?'

The Ramsden case. Everyone at Rother & Fenwick knew about the Ramsden case. It had been running for at least two years now and was going to end up earning the firm millions. It was so important that the managing partner had allocated five equity partners jointly to take the lead on it, each responsible for a discrete section. Only the best worked on the Ramsden case. This was a sign.

'I'd love to, Penny.' What else could she say? It was a sign. They wouldn't ask her to do this unless they were thinking of making her a partner, would they? Penny Warrender couldn't have seen the screen when she came in, could she?

'I'd like you to take an overview and let me know what direction you think we should take with the litigation,' Penny said. 'We need a fresh pair of eyes. You could be very helpful.'

It was a test. To see if she was truly partnership material.

'I will certainly try to be, Penny,' she said brightly.

'Good,' said Penny. 'It would be helpful if you could let me know what you think by next Wednesday. I'll get the key documents sent to you tomorrow morning. That will give you something to look at.' She smiled professionally at Rachel. There was no way she could have seen the screen when she came in, was there?

'I will get going on them as soon as I get them, Penny.'

'Good. See you next week.'

This was it – the chance to make partner. She deserved it, of course. But still. The Ramsden case. She had better get going. And she'd better sort out how she was going to get pregnant. She needed to get a grip on her life. Otherwise Virginia was just going to squat in their marriage till the day she died. And that was not going to happen. Rachel was going to get pregnant and she was going to become a partner. And suddenly, thanks to Penny Warrender and the Wise Women of the Web, both seemed far more possible than they had when she got up this morning.

Believe you can be who you want to be. Rachel was on the case. She knew she could make Francis happy. He was anxious about InterTrust but she was sure it was going to work out. And she knew what he needed. And, behind his reserve, what he really wanted. A new family.

twenty-two

wednesday 6.00 p.m.
'As your lawyer, I can't advise you to have anything to do with this, Francis.' Charles Wetherby sat at the conference table, his short, fat fingers steepled in front of him. 'This is a serious crime and I must advise you to have nothing whatever to do with it. You must go to the police.'

Francis stared at his lawyer. Charles Wetherby spent thousands of pounds every year having his suits tailored for him, carefully cut to flatter his comfortable paunch and chubby thighs. It never worked. Francis looked at him sitting dishevelled in his bespoke suit, a headman in the tribe of English lawyers rolling out the mellifluous but often scarcely comprehensible dialect of his people, a plump, portentous alien. 'What do you think will happen to James if I follow that advice?' he said, irritated. He wanted this sorted out, not to have his mind changed. It had been difficult enough making it up in the first place.

Charles Wetherby interpreted the question literally, as was the custom of his tribe. He said: 'That will depend on whether the police press charges.'

'And will they?'

'They may do. They may not. It is a first offence. They may conclude, however erroneously, he was not dealing himself. And he is a young man of good family. And your coming forward like this might be an argument in mitigation. So they might think a strong warning would suffice rather than cluttering up the courts with a prosecution that would serve no useful purpose. On the other hand, this is a Class A drug. And it might be hard for them to overlook that. And I should advise you that if the Crown Prosecution Service do proceed on this basis, this is a serious offence and he could go to jail. In the worst case, he could be looking at a sentence of several years. But if they decide he was not in business as a dealer he might just get a community sentence.'

'And you think that would be a good outcome, do you?'

'No,' the lawyer said carefully. 'I think that would be a bad outcome. He would still end up with a criminal record, but you did not ask me whether I thought the outcome would be good or bad; you asked me what the outcome would be and I told you.'

'Charles,' Francis said, equally carefully. 'I am asking for your help here. This is James.'

The lawyer looked at the table for a moment, making sure that his client could see him carefully considering his plea. 'I have considerable sympathy for the position in which you find yourself,' he said, looking Francis in the eye to ensure his client registered his sympathy. 'I understand your concerns. I do. However, you really must not get involved in this,

141

Francis. You must not pay this money. As your lawyer, I must strongly advise you to make sure that this thirty thousand pounds has nothing to do with you.' He continued to look Francis in the eye and paused. Francis sensed he was now being invited to contribute to this dialogue.

'And what would you advise me to do, speaking not as my lawyer?' he guessed.

Wrong.

'As your lawyer, I would find it impossible to advise you other than as your lawyer. So I am afraid my advice remains the same: should you, as my client, ask me, as your lawyer, what you should do to resolve this matter directly – you must go to the police.' The prosperously plump alien headman remained looking at his client, hands together on the desk.

Francis tried again. 'What if I stopped trying to resolve this matter myself – directly?'

Right.

'Then my advice to you would be different and it would depend on the circumstances.' Charles Wetherby's tone was more benign now and reminded Francis of a schoolmaster rewarding a slow but diligent pupil. 'If Virginia, for example, sought my advice, I would not be able to respond as she is not my client. What she did would be a matter for her. And, in the interest of clarity, my advice on this matter relates only to actions you take yourself directly in relation to James or the people with whom he has, so regrettably, become involved. I am not, for example, seeking to advise you on what actions in the immediate future you may wish to take in respect of your other family obligations. You have not, for example, sought my advice on any variations to the maintenance you pay to Virginia. I have therefore not given you any advice on that.'

Francis got it. It had taken twenty minutes and with the usual uplift it would probably cost him around a thousand pounds, but he had now got it. He wondered why he had bothered going to see Charles. He had not told him anything he could not have worked out for himself. But that was what you did when you had a problem – you called in your lawyer. Paying his fees at least made you feel you were doing something to find a solution.

'Thank you, Charles,' he lied. 'Very helpful.'

There was a pub on the corner by Charles's office. In the muggy early evening the pavements were clogged with people having a drink on their way home. As Francis negotiated his way through them he thought that, despite his irritating circumlocutions, at least Charles might have given him a way to handle it.

He came up against a particularly dense knot of young men, deep in raucous banter. 'Excuse me,' he said tersely.

He was suddenly conscious of how irritated he felt with all these people getting in his way. The meeting with his lawyer appeared to have wound him up.

Francis knew that Charles was professionally obliged to warn him, but his constant repetition of the seriousness of it all had taken root. It really was serious.

Charles had suggested a way to pay off the problem, but perhaps the best thing for everyone, including James, would be to go to the police? That was the obvious course of action. And you should never over-look the obvious. Of course, that would mean that James would have to take the consequences of his actions, but then surely that would be best for him in the long run? Charles would make sure he got the best barrister, and, after all, he had said that it was only in the worst case that James would go to jail. Virginia had made him feel he had no choice but to pay up. Now he felt the force of all the arguments against that course of action. After all, if he under-stood Charles correctly, probably the worst that could happen to James if he went to the police, would be community service and that would be good for him anyway. And it would solve all the problems about how to find the thirty thousand pounds. And what to say to Rachel.

Francis was changing his mind. He had reluctantly accepted that he would have to give the money to Virginia, but now he was beginning to think that it might be better for everyone if he did not. Better for James to confront the consequences of his behaviour and learn from it. Better for Francis. And better for Francis and Rachel. All round, it would be better for him to get James the best lawyer money could buy and then go to the police. And if Virginia disagreed, then she could sort it out herself.

Francis got into his car. He switched the engine on and then sat silently as the air-conditioning began to cool the fetid air. He thought about James. It seemed so long ago. Creased and middle-aged, staring out of the window at a blank wall, smelling petrol and sweat, Francis remembered the sap rising in that dingy one-bedroom flat in Wandsworth on rainy winter nights in 1976. He thought about Virginia and her omnivorous appetite.

And he thought about how, twenty-three years later, it had led to this unforeseeable but nonetheless apparently compellingly obligating dilemma. How could he have evaded it, this intricately gestating consequence of an unconsidered spurt of semen so long ago?

twenty-three

wednesday 6.50 p.m.

On the maple chopping board in her large light kitchen looking out over the spreading lawn, Rachel emptied her paper bags and set out the heaps of secret fertility.

The red clover was going to cleanse her blood, black cohosh would stimulate the pituitary gland in the brain, and red raspberry, squaw vine and the chaste tree berry – ironically named, she thought – would all nourish her fertility. Then, for Francis, saw palmetto would help the enlargement of the prostate which generated fluid in semen, and the pumpkin-seed diet – on which, unknowingly, he was about to go – would tackle any deficiency in zinc which, so she had read, was a key cause of low sperm-mobility.

One way or another, it was going to happen.

When Francis had rung to say he was going to see Charles on his way home and he would be late, she saw the opportunity. Why wait? She could buy the ingredients this afternoon and experiment with them at home in the evening before Francis got home, adjusting the proportions so the herbs and leaves would not be noticeable in the tasty new dishes she was going to concoct.

And so at half past four she had checked the where-abouts of Penny Warrender and her supervising partner Brendan Simpson. Both were in meetings scheduled to go on until six o'clock so they would not know if she left unprofessionally early. And, for extra insurance, she left her computer on so no-one could check when she had logged off. And then, head down to avoid drawing attention to herself, off she went to the little shop in East Finchley, with its modest front and its bulging hessian sacks of organic herbs and spices.

There she bought two carrier-bags bulging with red clover, black cohosh, red raspberry, saw palmetto and pumpkin seeds. And a pestle and mortar for pulverising and a wooden grinder for grinding, two pamphlets which explained the extraordinary proper-ties of herbs and a petite set of scales for measuring the minute quantities prescribed for the daily intake of these remarkable products of nature.

Going home, she sat on the Tube with her carrier-bags on the seat beside her, wondering what Marie, bright, pretty, ambitious Marie with whom she shared an office, would make of this: the up-and-coming solicitor with Rother & Fenwick – those sophisticated buccaneers of globalisation wielding the most elab-orately cerebrated weapons of commerce human ingenuity had yet devised – now returning from East Finchley with her harvest of potions and spells for the most elemental of all human purposes. Rachel was going to make a baby.

She knew it was ridiculous but she would sit in the

office and stare at her computer screen and calculate how many eggs she had left. That was still a comforting calculation. It sounded such a lot. But then she would calculate how many eggs she had already used up and she would start to panic. So many gone. So many gone never to come again. Never again. She was thirty-one and oh how she wanted a baby.

Now Rachel surveyed her fecund empire and breathed a little sigh of satisfaction. For every problem there was a solution. And here it was. And it was a lot cheaper than going to that ghastly Doctor Gray. And it was likely to be much more productive. Yes, Rachel thought, I am on the case. Now she would make something truly delicious for Francis to inaugurate the regime. This was the new age of agile sperm and hospitable eggs.

She scanned her cookbooks, arranged on a shelf overlooking the work surface. Inside those glossy covers lay the fruit of centuries of experiment and refinement, recipes for the great dishes of the world. And in three years of married life Rachel had not made one of them. But that was about to change.

She sat on the kitchen stool and leafed through the books. Saw palmetto and pumpkin seeds did not appear to feature in any of the world's great cuisines. She would have to invent something – she could cook one of the great dishes of the world and then just add saw palmetto and pumpkin seeds. What about a soufflé? That would be something special for this first night of their new start. Saw-palmetto soufflé with pumpkin seeds.

The crackly dark contents of her carrier-bags sat on the chopping board. Rachel inspected them. They did not look very appetising. Or smell it. There was obviously a reason why they did not feature in any of the great dishes of the world. But she supposed they must be good for you.

Something was making her feel uneasy. That shop in East Finchley would not have sold them if they had been dangerous in any way, surely? No, these natural herbs were recommended by Wise Women and backed up by the wisdom of Native Americans and their knowledge of the hedgerows. They should know. Shouldn't they? Something was worrying Rachel and suddenly she realised what it was. Allergies.

What would she do if Francis turned out to be allergic to these exotic ingredients? It happened. What would she do if he choked on his saw-palmetto soufflé? And especially if she had not told him what he was eating? This was simply wrong. She could not do this to Francis.

She stared at the mounds of leaves and berries. She could not risk Francis choking. But she could not tell him. He was diffident enough already about all this and he could just refuse. And then what would she do? Could she really just throw out her packets of hope from East Finchley? The question was how could she feed the herbs to Francis without telling him and without choking him?

Rachel toyed with the leaves. They were dry and scratchy on the tips of her fingers.

Then she remembered. Two years ago he had gone

for a medical. It had béen a full health screen and she was sure they tested for allergies when they did that. And there would have been a report. That might give her a clue to his propensity for an allergic reaction.

And anyway, even if there was nothing in the report from the health screen, Francis would have filed away his entire medical records upstairs. He kept everything and filed it. If he had any known allergies they would be recorded somewhere in his study.

Rachel looked at her watch. She might just have time to do this before Francis got home. She got off the kitchen stool and marched upstairs.

Francis had better not catch her doing this. She went into the spare bedroom at the front of the house and looked out of the window to see if his car was coming down the road.

There was a large black car parked opposite the house. It had a sleek, unusual shape and it was not a car Rachel recognised. Someone was sitting inside it, with long, dark hair streaked with grey and tied into a ponytail. Then as she watched, the engine started and the car pulled away. The road was empty. Nothing moved. Everything was OK. She should have time to go through his papers.

Francis had taken over one of the upstairs bedrooms overlooking the garden for his study. It was lined with bookshelves, the works of biography and history he never read and his poetry collections from university. In the middle of the books on one long shelf, a monitor sat, always on, blinking its red and blue signals from the markets. The windows were filled with the lush dark green of the tall large-leaved limes at the end of the garden. It was still and bathed in verdant calm.

Francis loved his study. And he loved this house. Rachel had never wanted to live in Surrey. She liked the city's tumult, millions of lives crashing into each other, like atoms: some glancing off again in a second's passing intimacy, others sticking together to make new molecules, stable, unstable, forming new organisms, new life. Frantic noise, grime and traffic and the insulated haven of a hardwood-floored apartment with a stainless-steel kitchen, overlooking the hustle of the street through double-glazing – this was the chiaroscuro Rachel had expected of her life. Not Surrey with its tones of green, hedges and lawns, and the spreading trees, and quiet streets with children on bicycles and a dog barking playfully in the middle distance.

But Francis wanted it. He loved this house with its hushed rooms and its acre of lawn and overflowing flowerbeds. And Rachel loved Francis and so she moved to Surrey where the large quiet house mocked her empty womb.

His desk sat by the window and beside it stood a four-drawer filing cabinet. Rachel went to work. She did not expect it to take very long as she knew how meticulous Francis was about his papers. The first drawer contained his financial records. The second one had all the papers to do with the house. And then in the third drawer she found it. A folder labelled in his neat hand: 'medical records'.

She took it out and sat down at his desk overlooking the garden.

And there it was, the bland form slid between the other papers. She stared at it.

So that was it. Now she understood. So that was the problem.

Why couldn't he have told her? He should have told her. She was his wife. How could he have kept something like this from her? His wife? This put everything into perspective. Why had he not told her? What had he been thinking about? How could he have gone on acting as if this form, with the toxic information it contained, did not exist?

Rachel realised she did not really understand Francis at all.

twenty-four

wednesday 7.45 p.m.

Francis sat in his car at the traffic lights as the meetings went back and forth in his mind. What a dreadful day it had been. Virginia. Lloyd. Charles.

Lloyd was obviously worried about the timing. Were they breaking bad news gently? And Charles had not been much use. All he had done was wind him up.

Thirty thousand pounds? Cocaine? How could James have been so stupid? What if Charles was wrong and James did go to jail?

The train of cars swept over Wandsworth Bridge and headed south, bearing their cargoes of appetite and yearning, weariness and disappointment, good news, bad news, out to the suburbs and home to the hearth. Past the avenues of cramped villas and rundown shops they swarmed. Sweeping into the Kingston bypass and the sudden open spaces, Francis felt the familiar sense of coming home. If the money did not come through, he would have to sell the house, he thought bleakly.

He turned off the main road into a small lane. High hedges screened large houses from passers-by. Ordinary people did not live here, Francis thought.

You had to have money. To move here now you had to have lots of money. Living here said something about you.

Tonight this thought that had so often soothed him at the end of a difficult day made him uncomfortable. What did it say about him if InterTrust failed and he was living here beyond his means? And he had to move? Like his father?

He turned into his driveway, hearing the gravel crunch under the wheels, a satisfying sound that signalled arrival onto his territory. He pressed a button and the garage door swung open. He parked and got out. As he emerged from the garage he could smell roses in the front garden. Someone in the distance was mowing their lawn. The peace of the prosperous suburbs began to lay its hands on him.

Francis never heard the man. Suddenly he was in front of him: a small dapper man in a dove-grey suit with a pink shirt and a pink tie. The scent of his cologne arrived an instant before his physical presence.

'Your son owes me a lot of money,' he said.

Francis looked at him. 'And you are?' he said, but he knew. And he knew the man knew.

'Mr Carroll,' Roger said patiently. 'I am here to help. You may not think so but I am.' Francis looked at him, aware that he was staring. A moment ago Francis had been calmed by the familiar routines of coming home. Now a fly had landed in his Martini. 'You know he owes me a lot of money,' the man said. 'And I want it. Now.'

It occurred to Francis that he had never met a drug

dealer before. He would not have expected one to look like this. No big straw hat. No two-tone shoes. Instead, dove-grey and pink on pink. In his front garden.

'You're a banker,' Roger said. 'You know debts must be paid.' He watched Francis as he spoke. 'If people believe they can borrow money and not pay it back, things fall apart. It's about trust. The way I look at it, when you lend money you need to know you are going to get it back. Or you won't lend it. No trust, no money. We'd all keep it under the bed. And then where would we be? End of capitalism. End of the free world. That's no good, is it?' Roger found that moving from a general principle to a particular demand usually worked. 'The way I look at it, when people don't pay their debts, it's no different from thieving. People think they have got a right to something when they haven't. They are too busy thinking about their rights when they should be thinking about their responsibilities. Like repaying their debts. It can cause trouble, Mr Carroll. And I am not sure you have grasped how serious that trouble can be.'

Roger showed no sign of moving after he had spoken. He stood still, waiting for Francis.

'I assume you are talking about James,' Francis said finally. 'And I suppose you got my name and address from his mother but I am afraid she misinformed you. His affairs are really no responsibility of mine. He is an adult and he must assume responsibility for his own actions.' As he said it, he felt ashamed of himself. He suddenly saw himself not as he wanted to be but as how he must look to others: pompous and cold.

155

For a moment, Francis remembered the little boy James had been, playing silently for hours with his toy soldiers, immersed, oblivious, loved.

'There you go, Mr Carroll,' Roger said equably, as if Francis had just agreed with him. 'Rights without responsibilities. To my way of thinking, don't do the crime if you can't do the time.' It irritated Roger when they tried to shuffle away from their responsibilities. This was why the country was in such a mess. 'He is your son,' he said.

Francis was taking against the man in the dove-grey suit. How dare he come here like this? It was a lot of money. His money. Rachel's money. What right did he have to demand it like this? And paying it would be illegal. Why should he just pay up? Virginia had made all the choices. She should live with them. She was the one who ought to be hearing these lectures about rights and responsibilities.

But then what would happen if he did not pay? Francis could not bear to think what might happen to James. And if he just paid this man now, it would all be over and they could get on with their lives.

Roger had watched these calculations taking place before. This was why he calibrated threats and reassurance to get them to cough it up. It was like being a politician, he thought. First, you frighten the punters about the opposition. Then you reassure them about you. The skill was in choosing the right balance and the right moment. He said: 'I know this might be difficult for you, Mr Carroll. You don't know me. But I know you. And I know where you live. And because you do not know me you might think that you will never get rid of me. You will pay me and then I will keep coming back for more.'

Francis looked at him. Why was this man dumping this on him?

'Let me reassure you,' said Roger. 'I am a businessman, not a blackmailer. All I want to do is run my business, just like you. I want my debts paid, just like you. I do not want to spend any more time on you than I have to. So it's quite simple. Pay me and I go. Don't, and I don't.'

Roger could see it had not worked as well as it usually did.

'Why are you asking me?' Francis said. Why did everyone assume everything was down to him? 'I have not had custody of James for years. If you can't get the money from him, why not go to his mother?'

'Because you have got the money,' Roger replied curtly. 'And I believe a father should take responsibility for his child. That is what holds society together. The way I look at it.'

'You are very good at explaining things to me but let me explain something to you,' Francis hissed. 'I love James, but he is old enough to take responsibility for his own actions. I don't know why he got involved with you, but from what I've been told it was all an accident. You sort it out between yourselves. This is nothing to do with me. And I have no intention of getting involved.' It had been a long, difficult day and the presumption of the man was irritating him. He and Virginia were just the same in the way they both expected to get whatever they wanted just by demanding it.

'That could be a mistake,' Roger sighed. They often began like this. They did it all day long at work: the tough, see-you-in-court talk. It never lasted. It was just a matter of time. Roger wished he could take them through it all so they could see what would happen from start to finish, but people like this would never believe it until it had actually happened. 'You could regret this,' he said sadly.

'Why?' said Francis. 'What are you going to do? Kill me? Kill James? That wouldn't be very good for business, would it?'

There was often this spurt of testosterone at the beginning, but they usually came round in the end. Usually. Roger said nothing but looked at Francis, a strangely sympathetic smile on his lips.

The front door of the house opened. Rachel came out. 'Hello?' she called.

Francis saw her and said to Roger, 'You had better go now.' He saw Roger look curiously towards his wife. It was only a glance but Francis sensed the threat in it. He suddenly felt tired. All the good intentions he had formulated after his meeting with Charles, all his determination to do the right thing, suddenly seemed a heavy burden. And he could not get Rachel tangled up in something like this. He just wanted to get rid of it all.

He could just give the money to Virginia, as Charles had so delicately suggested, and she could then pay him. And then goodbye. Although he supposed he should still have to have a word with James as Virginia had obviously let the boy run wild.

'I hope you will reconsider,' Roger said. 'I am not a very patient man. You owe me thirty thousand pounds now and interest runs at twenty per cent a week.'

The man was unbearable. How dare he talk to him like this? Perhaps he should just hand it all over to the police. They would know how to deal with this man.

'I hope you get your money,' Francis said, looking round uneasily towards Rachel. 'But you won't get it from me.' That struck the right note, he thought. It was the literal truth and it reserved his position.

'I would think about it, if I were you,' Roger replied serenely. 'You would not want to find out what can happen if you ignore good advice.'

'What are you talking about?'

'It's a bad world, Mr Carroll. Full of bad people. Not like you and me.'

'How dare you threaten me,' Francis said, conscious of Rachel standing watching in the doorway.

'I'm not threatening you, Mr Carroll,' Roger said routinely. This was familiar territory. 'I am just offering you advice to help you reach the right decision. Anyway, I won't keep you. I just thought you would want to know how much you still owed me.'

'I don't owe you anything,' Francis said.

'Your son,' Roger said carefully to him, 'took half a kilo of Scotty – a quality brand, he's privileged to be allowed to handle it – we don't take just anyone –

and that costs thirty thousand pounds. That's list price. That's understood. And if you do not pay up on delivery, that's twenty per cent a week on top. That's the terms. That's understood. He is your son. You take responsibility for him. That's how it should be. That's understood. If he doesn't pay, you pay. It's your responsibility. I take cash.'

Francis looked at him, considering Roger's statement of account. He said nothing. Why did he call it Scotty? 'Beam me up', presumably. He seemed very proud of it.

'Think about it, Mr Carroll,' Roger said. He was going to have to send a message to this man. That was clear but it would probably not require much to shift him. He would start with pain and loss and see how that went. Then, if necessary, he could get Davey to move on to misery and suffering. 'Here is a number you can ring when you are ready.' He handed Francis a small visiting card with a mobile-phone number on it. Nothing else. 'There won't be any more helpful reminder calls,' he said. 'But if I don't hear from you, you will hear from me again. One way or another, you will hear from me. Count on it.'

Roger turned away. And he was gone.

'Who was that?' Rachel asked as Francis walked back to the front door. 'I heard the car arrive. I wondered what was going on.'

'I'll explain inside,' Francis replied. 'Someone to do with James.'

twenty-five

That evening Rachel would remember as the first time she lost her temper with Francis. It began as she liked their evenings to begin. Francis sat in his chair in the living room overlooking the garden. Twilight softened the room. A gentle scent of grass and roses wafted in through the open windows.

Rachel settled on the sofa. She loved their evenings together in this room. The appearance of Roger in the front garden had not disturbed her. Why should it? Francis would tell her about it when he was ready. Her hands were clasped together in her lap and the thumbs circled each other, round and round. 'Who was that man?' she asked. Francis breathed out heavily. He was not unwinding well this evening. 'You don't have to tell me if you don't want to,' she said quickly.

'No,' he replied. 'I do want to. But it is complicated. James has got himself into a mess.'

'What's happened now?' she asked and her thumbs went round and round. So Francis told her what she needed to know.

'Poor James,' she said. 'And who was that man in the garden?' Francis told her.

'What did the police say?' she asked.

'I haven't told the police,' Francis said. 'Yet.'

She looked at him. 'What do you mean?' she said.

'My darling,' he said. 'What do you think would happen if I told the police?' She continued to look at him, not certain for a moment whether he was seriously looking for an answer.

'They would arrest him,' she said, after a moment. A note of caution had entered into her voice. Perhaps it was not as simple as it seemed. What was Francis not telling her now?

'What would it look like if I go to the police?' he said. 'This is a delicate time. I'm asking people to trust me with millions of pounds of their money. What does it look like for James to be involved with a drug dealer? After all, technically he has committed an offence as well. He could go to jail.'

'So what are you going to do?' she asked.

'I don't know.' Francis sighed again. 'It's a mess. Maybe it would be best to let the police handle it. But it might be easier just to pay for it to go away.'

'Yes,' Rachel said. 'It is a mess.'

They sat there silently, looking out at the peachy evening.

'I suppose I should just pay him off,' Francis said eventually.

'Why can't Virginia "pay him off"?' Rachel asked quietly.

'She couldn't possibly afford it.'

'Why? How much is it?'

Francis paused.

'Thirty thousand,' he said eventually. Instinct had suggested he should leave out the amount from his original account.

'Thirty thousand pounds?' she repeated incredulously. 'You are going to pay this man thirty thousand pounds of our money?' Envy was a mean little emotion. But there were times, like now, when it really was all too much. 'This is because Virginia has demanded it, isn't it?' she said. 'She just has to whistle and you run.'

'What do you suggest I do?' Francis asked. 'It's not that easy.'

'Go to the police. Get rid of it. It is not your problem,' Rachel answered, standing up. 'This is a crime and this man is threatening you. So you go to the police, that's what you do. I do not understand why you should think it is worse to go to the police than pay thirty thousand pounds to this man. Thirty thousand pounds of our money. What do you think that will look like? Paying off a drug dealer? Thirty thousand pounds? Of our money? For James?'

'I don't know,' said Francis to himself. 'It's not so easy.'

Rachel looked at him, sagged in his chair. 'Francis,' she said, 'you have to go to the police. That's the right thing to do. That's what they are there for. Then it's out of your hands.'

'That's what Charles said. But it isn't as easy as you think,' he said. 'What if they charge James? What then?'

'What do you mean "What then?"' demanded

Rachel. 'What then for you? Or what then for James? Wake up, Francis. You must go to the police – now. It's the right thing to do.'

Francis looked out of the window. 'Think what it would look like,' he said finally. 'It wouldn't be good for me to be mixed up in any of this right now. And what would it look like for James? Thirty thousand pounds? It's not nothing. They could assume he was dealing or something. What then?'

Rachel suddenly felt sorry for him. He looked so beaten up.

'Francis,' she said more softly. 'It is not your business. James is old enough to look after himself. He should have thought about all this before he got involved. And Virginia should have thought before she involved you. Again. When it is not your business.'

The injustice of it all resurfaced and her voice tightened.

'Do you think she stopped to think for one second before she involved you? Do you think she considered what it might mean for your business? What it might mean for us? How did she know we don't need that money. It's not nothing, thirty thousand pounds. I might have been pregnant – I'm not, of course – but for all she knew I might have been. And I might have needed to give up work. We might have needed that money. How did she know we didn't? And do you think she stopped to think for a second before involving you in this criminal activity? Do you think she thought for a second about how that could damage you? Do you?'

Francis did not move. He continued to stare out of the window. 'It's not like that,' he said.

'What is it like then?' Rachel's fury tore the words out of her. 'What is it like?'

Francis said nothing.

And then something else occurred to her.

'And what do you think this could do to my chances of making partner? Do you think having a drug dealer for a stepson will help me? Do you?'

'That's an argument for not going to the police,' Francis pointed out. 'If I just pay it off, no-one need ever know.'

'That's not my point, Francis. How long is Virginia going to go on dumping problems on us? Do you think she even thought about what it might mean for us before she came with her hand out for thirty thousand pounds?'

'No-one wanted this to happen, Rachel.'

'When are you going to wake up, Francis?' Rachel said. 'You are married to me now. Not Virginia. When are you going to stop her running your life? Our life? When are you going to realise you have new responsibilities? When are you going to get a grip?'

'That's not fair,' Francis muttered. Didn't she realise how difficult it was for him trying to keep them all happy – Rachel, Virginia, James – trying to do the right thing by all of them?

'No, it's not fair,' Rachel exploded. 'It's not fair on me.'

Francis looked up at her. 'You know I love you,' he said. He didn't know why but he was beginning to feel irritated. 'But I have got these responsibilities. You have always known that.'

'Yes, I know all about that. You say you love me but you always do whatever Virginia wants.' As she said it, Rachel knew she should stop there but she could not. Helpless fury overwhelmed her. What was the point of her trying and trying to get pregnant? All Virginia had to do was call and he went running. Virginia would go with them wherever they went.

'I am trying to do what I should,' said Francis wearily. 'I'm sorry if I don't always get it right.' If he kept his head down, Rachel would blow herself out sooner or later.

'You need to decide what matters most to you, Francis.' It was as if someone else was speaking. She knew that the Rachel who liked to sit here with Francis on summer evenings would not keep on like this. But still this other Rachel kept on coming as Francis stared miserably out at the lengthening shadows on the lawn.

'I can't walk away now,' he said to Rachel.

'Why not?' she asked. 'Why not? You are married to me now, not Virginia. And James is grown up now. He's a man. When is your life going to begin again?'

The irritation began to boil up in Francis. Rachel just would not let go. He did not know what she expected him to do. 'What choice do I have? Really? How could I just walk away?' he asked.

Rachel stared at him and her frustration boiled over. How could he say that? 'He's not even your son,' she said.

'What do you mean?' he said.

twenty-six

wednesday 8.15 p.m.

Virginia's taxi was stuck in the evening traffic and she got out in Soho Square and walked the rest of the way. The restaurant was a small square room and it was full. A man rose from his table as Virginia walked in and kissed her on the cheek. She placed her hand gently under his chin and steered his mouth towards hers and then kissed him back.

'Hello, Alex,' she said softly. He smelt of garlic. 'Don't eat garlic,' she added. 'It pollutes beauty.'

Alex smiled with his white, even teeth. 'Good evening, Virginia,' he said.

Francis always smelt of cloves and cinnamon from the cologne he bought in St James's. But Francis, the bank manager smelling of Indian Ocean spices, had let her down. And Alex, smelling of garlic and white Burgundy, was going to help her.

He poured her a glass of wine from a bottle already open on the table. His linen jacket was rumpled and he was wearing an open-necked shirt. His dark hair was streaked with grey and hung over his collar. He looked as if he had been left over from the 1970s but he had ordered a bottle of Puligny-Montrachet. He was obviously a journalist.

'I can't stay long,' he said. 'I am working tonight.'

'It's so good of you to spare me the time,' Virginia said.

Alex smiled affably. 'What are you eating?' he asked, opening the menu and handing it to her.

Virginia closed it. 'I'm on a diet of you,' she said. 'You gorgeous man.'

'What do you want?' he smiled.

Virginia took his hand and stroked it. 'You are so cynical,' she said.

'It's my job,' he said.

'No it's not. It's just an affectation favoured by people in your profession.'

'Come on, Virginia,' he said. 'What are you going to eat?'

'What's the hurry? The clubs don't get going for hours yet.'

'Virginia,' he said. 'Please choose what you want to eat.'

She squeezed his hand and blew him a kiss with her lips. 'I'm not hungry. I just wanted to see you.'

'I know you want something. What is it?'

'To spend some time with you,' she breathed. 'What could be better than that?'

'Nothing,' he said. 'Nothing at all, but I have still got to go to work.'

'That's not work, it's just phoning in gossip.'

'A common misapprehension,' he said. 'Everyone thinks that. But this is the most demanding branch of journalism. It requires the highest professional skills.'

Virginia smiled fondly at him.

'You may smile,' he said, 'but you are merely displaying your ignorance. Celebrity journalism is not gossip. It requires all the qualities of good journalism but to a higher degree. You need to know what's important. That's easy for political journalists. The Prime Minister is always important. And they are there day after day. But celebrities are different. Who's hot today is dust tomorrow. And you have to know who is who. Fine news judgement is required. Selecting this, rejecting that. And there's nothing automatic about it. Every day you have to do it again. This is not a job for the idle. And you need to have your sources to know where they are going to be. It's a bit more than just taking the call from the PR, you know. This is a very competitive game. You've got to build relationships. Based on trust and respect.'

'But you just make it all up,' Virginia said.

'If you think that's a killer fact, you're wrong,' Alex said loftily. 'All journalists make it up. Accuracy is only valued by people who don't understand journalism. We're not here to inform you. We're here to entertain you. That's what people want. They get enough information stuffed into them at school. That's what you do. Whatever they pretend, all journalists make it up. We're all slaves to the story. The only difference is that the celebrity journalist does it better than everyone else. We are the best at creating the significant narrative that helps the punters forget the drudgery of their daily lives. I think that's a worthy enterprise, myself. That's why we celebrity journalists are the cream. I rest my case. Now, let's eat.'

And as they ate, Virginia talked to Alex. And explained why she had wanted to see him tonight, before he went off to create the significant narrative for tomorrow's paper, exercising her own fine news judgement to select which piece of information to give him and which to reject. She rejected giving him any information about James.

'But why do you want to know all this?' he asked as she paused to sip her wine.

'I am going to have to teach a citizenship class next term,' she lied, creating a significant narrative for the autumn.

'Kids really need to know all this stuff, do they?' he asked.

'New Labour,' she explained.

'Oh,' he said. 'OK.' Virginia was not completely sure he believed her.

But still, lovely Alex reached into his backpack on the floor and took out a palmtop computer. He used it swiftly and deftly, his hand making precise jerky movements across the diminutive screen. He then wrote something on a piece of paper and handed it to Virginia.

'I don't know this guy very well,' he said, 'but I see him around and he should be able to help you.'

twenty-seven

wednesday 8.20 p.m.

'What do you mean?' Francis said again.

Rachel looked at him. 'I've seen the form,' she said slowly. 'The DNA test.'

'What were you doing looking through my papers?' he said.

'He's not your son, Francis,' she said.

'What were you doing, Rachel?' he said.

'How could you do this, Francis – all this money, all your jumping when Virginia says jump, and he's not even your son.'

'It's not really your business, Rachel,' Francis said wearily.

'Oh really?' she said. 'Not my business? I am your wife, Francis. Of course it is my business. It became my business when I married you.'

Francis ran his hand through his hair. She was right. Of course. Why was all this happening today? 'You are right,' he said. 'I should have told you. But what difference would it have made? It's not a part of my past that I want to remind myself about.'

'Oh, Francis,' Rachel said, softening. 'I am sorry. I can imagine how dreadful this must be for you. But all this agony you put yourself through about James and all the money you spend on him – and Virginia – and he's not even your son. Why are you doing this, Francis? Why are you doing this to us?'

'It's nothing to do with us,' he said. 'It's to do with me and James. In one way he is still my son. And he was my son in every way for thirteen years. I can't just forget that. For thirteen years I was his father and no DNA test changes that.'

As he spoke he heard Virginia's voice in his head. That was what she had said. 'In every way that matters, you are his father,' she had said. 'You love him as a son. And he loves you as his father. And that's what counts. That's all that counts.'

'What does that mean? In every way that matters?' Rachel said. 'You are not his father. Not his biological father. And you should have told me.' She looked at him sitting in his chair, his face tight, not looking at her. He had a point. Rachel could see that. She could understand why he could not simply cut himself off from James. Thirteen years was a lot of love. But he should have told her.

'I know,' Francis said, still not looking at her, staring out through the open doors. 'I know, but I still need to do the right thing by James. It is not his fault.'

The image was always fresh, the pain still raw. Sitting at the table, their table, and seeing Virginia walking in. With him.

Francis had had to go away for a business trip on his birthday. So he booked a table at Bibendum for her. He said his present would be for her to go there for lunch and drink a bottle of Krug on her own and think of him. They loved the restaurant and they loved Krug and they loved this table by the big stained-glass window. And he wanted her to be somewhere special to think of him on his birthday.

When he had finished his business early and realised he could get back on his birthday, he had not told her. He had wanted to surprise her. He had got there early and sat at the table by the window, winter sun pouring through it and casting a rainbow of colours on the crisp white tablecloth, thinking happily how surprised she would be when she came in to find him sitting there, and how thrilled.

She had walked in happily enough, and thrilled, on the arm of a man Francis had never seen, turning towards him, laughing at something he had just whispered to her. With cold shock, Francis saw a smirk of sexual possession on the man's face. They were waiting to be seated when Virginia looked across the room and suddenly saw him.

With painful slowness, Francis had watched her assessment of the options flit swiftly across her face. Almost without faltering, she waved at him, a bold movement above her head, and walked over to him, saying something to her companion as they walked.

'Darling,' she had said. 'What an extraordinary surprise. And what a nice surprise.' Francis had glowered, unable to speak. 'This is Simon Hardy.' He could still recall precisely the exact way she had pronounced every syllable of the name. 'Simon, this is my husband, Francis.'

The man offered his hand to Francis. He had a carefully barbered honeyed beard and gleaming eyes and the knowing complacency of a sexual predator, a conqueror.

'I thought it would be such a shame to waste the table, when you had been so clever to get one. So I asked Simon to keep me company.' Virginia had appeared unruffled. 'But now you have been even cleverer and managed to get here yourself, I won't need him. Simon, it was noble of you to volunteer. You don't mind, do you?'

Francis had noticed that the contented smirk never left Simon's face. 'Of course not,' he had replied, offering his hand to Francis again. 'Nice to have met you, Francis. Enjoy your lunch.' He turned to Virginia and offered her his hand. 'I'm glad I was available to help out.'

Virginia shook his hand. 'Thank you. It was sweet of you.' She turned back to the table and sat down. 'What a lovely surprise.'

'Who was that?' Francis demanded, ignoring her remark.

'Just a friend,' she said dismissively, picking up the menu. 'He agreed to keep me company – as you were away on your business trip.'

Francis looked at her. She studied the menu without meeting his gaze. He had so wanted it to be true. The words had churned around in his mind – 'just a friend', she had said. But Francis knew he could not forget that smirk. That man was not just a friend.

'How long have you known him?' he had asked quietly.

Virginia did not look up from the menu that was engrossing her. 'He is just someone I met through school.' Ten years later, Francis could still remember every word.

'He is not just a friend, is he?' he said.

Virginia put the menu down and looked at him. 'Oh Francis,' she said. 'Please let's not fight. It's your birthday.' She stretched out her hand across the table and put it over his and squeezed it. He had not moved, frozen by her evasion. He could still remember the touch of her faithless hand.

'You are a good man,' Rachel was saying to him as she touched his cheek. 'It is wonderful how you still care for him. It must have been so difficult.'

He said nothing. His face was raw with hurt.

'My poor Francis,' she continued. 'But we must put this behind us.'

Rachel had never realised the full dimensions of her problem. How was she ever going to disentangle Francis from his past? If he was still so affected by it when James was not even his son, it was worse than she had ever imagined.

'I have put this behind me,' he said sharply. 'I am doing what I think is right. You are the one who appears to have a problem.'

'What do you mean?' Rachel was taken aback by his abrupt tone. 'I have a problem with the fact that you did not trust me enough to tell me about something as important as this. That's what I have a problem with. I have a problem with the fact that if Virginia wants this thing then our marriage is jerked this way and if Virginia wants that thing then our marriage is jerked that way and whatever Virginia says James needs, James gets. And he is not even your son.'

'I have tried to explain, Rachel,' he said. 'Until James was thirteen I thought he was my son. I loved him. Should I just stop loving him because it turns out I am not his biological father? Should I just stop caring about him?'

But that was the question he had been struggling with ever since that dreadful day.

Francis had so wanted to believe what Virginia had said. 'Just a friend,' she had said. He had longed to believe her. But he could not erase that smirk. Those shining eyes gleaming with self-satisfaction above the carefully barbered beard.

'But why does she always turn to you?' Rachel asked. 'I don't understand. Why doesn't she go to James's real father?'

'What's real?' Francis muttered automatically.

'You know what I mean, Francis,' she said. 'Why doesn't Virginia go to him?'

'Because she does not know who the biological father is.'

How could he begin to explain about Virginia to Rachel?

It had started when they got home. Walking through the door had triggered it. Had they done it here? In their flat?

'It wasn't important,' Virginia had responded. To every question he asked, she replied in the same way: 'It will only upset you more. It was not important.

I won't see him again. It was not important. You are important.'

There must have been more than this – Francis remembered not being able to eat or sleep, thinking about nothing else – but this was the image that stayed. 'It's not important,' and the nauseating sense that everything had changed, nothing could ever be the same again.

What if there had been others before? Why not? And then, if there had been, what about James? Who was James's father?

Virginia had refused to discuss it.

'James is your son,' she'd said. 'There is no doubt about it. I have no doubt about it. Please leave it alone. How can you bring something so precious into this?'

'I didn't: you did.' He recalled every word. 'I didn't fuck someone else. You did. How do I know you haven't fucked half the school and his father is some PE teacher? How am I supposed to know? I didn't have a clue about that smug fucker you took to lunch – how am I supposed to know about how many others there have been?'

'Because I am telling you,' she had said. 'You are James's father.'

'So you say,' he had replied bitterly. 'So you say. If you are so confident, let's have a DNA test. Let's settle it.'

And they had.

'You are still his father,' Virginia had said. 'The biology is irrelevant. Could you love him more? Or less? Could you stop loving him? The DNA is beside the point. Look at that little boy. That's the real test. Do you love him? Or not? You have been his father for the last thirteen years. You are his father now. Be his father.'

He had tried. Oh how he had tried.

'It wasn't important,' Virginia said again and again. 'They were not important. You are important.'

'What do you mean she does not know who the biological father is?' Rachel said now.

'I know it must be hard to understand,' he said. 'Virginia is an unusual person.'

'I've noticed.'

'Please, Rachel, don't be like that.'

'Like what?'

'Please. It's too important for these debating points. Please.'

Rachel felt abashed. He was right. But really, what kind of woman was Virginia?

'It was different then,' Francis said.

'Evidently,' Rachel said.

'Rachel, please. I have just tried to do the right thing.'

And he had. He knew Virginia was right, but he did not feel it. And he knew it was not James's fault. But something had changed for ever that day.

He still loved James – how could he just stop? – but it was not the same. And how could he stay with this woman he had discovered he did not know at all, this new Virginia, a woman he had unknowingly shared, and who had borne someone else's child? Someone whose identity she did not know or would not tell him.

As Rachel questioned him on this summer evening, the rage came welling up from the depths where he had tried to keep it buried. How could Virginia have done this to him? And wrecked their life together.

And his fury had been harder to bear because he knew he should keep it bottled up. Virginia had been unfaithful, but he could live with that, he supposed. He had been betrayed, and many times, obviously. Over many years. But should he abandon his marriage for that? James was not his son but he knew Virginia was right. He should not stop loving him. Love is not decided by blood. And he did still love him, but it was not the same. He knew he should love James for who he was and for the years they had shared so happily. But it did not feel the same. He knew it should, but it didn't. He knew Virginia was right. But it did not feel like that.

There was no escape. Francis knew there could be no end to this conflict in him. What Rachel was saying to him on this glorious summer evening was what he felt. But he could not tell her that. It was wrong. He should not feel like that. It was not James's fault. What Virginia had said to him during those dreadful days was what he knew was right. But he did not feel it.

It was always waiting there, lurking in an antechamber to be summoned. And Rachel had just turned the key to open the door.

And now she sat beside him and held his hand in silence. 'You must do what you think is right,' she said eventually. 'I am sorry I have given you such a hard time. It's not fair. Whatever you decide, I know you will do the right thing.'

Francis squeezed her hand.

'What do you think is best for James?' she asked.

'I don't know,' he said. 'One moment I think I should just pay up and make it all go away. And then I think: what message does that send James? That I am always going to be around to underwrite his criminal activities? Will it just encourage him to go on doing it?'

'What did Charles say would happen if you went to the police?'

'He said James might go to jail. But he also said they might not press charges. Especially if James went in voluntarily to own up. And even if they did prosecute him, he might just end up with a community sentence.'

Rachel said nothing. She waited. Sometimes it was important just to wait.

Francis stared out of the window. 'It's not good however you look at it,' he said eventually. 'It's a question of finding the least bad option.'

Rachel gently stroked his hand. 'Whatever you think is best, my darling,' she said.

Francis felt a great weariness sinking into him. He did not want any more discussions with anyone about this. He just wanted to be finished with it. But he still wanted to do the right thing.

Going to the police must be the right thing. For Rachel. For InterTrust. And for James. The odds were that he wouldn't end up in jail. He'd get a shock and get the message. But if he just paid up, James might not learn the lesson and then, sooner or later, he would end up in jail.

But Francis did not feel reassured by this decision. Something was still bothering him.

He hated revisiting his past. Rachel had dragged him back and he hated it. But it was not that.

Francis did not like the way Rachel had gone through his papers. He wanted to share everything with her but she still had to learn to respect his space. As Virginia used to say. Rachel still had to learn how to do that. But it was not that either.

Something else was bothering him. Something new. And then he realised. It was something that dapper little man had said to him in the front garden. He had said something Virginia had not said. And so it was something he had not told Charles. The dealer had said that James had taken delivery of half a kilo of Scotty. James had. And that changed everything.

twenty-eight

thursday 7.00 a.m.

Three bedrooms, ocean-front condo in Honokawa: $1,195,000. In Kaanapali you could get two bedrooms and two bathrooms for $795,000. The brochure had page after page of tropical wood verandahs looking out over the blue rolling surf and white sand and Roger put it down reluctantly. Soon he would be there, but first he had to sort this out.

The way Roger looked at it, there were two kinds of trouble: predictable trouble and unpredictable trouble. Unpredictable trouble was unavoidable. But predictable trouble was unnecessary trouble. That was how Roger looked at it. And, as life was full of grief anyway, getting into unnecessary trouble was stupid. He drew on his cigar. That was how he looked at it.

Roger liked this time alone with his cigar, looking out of the window. It helped his creativity. This was when he had his best ideas. And he liked an early start to the day. He could get things done while everyone else was still getting into work. He was flowing now.

Dealing with Chris could be trouble. Little pricks like that always had family. He could only do it on his own if there was some way it could not be traced back to him. But it looked like it was going to be necessary trouble.

Roger placed the Romeo y Julieta carefully in the marble ashtray on his desk. He had read somewhere that gentlemen never stubbed out a cigar. They let it die a natural death.

He wondered if it was true that they rolled these cigars between the thighs of Cuban maidens. He couldn't see what difference it would make. And how would they control the finish? The thigh was not a precision instrument. That was more like the finger and thumb. What they said was probably just a marketing campaign. It sounded better. At least, until you thought about it. Once you thought about what was actually involved, it seemed a little less appealing.

Roger picked the cigar butt out of the ashtray. It was still smouldering. It took a long time to go out. That was the mark of an expensive cigar, he had read somewhere. He smelled it. Not much aroma of maiden there.

There was trouble ahead but all things considered, Roger felt he had a grip on the situation. Davey would report back on Chris. And then he would decide what to do about him.

And then there was that banker. But he would probably get the message and come across with the money by Friday. He didn't look the sort to cause trouble. That was under control. The process was in place.

Roger picked the cigar butt out of the ashtray again. It was still smouldering. It was obviously one of the best. He drew on it.

Mao Zedong said the Long March started with a single step. And Roger knew what he meant. He was on his own Long March. Onwards to Honolulu.

Little pricks like Chris wanted it all immediately. They had not learnt to delay gratification. That was what made you an adult, he had read somewhere. But these fucking little kids couldn't wait for anything. That was why Jason had got his ears pinned to the wall.

Roger's Long March would stretch across the next twelve months to Honokawa and Kaanapali. And on the way, some would have to be sacrificed for the cause. Roger liked the sound of that. That must have happened a lot on the Long March.

The way Roger looked at it, Mao Zedong would have understood what was now required.

twenty-nine

thursday 8.00 a.m.

'Why didn't you tell me?'

'Not now, Francis.'

'That's just typical. Why do you always put off confronting the truth, Virginia?'

'This is not a good time, Francis.'

'There's never a good time for you to tell the truth, is there? When are you going to confront the fact that James is up to his neck in cocaine.'

'Not literally, Francis, surely?'

'This is not funny.'

'And this is not a good time to discuss this. Really not.'

'Well I am going to discuss this. Now.'

'Frankie's right. It's not funny. It kills you.' Julie appeared out of the kitchen, polishing a glass with a dishcloth.

'I told you it wasn't a good time, Francis.'

'Well I want to talk about it. Please could you leave now, Julie.'

'You're right, Frankie. This stuff kills you. A kid from our block overdosed two months ago. Dead. Get James away from it.' Julie moved her arm to emphasise her advice and the glass smashed against the door frame. 'Whoops. Sorry.' She knelt down and started to pick up the pieces of broken glass and put them in the dishcloth. 'My mum always said I talk with my hands.'

'Don't worry, I'll do it later,' Virginia said.

'Anyway, believe me. Get him away from it,' Julie said from the floor.

'Thank you for your advice,' Francis said. 'Please could I now have a private conversation with James's mother?'

'All right, all right. I'm done. I think I've got it all.' Julie got up and went back into the kitchen.

Francis and Virginia heard the broken glass tinkle and spatter into the bin.

Julie came back into the living room. 'I'll be off then,' she said. 'See you on Tuesday, Virginia.' She patted Virginia on the shoulder as she left. 'Be careful,' she said.

'Does that woman live here now?' Francis asked as he heard the front door shut.

'Relax. She just thinks you should not have left me and James. That's all. So what? Now, please sit down and calm down.'

'Why didn't you tell me?'

'Tell you what?' Virginia sat on the sofa in a fuchsia silk dressing gown and ran her hand through her hair. 'You could have come round a bit later,' she said. 'This is an inset day. And so is tomorrow.'

'Please, Virginia,' he said. 'This isn't a game. Why

didn't you tell me? And aren't you meant to be in school anyway?'

'I am not required. I don't need training. I am relaxing and enjoying my well-earned day off. And you are disturbing me. Do you want a coffee?' She yawned. This early in the morning she looked young no longer. Lines on her face inscribed her history and the tangled blonde hair was now delicate not lustrous. But Virginia still emanated soft warmth and mellow sensuality. She stretched and got off the sofa.

'Are you sure you don't want some coffee?'

'No, I don't. I just want the truth.'

'I make proper cappuccino. It's a Gaggia.'

'Please, Virginia, this is not a game. This is dangerous and we should get out of it as quickly as possible. What else has James not told us?'

She looked at him.

'Why are you looking at me like that?'

'I'm not looking like anything,' she said.

'You know what that man said yesterday? He said that James took delivery of half a kilo of "Scotty"? Did you know he was dealing himself? James was taking the whole lot. It wasn't for anyone else. It was all for him.'

'What's "Scotty"?'

'Drugs. Cocaine, I suppose. You know, "Beam me up"?' Francis said absently, and then focusing again, 'Did you know James was dealing? You did know, didn't you?'

'I didn't know.'

'You suspected then.'

'How could I know?'

'Virginia, please. Did you know all along that he was dealing? Why do you bother lying to me? Again.'

'I am not lying,' Virginia was indignant. 'I did not know. I did not know because I did not ask. And I did not ask because I didn't want him to feel he had to lie to me. But I guessed. You're right. I guessed. It was a pretty stupid story. It didn't sound very likely, did it? So I guessed he had been dealing. But what difference does it make whether he was or he wasn't? Why waste time on that? He owes this man thirty thousand pounds – that is true whatever – and he needs our help – that is true whatever. And that is what really matters.'

'How could I have been so stupid? How could I have believed such a stupid lie?' Francis sat down on the sofa and stared at the floor. How could he possibly take James to the police now? His son would go straight to jail. There could be no understanding or sympathy for dealers. There would be no community sentence now.

Virginia sat down beside him. 'Francis,' she said gently, 'what difference would it have made? He's our son. He needs our help. That's all. It doesn't matter why. I wish he hadn't felt he needed to lie. He must have felt scared of you. But he did. And it's not important. All that matters is that he needs our help. And we are going to help him.'

'Why should he be scared of me? What has that got to do with anything?'

'It's not important,' Virginia said soothingly.

'It is important. James has been dealing Class A drugs. Half a kilo at a time. He could go to jail. And you say that's not important? How on earth have you let him grow up like this?'

'Like what? Like what exactly?'

'A drug dealer.'

'Is he a cruel boy? That would be a problem. Is he violent? That would be a problem. Or racist? That would be a problem. Does he abuse women or children? Those would be problems. He does not do any of those things. He is a sweet, good boy who does not know what he wants to do with his life. Is that a crime? I don't think it's anything to be ashamed of. We can't all be like you, Francis.'

She took his hand as she spoke. 'Francis, you must not blame him.'

He took his hand away. 'He is a drug dealer,' he said. 'What about all the people he sells it to? What about their lives? He's peddling drugs which destroy lives.'

'Don't be so melodramatic. He sells it to his friends. They use it like you use whiskey. It's recreational, not something they shoot up in an alleyway.'

'I thought you didn't know. I thought you only guessed what was going on. You seem to have guessed to a remarkably high degree of detail.'

She took his hand back into hers. 'Don't resist me, Francis. You are just making yourself wretched for no reason. This is not important.'

'I remember hearing that once before.'

'Yes, you did. And it wasn't. But I can't stop you

making yourself miserable. I could not stop what went wrong between us. But this is our son. Whatever mistakes we have made, you and I, he was not one of them. He needs us. What matters is we help him through this.'

'Of course I will. I have always done everything you wanted to help him. But it doesn't make me feel any better about the fact that he is dealing drugs. And it doesn't make me feel any better about the fact that he lied about it. And such a stupid lie. I don't know how I could have been so stupid as to believe it. And I can't help it: I just think it is wrong. It is wrong. It's a crime. And he could go to jail. How could he have got mixed up in this?'

Virginia took his other hand as well and gave them both a little shake. 'Please, please stop making yourself unhappy,' she said. 'Why? What purpose does it serve? This sort of judgement is such a lazy way of making sense of things.'

'Spare me the hippie philosophy. There's right. And there's wrong. And this is wrong.'

'Yes,' she said patiently, as if she was back in class. 'There is right and there is wrong but these are precious judgements. They should only be used for important things, not things like this.'

'And, of course, you are the judge of what's important.'

'No.' Virginia continued to speak with great patience. 'We all make our own judgements. But only children believe that deciding right and wrong is a science. It is not. It is a convenience. Societies need it to function. But it is not much use for human beings who have to get through every day. It's not much of a guide for our relationships with each other. What's it got to do with love?'

Francis relaxed his hands in hers. Only Virginia could say something like that. It almost meant something when she said it. 'Don't be so ridiculous,' he said. 'This has got nothing to do with love. It's got to do with the fact that James is a drug dealer and that is wrong.'

'Don't be so rigid,' Virginia said. 'You are just making yourself miserable for no reason, because this is the story you are telling yourself about what has happened. But there are other stories you could tell yourself about it.' She spoke as if consoling a small child over the death of a pet budgerigar. 'Stories with one beginning and one middle and one end are for children,' she said. 'They need a simple structure. Children need boundaries. But all that stops being much use when you get to our age. Nothing makes sense, really makes sense, except what we feel. The story is not the neat narrative you think it is. It's moments, each with their own unique meaning – like the moments we had. Remember? You say you're stupid to have believed James. I don't think it's stupid. You did it for the best reason – because you love him. That's the best of reasons. I'll tell you what's stupid. It's stupid to think there's order and cause and purpose in our lives. There isn't. Things happen. That's it. Love matters. That's it.'

Francis remembered how her insidious logic could

penetrate any gap in the armour. It was so easy to give in to it. Dying must be like this, he thought. The temptation to stop resisting, just to let go and drift away. The temptation of Virginia never went away. Its power flowed from its relentless persistence. She was so certain.

'You think too much. Things happen,' she said. 'The only thing you can really be certain of is what you feel. And you must be certain of that or you are lost. And that means you have to forget what other people think. They are not important, Francis. All that matters in the end is love. And you love James. Hold on to that and you will never be lost.'

Francis said nothing.

'These judgements you make have always made you miserable. What good have they ever done you? When you left me, who was right, who was wrong? You knew. All our friends knew. Who cares? These judgements are just lazy ways of making sense. Love is more difficult. But it is the only thing that really makes sense.'

'If only it was so easy,' he said.

'It is,' she said passionately. 'It is.'

'Not for me it isn't.' He got up firmly, breaking the spell. 'And not for James it isn't. Quite apart from whether it's right or wrong he's now faced with a future where he either goes to jail or he gets his head blown off by the Mafia.'

'Or we help him,' Virginia said. 'That's what parents do, Francis. Help. Don't judge. Help.'

'Yes,' he said. 'Very good, Virginia. But I know that.

What I don't know is how.' He sighed. 'I need to go. I have got to get into the office. And I suppose I should see James and find out what exactly he has been doing and find out if there are any more surprises before I decide what to do. To help.'

'Remember what's important,' she said, looking up at him from the sofa.

'I know what's important.'

She held his eye. 'Please, Francis,' she said. Her early morning softness seasoned her urgent tone with a carnal charge.

He buttoned his jacket defensively. 'I am going to see James.'

It was only when she watched his car driving off that she remembered he had not said anything about paying the money. Presumably that meant he was not going to and that meant his only contribution would be a ponderous lecture to James about drug dealing. And she would still have to sort it out herself.

Francis drove to his office, simmering with frustration. His initial anger at the duplicity of James and Virginia was now being overtaken by his alarm that it was all so much more serious than it had seemed at first. How could they have got themselves into this mess?

One image of James would not leave him alone. Although Francis had knocked and knocked, he had refused to come out of his room. 'Daddy and Mummy still love you,' Virginia had called. 'We still love each other.' Finally, they went into his room together.

Virginia said: 'Daddy and Mummy are not getting on at the moment. We still love you. We still love each other. But it is better we do not live together. Just for a bit.' Francis had watched, miserable and mute, while James stared silently at the wall in his Teenage Mutant Ninja Turtles T-shirt and Virginia tried to reassure him. He had stopped wearing the T-shirt two years earlier. It was far too small for him. Francis had thought they had given it to Oxfam. How could that lost little boy have grown up into a man who spent thirty thousand pounds on cocaine?

Francis turned off the Embankment up towards the City. 'Daddy,' James had said when he left. Nothing else. It was the last time he ever said it. From then on, James had always called him 'Dad'.

A red car in front of him suddenly slowed down and Francis braked sharply.

As Francis had left his family, he had turned round in the street and looked back at the flat. Up at the window he could see James looking down, in the Teenage Mutant Ninja Turtles T-shirt which was too small for him. But it was too late to turn back. He had left the house. How could he have gone back?

A young woman with blonde hair and sunglasses sitting in a convertible BMW looked at him as he drew up beside her at traffic lights.

What was he going to do about James?

There could be no question now of him getting away with community service. So should he give Virginia the thirty thousand pounds now? It was only when he was parking the car that he remembered he had not even got round to discussing that possibility with her. But he supposed now he had better just pay up and get it over with.

Francis drove into the car park and locked the car and started to walk round to his office. He brushed past two men standing by the entrance to a narrow street that ran along the side of Silvergate House. At first he thought he had tripped. Then he realised the taller one had stuck his leg out deliberately.

As he stumbled, they caught him under the arms and pulled him into the little alleyway. Fluently they propped him against the wall and one of them punched him in the face. The intensity of the pain startled him. His nose was leaking blood. At the same time, he was aware through the pain that the other one had taken his arm and was twisting it behind his back so he was being forced round to face the wall. He felt the rough stone grazing his cheek. The man was continuing to push his arm up behind his back. He cried out. The other man punched him hard, very hard, in his ribs and Francis gasped as the air was forced out of his lungs. The two men were silent as they went about their task. One of them slipped the watch off his wrist. The other man then kicked his calf hard and as Francis instinctively reached down for it, doubling up, he was pushed sprawling onto the ground. Then they were gone.

Francis lay on the uneven cobbles for a moment, uncertain how to begin getting up. Everything hurt. His ribs ached. He could feel the blood oozing over his face. His arm felt as it had been wrenched out of its socket. And the shock was beginning to make him shiver.

He sat up carefully. The early morning sun was beginning to warm up the alley. He wiped the blood off his face. He had never realised muggers worked in the morning, and yet here he was, bleeding on the ground, on his way to work at nine o'clock in the morning. His calf throbbed where he had been kicked. His nose was still bleeding and his arm was getting more and more painful.

He stood up. His suit had some white smears on it. He brushed them off. It was not torn and he thought it could be made presentable. He supposed he had better get into the office. But first he ought to go to hospital to check whether anything had been broken.

thirty

thursday 9.15 a.m.

They were in Morden, another of Prendergast, Markby and Matthews's small, windowless conference rooms. Engravings of Victorian law-courts hung on the walls, picked up by one of the partners in a Brighton antique shop one weekend. Clients were given no reason to worry about excessive overheads in this room. James had been in some of the grander conference suites but this one was definitely for the cheaper end of the market. This one was for the private business of Raymond Chivers.

The door opened and the client came in, short and plump with an unhealthy sheen on his forehead. 'Colin,' he said, stretching out his hand, 'I'm grateful you could see me so soon.'

'Good to see you, Raymond,' said Colin Evans. 'Let me introduce you to James Carroll, one of our most promising young lawyers.'

James and Raymond shook hands and they all sat down.

James briefly considered being promising and Colin Evans finally recognising it. But then rejected the idea. He didn't suppose even Raymond Chivers believed it. The truth was there was no-one else to do this rubbish, whatever it was. Or at least no-one Raymond Chivers could afford in his personal capacity.

'Coffee?' Evans indicated a white insulated flask on a side table with some white china cups.

Raymond Chivers shook his head. He opened his briefcase and took out a thick manila folder and placed it on the table in front of him. He smoothed his hair down with his hands and then opened the file. He didn't say anything but riffled through the papers, breathing heavily through his nose. His hair was cut close to the skull and severely receded at the temples. In compensation, wiry strands from his chest and back escaped around his collar.

Colin did not offer any coffee to James. He wouldn't have taken it anyway as he loathed the stewed bilge that came out of those flasks. In the smarter conference rooms they brewed the coffee to order and one of the kitchen staff brought it in. That was for the larger corporate clients, but not for Raymond Chivers in search of his patrimony.

Colin Evans waited patiently. It was the client's time and money.

Raymond Chivers was still fussing through his papers.

James wondered about a short series on coffee. It could be an observational documentary showing who made what sort of coffee: how the Maxwell House housewife had succumbed to the cappuccino. And it could analyse why coffee had become so central to Western social discourse. That would be interesting.

It could explore why the phrase 'Would you like to come up for coffee?' had become such an indispensable part of sexual etiquette. That could be really interesting. Why did no-one ever say, 'Do you want to come up for a cup of tea?' Perhaps because no-one drank tea at night? But then lots of people did not drink coffee at night in case it kept them awake. Maybe that was it – it was a double message: not only 'Do you want to come into my bedroom?' but also 'Do you want to be awake all night, having passionate sex. Because I'll be up all night. Because I drink coffee.'

Definitely BBC2 with all that popular culture. It could include archive film of the Nescafé commercials. But the sex might make it more suitable for Channel 4. Whatever. It could be really, really interesting.

Raymond Chivers made a little noise clearing his throat as he found the papers he had been looking for. 'Here it is,' he said. 'Look.' He showed the papers to Colin Evans. 'This is the will they both made.'

'Raymond,' said Evans, 'take us back a stage. I got the basic picture from what you said on the phone but James and I need to understand the background a bit better.'

'I need you to undo the will.' Raymond Chivers had a low voice which sounded as if he was always complaining about something. He directed himself at Colin Evans, ignoring James. 'Ten years ago, my mother and father made wills leaving everything to each other, and then, when they both died, to me. My mother died in 1995. And my father then married again. He died two months ago and I discovered he had made a new will leaving almost everything to his new wife.'

'How much are we talking about, Raymond?' Colin Evans asked gently.

'It's not the money,' Chivers said. 'I do want you to understand that.'

'How much are we talking about, Raymond?' kindly Colin Evans asked again.

'With the house, it's about three hundred thousand before tax,' said Chivers. 'But it's not that.' He looked earnestly at the solicitors across the table. James noticed the forefinger on his right hand was picking away at the skin round the cuticle of the thumb. He watched as it worked loose a tiny flap of skin, like a subterranean insect blindly obeying some biological law. 'My mother would never have wanted this. She could never have imagined he would do this. I could never have imagined he would do this.'

'What does your stepmother think about it all?' asked Evans.

'I think she is a bit embarrassed.' Chivers spoke in the careful, factual tones he doubtless used with his own clients. 'I hope she is. She should be.'

James wondered if Rachel would be embarrassed in similar circumstances. Probably not.

'I ask,' Evans said, 'because it is often best to try to sort out this kind of thing amicably, without lawyers.'

He smiled self-deprecatingly. James knew he didn't

mean it. He had seen this technique used too often now in the initial meeting. In six months he had never yet seen a client stand up at this point and say, 'OK, I'll do it myself.' Whenever one of the partners said this, it always seemed to intensify the client's urge to pay thousands and thousands of pounds to lawyers to do it all for them, convincing them, perversely, that only a lawyer could sort it out for them. James had not yet managed to work out why this was. But he recognised it as a smart trick. These lawyers were smart. No doubt about that.

'I could try, I suppose,' Chivers said doubtfully, but James knew he wouldn't. 'But I would rather you had a look at it for me.'

'Of course we will,' said Evans. 'What do you make of it, James?'

'I have been looking through the papers,' James said. 'Do you mind if I ask you a few questions?'

This was the cue for Colin Evans to leave. He stood up and extended his hand to Chivers. 'Nice to see you again, Raymond. I'm going to have to leave you in the very capable hands of James here. He does all the real work anyway, but I thought I would just drop by to see if you had anything you wanted to ask me.'

His expeditious tone dared Chivers to demand more, but Chivers had got the message. He knew about charge-outs and his personal money ticking away in the windowless conference room.

'Good to see you, Colin,' he said. 'If there is anything I will let you know.' They shook hands and Evans left.

'You had some questions for me?' Chivers turned to James. He had moved on.

Despite himself, James had begun to enjoy this. It was the first thing he had been given to do on his own and he had even stayed late last night to make sure he had gone through all the papers properly in preparation for this meeting. It had even stopped him thinking about that dreadful visit yesterday from the man in the dove-grey suit, Chris's boss, as the work blotted out the intense panic the man had ignited. Concentrating on something else, surrounded by books and his computer in his office, displaced the tension. It was almost better than a spliff. And he believed that he had got a grip on the case. He understood it. He knew what had to be done. And he was doing it on his own, without Evans.

James looked at his notes. 'Do you have any evidence your mother wanted your father to leave everything to you when he died?'

'Of course she did. The evidence is in the wills. They left identical wills, both leaving it all to me when they were both dead.' Chivers spoke with an edge of irritation, as if dealing with a recalcitrant pupil.

'That is evidence they left identical wills. But Goodchild v. Goodchild suggests that is not sufficient.' James surprised himself with his fluency. This was how lawyers talked. He saw Chivers was listening. 'Goodchild v. Goodchild is an important case for determining the nature of mutual wills,' James continued.

'Yes, yes,' Chivers muttered.

James was disconcerted by his impatience. 'The point is you have to have a mutual will, not an identical will,' he said. 'I mean you don't have to have a mutual will, but if you are going to get anything from your father's will, you will need to show your mother and father left mutual wills.'

He had spent a lot of time looking into this. Even Miranda noticed he was working. 'Interesting?' she had asked curiously. 'Yes,' he had said, enjoying this rare moment when he had attracted Miranda's attention.

'Goodchild v. Goodchild found that a key point determining whether wills are mutual wills is whether the mutual intentions are irrevocable.' James read out his notes carefully. This was important. He did not want to get it wrong.

He looked up at Raymond Chivers. 'The point is,' he said, 'it all depends on what they intended when they made the wills. The judge in Goodchild v. Goodchild said suppose you did something really awful after your mother died but while your father was alive, would your mother still have wanted your father to leave it all to you?'

Chivers did not react. Perhaps he thought this was not a sensible question.

'I mean,' James continued, 'I don't mean you would do anything awful, but let's just suppose you did, let's say, for example, you . . .' He could not think what might have caused Chivers's father to cut him out. 'What do you think would be so awful that your father would have cut you out of the will?' he asked.

'This is irrelevant,' Chivers snapped. 'This has got nothing to do with it. I can assure you I have not done anything of the sort. And there really is no point in discussing this any further.'

James was reluctant to see all his work wasted. 'That's not the point,' he argued. 'The point is did your mother think you might, and even thinking that you might do something really awful, did she still want your father to leave it all to you?'

James felt he had expressed it well. Chivers ought to be able to understand it now.

'I'd like to see Colin Evans,' Chivers said.

'Now?'

'Now,' Chivers confirmed.

Waiting outside the conference room as Evans conferred with Chivers, James mulled it over. Evans had been visibly irritated to be summoned back so soon. It was ironic that the one case he thought he might actually enjoy was turning out so badly. Typical, really. Perhaps Evans had been wrong, and Goodchild v. Goodchild had nothing to do with it. But how would Chivers know that? He was an accountant.

Evans put his head round the door. 'Come in, James,' he said.

Chivers looked at James as he came in.

'I have just been explaining to Raymond how much work you have done on his case,' Evans said. James wondered how Evans could possibly have known that. Then he realised he didn't. It was just one of those things he said to clients. 'And how you are one of our most promising associates.' Associate? James saw that

Chivers also liked this description. Perhaps it wasn't as bad as it looked. A bond was developing from their mutual appreciation of this image of James as an associate. 'I have explained that you might not have fully communicated the significance of Goodchild v. Goodchild but that I was sure you would be happy to go through it again.'

James nodded.

'Raymond and I have also discussed the time we need to spend on this and the cost implications. And I think we are now all set.'

As Evans said this, Chivers looked on comfortably. Whatever Evans had actually said, it had worked.

Evans stood up again. 'I'm afraid I really do have to go now. Good luck.'

Once Evans had gone, James looked at Chivers uncertainly. Chivers smiled at him. James was sure it was meant well but it made him look like a malign dormouse bent on mayhem.

'We seem to have got off on the wrong foot. Let's start again.'

James nodded, uncertain of what to say. 'OK,' he said.

There was a moment's silence. Then they both started to speak at the same time. Chivers persisted. 'Colin explained about Goodchild v. Goodchild,' he said. 'What else do you need to know?'

James realised this was being professional: you had to forget about any personal feelings and do the job. 'We need to establish the intent at the time the wills were made.' He had picked up the tone from Evans but he was still impressed by himself. 'We' was good, suggesting mutual purpose, shoulder to shoulder with the client: his case, your case; his concerns, your concerns; his money, your money.

'I understand,' said Chivers. 'But I don't know I can prove it. I am sure my mother would never have wanted my father to cut me out like this. But how do I prove it? I know that's what Mum would have wanted. I was her son. God knows what Dad wanted.'

There was something jarring the way this plump, balding, middle-aged man talked about his parents. The protective coverings of adulthood were dissolving, revealing the man's raw core. The more he talked, James's ambivalent feelings, his enjoyment of his own expertise, his unease at being the authority and his dislike of Chivers, were joined by a strange new sensation as, unexpectedly, sympathy sneaked in.

It was his bafflement about his father that jolted James. 'God knows what Dad wanted.' That was it, that was it exactly, what he felt so often.

'Goodchild v. Goodchild says it doesn't matter about your dad,' he said sympathetically, with suffi-cient force that Chivers looked up from his papers. 'All that matters is whether your mother wanted it to be irrevocable. And we need to have proof – other-wise the courts will just assume it wasn't irrevocable.'

Chivers was now looking at him as if he wanted him to continue. James liked this unexpected feeling. 'Did your mum say anything to you before she died about what she wanted?'

Chivers shook his head.

'Or did your dad say anything about what they wanted?'

'They never discussed these things with me,' Chivers said.

'Is there anyone else they might have discussed it with?'

There was a knock at the door before Chivers could answer and Katie came in, without waiting for an answer, and handed James a note. She smiled knowingly at him as she left.

'Darling,' it said. 'I'm outside.' His Mum.

Chivers looked at him.

'I can't think of anyone,' he said. 'I could ask their friends,' he added doubtfully.

'Yes,' James said. 'That sounds like a good idea. Why don't you do that and let me know what they say.' He stood up. He had forgotten about his problem. That must be why she was here. There could be no other reason why she would just turn up. Perhaps she had sorted out the money.

'Then we should meet again,' Chivers suggested. 'I could do nine o'clock on Tuesday.'

'I'll make sure I am free,' James replied. He had heard Evans say this. It had the right ring to it.

'Thank you.' Chivers shook his hand. Chivers's hand was clammy and limp but it felt good to James. This is what lawyers did.

James tried out a new walk as they left the room. A purposeful new walk to go with his new responsibilities as a lawyer, as a promising associate. Straight ahead, brisk feet, shoes shining.

As they came into the reception area, James saw his mother sitting there, her long legs resting on the glass coffee table. Underneath it sat two purple shoes with stiletto heels. Beside him, Chivers straightened up as he noticed Virginia. All his life, James had noticed the effect his mother had on men. Even now, at her age, it still happened. He knew she did not try for it. It had always bored her. But it still happened and it still embarrassed him.

'Darling,' she said, putting on her shoes and getting up. She came over to kiss him, ignoring Chivers. He seemed used to such treatment but James said protectively, 'Mr Chivers, this is my mother. Mum, this is Mr Chivers. He is a client.'

They shook hands and Chivers left.

'Darling,' Virginia said. 'I have worked it out.'

'Not here, Mum,' James pleaded. Katie was on the phone but he was sure she was listening. 'Please let's go outside.'

'All right,' she said, eyes gleaming. 'But I have got it sorted.'

thirty-one

The beautiful young receptionist still stood motion-less behind her desk, contemplating the middle distance as if she had not moved for days. Roger watched Davey Boswell as he loped amiably across the white lobby of the hotel towards him, his eyes on the ground as he approached, his long legs gangling, feet stepping one after the other in a long, loose-jointed stride, cowboy boots shining in the white light of the lobby, never faltering.

'Hey, man,' he said as he sat down. 'How's it going?'

Roger did not reply to the question. 'What's the little prick doing?' he asked.

'Two grand,' Davey said affably. This was a prin-ciple of Davey's. He had done the work and now he wanted the money. And he wanted to get paid before it was too late. He knew they didn't respect you after-wards – money first means everyone gets satisfaction, money later means someone gets screwed for nothing. Davey had learnt that.

Roger took an envelope from his inside breast pocket and slid it across the coffee table to Davey. It was expensive but then Davey would have had expenses.

'All there?'

'Of course.'

'Thanks, man.' Davey put the envelope in his pocket without opening it. And then he was away describing what he had found out about Chris. 'That dude of yours is pretty laid-back, doesn't work a lot, cruises round in the BMW with his mates most of the time, roof down, music on, you know, picking up chicks.'

Why didn't the little prick put a sign up: I'M A DEALER. I WORK FOR ROGER OATES. PLEASE ARREST ME. AND HIM. But Roger knew better than to interrupt. It would all be there somewhere, the jewels of information nestling among the packaging of insignificant trifles and meretricious trinkets. The drugs may have eaten away at the neurons in Davey's brain that ranked the important and the trivial but Roger knew it would all be there somewhere.

'Did a bit of work for you, man. Deliveries I think, don't know how much. Went to some temple yesterday evening with his old man and his brothers.'

Roger wanted to drum his fingers on the table – come on, man – but he had learnt to be patient with Davey.

'I took a look around the house when they were out. Man, they have got the biggest fucking television I have ever seen.'

Come on, Davey, just hurry up.

'The man certainly looks after himself. The bathroom is full of perfume. Smell this.' Davey wafted his hand round Roger's face. A scent of geraniums and lime-flowers drifted over towards Roger. 'Cool, isn't it? I took a bottle. He's got so many, he won't miss one.'

Just get on with it, Davey.

'Hey, man, I'll tell you something funny. His real name isn't Chris at all. It's Krishnan. How about that?'

'Yeah, yeah, I know,' Roger said.

'OK. OK. Your dude has got fifteen grand in an envelope – maybe your money, man, from deliveries.'

That is my fucking money and that little tangerine prick better give it to me.

'And he's got another five grand in a wallet. That's it. And, oh, yeah, I'll tell you what else, he's got an MP5K in a plastic bag at the back of his wardrobe.'

What the fuck did he want that for?

'Oh, yeah, and he goes to, like, this very, very expensive gym – man, it costs like a grand just for the membership and two grand a year and all the staff are, like, these seriously foxy ladies.'

He was paying the little prick too much.

'Thank you, Davey,' Roger said.

'Hold on, man. Is that it?' Davey asked himself the question seriously, searching his memory. 'Have I told you everything? Got to make sure you get your money's worth, man.' Davey scratched his head. 'Yeah, I do believe that is it. But don't worry, man, that's just a first instalment. I'll keep an eye on him over the weekend and get back to you on Monday.'

'Thank you, Davey,' Roger said. 'Anything else?'

'Yeah, man. The tea.'

Roger looked at him, suspecting some hippie jargon he did not understand.

'The tea, man. Tea. Green tea.'

Oh yeah. Tea. Roger raised his hand and the beautiful young woman behind the desk observed it without moving and then, in turn, she raised her hand, and then another beautiful young woman, also dressed all in black, arrived to take the order. That was how things worked in the all-white lobby of this beautiful hotel.

'Keep an eye on him,' Roger said.

'Sure, man. You get another seven days for the money,' Davey said. 'Got to make sure you get your money's worth, man. Do you want to meet tomorrow?'

'Monday,' Roger said. The beautiful young woman arrived back with the tea and poured it into a cup for Davey. 'I might need you to do the other job for me then.'

'Not paid you yet?' Davey asked sympathetically. 'That's too bad.'

'I'm not sure it's going to be a problem,' Roger said. 'He got a message from me this morning. We'll see whether he learns from it. Or not.'

If the thirty grand had not turned up by Monday, he would let Davey go after it. He knew Davey would already have begun on the preparations. He was good like that. A professional. Meticulous in the way he would escalate pain for the banker and his family until he got the money.

But Roger thought the banker would get the message. He did not look like someone who could take much pain.

thirty-two

thursday 10.15 a.m.

'Marketwatch.com was four hundred and seventy-three per cent up on the first day. If we did that, my options would be worth . . .' Alison calculated quickly '. . . around fifty thousand pounds. I could buy a flat.'

'Yes you could. If, if, if,' Lawrence said. 'If.' He hated it when they talked about money like this. He had a first-class degree in computer science from Imperial College and he had come to InterTrust to build a world-class system. It was demeaning to talk about option and money all the time. 'This is just speculation,' he said. 'Froth. Markets go up and down. What some of us are here to do is build a world-class company with leading-edge software.'

'And make shed-loads of money,' said Marion.

Alison giggled.

'You can laugh,' Lawrence said. 'But I would not bank on it if I were you. Just build the business.' He hated it when they talked like that, it sounded so crude, but Alison was really pretty and Marion was not bad either and he liked sitting round with them having coffee. He just wished they could talk about something else.

'Froth, eh?' said Marion. 'What about this?' She read from a sheet of paper: 'The Street.com up two hundred and fifteen percent up on the first day, Internet Financial Services.com up fifty-seven per cent, DLJ direct.com fifty per cent up. Froth, eh?'

'Just because there's a lot of froth about doesn't mean it's not still froth,' Lawrence answered and he polished his glasses furiously.

'The Chairman of the Federal Reserve, that is the Federal Reserve of the United States of America, he doesn't agree with you,' Marion said, persisting. 'Look,' and she pointed at a large sign that someone had hand-lettered and stuck on the wall behind them.

'You wouldn't get hype working' it read 'if there wasn't something fundamentally potentially sound under it', and then 'Alan Greenspan, January 1999'.

'See,' said Marion.

'Yes, we'll see,' muttered Lawrence. And then Francis walked in and Alison thought it was an omen. When he walked in like that, it was obviously a sign.

All her friends were envious when Alison got her job with InterTrust. They became articled clerks and trainee civil servants, but she walked into this sumptuous office. Walked into it. Typical Alison, her friends said. Lucky. She was a marketing assistant. The marketing assistant. There were only two of them in the marketing department. And there wasn't much marketing to do just yet. They were drawing up strategies, her and Marion.

Everyone agreed it was a great first job. Lucky Alison. Everyone wanted to be part of the dotcom revolution. And Alison actually was. The money was not great. She was earning less than the articled clerks. But she had stock options. Everyone at InterTrust had stock options. Francis insisted on it. And everyone knew there were at least 873 millionaires at Microsoft who had cashed in their stock options and retired at thirty. Lucky Alison. Her friend Mina said it proved looks mattered. Alison knew she would have been envious too if she had been Mina. Lucky Alison. Alison had never seen it like that. She would not be pretty for ever. Look at her mother. No-one looked twice at her now, not even her father. Especially not her father. Alison knew luck did not come into it. You had to work for it. And she was going for it. At InterTrust.

But when Francis walked in, his arm in a sling and a bruise spreading over his left cheek, as she said to Mina later, it just came to her: it was an omen.

It was like Francis himself. He had obviously been really good-looking when he was young. Even as his skin coarsened he retained the innocent vanity of a man who had never had to work to attract women. Alison said to Mina that he was like a ghost of sex who did not realise that he had passed from this world to the next.

Everyone knew Francis had been stuck in some long, important meetings. Everyone knew that everything depended on the IPO. Everyone was waiting for him to say something. Which he didn't. So when Alison saw him walking in, beaten up, it was like an omen.

'Must have been that ex-wife of his,' Marion said.

Alison laughed. She knew what Marion meant. They had all seen Virginia when she had come to the office two days ago.

Francis knew they were all looking at him. 'I was mugged,' he said to his secretary, Joanne. 'I hope I don't look too dreadful.'

'How awful,' she said. 'Did they catch them?'

'Not yet,' he said as he went into his office. He did not suppose they would be satisfied with this but he did not want to discuss it. His arm throbbed. The drugs they had given him at the hospital dulled the pain but did not remove it. He had thirty-seven emails. He started working his way through them, delicately tapping his way across the keyboard with his left hand.

Rachel rang to see how he was. The PR agency rang to discuss the launch event. He had a short meeting with the marketing team on strategy. The merchant bank rang to ask about a phrase in the offer document. Lloyd did not ring. Neither did Matt or Dan. And his arm continued to hurt, with a steady, insistent pain.

He could feel the drugs beginning to wear off. The pain was becoming sharper. He looked at his watch to see how long it had been since he had taken them. He did not have his watch. Those thugs must have taken it. He looked at the computer screen. Eleven thirty.

An item flashed across the screen. Sales of gemstones were up nearly fifty per cent in the first half of the year. Jewellers reckoned everyone would be buying diamonds for the millennium.

He ached everywhere. Why him? Today of all days?

What were the odds against him being mugged in broad daylight in the City of London? As if his life was not difficult enough. He had so much to do for InterTrust. That frustrating breakfast with Philippe had started off a terrible three days. There was James and all his problems. And now this. Why was this turning into such a terrible week? Mugged in broad daylight. In the City of London. What was God trying to tell him?

He looked out of the window. Everything hurt but he had so much to do. For a start, he had to talk to Virginia about the thirty thousand pounds. But he did not want to visit her again. This morning had made him uncomfortable for reasons he did not want to explore too closely. But he could not really talk about this over the phone. What if anyone should overhear? He would see her in the office. That was the answer. He asked Joanne to see if Virginia could come in that afternoon.

That was the right message. Joanne could deal with Virginia's notorious telephone manner, and getting her to come in would send the right signal. Grip.

'Mr Carroll,' said Joanne. 'It's Mrs Carroll. On the phone.'

'Francis, I don't have time to see you today,' Virginia said. 'There's no need anyway: I have found a way to sort it all out for James. I would have told you this morning only you were too busy lecturing me. Anyway, you can relax.' Virginia always spoke on the phone as if every minute cost her a hundred pounds. 'Alex has helped out,' she said.

Francis could not think what to say. Too many thoughts were flooding his brain. There was a silence.

'There was no need for that,' he said eventually. 'I said I would consider what I could do and that is what I was doing.'

'It's done, Francis,' she said. 'You don't need to agonise any more.'

'I was trying to do the right thing,' he said stiffly. But the relief was starting to sweep through him. He was out of it, no need for more arguments with Rachel or to find the money; and James would be OK. And it was Virginia's decision. Even if Alex had helped out. Whatever that meant. How could he have found thirty thousand pounds? He was just a journalist.

'Oh, and Francis,' Virginia added, 'next time you want to see me, you don't have to get your secretary to ask for you.'

'I'm glad it's sorted out,' he said quickly. 'I hope you understand why I needed time to consider.'

'I understand,' said Virginia, without expression.

Francis could not tell if she was being sarcastic or sympathetic or simply stating a fact. Why did she always make him feel in the wrong? 'This is difficult for me, Virginia,' he said. 'I will go and see James.'

'I'm sure he would like that,' Virginia said. 'Goodbye Francis.'

As Francis put down the phone, Joanne put her head round the door. 'Mrs Carroll is here to see you. She asked if you had a couple of minutes free?' Even if he had not just spoken to Virginia, he would have known from this introduction that it was Rachel. His mood softened.

'Hello,' she said as she came in. 'I thought I should come round to see you. You sounded a bit wan when you rang. I hope I'm not disturbing you.'

Francis smiled at her as he got up. 'Of course not,' he replied, and went over to her and kissed her. She smelled of lilacs.

'You look awful,' she said. 'Does it hurt terribly?'

'I'll be OK,' he said. Bravely.

'I just came to see how you are. I can't stay long. They'll think I'm accumulating too much personal time.'

'It's lovely to see you even for five minutes,' he said. 'Virginia rang.'

Her smile vanished.

'It's all right,' he said. 'She is sorting it out, the business with James. I don't need to do anything.'

Her smile returned. 'So she should,' she said happily. This was a milestone.

Francis looked at her. She shone. Shame washed through him. He had not made this decision. Virginia had. He had been going to pay up. But he could not explain all this to Rachel. She was so happy. He should just leave it alone. Rachel had got what she wanted. Virginia was dealing with it. It was nothing to do with them any more. They could get on with their lives.

But still, he should go and see James. As he remembered, he felt a surge of intense irritation. The boy had been incredibly irresponsible. He needed to be put right. And then they could get on with their lives.

219

thirty-three

thursday 12.05 p.m.

The crack was louder than Davey would have expected. At the tables nearby, people looked up to see where the noise came from. He wrenched the claw from the body of the lobster and started to scoop the meat into his mouth.

The restaurant had limed-oak floors and glowing reviews from the *Evening Standard* for its fresh seafood and imaginative wine-list. But that was not why Davey was there. The restaurant was right across the road from the office where the boy lawyer worked, and from his table by the window Davey could see everyone who went in and out of the building.

He was not sure he liked lobster but it was the most expensive item on the menu and Roger was paying. Davey took a swig of his Jack Daniels and tried to excavate more meat out of the shell.

He snapped his fingers and smiled lazily at the waiter. 'Bring me another one, man,' he said, briefly taking his eyes away from the window.

When he looked back, he saw something that made him put his hand into the deep pocket of his jacket.

He took out the small folder of photographs Roger had given him and leafed through them.

Yes, that was definitely one of them. In the wrong place. But definitely one of them.

thirty-four

thursday 12.10 p.m.

James had never seen his father like this. He had marched into the office and told Katie to get James to come to reception. 'Wait here,' he'd said when he saw James. He then marched off towards Colin Evans's office, saying as he went, 'Is Colin in?' but not waiting for an answer.

James watched as he strode down the corridor. There was a cut on his face and the back of his suit was rumpled.

Francis and Colin Evans had worked on deals together. That was how James had come to the firm. He didn't know what his father said but he marched back a few minutes later and said, 'Come with me.' It was humiliating. One parent after the other summoning him out of the office, all in one morning. Katie kept her eyes studiously averted. Francis's rage was too close to the surface. This was not something she wanted to share with James.

James followed his father out of the office. 'Where can we get a cup of coffee round here?' He could hear Francis trying to keep his voice under control.

'I'll show you,' he said. He did not know what had

triggered this but he was not surprised. He spent his life expecting it. Things were never quite as they should be and this was always on the verge of happening. Every time he saw his father, this was seething beneath the surface. Now here it was: out. The impatient rage that pulsed beneath the skin, the cold fury he had always known waited behind the distant gaze and the abstracted courtesy.

It looked as if a bruise was coming through on his father's face. What had happened to him?

They took the café lattes Francis had bought and sat in the chocolate leather armchairs in Starbucks. Soft rock music filled the empty coffee shop. A muscular bald man briskly set out trays of cakes and sandwiches.

'How could you do it?' Francis demanded. 'How could you have been so stupid?'

James looked at him blankly but he knew. He said nothing but he knew.

'Don't you know what you are doing?'

James said nothing. The coffees cooled untouched on the low table in front of them. The music curled around them.

'Don't you know how stupid you have been?'

James said nothing.

'Why don't you say something? Don't you know what I'm talking about?'

James shook his head but he knew.

'I've spoken to your man,' Francis said. James looked at the coffee on the table. 'You know, the man who sells you drugs. So you can sell them. The man who sold you half a kilo of "Scotty". You know: "Scotty"?'

James nodded miserably. Still he said nothing. There was so much to say but how could he begin to say it to this man, this furious stranger, his father. He did not know how to explain it to himself. And how could he even start to talk to his father about film school?

'I'm sorry,' he said.

He looked a boy again. Francis saw him putting on his Mutant Ninja Turtles outfit when he first got it, consumed by innocent excitement.

James wanted to say more but his father's scorn knocked away any possibility of explaining. It had never seemed that important. It earned good money, so he did not have to ask his mother for money she did not have but that she would have given to him if she had. And it avoided him having to ask his father, who gave away money as if it were his kidney.

It had only been a gramme here and there, until this last deal when he had wanted to put something aside for film school. Was it so wrong to want to provide for your own future? They were always telling him to stand on his own two feet. That was what his father was always saying to him. But how could he even begin to explain about film school?

'James,' his father spoke more quietly, 'you do realise how incredibly stupid you have been?'

James wondered what was the point in asking this question. Why would anyone think that he was doing it if he thought it was incredibly stupid. 'What difference does it make?' he muttered. He felt twelve again.

His father stared at him. 'James, it's wrong. It's a crime. You're breaking the law.'

James said nothing. He fixed his eyes on the cut on his father's cheek and said nothing.

'Did you hear me? I said you're breaking the law.'

'And I said: What difference does it make?'

'What do you mean – what difference does it make? It's a crime. You're breaking the law. You could go to jail.'

'That's my business.'

'It's not your business. It's my business too. And your mother's. How do you think she would feel seeing you in jail?'

'She doesn't come storming into my office. She doesn't frogmarch me off to Starbucks.'

'That doesn't mean she isn't worried sick.'

'Mum never worries herself sick about anything,' James muttered as he toyed with his mug of coffee.

'What is wrong with you, James? Can't you see it's wrong what you're doing?'

'Compared to what?'

'Please don't give me this rubbish. I've heard it all already. Who does it hurt? Consenting adults in their own homes? How do you know where this muck ends up?'

'What about whiskey? You drink whiskey. How many lives are ruined by drink? Who says it's OK to destroy yourself that way but not OK this way? Who says?'

'I don't care. I've heard all this stuff about manmade laws. Whoever made it, it is still the law and you have got to obey it. Or you go to jail.'

'What's the deal here anyway? Do you know how many children die every day in sub-Saharan Africa because they don't have clean drinking water? Do you know?'

'You are your mother's son, aren't you?'

'What's that supposed to mean?' James looked up from the table at Francis.

'It's not a contest, James. Of course it's wrong that young children die. But that doesn't make selling drugs any better.' Francis put his thumb and index finger into the corners of his eyes and squeezed his eyes tight shut around them in a gesture of intense weariness.

'Can I get you gentlemen some fresh coffee?' The bald man had finished stocking the shelves.

'No thank you,' Francis said. James said nothing. The man went away. Francis said nothing. The rock music covered the silence. No-one else had come into the coffee shop. Outside, mid-morning traffic was grinding ponderously through the City.

'Why you are doing this? Is it the money?'

James looked over to the counter. 'Could I have another latte?' he called.

'Coming up,' the bald man called back.

That should hold off his father for a few minutes. He would not want to continue the interrogation until the man had brought the latte and gone again. Then there was a chance his father's wrath might have been deflected somewhere else.

They sat in uncomfortable silence.

'There you go,' the bald man said, putting the coffee on the table and walking back to the counter.

'If it's the money, I can give you more.'

'I don't want your money.'

'Why do you say it like that?' Francis said. 'Don't I give you enough?'

James wiped the froth off his mouth. 'That's not the point.'

'Well, what is it then?'

James looked at the coffee on the table. He said nothing. The steam was rising off his mug. Francis's coffee looked cold and stale. Temperature was everything with coffee.

Francis looked at the stubbornly mute young man in front of him. It was like talking to a naughty child. Not that James had ever been naughty. He realised that he had last seen James looking like this when he had left Virginia.

'Why did you lie to us?' he said.

'I didn't lie to anyone. You never asked me.'

'James, you are a drug dealer.' Francis measured the words out carefully. 'What you are doing is not right. It is not right anyway and it is not right because you could end up going to jail. And these are bad people you are involved with. That is a fact. Not a moral judgement, but a fact. Is this really what you want for yourself?' The more Francis talked, the more he alarmed himself. How could James have been so stupid? 'These are dangerous men. I have met your dealer and I am telling you he is a dangerous man. These people kill people.'

'What do you know about it?'

'A lot more than I did a week ago, unfortunately.'

'I have been doing it for years and I have never had any trouble. It's not as bad as you think.'

'Years? Not as bad as I think? How much worse can it be? How many years?'

'Please keep your voice down, Dad.'

Francis breathed in deeply. He could feel his heart beginning to pound. Years? 'How many years?' he repeated.

'Don't be so dramatic. Not that many. Since my second year at college. So, three years?'

'Three years?'

'I have never had any trouble all that time. I've never had a single problem until now. And it's only because there really was an accident that I had nothing to sell so that I couldn't pay him this time. It really is no big deal, Dad.'

'James, you don't seem to understand. It is a big deal. I don't care if nothing has happened to you up until now. These people are dangerous. The only reason he has not gone after you is because he thinks you don't have the money to pay him and I do.'

The door to the coffee shop opened and a middle-aged man in a black linen suit came in and ordered a tall latte. He wore his long hair in a ponytail and he sat down at the other side of the room.

Aware of the new arrival, Francis managed to keep his voice down. 'Actually, I don't know why you don't have the money. You must have made a bit over the last three years. What have you done with it all?'

'It wasn't a business, Dad. I just did it when I needed some money.'

Francis looked at him, exasperated. 'Why didn't you ask me? I would have given it to you. If these people don't get you, the law will. You could go to jail. Did you think about that? What sort of lawyer do you think you will be when you get out of jail? Who will want you then?'

Surprised, he saw James suddenly become alert. A nerve had obviously been touched.

'Convicted drug dealers tend not to be in much demand as lawyers,' he continued, but he could see James had got the point. His anger began to drain away. He had been ready for a fight about why James should take his career more seriously and get more interested in the law. Suddenly it did not seem necessary.

'What do you mean?' James muttered miserably but he knew the answer.

Francis looked at him. He was a woebegone still-life. A twelve year-old with coffee. Francis could not remember when James had last needed him and he did not understand what had changed now, but suddenly all he wanted to do was hold him in his arms and tell him it would all be all right.

'I wish you hadn't done this,' he said. 'But I don't think there is going to be a serious problem. You're lucky. It is going to be OK. Your mother is going to sort it out. She will pay this man off. And that should be that. It will be OK, James.'

James nodded mutely, still looking down at the table.

Francis imagined him thinking about his wrecked

career. 'I can't promise you there will never ever be any consequences. You never know what is going to happen. But as risks go, I would not worry too much about this one. I wouldn't have thought this one will come back to haunt you.' He smiled at James. His son. He had not felt like this for ten years. James remained looking miserably at the table. 'James, look at me. It really should not be a problem. I am sorry if I alarmed you. But this really must be an end to all this. James – is it?'

James looked up at him finally and nodded. 'Thank you,' he said quietly.

Francis wanted to hug him. But the last ten years had been dry of such moments and now he did not know how to do it. He did not know if he could do anything.

Now, finally, he understood what Virginia had meant. Biology was irrelevant to his parenthood. Francis loved James. No matter what, he was James's father. It had taken ten years, and all this, to make him see what Virginia had meant. She had been right all along.

'Thank you,' James said again, and looked away.

'There's one more thing,' Francis said. 'Until we know this has all gone away, I think you should get out of London for a few days. These are dangerous people and I do not think you should be around until we know it's all been settled.'

'It's not like that, Dad,' James muttered. 'It's not some gangster movie.'

'I am not prepared to take the risk that you might be wrong,' Francis said.

James could not think what to say. He was remembering Chris's boss in the Barnet conference room yesterday.

'Please, James,' Francis said. 'If you won't do it for yourself, please do it for me and your mother. We would worry less.'

'What do you want me to do?' James asked.

'Get out of London. Go somewhere nice. Relax. Just until this is over. I've spoken to Evans and you can take a week's holiday. From now.'

'What did you say to him?'

'Don't worry.' Francis smiled at his son. 'I just said it was a family matter.'

'Where should I go?' James asked. Again Francis saw the twelve-year-old in his face.

'Wherever you want, as long as it's away from London. Here, take this.' Francis took a long thin envelope from inside his jacket and handed it to James. 'I went to the bank on the way here. There's fifteen hundred pounds. That should be enough for a decent hotel and an airfare. Or two if you want to take a girlfriend.'

Unerringly his Dad got it wrong. However hard he tried. James did not need him intruding with advice about who to take with him.

'Go on, please take it.' Francis pushed the envelope towards James. 'Please. It's important.'

James could not see how he could avoid taking it. A refusal would trigger a lengthy lecture and then more arguments. 'Thank you,' he said.

'Take the envelope and be careful with it. The cash will be safer than a credit card. It's untraceable.'

James smiled.

'It's not funny, James. You can't be too careful with these people. Please.'

How would he know? But James could see no way out. He took the envelope and put it in his pocket.

'Thank you,' he said again.

'And go today,' Francis continued. 'Or tomorrow at the latest, James. Do not hang around. That's why I have given you the money now.'

'I've got the point, Dad,' James said. 'These are dangerous people.'

'It is not funny, James.'

Francis looked so worried that James felt a twinge of pity. 'I know,' he said. 'I will be careful.'

Francis could feel the muscles in the back of his neck start to relax. 'I am glad we've got it sorted out, James,' he said. 'I want to be there for you when you need me. I want you to understand that. I am sorry it wasn't me that sorted this out for you this time. I wanted to explain that to you myself. I don't want you to think badly of me. I am glad your mother was able to sort it out. You are lucky to have her for your mother.'

Francis meant it. He thought he had said it as if he meant it. But James's face tensed up. Francis saw he had upset him again. Then, disconcertingly, he thought he saw pity struggling with the irritation in James's face.

'You just don't get it, do you, Dad. You really just don't get it?' Suddenly James seemed the older, worldly man and Francis the innocent youth. 'You

don't know how Mum has got it sorted out, do you?'
He looked at Francis accusingly. 'You think she is
going to pay him off, don't you? But you don't know
that, do you? You don't really know how Mum is going
to get it sorted out, do you?'

Francis shook his head. So James told him. And
dismay welled up in Francis.

thirty-five

thursday 1.05 p.m.
'What do you think you are doing?'

'I am making my lunch and you are getting in my way. Again.'

They stood in Virginia's living room in the flat they had bought when they married and which Francis had given her in the divorce.

'You can't do this,' he said.

'Why not?' Virginia asked.

Francis looked at her. Once he had been exhilarated by this challenging obstinacy. His good looks had never made Virginia want to please him as other women did. He never felt their response had anything to do with him and who he really was. It was just a reflex. But Virginia wanted to be with him. She teased him, flirted with him, provoked him and stimulated him. And loved him too. She was engaged with him, all the time, in every way.

Virginia wondered why he bothered to come round. He was always so ill at ease and hostile. And now he had come just as she was getting ready to enjoy her lunch on her day off.

Francis had never understood why she did it. He

had been so certain they were happy. Was it her fault? Did the deep itchiness which made her so fascinating also drive her to destroy anything that might last? And become boring? Or was it his fault? He could never shake off the thought that the failure of his first marriage revealed him to be little more than a handsome face, a stolid zero, too uninteresting to be able to keep her around?

Virginia had been making fish soup and the unctuous smells of the Mediterranean drifted through the flat. The bones had been boiling all morning and she had just strained it and she was about to add the Pernod and saffron.

And then Francis arrived. Why did he do this to her? She had not left him. He had ignored her for years. Why had he now come round twice in one morning?

'Ginny,' he said more softly, 'this is the wrong way of dealing with it.'

She bridled at the use of her childhood name. It belonged to another time. When they first went out together and exchanged histories, she had told him her father called her Ginny. Francis adopted it when he felt particularly affectionate. 'How wrong?' she said. 'What do you suggest, Frankie?' He hated the diminutive. Everyone had always called him by his full name – except for Julie, and Virginia when she was cross. 'I haven't noticed you coming up with anything better.'

'You can't do this, Virginia.'

'Francis, I am making lunch,' she said. 'I did not ask you to come here . . .'

'I could not possibly have talked about this on the phone,' he said quickly.

'You did not need to talk about it at all,' Virginia said. 'You made it quite clear you did not want to help.'

'That's not fair. I said I needed to consider it. I didn't say I would not help. You know I have never denied James anything. Just because I did not instantaneously agree to your demands does not mean I would not have helped.' She really was infuriating. He had been so relieved that, for once, she was taking responsibility for sorting something out herself. And now this. What was she thinking of? Now he was once again faced with all those hard choices. And this.

'I am not getting into that now. I am making lunch,' Virginia said. 'You said what you said. There was no time to hang around while you considered the situation. So I made my own arrangements. And they are none of your business. But, in case you are worried about it,' she added, 'it will have no impact on you. It's got nothing to do with you.'

'That's unfair,' Francis said. 'I was thinking about you. This is not a game. These people are dangerous.'

'You look as if you would know about that,' she said. 'What happened to you?'

'I was mugged,' he said curtly. 'Just a couple of street thugs. This is quite different. These people are professionals. You can't just declare war on them.'

Virginia ignored him. 'I promise you, Francis – even if anyone were ever to find out, which they won't, these people are very discreet, I'm told – and very dangerous,' she could not resist adding. 'Even if anyone did ever find out, no-one will be interested in a story about your ex-wife. And it will all be down to me. Your son will not be involved.'

'Of course he'll be involved. He knows about it, doesn't he? How do you think I found out?' Francis realised as he spoke that he should not be debating this with her. It was not a question of whether he would be implicated. It was just wrong and she should not do it.

'This is not about me or my business,' he said. 'It is unfair of you to talk like this . . .'

When they had first met, Virginia had loved his earnestness. It was so different from the boys she had privileged by letting them go out with her before. His seriousness proofed Francis against her provocations. She liked that. It made him worthy.

'This is not a game, Virginia. This is dangerous and we should get out of it as quickly as possible.'

'Francis,' she said. 'Sit down. Let me explain it to you.'

He sat down. Whenever he spent any length of time with Virginia, he was reminded what hard work she could be. Nothing was ever easy or simple.

'Francis,' she began. 'You are a logical man. Work it out. Here is a problem. I know it is not a problem you wanted, and I do understand this is a bad time for you. But do you think I wanted it? Or James wanted it? But here it is anyway. A problem. What do we do about it? Let's look at the options. That's what bankers do, isn't it? Look at Options?'

He could see Virginia was pleased with her impression of a banker.

'Option One: Do Nothing. And then what? Do you really want to take the risk of what these people might do to your son? They are dangerous, you know.' He could hear the quote marks in her voice as she repeated his words back to him.

'Option Two: Do Something. If we adopt this option, then how do we achieve it? We could do what the man asks and pay him the money. This seems to me the Best Option. Because we could then get rid of the whole problem and get back to our lives. This is the Best Option, in my considered opinion.' Virginia crossed her legs as she got into her stride. 'But there is a problem with this option. James does not have the money to pay him. I don't have the money. I really do not have the money. Despite your generosity, despite the fact that we have never wanted for anything, I don't have thirty thousand pounds. James does not have thirty thousand pounds. Now, you do have thirty thousand pounds, I assume. That's what bankers do, isn't it: they have lots of money. So you have thirty thousand pounds but you do not want to give the man any money at all. I understand why you do not want to give him the money. I do understand.' Virginia paused as if to emphasise to Francis that she did sympathise with his predicament. 'But there it is: no money for Option Two. James and I would give him the money, but we don't have it. You do have the money, but you won't give it. So is there anything else we could do about Option Two? I could try to get the money elsewhere. And I've tried. My bank won't give me an overdraft like that. They were keen to give me a loan but they wanted me to come in to talk about it. And I do not think that my bank would be very keen to lend me thirty thousand pounds to pay off my son's drug debts. What do you think, Francis? You are a banker. You understand banking. Do you think that I've got a good case for a bank loan?' Virginia did not wait for an answer. 'So what to do? I could try to persuade you to cough it up. What do you think, Francis? Do you think I have any chance of persuading you to change your mind? You are not very good at changing your mind. Or perhaps I am not very good at getting you to change your mind. Either way, I don't think it's worth the effort.' Virginia paused again, briefly, as if reconsidering whether to try once more to persuade Francis. 'So Option Two, the Best Option, won't work. So what should I do, Francis? Go back to Option One? Remember Option One, Francis? That's the one where James gets kneecapped or put in concrete and buried under a motorway. I don't think so, Francis. So, logically, where does that leave us? It leaves us with Option Three. What is Option Three? Option Three is Something Else.'

Francis wondered what the eight-year-olds made of her pedagogic technique. He was not enjoying it. But then, he did not suppose he was meant to.

'I have thought a lot about Option Three over the last two days, Francis. And this is what I have come up with. It's not perfect, but there it is.' She crossed her legs and leaned slightly towards him. 'And, actually, Francis, the more I think about it, the more I think Option Three is not such a bad option. I hear people do it all the time. Hardly anyone ever gets caught. Do you know the police only solve twenty per cent of all recorded crime. That means eighty per cent get away with it. Eighty per cent, Francis. That's a good figure for a banker, isn't it? Eighty per cent. It sounds betting odds to me. And do you think anyone is going to try too hard to solve something that happens to someone like this man? Do you really think the police are going to make whatever happens to this man a priority? They must know what a creep he is. I don't think the police are going to bother very much when some drug dealer gets what he deserves, do you? And do you know what else I think?' Again, Virginia did not wait for an answer. 'I think this man does deserve it. How dare he threaten James and think he can get away with it. Let's see how he likes it.'

She finished. It seemed churlish to question such a performance. But he did.

'Very good,' he said. 'But what makes you think it will persuade him to go away and not keep coming back until he gets paid?'

'Because I think it will be difficult for him to keep coming back when he has been ground up into break-fast for a herd of prize pigs.' Virginia picked at a cuticle as she said this, looking intently at her finger as she worked.

Francis stared. 'You cannot be serious, Virginia,' he said. 'How can you even talk like this?'

Virginia laughed. 'Of course I'm not serious,

Francis,' she said. 'Only you would seriously think I was going to murder this man. I'm not the Mafia, you know, Francis. I am just going to frighten him.'

She may not be in the Mafia, Francis thought, but she acted as if she was. He noticed her tone had softened. It was now almost affectionate. He was not sure whether his sense of relief flowed from the fact she was only planning grievous bodily harm or the possibility she might not despise him after all.

'Frightening may not be enough,' he said. 'What if he doesn't get frightened, he just gets cross?' As he spoke, he realised that again he had fallen into one of Virginia's traps. Blundering about, again he had strayed onto her territory, from his own carefully fenced and cultivated land, and he was lost in her wild and uncharted terrain.

He should be insisting this was wrong, forbidding it (although this effort would only be for the record: the chances of him successfully forbidding Virginia to do anything she did not want to be forbidden to do were nil). He should just give her the money. He should not be entering into any discussion about anything else at all. He supposed he had always known he would have to give her the money. Now was the moment to tell her that. But instead he was discussing whether this extraordinary bad idea would work. He realised he wanted to prove her wrong and show her that he was not a boring banker but a buccaneer. He wanted to show her he could do it better. He was appalled at himself.

'People like this don't frighten,' he insisted. 'What

makes you think there is anything you can do to someone like him that will frighten him? He lives with this all his life. It is his life.'

'What do you know about it, Francis?' Virginia said, reasonably.

'I've read enough,' he said, still clinging to a fragment of hope that he might be able to persuade Virginia to give up her plan, 'and anyway, it's not difficult to work out. These people live outside the law: the only way they settle arguments is violently – this is what they do. They are professionals. You are an amateur. How exactly are you going to frighten him? Break his legs? But why should that stop someone like him? He'll just retaliate. He'll break your legs. Or James's legs. Or both your legs.' He corrected himself. 'Or both your legs and both James's legs. And then he will still want his money.'

'It doesn't work like that,' Virginia explained. 'This is not the Wild West. They have their own way of keeping order. There are rules here too.'

'How on earth do you know, Virginia?' Francis burst out in exasperation. 'You are a teacher, not a gangster. Or a policeman. How on earth can you be so confident about all this?'

'Because I have looked into it all,' Virginia said equably.

'In two days?' Francis said. 'In two days, you have become an expert, have you?'

'That's your problem, Francis,' Virginia said. 'No confidence. You think there is a right and wrong way to do things. And the right way is to do it the way that everyone always does it.'

'No, I don't think that. And please don't patronise me,' Francis said. He felt irrelevant in this scheme of hers, this immaculately argued and horribly wrong-headed scheme, and impotent to do anything about it. 'You think that because something has always been done in a particular way, it must be time for a change,' he said. 'It never occurs to you that, perhaps, if things are done in a particular way it is because that is the best way. That people have experimented over many years and discovered what works and what doesn't. And it may seem boring to you, but personally I would prefer to have something that works rather than something which doesn't.'

'Actually, I don't think that,' said Virginia. 'And please don't you patronise me. I have spent the last two days – every hour of the last two days – trying to think how to sort out this terrible mess James has got into. Our son James. You have managed to spare me an hour for lunch. To say you will consider it. But this man wants his money now. So instead of discussing my failings, you might want to consider whether you have anything constructive to say to me. Or you can let me get on.' She looked at him and relented. 'Don't look so hurt,' she said. 'This isn't easy for any of us. But I have done the best I can. And it really is not such a stupid idea.'

'I never said I wouldn't help,' he said defiantly, but he could feel relief seeping through him that she was suddenly speaking more affectionately. Virginia's moods could make the weather turn. He remembered that.

'I really did look into this, Francis,' she said. He sensed she was trying to persuade him. Was it because she wanted his approval? Or was she was not sure herself that this scheme would work? 'I talked to James about this man. It seems he is not a street dealer. He only deals with students. The whole thing is very discreet. James said he is more like a banker than a dealer.'

Francis would not have described the dapper little man in the dove-grey suit quite like this. He wondered what James thought of him, if he thought he and that man looked as if they belonged to the same profession.

'I think there will be a limit to how far he will go,' Virginia continued. 'You see, if he really carried out his threats, then sooner or later someone is going to involve the police and his nice discreet operation is going to get a lot of attention. Heat. And from the sound of it, he would not want that. It sounds to me as if he wants a nice discreet business that makes a lot of money without any heat.'

Francis wondered where she had learnt to speak like this. And think like it.

'He's a businessman,' she said. 'And businessmen always need to balance risk and reward. You told me that.' Despite himself, he was pleased. She remembered those early attempts to share a life together. 'And there's always a time when a banker has to write off a debt because it's just not worth pursuing it any more. You told me that too.'

He had wanted so badly to include her in everything: the jargon, the craft, the personalities. At the time, he'd thought she was only listening out of love and it had been all the more precious for that. Now it seemed she had really been interested.

'That's true,' he agreed. 'But I also said bankers hate writing off debt. It sets a bad precedent. Debtors should never think they can get away without paying. Think about it from his point of view. If he let James get away with this, everyone would think he was a soft touch. He couldn't let that happen. Nobody could.'

Virginia was learning forward now, engaged. 'You seem to know quite a lot about this, Francis,' she teased.

He ignored it. 'The problem is,' he said, 'it's just too much. No-one can just write off thirty thousand pounds.'

He noticed Virginia's eyes had begun to shine. She was loving this, he thought, arguing, grappling with the problem, working it through.

'But there must be a limit,' she said. 'If you held a gun to his head and you told him you would blow his brains out in five seconds unless he forgot all about it, of course he would forget all about it. So there is no reason in principle why he couldn't write it off. It's just a question of finding the right way of applying pressure.'

Francis remembered he had read that sociopaths exhibited symptoms of impassive detachment and an inability to connect with the world around them. Like Virginia. She seemed to have no idea what her words meant in real life. But Roger was not abstract. That dapper little man had stood in his front garden talking in his soft South London voice as pigeons cooed in the distance, and now here was Virginia talking about blowing his brains out, spattering them all over his immaculate dove-grey suit. She might claim the idea was only hypothetical but he was beginning to wonder.

'Thirty thousand pounds will need a lot of pressure,' he said.

'It's just a question of who blinks first,' Virginia said authoritatively. 'I have been thinking about this. You know what they say: look for the strength in your weakness. Like yin and yang. You're right, we are vulnerable because this is not our world. But that also means that if he gives into us, no-one will know. It is not our world. You said he couldn't write it off because then no-one would pay up. But in our case: who would know? We aren't going to tell anyone. And he won't. I think he will understand this.' Francis could hear her persuading herself as she talked. 'So all we've got to do is find an incentive for him to give in. Breaking his legs, for example,' she said with gusto. 'If we make him think he is mixed up with someone more ruthless than him and it won't cause him to lose face, it seems to me that thirty thousand pounds would be cheap to get rid of us. Think of the damage we could do his business. Think how much money he would lose if he kept getting his legs broken.'

'Brilliantly argued, Virginia,' Francis said. 'But ridiculous. You can't talk like this.'

'Why not?' she asked. 'We would not need to go as

far as killing him – although you won't believe how often I have thought about that over the last two days. I am only talking about hurting him enough to make him stop. After all, that's what he's threatening to do to us: hurt us until we pay. All I want is to do to him what he says he will do to us. Own up, Francis: when he came to see you, didn't you think, even for a moment, that you would like to hurt him enough to make him go away?'

He stared at her, unable to speak.

'You did, didn't you?' she said. 'Of course you did. Well, do it,' she said. 'Hurt him.'

She was right. He did wanted to hurt him, the dapper little man who came onto his land, threatening him, threatening InterTrust, threatening Rachel. Virginia understood temptation viscerally.

Francis looked at Virginia. She was glowing. There was no other word for it. There was a slight flush in her cheeks and her eyes were alight. He realised he was staring but he could not look away. She looked back at him and half smiled. 'Come on, Francis,' she said. 'Let's do it.'

Photographs never did her justice. No celluloid could capture her glow. Francis had sometimes seen film stars interviewed on television and they were glib, artificial, dull. He had wondered how they could project such humanity and warmth in the cinema. It was the way the camera loved them, it was said, that made them stars. Virginia was the reverse. The camera diminished her but she came alive with people. Oh how she came alive.

'How are you proposing to do this?' he asked cautiously.

'I've got the name of a man who will do it all for you. Apparently, all you do is give him the name and the money and he arranges it all: broken legs, dislocated shoulders, faces marked for life. It's a complete service,' she said happily. 'He lives in Spain.'

It was a game. Francis saw that. It was an exciting new act in the adventure that was Virginia's life. And it was exhilarating. Magnetic. Nothing had changed. And, as always, Virginia seemed unaware of the consequences – or reckless of them.

'And how much do you pay for this service?' he asked, trying to sound ironic but failing to keep the curiosity out of his voice.

'Depends what you want,' she replied seriously. 'You have to negotiate. But a hit is only five thousand pounds so I would have thought broken legs would be a lot less, wouldn't you?'

She talked about this as if she was buying a second-hand car. Boundaries had never meant very much to Virginia. And now she was dragging him over the line.

'And how do you propose to negotiate this?' he asked.

'Apparently you have to do it face to face. He won't talk over the phone. Like you,' she added mischievously. 'You know: bugs and all that sort of thing. You have got to see him. So I'm off to Spain,' she said gaily.

'Just like that?' Francis asked ironically.

'Just like that,' Virginia replied cheerfully.

He thought of her negotiating to get the dapper little man's legs broken, with some villain on the Costa del Sol. The enthusiasm that he found so enchanting, they might see as dangerous innocence. All these criminals knew each other, he had read somewhere. They were part of crime families who, when they weren't killing each other, were in nefarious partnership.

What if this man was associated, somehow, with the little man in the dove-grey suit? What if Virginia blundered into some cosy arrangement where she ended up with her legs broken – or worse – instead of the dapper little man getting hurt.

'Virginia, you can't go,' he said.

'Francis, we have been through all this.'

'No,' he said. 'I mean I will go.'

She looked at him surprised, with all the mischief suddenly emptied from her face.

'You're not serious?'

He nodded. As he had spoken, he was watching himself with astonishment. How was he, Francis Carroll, saying this?

'What's happened to you, Francis?' she asked.

'I can't let you go,' he said. She looked up at him. 'Something awful might happen.' He could not look at her as he spoke. The waters were really beginning to close over him now.

'You mean, I could get killed? Or something really awful, like I might pay too much?' She smiled at him as she spoke to show she was only teasing. But as she looked at him, she saw she had wounded him. She had seen him look like this during the divorce.

'Francis,' she said, pleading. 'I didn't mean it. I am really grateful. I know what this must mean to you. It's just that it was a surprise. I did not expect this from you.'

He did not respond.

'Oh, Francis,' she said. 'Please forgive me. I really am grateful. But how are you going to manage? Why is it going to be easier for you?'

'I would just feel happier if I did it,' he muttered, still not looking at her.

She was right, of course: there was no reason why it would be easier for him. But he knew he would never feel comfortable knowing he had let Virginia walk off to do this, when he knew the risks and apparently she did not. If he could not persuade her out of this, and it seemed that he could not, then the right thing for him to do was to do it himself. Someone had to do it. James was their son. He knew now Virginia had always been right about that.

It was ironic, he thought, that it had been his worry about James that had driven him out of their home, and now, ten years later, it was their worry about James that was bringing them together again. But this was not about him and Virginia. He really was not doing this for Virginia. He was not. He was doing it for James. His son. His duty. This was his duty.

The risks scurried through his mind. What could go wrong? He could incriminate himself by soliciting a crime – but there must be a coded way of commissioning the job that would never get him convicted in court. And that was another reason, he thought, why he should do it instead of Virginia: she would spell it out, give anyone taping it an open-and-shut case. Or the thing itself could go wrong and they would get caught. But as he understood it there was a long chain of command between those who commissioned and those who did it. He could not imagine the man in Spain would talk: it would be unprofessional. As Virginia would say: it was betting odds. Now he felt the adrenaline rushing through his veins. He was a buccaneer.

It was only later he remembered that after James had told him about Virginia's plan, he had decided it would be best to pay her the thirty thousand pounds to get rid of the problem.

And then he thought of Rachel.

thirty-six

thursday 4.40 p.m.
The reception area was dominated by a painting which
spread from floor to ceiling. An off-white canvas was
divided up by an asymmetric grid of black lines. Some
of the rectangles were filled in with bright acrylic
colours, red and blue and yellow, while others were
not. It spoke authoritatively of control. A small brass
plaque by the side said 'Purchased by the Fine Art
Selection Sub-Committee, New York, 1996'. This
painting was in the reception area of an organisation
that clearly knew what it was doing. It exercised its
grip on the world by fitting it into a grid of even black
lines and accommodated its unpredictability in the
way apparently random rectangles chose to contain
different colours or none at all.

Those waiting patiently in the reception area might
not understand why some rectangles were filled with
colour and others not, but the Fine Art Selection Sub-
Committee clearly did. Otherwise they would not have
purchased it in New York three years ago. And it was
a privilege to be allowed to purchase the legal serv-
ices of an organisation that so manifestly knew what
it was doing.

Davey sat in an architectural black leather chair in the reception area of Rother & Fenwick, contemplating the large canvas. His mind was still. No ripple disturbed the surface of the pond which was his consciousness. He was in *zazen*. So still and at one was he that it took half an hour before one of the receptionists noticed he had not checked in with the desk.

'Can I help you?' she said, walking over to him, sleek in white shirt and black pencil skirt.

'No thanks,' he said. 'It's cool.'

'Are you here to see someone?' she persisted.

'Yes,' he lied. 'They'll be down soon. It's cool.' And something in his tone persuaded her she had done all she could to help him. And as he wasn't doing any harm where he was, she went back to her desk and her telephone. And so Davey sat and contemplated the floor-to-ceiling canvas and watched the people come and go in the great reception area of Rother & Fenwick.

thirty-seven

thursday 8.00 p.m.

Even at eight o'clock in the evening, the heat was intense. Francis felt stifled as he walked out of the airport. He wished he had not been wearing a suit. Too obvious, he thought. It made him stand out among the thousands of holidaymakers thronging Malaga airport, with their expensive casual clothes and exhausted children. But there had been no time to change. Leaving Virginia, he had gone straight back to his office, collected his passport, always there in case he suddenly had to go to New York for a meeting, and then, without stopping except to tell Joanne he would be in early tomorrow, on to the airport where he just managed to get on a four o'clock flight.

He had called Rachel on the way. She was used to the unpredictability of his life at the moment. All the time there were late meetings and dinners with visiting investors. He was careful not to lie. 'Something has come up. I could be back very late. Talk to you later. I love you.'

He ran a finger round the inside of his collar which was wet with sweat. Instinctively, he scoured the hordes of taxi drivers holding up a forest of placards, handwritten, printed, calling for the chosen ones who had their cars already booked. Wherever he went, there was always one for Francis. But not this time.

He looked up at the airport signs. As he did so, a man in chinos and a Hawaiian shirt touched his elbow. Francis stiffened, startled. 'Taxi, sir?' And then another one. 'Do you need a taxi, señor?' Like ants to sugar, two more materialised. 'Taxi? taxi?' He hesitated, but then he decided this was not a good idea. They were probably all known to the police already. Too conspicuous. Better just get in the queue like everyone else.

Outside there was no-one in the queue. A large family with a hillock of luggage were arguing among themselves by the automatic doors. Francis got into the first taxi and gave it the address he had written out.

'Do you know this?' he said carefully. The taxi driver looked at him blankly, politely, waiting. 'Do you know this address?' Francis repeated.

The taxi driver looked at the piece of paper. 'Si, señor,' he said, and then started a long sentence in Spanish which Francis could not understand. But it sounded conversational and friendly enough.

'I am sorry, I do not speak Spanish,' Francis said apologetically.

'Manchester United,' said the driver and started off in Spanish again. Francis heard the word football. This mutual incomprehension comforted him. He was grateful for its normality.

The taxi drove fast along the Autovia del Sol. 'Boom, boom, boom, boom,' went the Vengaboys on the radio. The driver tapped his fingers in time on the steering wheel. There were cranes everywhere and the desert scrub of the coastline surfaced only intermittently among the concrete developments. On one site the diggers were still at work, wheeling, clawing, scooping out the dry Andalusian dirt to satisfy the insatiable craving of North Europeans for the baking sun. Signs beckoned Europe's affluent in English, German, Swedish and French, and even, occasionally, Russian.

It had seemed inescapable when Virginia had argued it. Now it was about to become ghastly reality.

As they drove along the coast, the Mediterranean glittering blue in the evening sun, hot air blowing in through the open window, Francis felt his gut knotting. As they sped past the benign human dreams of families on holiday, he felt, mile by mile, that he was driving out of their normal, decent world.

How ready Virginia was to cross over the boundaries – for him they were ten-foot walls, for her they appeared to be just a line in the sand. And how ready she was to step over it into a new world. Francis felt the brand of the outlaw on him as he was being driven out from the wide streets and arcades of his civilised world into a lawless desert.

Around him, the reverse process was taking place as developers turned the Spanish scrub into a version of civilisation: ochre tiles and glaring white stucco, the Costa del Sol vernacular, a quick-money fantasy of Andalusia. Every so often, tiered rectangular blocks of flats squatted by the side of the motorway, balconies draped in washing, housing the great-grandchildren of peasants and fishermen who had once eaten grass to survive famine.

The taxi turned off the baking Autovia after half an hour and began to wind its way up into the foothills of the sierra. Francis could feel the air cooling as the shadows began to lengthen.

They passed high white walls with elaborately wrought iron gates. There was no other traffic. A few minutes later, the driver stopped by a large stone archway. 'Urb. California,' Francis read. The driver said something in Spanish to Francis and got out of the taxi. Francis watched him walking past the arch. Beyond was a gatehouse. The driver went in. Francis could see movement through the window.

He realised suddenly that Virginia had not told him what had been agreed. She had just given him the name and said she had spoken to the man to tell him to expect the visit. What was he supposed to do? Was his role just to negotiate a price? And what precisely was he asking for? It was typical of Virginia to leave him to sort out all these vital details.

He waited. He could feel the sweat drying on his skin in the cooler air. The taxi driver emerged from the gatehouse, walked purposefully back to the car and got in. He said something in Spanish to Francis and started the engine.

The taxi went back down the road a few hundred yards and turned up a narrow lane that Francis had not noticed on the way up. More high white walls and wrought iron. Five minutes further on and the taxi slowed to a crawl, the driver peering out through the offside window. He gave a little grunt and stopped the car. He leant out of the window and pressed a buzzer on a gate. An electronic voice said something in Spanish. The taxi driver looked at Francis and said something, obviously a question. Francis smiled apologetically. The driver pressed the buzzer again and spoke some more. Francis imagined he was giving a description. The electronic voice said something.

The driver got out and opened Francis's door, and gestured for him to get out. Francis looked around. There was nothing on the road. The verge where he stood was dusty and stony. There was a heavy aromatic smell, the mingled scents of barbecues and garbage. It was still hot. Francis could feel his shirt sticking to his back.

Nothing happened. There was an uneasy stillness. The driver leant against the car, picking his nails. Waiting. There was no sound except for the insistent cicadas surrounding him. Then, far in the distance, up the mountain, Francis heard the distant buzz of a motorbike, fading rapidly.

The driver waited against the side of the car. It was very still. Francis could see his shoes had gathered a light coating of dust. He heard a car coming up the road. He smoothed his hair. The driver did not move. Francis heard the car change down as it came round the bend. It was moving fast, he thought.

Then it was past them. Francis glimpsed a young couple. The tan skin and black hair of a woman in a white dress and then they were gone. The air settled back into stillness behind them. Francis could feel his forehead getting clammy with sweat. He wiped it away with his handkerchief.

Then the buzzer crackled again into the stillness. Francis started. The driver listened and nodded. He came over to Francis. Francis could see that he had been sweating too. Moisture nestled in the lobes of his nose and glistened in the day-old growth of his beard.

He opened Francis's door and indicated that he should get in. As he did so, Francis saw two video cameras on the pillars of the gate following him in jerky, pecking little movements, observing.

The gate swung open. The driver started the engine and drove up a short drive, past a tennis court. The garden was overwhelmingly green: dark, restful shades of it overhanging the drive, denying the stony desert outside the gates, splashed occasionally with vivid colour as some carefully tended bougainvillaea, luscious purples and whites, burst out of the foliage.

He stopped outside a low white ranch-style bungalow. There was a heavy, dark wooden door. The driver turned in his seat to Francis and said something, obviously asking for the fare. Francis offered him a handful of notes and pocketed the change without counting it. 'Gracias,' he said, 'muchas gracias.'

The driver was obviously keen to go. Francis got out of the taxi which reversed rapidly back down the drive.

He stood in front of the door. He could hear the taxi turning in the road and then accelerating away down the hill. Then silence. Even the furious racket of the cicadas had been softened by the enveloping lushness of the gardens.

He waited. Nothing happened. He looked to see if there was a bell. The door was solid. He looked up. Set into the wall above the door a little red light winked above a tiny recessed-glass lens.

He thought he could still walk away. He could walk down the drive and onto the road and out of this. He could tell Virginia it had not worked. They would think of something else.

Then the door opened.

'I'm Ken. You must be Francis.'

He was taller than Francis, his thick grey hair swept back in waves which reached back down to his collar. He was wearing white chinos with a sharp crease and a silk shirt, in an expensive blue, with the sleeves rolled up to the elbow. He was very tanned. His voice was deep and had the authority of someone who was used to being listened to. He spoke with the sort of London accent Francis had heard in films. It was the deeper, older cousin of the voice of Roger Oates. 'Come in,' he said. 'I am sorry to have kept you waiting.' It was polite but he did not sound very distressed by Francis's sojourn at the front door.

Ken led Francis through a hall in deep shadow. The marble floors were cool and there was a heavy, dark dresser. They went through a large living room with brightly coloured rugs on the floor and lots of photographs on the coffee tables around the plushly uphol- stered sofas.

'Come on into the garden,' said Ken.

There were four wicker easy chairs around a glass table on the verandah.

'Sit down,' said Ken.

A closely barbered lawn of thick coarse grass swept down to a large irregular swimming pool. It looked like an amoeba, Francis thought. He could see someone swimming a careful breaststroke across the widest part of it. The air in the garden was cool and sweet, fragrant with the scents of tropical flowers. Beyond, down the mountain, he could see the coast sweltering beside the blue sea, the concrete blocks lining the beaches shimmering in a haze of heat.

Ken smiled at Francis and put two fingers in his mouth and whistled. A middle-aged Spanish woman in a dark green maid's uniform appeared with a silver tray. There was a large jug of ruby liquid on it, with fruit and foliage in it and two glasses.

'Sangria?' Ken said. The maid put it down on the table and disappeared silently back into the house. Ken poured out two glasses and handed one to Francis and looked at him.

'Thank you,' Francis said. He hoped Ken would start. Ken sipped his sangria and continued to look at him in companionable silence. It was very quiet in the garden. Francis could hear the plashing of the swimmer making her way up and down the pool. He sipped his sangria.

'It is good of you to see me,' he began. Ken smiled pleasantly at him. Francis wished he had spent less time worrying generally about what he was doing and more time on how he was going to do it. Virginia had arranged the trip. She had not told him what to say. 'I understand that you might be able to help me with a problem,' he said.

Ken nodded sympathetically. 'And what sort of problem might that be?' he asked. Francis looked at him. Ken was obviously going to make him work for this.

'I understand,' Francis said, starting again, 'you can make some difficult problems go away, because you know how to explain to people why they should go away.'

Ken laughed, a deep chuckle. 'I've never heard it described like that before.'

Francis wondered why Ken was making it so hard for him. 'Money is not a problem,' he said.

Ken laughed again. He clearly found Francis amusing. 'It rarely is, sunshine,' he said. 'Money is hardly ever the problem.'

Francis could see the swimmer getting out of the pool. She was a handsome tanned woman – in her thirties, Francis guessed – in a one-piece suit.

Ken followed his eyes. 'My wife,' he said, without turning round as she came up to the verandah. 'Darling,' said Ken, 'this is Mr Carroll come all the way from London to see me. Francis, this is my wife.'

She was very blonde. A thin gold chain round her neck accentuated the tan. Francis tried to avoid looking at her breasts, which were full and firm against the sheer bathing costume.

'Hello,' she said, putting out a hand still wet from

the pool. Francis got up and shook it. Her eyes looked past him. He was not a man, Francis thought. He was today's supplicant at court. Ken watched them.

She smiled again politely and walked off into the house. Ken watched Francis. Francis sat down again, carefully not following her with his eyes.

Ken looked at him and filled up his glass from the jug. Shadows began to lengthen across the lawn.

Francis began again. 'My son has got a problem,' he said, thinking that the mention of family might make Ken more responsive. 'I want to help him make it go away.'

'They can be difficult, can't they, children,' said Ken sympathetically. 'You want them to have everything. But they can be difficult. I've got three. How many have you got, Francis?'

Francis felt he was being corralled by an expert. 'Just one,' he replied. He did not know what Ken expected him to say. He had just assumed that this sort of conversation was conducted in code, where everyone understood what was being said. 'I need your help,' he said. 'I understand you can help.'

Ken looked at him patiently. Francis realised he was not going to be able to say it. Ken was waiting for him to say it and he could not.

Francis took a mouthful of sangria. He started again. 'I have come to see you because I am told that you can be very helpful in making problems go away.'

Finally, Ken relented. 'Come on,' he said, getting up, indicating Francis should follow him. They walked out onto the lawn. Ken looked back at the house.

Francis could see it was much bigger than it looked from the front. It was built into the side of the mountain and it stretched across two storeys. 'That's a lot of property,' Ken said. 'And that is a beautiful view.' He looked reflectively down the mountain at the concrete Costa. 'The reason I am up here and they are all down there is that I am a careful man. In business, you have to be. You are a businessman, Francis, you should know that. Now I understand you have a problem. I would like to help you.' He turned to Francis. 'I would like to help you, Francis. I am a father. I know what it's like. But it is not as easy as all that. You may think it is just a matter of coming up here and paying the money. But it is not as easy as that.' Ken put an arm round Francis and walked him back towards the house. 'Problems can be very difficult,' he said. 'If they are going to go away, you have got to want them to go away, really want them to go away. You have got to realise what that means. It's not a game. You have got to really want it.'

They stepped back on the verandah.

'I am sorry I can't help you, Francis,' said Ken.

It had been swiftly, brutally done, thought Francis, but expertly.

'I'll call a taxi to take you back,' Ken continued, taking a tiny mobile phone out of the breast pocket of his shirt and flipping it open. He spoke rapidly in Spanish. Francis heard the word 'Aeropuerto'.

'Ten minutes,' Ken said to Francis.

His wife came out of the house, dressed in a bright yellow dress. 'Are you ready to go?' she asked.

'Fifteen minutes, doll,' Ken said.

She must have been twenty years younger than him, Francis thought. She went back into the house without acknowledging him.

It was if the couple had choreographed his unmanning, he thought. He was not man enough to do the deal with the husband – or even to be noticed by the wife.

'There are some lovely restaurants round here,' Ken told him kindly. Francis supposed he was going to one of them with his wife once Francis was on his way. 'Next time you are here, try Casa Pedro on the coast. Lovely fresh fish. Just mention my name. Pedro will look after you.'

Francis could feel humiliation bubbling under the relief. This man had not even considered him worth a discussion. He had looked him over and rejected him and Francis had not even been aware that he was being interviewed.

The taxi rang the bell and it jangled through the dark marble hall. They shook hands. Francis thought that if he had not known what he had been told about Ken he would never have guessed anything about him. He had not said one thing during their conversation which had indicated anything illegal. Or violent. Francis supposed that was what he had meant about being careful.

The taxi drove back down the mountain in the sudden twilight. The sky was a symphony of gold and mauve and pink over the sea. Along the coast, Francis could see the first white lights of the evening winking in the dusk. The driver drove fast and expertly down the winding road back to the Autovia. He did not speak.

Francis supposed he should now get back as quickly as possible. At the airport he found a late flight to Gatwick and he sat in the bar waiting for it to be called. His thoughts chased around. This had never been a real option, just a crazy instinctive reaction from Virginia. It was typical of her that she had tried to turn an emotional spasm into some lasting reality. What if Ken had done it? They would have been criminals. For the rest of their lives, they would have had to live with the guilt. Even assuming they had not been caught. In which case they would have lived with their guilt for the rest of their lives in jail.

Francis knocked back the generously filled balloon of Spanish brandy. How could he have let Virginia persuade him to do this? She had always been able to take him out of himself. That was why he had married her. Whenever he had looked back he had assumed it was down to the sexual rapture of youth. But perhaps it was something else. After all, she could still do it. She had just done it. He finished the brandy and called for another.

Virginia had always been able to make people do things for her. He could feel the brandy begin to warm and soften his mind.

At a table nearby, four young men in shorts were singing as they sank foaming pints of beer. By Francis, a young mother, not much older than James, was trying to persuade a toddler to eat a sandwich.

His head was beginning to swim. At least, he thought, Virginia did not make me into a criminal. He thought back to his conversation with Ken. He was almost sure there was nothing he had said that could have been construed as soliciting a crime. Even if Ken had been wired. Perhaps that was why he was being so careful. He was really working for the police. But Francis was almost sure he had said nothing. He had just talked about help with a problem. That would never stand up in court.

Francis looked at the young mother and child. He felt a sudden rush of relief, washing away his mounting agitation. If he was this worried when nothing happened, what sort of state would he have been in if Ken had actually agreed to do something?

But how was he going to tell Virginia about his humiliation?

He would work it out on the plane.

thirty-eight

friday 6.15 a.m.

Francis hardly slept. Images of the pool, the drive along the Costa del Sol motorway and Ken's wife flickered feverishly in and out as he dozed. His head still ached from the brandy. Beside him, Rachel breathed deeply. She was a neat sleeper, rarely moving, never snoring.

As the dawn chorus began, he finally drifted off. Half an hour later he was abruptly, completely awake. He lay without moving, staring at the ceiling as the room began to fill imperceptibly with grey pre-dawn light. The agitated images of the night had gone. He was exhausted. The ceiling was like a blank screen. He lay staring at it, finally empty of thought.

At six o'clock, fresh light began to filter through the curtains. Suddenly restless, he decided to get up.

In the kitchen he made himself coffee. The first sun was now flooding into the room, not yet warm but soft and golden. Outside, dew sparkled on the lawn. The world was being born again. He sipped the hot, bitter liquid. Yesterday had become history. Francis looked out at his garden. Everything was green and fresh.

He picked up the notepad by the telephone and started to make a list of what he had to do later.

Rachel came sleepily into the kitchen. 'How are you?' she asked tenderly. Francis prickled with irritation at this interruption and immediately felt ashamed.

'All right,' he said, but the mood was broken. Her question had reminded him that, in the real world, he was not all right. Things were not all right. He had sorted nothing out. James still owed thirty thousand pounds to a drug dealer. He still had to tell Virginia what had happened in Spain. He still had to sort out the financing for InterTrust.

He went over to Rachel and kissed her. 'I'm sorry,' he said. 'I'm just a bit grumpy. It's been a difficult few days.'

'I know,' she replied.

There was little traffic on the drive into town: this was an advantage of not sleeping, he thought. But by the time he got to the City, London was alive, the marble-faced streets between the tall buildings bustling with the men and women of money, hurrying along to spend another day getting and getting more.

Joanne was already at her desk when he arrived. He had not realised she got in so early. Francis felt a sudden surge of gratitude and affection. All his senses were heightened this morning. Too much coffee, too little sleep and too much emotion, he thought.

'Good morning,' he said briskly.

'Good morning, Francis,' she said. 'How is your arm?'

He had forgotten his mugging. 'Much better,' he said. 'Busy day today.'

'It always is at the moment,' she smiled eagerly. Francis knew they all loved being part of the excitement of InterTrust. He wished he could share in that exhilaration now. The events of yesterday had begun to press in on him again like a bruise.

At eight thirty, Jonathan Miles arrived, their very own venture-capital consultant.

'Good morning, Joanne,' he said sunnily. 'How are you?' He caught sight of himself in the polished glass behind her desk. He tightened his tie and then smoothed it down over an affluent midriff. He emanated money and his presence sanctified their efforts.

Francis liked him. Jonathan made the effort. He visited his clients and did not expect them to call on him. He immersed himself in their business. In return, he expected a lot of them. And he took a lot from them as well. He was counting on Francis. He had high hopes of InterTrust.

'What's happening?' Jonathan Miles asked.

Francis ran through the figures on cash. He explained how they were planning to exploit free media. He gave the latest projections for break-even and profit. And he thought about James and thirty thousand pounds. As he talked and tried to keep enthusiasm bubbling through the figures, the acid, indigestible questions ate away at him. How was he going to tell Virginia? What was he going to say to James?

Jonathan Miles listened intently. 'This all sounds fine, Francis,' he said. 'But – and I hope you will forgive me for being blunt – you need to get more of a move on.'

Francis noticed his tone never varied, it flowed smoothly and silkily, no matter what he was saying.

'If you want to do this, Francis, you will have to be a little more hungry.'

Francis looked at him. Hungry?

'Return your calls, Francis,' he said, and it was more than advice.

'What do you mean?' Francis said. He always returned his calls. It was good practice and he always returned his calls immediately.

'I called you yesterday afternoon because I had someone coming through from New York. Your office said you could be reached on your mobile and I left a message on your voicemail. You never rang back.'

When he was in Spain.

And in all the tension of yesterday he had never thought to check his mobile.

'It might have been interesting for you two to meet. He could have easily come in for five million if he liked you. Sterling.'

That would mean he could do without Lloyd and Matt and Philippe and all their jerking him around. 'I can clear my diary this morning, Jonathan.'

'Too late. He was only here yesterday evening. I'll see if we can rearrange it when he's next coming through. But check your messages, Francis. This game does not hang around.'

How could this business with Virginia have made him so careless? He felt sick. If he did not get the money soon, he would have to sell the house. How could he explain that to Rachel?

He was not his father. This was not going to happen to him. He had to get a grip.

'How long do you think you need?' Jonathan Miles asked.

'It's not so easy,' Francis replied. 'Better right than quick. Remember: trust is the glue. If we make a mistake, who is going to trust us again? This is people's savings. Their lifeblood.'

'So how long do you think you need?' Jonathan Miles asked again.

'Nine months, once the financing is in place – if we really move. A year would be safer.'

'You are doing well, Francis,' Jonathan Miles said. 'InterTrust is being set up meticulously, if I may say so. But you've got to get a move on. When you are hot, you are hot. When you are not, not. There is a real appetite out there for what you are doing. But first-mover advantage matters. Nine months is Old Economy time. Get on with it. Good luck.'

He got up to go. He never wasted clients' money. But something – that missed call? – must have worried him because he stopped on his way to the door and turned around. 'I am serious, Francis,' he said. 'A lot is at stake. We're working on a valuation of eighty million pounds. In the current market, that's conservative. It could be north of that, possibly nicely north. But only if you get away first. I've told you about

WebMoney. We've heard of two more possible start-ups in the last week. And sooner or later the clearing banks will get round to doing it. This is a good idea. We think this could be where the Net really scores and the market is only just beginning to wake up to the possibilities. But you've got to be in first. You have got to keep a grip on it.'

Eighty million pounds. That made his stake around ten million, Francis calculated automatically. Ten million pounds, possibly even nicely north of that, and he was wasting all this time over thirty thousand.

'Get a move on, Francis,' Jonathan Miles said again as he left. 'You don't get reminder calls in this business.'

'Not, not.' How could people talk like that? Francis looked out at his view. It was going to be a hot day. He would go through the resumés of the candidates for finance director. Then he would have a cup of coffee and skim the papers. Then he would ring Virginia and arrange to meet her to tell her what had happened. And what he was going to do. That's what he would do. That's definitely what he would do.

There was a knock on the door. 'Mrs Carroll is here to see you, Francis,' Joanne said. That Mrs Carroll, her tone indicated.

Virginia walked in, her eyes shining. 'Well?' she asked. 'All done?'

Francis said: 'Have you offered Mrs Carroll a coffee, Joanne?'

'I'm fine,' Virginia said.

'Why don't you sit down?' Francis said to Virginia as Joanne left the room.

'Why didn't you ring me last night?' Virginia demanded.

'It was very late when I got back. Anyway, you know we shouldn't talk about this over the phone. And I was just about to call you to arrange to meet so I could tell you. Not that there's much to tell.'

'What do you mean?'

'He wouldn't do it.'

'What do you mean, "he wouldn't do it"?' The light in Virginia's eye paled into fury.

'I mean, he wouldn't do it.'

'You mean you wouldn't pay what he wanted.' Wrath had taken hold of Virginia now.

'Virginia, we never even got as far as discussing money. He just wouldn't do it.'

She looked at him, willing him to say something to make it different, waiting for him to tell her that there was a friend who would do it, even that there was a friend who would discuss doing it. She would even settle for a friend of a friend who might know someone who might be prepared to discuss doing it. But not this.

'Ginny, I'm sorry. I know how disappointing this must be for you,' Francis began. And as he spoke, he realised that he really was sorry he had not been able to do this for her. The relief he felt last night at being spared this dangerously illegal entanglement was now overlaid with a sense he had let her down. Watching the light dim in her eyes, he knew he had failed her.

'I knew I should have done it myself,' she said, suddenly calm. 'Not really your sort of thing, Francis.' She smiled at him sweetly. 'But thank you for trying. It was good of you to offer.'

'I hope it's not your sort of thing, either,' he said, stung. 'It was a stupid idea. I should never have considered it. It would have been breaking the law, Virginia.'

'What do you think this man does every day?' she said. He recognised the sound: Virginia building up to full flow. 'These are constructs, made by men and broken by men, Francis. There is nothing divine about the law Francis. If you break it, you run the risk of paying a price. That's it. Nothing wrong. It's just a calculation. Just like you make every day. Risk and reward, Francis. Remember? God won't strike you down if you break the law. The law will. If you get caught. And we weren't going to get caught. And now we've still got a problem.'

'It was still stupid and wrong,' Francis said wearily. He remembered how he never won these arguments with Virginia. The best he could ever hope for was to fight her to a standstill. And you never did this through logic, only by attrition. 'Please don't let us fight, Virginia,' he said. 'I'm sorry I couldn't do what you wanted. But I have been thinking about what to do next. I have decided to give you the money.'

She said nothing. He knew he should just leave it there but he wanted to explain.

'As I came home last night,' he said, 'I thought about what a mess it all was. How I should never have gone to Spain. How I wished I had the courage

275

to go to the police. That is what Charles advised and in my head I knew he was right. But how could I have done that to James? So, as I didn't have the courage to go to the police, I should have just given you the money.'

He looked at her but she was looking out of the window as she listened to him.

'How could I have lived with myself if he had ended up in jail? So, there it was, staring me in the face. I should have just given you the money when you asked for it. I am really sorry I did not. I don't know how we got into this state. But you were right. I should have just given you the money when you asked for it. And that is what I am now going to do. I am going to give you the money now and we can put an end to all this.'

For some reason, Virginia did not look as pleased as he had wanted her to be.

'Look,' he went on, 'this is not easy for me. I have no spare money right now. I have remortgaged the house up to the hilt to get the money I need for InterTrust. There is just nothing spare at the moment. I know you think I'm made of money but it is not that easy at the moment.'

As he spoke, he felt relieved that at last he could be honest with Virginia. He was not pretending any more. And that felt better. As if their relationship was moving into more comfortable territory. And then he felt a rush of guilt. What was he doing telling Virginia about the remortgage? He had not even told Rachel yet. He had wanted to avoid worrying her. But why did he feel good about telling Virginia and bad about telling his wife?

Virginia did not react.

Did she not realise how difficult this was for him? This was not just about thirty thousand pounds. He did not expect her to care about that. It was about InterTrust, his baby, and purging those memories of his father's failures. And it was a symbol of his new start with Rachel. This was him beginning to heal the damage Virginia had done to him. And she did not seem to appreciate that he was willing to put all that at risk to get James out of a mess she should never have let him get into in the first place. She just sat there as if it was nothing.

'This must not be traced back to me in any way.' He was going to move on. 'So I am going to pay you thirty thousand pounds, Virginia. What you do with it is now entirely a matter for you.'

Francis realised his tone had changed. Now he was talking to Virginia not as a woman with whom he had shared so much but as if he was a bank manager and she was a client. She used to tease him about this manner of his. And it was as if he had slipped back into it to force his return to a normal, ordered world of law and contract where he was married to Rachel and Virginia was just a woman he had once known and where a simple payment of money could put the lid back over that seething, foul underworld he had glimpsed.

'I will make the arrangements to have the money transferred into your account this morning. As far as

I am concerned, I am responding to a request from you for money for James, as I always have done, without question or enquiry.'

'Thank you, Francis,' Virginia said. He could feel her wanting to make some comment about his tone but she didn't. 'Really, thank you,' she said quietly. 'James will be so relieved. He has been distraught about this. I am glad it is over.'

He sensed the softening in her tone. It was extraordinary how she could bring out the sun.

'Please, Virginia,' Francis said. 'I am trusting you. Please don't say a word to anyone about this, not even to James.'

She nodded meekly.

'I mean it, Virginia. Please?'

'You can trust me, Francis,' she replied.

thirty-nine

friday 11.15 a.m.
Rachel opened the vacuum flask and poured herself a cup of red-clover infusion. Marie was still away fortunately so she had the office to herself. Cleansing the blood seemed the right place to start and that was what red clover was for. She sipped it and tried to visualise how it was washing away all the microscopic impurities in her blood that had stopped every single one of Francis's eighty billion sperm reaching one of her passionately waiting eggs. Visualisation. She had been on a course about it. Visualise her blood being cleansed, that was what she had to do. Visualise it and make it happen.

She sipped the infusion and looked out of the window, visualising the red clover dissolving the nano-blockages and micro-pollutants in her blood that stood in the way of pregnancy. It tasted odd, stalky, disagreeable. Perhaps she had made it wrong. Perhaps something so good for you was not meant to taste good as well. Visualise the good it was doing, ignore the taste. Do it for Francis, do it for her and Francis, do it for the baby. But most of all, do it for them all together.

Her office looked out at the side of the building.

You only got an unrestricted view as a partner. That was the trick she had to pull: pregnancy and partnership. Be made pregnant by Francis and be made a partner by Rother & Fenwick. Why did she put it like that – so passively? Far too passive. Why should these things that were so important to her be things that were done to her? She would get pregnant. She would become a partner. She could see it.

There was a knock and the door opened.

'Hello, Rachel. Have you got a moment?' Brendan Simpson was the managing partner of her division.

'Of course, Brendan. Come in.' But he had already done so and sat himself down at the chair by Rachel's desk. There was only just room for the two of them. Brendan Simpson was a tall, bony, awkward man, punctiliously polite and ferociously clever, in the running for senior partner.

'How are you?' he asked sympathetically.

'Fine,' she replied automatically, and at the moment she spoke she remembered. 'Better,' she said. 'Much better'.

'I'm pleased to hear it,' Brendan Simpson said. 'It's just that I noticed you have had quite a bit of personal time recently, doctor's appointments and so on, and I just wondered if there was anything I should know about, anything we could do to help?' Rachel pushed the red-clover infusion away guiltily. He could not possibly have guessed what it was.

'No, I'm fine, Brendan, really.' She sensed him scrutinising her. 'Really, I'm fine.'

He was looking at her with benign, penetrating

curiosity. He was a lawyer. A very good, very expensive lawyer. He would remember everything she said, exactly. He had asked if there was anything he should know about. Pregnancy was something he should know about because it would obviously affect her work. But she was not pregnant. But she was trying to get pregnant. Because she might succeed in getting pregnant, that was probably also something he should know about. But how could she tell Brendan Simpson that she was trying to get pregnant? Rother & Fenwick would hardly welcome the fact she was taking time off in order to take more time off on maternity leave.

'Just women's things, Brendan. You know.' Rachel smiled prettily at him. That should cover it.

'Good. I am glad everything is all right,' he said. 'But I hope you would feel able to share with me anything that was on your mind. You have done well, Rachel. You have great potential and I would very much like to see you fulfil it.'

She looked down modestly.

'I have been a partner here for twenty-three years,' he said, 'and I have seen a great many articled clerks and solicitors go through this firm. Most of them highly talented, clever, hard-working individuals. Some have gone to great things, in this firm and beyond. But sometimes, even some of the cleverest and hardest-working of them have not gone on to fulfil their potential. There have been all sorts of reasons for this, but I would hate to see this happen to you, Rachel.'

The time off had been noticed. That bloody Dr

Gray, keeping them waiting for so long. That was what had done it.

'I'm fine, Brendan, really,' she said.

'I am glad to hear it,' he said, getting up. 'But please do not hesitate to let me know if there is anything you think I should know.' He opened the door. 'How are you getting along with the Ramsden case? It's important for us to get a result. And I am sure it will not have escaped your notice, it's the sort of case which gets people made partners.' He was looking at her again with that benign, penetrating curiosity. 'There will probably be three or four new ones this year.'

'I'm getting on fine, Brendan,' she said. 'I think.'

'Good, good,' he said and smiled at her. He closed the door carefully behind him as he left.

That bloody Dr Gray, keeping them waiting. She swigged down the rest of the red-clover infusion. They were watching her. They would need reassuring that she really did love being part of Rother & Fenwick and she would make the sacrifices needed to be part of it. She simply could not afford any more doctor's appointments.

Rachel looked out of the window at the side of the building. That doctor had not been much use anyway. She would keep on the herbal diet and keep feeding Francis the saw palmetto and pumpkin seeds and it might just work out.

She picked up the cup of red clover and then remembered she had finished it. She looked at her watch. She might as well try again.

Some things were so important you had to make

them happen. She would become a partner. She would get pregnant.

Rachel opened her handbag. She never went anywhere without it nowadays. There it was in the inside pocket. She took it and went to the marble-floored, chrome and smoked-glass lavatory at the end of corridor. There was no-one there. She took out the testing kit. Be there human chorionic gonadotrophin. Be there two pink lines. Be there little baby in me.

She counted to sixty. One line. Come on. She counted to a hundred. Come on, please come on. Nothing more. She counted to a hundred again. Still just one pink line. She threw it in the bin.

forty

Virginia had dissolved. The sun had come out and
filtered through the curtains in Alex's bedroom. In the
sub-aqueous, pale golden room, she was suspended in
her skin. Every part of her felt light and soft. Her bones
had liquefied. She was drifting lazily through air and
time had stopped. She was glad Alex was making tea
in the kitchen. She loved this moment. She did not
want to have to talk to him. She stretched luxuriously.
This was perfect. After all this time, it still felt wonderful.

A slight breeze stirred the curtain. There was a
Manchester United Yearbook beside the bed. She
flicked through it. Her body was resuming its usual
shapes and textures. She was beginning to feel flesh
and bone again. Under the sheet, she ran her hand
over her stomach. Still flat, at least lying down. Who
would have a Manchester United Yearbook by the bed?
Alex was quite boring. Good-looking and willing
enough but boring. Actually, very boring. It was a
mystery to her how men could be so dull when, at the
same time, they were capable of giving her so much
pleasure. She really ought to want to spend more time
with them afterwards.

It had never been like that with Francis. She had been thinking of him a lot recently and it was unsettling. Alex came back into the room with two mugs of tea on a tray. 'You are nice,' she said and she meant it. He was nice. And so easy to be with. So relaxed about everything. Just a bit boring. Comfort food.

Virginia had never had to try to get men interested in her. Sometimes, reading a magazine or listening to her friends talking, she wondered why she did not panic as birthday followed birthday. She supposed twenty-five-year-olds would no longer be very interested in her, but then she was not interested in them. Most men seemed to need twenty years to emerge from acned teenage obsessions into a brief period when they knew who they were and were still young enough to enjoy it. They could be interesting then for a few years before they ossified into old age.

Francis had not been like that. There had always been something more.

Alex put the tray down beside the bed and took off his dressing gown and got in beside her. She snuggled up to him and took his arm and put it around her. She loved this feeling of skin on skin and her blood pulsing next to his. She had not thought of Francis like this for years. She raised herself up and reached for her mug of tea.

'You're restless,' Alex said. She kissed him and sipped the hot, sweet tea. It surged through her. She closed her eyes and felt Alex's skin next to hers, the sweet and tannin taste of the tea and his sweat and salt in her mouth, the cool cotton of the sheet under her and around her, the soft refracted light of the afternoon. It had never been like this with Francis. They had never had afternoons like this. Francis was always working in the afternoon.

'You don't seriously read this, do you?' she asked, picking up the Manchester United Yearbook.

'Why not?' he said.

'Because it's the definition of tedium, the dictionary definition,' she said.

He laughed. 'It's just a book,' he said.

'But such a boring book,' she said. 'What can there possibly be that's interesting in the Manchester United Yearbook?'

'It's quite interesting if you are interested in Manchester United. If you are not, not,' he said. 'It's just a book.'

'It's a denial of life,' Virginia said. She took another sip of the tea. It had been different with Francis and never like that with anyone else, before or since. Perhaps because he was the first with whom sex had been transforming. She had never understood why but something about him had always been able to flick a switch in her. She loved it with him. She married him. And they were happy.

'Sweet dreams,' he used to say to her every night before they went to sleep. One Sunday they made love to the Emmylou Harris version of the song, and the sweet longing in her voice and the luscious melancholy of the ballad harmonised with their tender

286

coitus. And then when Virginia began to doze off, Francis said, still inside her, in his intense and serious voice, 'Don't go.' And when she said, 'I am so sleepy, you have made me so happy,' he said, 'sweet dreams then,' quoting the song. She knew he was trying to tell her how much he loved her and how much and how selflessly he wanted her to be happy. To anyone else, and at any other time, it was a casual remark, a trite song title. But to Virginia and Francis, on that Sunday afternoon, it distilled their passion. Sweet, sentimental Francis. And Virginia.

Then that worm of curiosity had hatched. Was he really the one, the only one, for her? Or was he just a companion for this stage in her journey towards a higher plane of experience?

And so yearning unexpectedly returned into their happiness. From unknown deeps, a gene for exploration surfaced and a restless hunter-gatherer battled the settler in her. It was a bad thing she did to him. In their restaurant. She knew that. She had known it as soon as she walked into the room and saw him sitting there, bursting with pleasure at his surprise for her. She had done him wrong. She tried to show him she knew that. She tried to make him see what was important and not important. She tried to help him understand the hurt was to his pride, not to his love, and it would heal. And still they could have been happy. But he would not listen. He was so stubborn. She had tried. Oh how she had tried.

After he left, her need to explore weakened. She hunted and gathered – what else could she do once he had gone – but she found the gap between hope and disappointment grew shorter and shorter. And always she knew they could still have been happy. And then came Alex. Slow, comfortable, taut Alex. Never taking offence. Never losing his temper. Sweet, relaxed Alex. Not a disappointment – how could he be, nice, handsome Alex? But not a thrill. Not Francis.

Had those special times with him just been something for that part of her life? Perhaps it could never be the same again whatever you did, if you stayed or if you left? Perhaps it was like that when you were twenty-two. And only then. And it could never be like that again. Or was it that Francis had been the one, the only one? And she had lost him.

Alex kissed her on the cheek. She purred appreciatively. He sought her mouth. She kissed him back with her lips together. 'That was lovely,' she said. 'You are so clever.' She reached over him for her mug of tea. He kissed her shoulder again and again as she drank, little persistent kisses. He was not really that clever, she thought. Actually, he was quite stupid. He certainly had not got the message. No more. At least, not just now.

Why did she fight so much with Francis? He was irritating. But it was not just that.

'Would you like some toast?' Alex asked.

'That would be lovely,' she said.

Alex was such a nice man. All her friends said so. She was lucky. She knew that. Perhaps she had never forgiven Francis for leaving her? Was it really no more than that? Wounded pride? No-one should leave Virginia.

She watched Alex as he left the room. Would he leave her? She would understand if he got fed up with the way she treated him. And he would probably want children at some point. What then? What would she be left with then? Even though he was not fully aware of it, at least he had helped her with James's little problem. Unlike Francis.

Perhaps she was too hard on Francis. He was only trying to do the right thing. As he saw it. Perhaps that was the problem. He was so emotionally constipated. But was she too hard on him?

Alex came back into the room with a plate of toast. He always made it so the melting butter flowed over the edges and mingled with the jam. 'This is lovely,' she said. 'Thank you.' She gave him a kiss as he got back into bed.

Virginia munched the toast. Francis's wife was a dumpy little thing. Sure, she was clever and pretty enough. But she was dumpy. And earnest. Virginia licked the jam from her lips. She understood why Francis had picked Rachel up on the rebound. After her, he obviously needed a rest – a devoted, pretty, dumpy rest.

Rachel would never be hard on Francis, even though he might deserve it. Virginia could see that. From now on, she resolved, she would treat Francis better. And she would start by paying all the money to James's dealer, as Francis wanted. She knew the money would be in her account by now. Francis always did what he said. She really did not want to pay it. She had warmed to the idea of taking on the drug baron at his own game and outwitting him. But she would do what Francis asked.

She stretched again and turned towards Alex. She kissed his ear and stroked his hair. Thirty thousand pounds? It was all right for Francis. That sort of money meant nothing to him. But it was more than she earned in a year – before tax. She ate a satisfying slice of toast, dark and crisp with the butter and jam melting in her mouth.

It was objectionable. How could anyone justify handing over so much money to someone who had done so little to earn it? It was wrong. And anyway, she was sure there was a better way of sorting it out than giving in like this and just paying up what he asked.

Virginia sighed and then, as she did so, remembered Alex was lying beside her. She hoped he would think it was contentment.

She would make the sacrifice and argue no more. She would finish the toast and then ring that number Francis had given her. She would pay up. She still had a couple of hours to get the money out of the bank. She could do it today.

Anyway, she supposed she was curious to see what so much money would look like. Thirty thousand pounds. She tried to imagine how high it would reach up to the ceiling, those tottering piles of notes. She would indulge herself by getting them out of the bank and bringing them home and then ogling them on the kitchen table. And then when she had finished ogling it, she would meet this man somewhere and hand it all over to him.

God, she was being good today. She would pay up. She would give in and pay up. For James. For Francis.

forty-one

friday 4.30 p.m.
Paddington Station simmered under Brunel's great arched roof, summer light flooding the terminus as the travelling masses scurried and waited: account-management teams in business suits strode from first-class carriages to the taxi queue; two grungy teenagers, hair plaited in dreadlocks and grubby yellow ribbons, sat patiently on the concourse with a skinny sleeping hound; weary executives plodded off the Heathrow Express, shouldering their carry-on bags, fighting the exhaustion of their third transatlantic flight in a month; bad-tempered queues seethed around the fast-food stands; sweating mothers snapped at grizzling children; station staff in ill-fitting uniforms talked to each other, occasionally breaking off impatiently to direct a passenger somewhere else; a squad of foreign-language students milled around their teacher, chattering; and an elderly Asian lady patiently pushed a large broom across the floor. By the barrier to Platform Four, a young couple kissed passionately, oblivious to passers-by, ridden by the insatiable hormones of youth.

It reminded Virginia of a mediaeval Flemish vision of hell. All humanity suffering but each human being in torment in their own particular way. This is what hell really could be like: no extremes of pain or punishment, just a steady accumulation of sweat and grime and proliferating irritation – for ever and ever and ever; a ceaseless dripping of aggravation for ever and ever, without stopping, not even for a second.

She came out of the Underground and stopped, awed by the grief people put themselves through to travel by train. But it was a good place to meet, she thought. Roger clearly knew what he was doing. It had been so slick. One phone call and a meeting two hours later.

She felt in her bag anxiously. She had never seen so much money before. It would be ironic if someone were to lift it in the mêlée. But the comforting bulk was still there.

Through all the tumult and noise, she became aware that her mobile phone was ringing. Perhaps it was him. She felt in her bag for it, and all she could feel was wads of pound notes. She had better answer it in case there was a change of plan, or something had gone wrong. It was still ringing. Where was it? What could have gone wrong? The phone kept ringing. More pound notes. Where was it? And still her phone kept ringing. Finally she managed to extricate it.

'Hello,' she said. 'Oh, hello, Mrs Court.

'Mrs Court, I am really sorry, I can't talk to you now. I will call you back later.

'Yes, I do recognise Patsy's talent, Mrs Court, but I am afraid I really can't talk to you right now. I will call you back.

'Yes, I do have your number, Mrs Court.

'Mrs Court, I am really sorry. I promise I will call you back later.' Virginia put the phone back in her bag. She could feel her heart beating faster. She was more wound up than she had thought.

He had said to meet by the entrance to Platform One. She saw why. People dropped off by taxi had to come down the platform to get to their trains. The public lavatories by the entrance created a constant flow of traffic. Trains came and went, disgorging tanned holidaymakers from the Cornish Riviera, absorbing busy, brash businessmen on their way to the boom towns of the M4 corridor. No-one would notice Virginia and her man.

She wondered if he was already here and observing her. That would be sensible, she thought. He could check whether she had been followed or had brought back-up. It was quite complicated, when you thought about it. How did he know it was not a set-up? How could he know that she had not brought the police with her, that five muscular Drugs Squad detectives were not strategically positioned at all ends of Platform One, ready to pounce as soon as the money was handed over? It must be quite stressful being him, she thought.

A burly man perspiring in a creased grey suit, with a bulky shoulder-bag and carrying a laptop computer and a carton of coffee, jostled past her, pushing her to one side.

'Excuse me,' she said with heavy irony. He lumbered down the platform, unheeding. Shoving her had clearly given him some consolation for the sweaty maelstrom.

But then, she thought, what would they arrest him for? He wouldn't be so stupid as to carry the drugs around with him. Would he? She considered the possibility that the man who had just given her such a shove had been the man she had come to meet, not recognising her, in a hurry to get to his rendezvous, not realising he had just missed it. And that the shoulder-bag which had bumped into her had been crammed with neatly packed packets of heroin and cocaine. What if he was not smart and he really was lugging around a shoulder-bag of heroin and cocaine, with all those little plastic packets sweating away in the bag on his shoulder?

Virginia's reverie was rudely disrupted by this notion. The seamless flow of argument she had been conducting with herself came to a sticky halt on this indigestible thought. She was reliant on her man not to make mistakes. This dependency had not occurred to her before and she did not like it. What had been a pleasant interlude among the heat and the noise now became a sudden source of anxiety. This man could be an idiot, she thought. Why wouldn't he be? And it was highly likely the police would be on to him in some way or other. Why wouldn't they be?

'Mrs Carroll?' The voice was soft and right beside her and spoke with a subdued London accent. Dapper was the word for him, Virginia thought. A small man, with thinning blond hair. Good-looking, she thought, like the drummer in a 1960s mod band. He was wearing a pale grey suit, and a delicate lilac shirt and mauve tie.

She nodded. Where had he come from?

'Can I offer you a cup of coffee?' he asked politely.

'Of course,' she said. His appearance was reassuring – no-one this neat and tasteful could be a complete idiot. 'I've been dying for one.'

'Have you got it?' he asked as they walked back onto the concourse. She nodded, noticing how carefully he chose his words.

'In the envelope, as I said?' he asked. She nodded again.

They arrived at a coffee stand.

'If you sit down at the table, I'll get us the coffees. Please put your bag on the table,' he said politely.

She sat down and put her bag on the table. Around her the travelling public swirled and sweated. She watched Roger as he queued for coffee, neatly, unobtrusively. No-one would know, she thought. He looked straight in front of him, at the back of the head of a plump, middle-aged woman having a loud conversation on a mobile phone. Virginia could hear her from the table. She was telling someone to meet her off the train at Didcot.

Roger showed no sign of listening, or even hearing. He stared ahead with Buddhist patience, taking two precise little steps forward every time the queue moved. Blending in, Virginia thought. Doing nothing to draw attention to himself. She felt the panic ebbing away. And he did not have a shoulder-bag. Nor was there any sign of muscular detectives. Just the swarming throngs of perspiring, agitated passengers.

Roger returned and placed the coffees on the table.

'Just drink it as you would normally. I will talk to you. There is no need for you to say anything. Just nod from time to time as if you are interested.' He spoke very softly but with such precise diction Virginia hardly had to strain to hear him.

He carried on in his low, meticulous tones. 'I am going to put my hands into your bag and count the money in the envelope in the bag. Please could you nod as I am doing this and look as if you are interested in what I am doing.'

Virginia thought she could manage this. Roger put his hand into her bag, into the envelope, left open as he had asked, and began counting.

Virginia had sometimes seen clerks in the bank counting money, riffling through it with ostentatious speed, fingers flickering through the notes. Roger was in a different class. She barely noticed his fingers moving, just a slight regular twitching. He was staring into the middle distance as he did it. Unless you were right there beside him, it would have looked as if he was just resting his hands in the bag. He finished almost before he started. Virginia remembered to nod. His mouth tightened. He counted the money again. Again he finished almost before he started.

'Twenty-nine thousand, five hundred . . . thirty thousand pounds.' He was clearly unhappy but his tone did not change.

Virginia looked at him. 'Yes,' she said. 'As agreed.'

'No, not as agreed,' he said. He was clearly cross but his voice never changed its low, even tone. 'There's interest. Six thousand pounds. The money's three days late and I don't do parts of a week.'

Virginia was outraged. 'You can't do that,' she hissed at him. 'You can't just slap on another six thousand.'

'It's six thousand pounds,' said Roger evenly. 'Interest runs at twenty per cent a week. That's six thousand.'

'My bank charges me nine per cent for my overdraft – a year.' Virginia was furious.

'I am not your bank,' Roger pointed out.

'I've paid you what you asked. It's a huge amount of money. You've got a nerve asking for another six thousand pounds. Six thousand pounds!' she repeated incredulously.

'It's what you owe me,' Roger said. 'And please don't raise your voice.'

'What do you mean – I owe you?' Virginia was struggling to keep her voice down. 'I don't owe you that. I don't even owe you the thirty thousand but I paid it just to get rid of you. I am not paying this.'

'You do owe it and you will pay it.' Roger's voice never varied. 'At least, I suggest it would be advisable for you to pay it.'

'You never mentioned any interest – you can't just demand it because you feel like it.'

This edgy blonde was more persistent than most. 'I'm afraid you are wrong, Mrs Carroll,' Roger said carefully. 'I did mention it. I always mention it. I explained to Mr Carroll the financial consequences of late payment. And you were late paying. So, six thousand pounds. Please.'

'He never said anything to me.'

'It must have been an oversight. You still owe me the money.'

Virginia felt her fury with Roger becoming infused with irritation with Francis. Had he been told and forgotten to give her the extra six thousand pounds? Or had he just decided not to pay it and not told her? Or was the dapper little man trying it on? Was he lying?

'Are you calling me a liar?' she demanded.

'I'm not calling you anything, Mrs Carroll.' Roger's tone remained implacably even. 'I'm just reminding you that you still owe me six thousand pounds.'

Virginia was so cross she could not summon words. How could this man treat her like this? She looked at him with cold fury. At the next table, a middle-aged man in a suit was holding hands with a much younger woman and speaking earnestly to her as he gazed into her eyes. Somewhere nearby, a child was crying inconsolably. The station Tannoy was making some reverberatingly indecipherable announcement.

Roger looked calmly into the middle distance, away over the bedlam of the station. Clearly, he did not feel the conversation had concluded. Perhaps he thought Virginia had the six thousand elsewhere on her person and was just negotiating before she handed it over.

Suddenly, Virginia wanted to cry as the frustrations of the last three days boiled up: all her plans and plotting for James since he first asked her for help, all the twists and turns pulling her this way and that, and then finally Francis giving her the money and her believing that this could now all be put away and she could get on with her summer. And now this destruction of her plans by this strange, dapper, greedy little blond.

The cloud of helplessness passed over. She could ask Francis for the extra money – it wasn't much compared with what she had just handed over. Why would he refuse when he had just handed over thirty thousand pounds? And it was probably his fault anyway. Although it was unlike him to forget anything important, particularly about money. But then the little blond didn't seem like the sort of person to overlook anything either. If Francis had just paid up when she had asked him, instead of getting on his high horse, then there would not have been any of this discussion about 'interest'.

'We're wasting time, Mrs Carroll,' Roger said politely. 'It's six thousand pounds. On Tuesday it's another seven thousand two hundred. Thirteen thousand two hundred all together. Seven days after that it's another eight thousand, eight hundred and forty pounds on top.'

'Eight thousand six hundred and forty,' the teacher corrected automatically.

'Yes, thank you, Mrs Carroll. You are right. My mistake. I am sorry. I am not compounding the interest on the interest on a daily basis. Eight thousand six hundred and forty. And the week after that, ten thousand six hundred and sixty-eight pounds.'

She did not correct him this time.

'As you can see,' he said, 'you will save a great deal of money – and a lot of unnecessary problems – if you pay me what you owe me. But it's up to you.'

Virginia looked at Roger with hatred. He seemed oblivious. Where did this line about interest come from anyway? Any normal person would think thirty thousand in a week was good work. Why did he need this six thousand? It was extortion. It was unfair.

'Why can't you be satisfied with what you've got?' she ended up saying.

'Who is, Mrs Carroll, who is?'

'This is outrageous,' she said. 'You've got your money. What more do you want? Do you have any idea of what I've had to go through to get you this money?'

'Did you have to fuck him again?' Roger enquired sympathetically. 'Your ex-husband?' He had expected some resistance but this fidgety blonde was beginning to irritate him.

Virginia looked at him, startled. Had he really just said what she thought he had said? What an extraordinarily unpleasant little man he was. She glared at him but could not think what to say. The adventurous mood in which she had entered the station just twenty minutes ago had vanished. Who did this scrawny little blond think he was?

'Fuck off,' she answered. Roger smiled briefly. Most of them got round to this eventually. It meant that they had given up. It was a last impotent cry of rage before they rolled over and surrendered. He would take the capital and come back for the interest.

'Think about it, Mrs Carroll.' He pushed his chair back to leave. 'I would if I were you.'

The bag sat on the table. Virginia looked at it.

'Fuck you,' she said, and picked up the bag and ran. Within seconds she had disappeared into the crowd.

Roger stared after her. The second he realised what she had done, she had gone.

forty-two

friday 6.30 p.m.

Rother & Fenwick emptied early on a Friday evening. To beat the rush-hour, the senior partners left in mid-afternoon for their country houses, carrying full brief-cases of work for the weekend. At five thirty all the office staff left, on time as there was no longer anyone to keep them late on the overtime which paid for their childcare and winter holidays. And then, finally, after-wards, left, one by one, those anxious, busy solicitors who still had to make partner.

This evening Rachel came down in the lift on her own. Almost everyone else had already gone. The large reception area was almost empty. Only one slim doe-eyed receptionist sat behind the desk. And there was only one person sitting quietly in the waiting area, where all day it had been thronged with the busy and the quick and the rich and the desperate.

Rachel stopped and bent down to adjust the strap of her shoe. As she straightened up, she noticed that the man waiting in the reception area was staring at her. It was a calm, peaceful gaze.

She noticed his long black hair, streaked with grey, tied in a ponytail, and his black linen jacket with the sleeves rolled up to his elbows. He was sitting very still by the large canvas and looking at her. She saw that he saw she had noticed him looking at her, but his gaze did not change. She wondered what he was doing there at this time of night.

Davey kept his calm, still gaze on her.

'Goodnight,' she said to the solitary receptionist and pushed her way out of the glass doors, out into the muggy summer evening and on her way home to Surrey.

forty-three

friday 6.30 p.m.

Virginia knew what she had to do now. And she wished she had gone by Tube. Her taxi was stuck in a jam outside Waterloo Station. She was wearing a fine cotton shift, the colour of bleached grass. She tapped her fingers on the arm-rest and looked out of the window. She looked at her watch. She pulled back the glass partition and asked the driver how long it was going to take. He shrugged. 'How do I know?' he said. The traffic did not move.

The taxi driver swigged from a plastic water-bottle. Virginia ran her fingers through her hair. She took a small bottle of perfume from her bag and dabbed some behind her ears. She put the back of her finger to her nose and smelled it. She left it there. She breathed deeply. She wished she had gone by Tube.

Outside, South London was sweltering in the late afternoon. Finally, the traffic moved. She pulled the window down to get more air. The taxi was now past Waterloo in an area showing signs of new investment. Derelict shopfronts sat side by side with sleek new bars and jewellery shops. Off the main road could be glimpsed – through the canyons of dour old warehouses – the neon and newly sanded stone of vogueish galleries and artisan workshops.

Near the Tate Modern, the taxi turned off into a short side-street shadowed by the blank walls of a morose, unrefurbished building on the main road.

Virginia paid the taxi driver and walked down a few yards. Set into the wall there was a royal-blue door. She rang the bell. The camera above the door swivelled to point at her. She spoke into a box by the door. The door opened and Virginia went inside.

Inside, it was cool. A short corridor with dark polished-wood floors led to a desk. The woman behind it had cropped black hair and was wearing a fitted black suit with a short skirt. She indicated that Virginia should follow her.

The club lounge was vast, the size of half a football pitch, and a canopied skylight bathed the room in refracted light. Even at this pendulous time between lunch and drinks, almost every chair in the room was occupied, but so discreetly had it been arranged that it did not seem full. There was space around every island of furniture. There was a low hum of comfortable conversations.

Virginia was led over to a small sofa.

'How nice to see you again,' Alex said.

'Yes, it was a nice afternoon, wasn't it.'

'How did it go?' he said, looking at her.

'What?'

'Whatever it was you had to rush off and do so urgently at three o'clock.'

'OK.'

'Really?' Alex took her hand. 'Really?'

'Really, OK. Thank you. I am just hot and furious at having to sit in a traffic jam for an hour,' she said. 'I did not want to be late for you.' And she squeezed his hand.

'OK,' he said. 'What do you want?'

'Why do you always assume I want something from you?'

'Because . . .'

'Well on this occasion your journalistic instinct has not let you down,' Virginia said. 'I do.'

Alex poured her a glass of champagne from the bottle beside him. She took a swig of it.

'I need to know about the drugs business.'

'For the citizenship course, I suppose,' Alex said.

'Yes, yes. Do you know anyone who knows about these things?'

'You're being very diligent this summer,' Alex said. 'Doing all your preparation for next term before this one has even ended.'

'Come on, Alex,' Virginia said.

Alex looked at her. 'Virginia, are you all right?'

'Of course I'm all right. Why shouldn't I be?'

'OK. It's your business. But if you want to talk about anything, I am very discreet. I have to be. I'm a journalist.' He laughed.

'Exactly,' Virginia said. 'Now, do you know anyone?'

Alex pulled out his palmtop computer and scrolled through it.

Virginia sipped her champagne.

Alex then reached into his bag and took out a small notebook, wrote a name in it and then tore out the page and gave it to Virginia.

'This is a long shot,' he said. 'I have met this guy a few times around the clubs. He seems connected. But I would not use my name. And I would not tell him you are doing research for a citizenship course. He might think you are doing something else. Like undercover work for the police. I would say you are a journalist. Then he won't expect you to be telling the truth.' Alex laughed again. 'But you might as well try him. He seems a nice-enough guy. Laid-back. No guarantees. He may not be connected at all. A lot of these young guys like to make out they are even if they are not. And even if he is, he might not want to talk to you. But it's worth a try.'

'Thank you, Alex,' Virginia said. She put the torn-off page in her handbag and took another sip of champagne.

'Actually,' Alex remarked, 'you had better take the whole pad. You might need it. Seeing as you are a journalist.'

Virginia took it from him. 'Thank you,' she said again.

Alex looked at his watch. 'I've got to go,' he told her. 'Will I see you later?'

'Come over when you're finished,' Virginia replied. 'I'll be home before you.'

Alex leaned across and kissed Virginia. 'Good luck,' he said.

Alex watched Virginia as she walked out of the room

with her elegant, purposeful stride. He looked thoughtful. 'Be careful,' he called after her.

Two hours later, Virginia was sitting on a bench outside the National Theatre by the River Thames. It was still very hot. She was sipping a glass of water. At the next table, a plump middle-aged couple were gulping Coca-Cola and mopping their brows. When the man put his hand to his face there was a large damp patch under his arm. Virginia did not look sweaty. She never did. She was still wearing the green cotton shift.

Virginia was not on her own. Sitting beside her was a young man wearing a black T-shirt and immaculately clean white jeans. He was also wearing obviously expensive black loafers, polished till they gleamed. His muscular upper arms stretched the fabric of the shirt. It was Krishnan Singh.

'Why would anyone who knew anything about this want to talk to you about it?' Chris said.

Virginia looked into his eyes. 'To help me,' she said.

'That would not sound like much of a reason to anyone who knew anything about this sort of thing,' Chris said.

Perhaps he was too young for this approach, which had usually served Virginia well.

'There's a lot of misunderstanding about drugs,' Virginia improvised. She had not expected a grilling from this teenage clubber. 'It would help everyone if the general public understood it better.' And then, inspired, she said, 'I would be looking at it from a business perspective. As an industry.'

'Business?'

'Yes,' Virginia said. 'Supply and demand. Market forces. You know. Analysing without moralising.'

'Analysing the business?' Chris asked. 'You mean looking at margins and turnover. And credit collection? That sort of thing?'

'Yes, yes,' Virginia said. 'That sort of thing.'

A large tourist boat went down the river, the commentary blaring out, carried by the wind. Virginia turned to look at it, irritated. The young man waited impassively.

'And you want to put all this in the papers?' Chris asked.

'Of course, I would protect the identity of my sources.' She was glad she had been listening when Alex had been blathering on. He had been so useful in so many ways. Unlike Francis.

'And which paper did you say you worked for?'

Virginia was impressed. She had not said which paper she was pretending to work for. She had to be careful now. It was important that he believed she was a journalist and told her what she needed to know. She was operating on the outer limits of what she had picked up from Alex. What paper was he least likely to read?

'The *Observer*,' she said.

'And you would analyse it from a business perspective?' Chris asked. Was he was beginning to sound more interested?

'Yes,' Virginia said. He had lovely brown eyes.

'And this newspaper would definitely publish it?'

'Yes. But I can promise you your name will not come into it,' she added cautiously.

'Stand up,' he said.

'What?'

'Stand up,' Chris repeated patiently. 'I need to check something.'

'Why do I have to stand up for you to check something? You can just ask me,' Virginia said. There was something in his voice she did not like, even though he had continued to speak softly and politely.

'Look,' Chris said quietly, 'if you want me to talk to you, stand up. Please.'

Virginia felt a squirt of excitement as she realised he was about to talk to her. She was not sure what had persuaded him but he was clearly not as immune to her as he had appeared. He was the one. Not a connection, but the one who was actually going to talk to her. She could stand up for that.

'OK,' she said. 'Now what? What do you want to check?'

He put his hands on her waist and ran them firmly and expertly round her stomach and up to her armpits and then down the inside of her legs. It was over before Virginia had worked out how she should respond. And it had not been unpleasant. Not at all. She wondered if it had just been an excuse.

'Put your bag on the table,' Chris said. 'Please.'

As he had just run his hands all over her and she had said nothing, Virginia could not think of any reason why she should now refuse this less intimate request. Young brown-eyes was a commanding presence.

Chris riffled through the bag.

'OK,' he said finally. 'Now, what do you want to know?'

Virginia sat down and pulled the bag towards her. She took out the notebook Alex had given her and hoped Chris would not notice that she was not using shorthand.

As they talked, the sun's heat finally began to calm down and the shadows lengthened around them. The tables in the little piazza were emptying and not refilling. And on they talked. And on and on Virginia scribbled, page after page.

Finally, Chris finished talking.

'Thank you,' Virginia said.

'OK,' Chris said. 'I would not mention my name if I were you.'

'Of course not. I gave you my word.'

'That's not the reason I wouldn't use it. If I were you,' Chris said.

'No,' Virginia said. 'I won't.'

She realised, suddenly uneasy, that there was no-one at any of the other tables and they were now on their own.

'And they will print it just as you write it?' Chris persisted.

'Yes, yes,' Virginia said. There was something scary about the quiet determination of this nice-looking young man. And there was something odd about his concerns. Although he had been careful to avoid any suggestion about how he knew so much, he had been very open with her about what went on and what other people did, but he was still anxious about something. She could not quite put her finger on it, but she did not think she should stay around to find out what it was. It was time she went. It had been quite exciting when there were other people around. But now she was beginning to feel nervous. Now she had to go.

'I am not naming names. It's just analysis,' she said. What was the best way to reassure him that she was not going to cause trouble for him?

'When will it come out?' Chris asked.

'I can't be sure. Next week? Maybe the week after? Or the week after?' That ought to be vague enough. And now, it was really time to go.

'I am very grateful,' she said, getting up. 'You have been very helpful and I promise you that your name will not appear anywhere.'

'That's OK,' he said. 'It's important people know what's going down.'

Chris got up from the table. 'Nice to see you,' he said as he walked off, with long, athletic strides. In seconds he had turned a concrete corner and was gone.

Virginia watched him go. As soon as he disappeared, she took out her mobile phone and started to dial.

forty-four

saturday 9.15 a.m.
The Ramsden files sat on the table. Rachel had gone
through them once this morning already, getting up
at seven o'clock, creeping out of bed so as not to
disturb Francis who lay snuffling quietly in his sleep.
Her visits to East Finchley and Harley Street had
caused her to get badly behind and Brendan
Simpson was now on her case. She had to catch
up this weekend. She sat at the kitchen table in the
quiet Saturday morning, the rich aromas of coffee
and toast comforting her as she read through the
files.

First she had to get a sense of the geography of the
case. How it looked as a whole. Where it started. Where
it ended. And how it got there. Later she would go
through it, document by document, looking for the
nuggets that would convince Brendan Simpson that
she deserved to be made a partner. This was going to
take hours.

Rachel made another cup of coffee and looked out
at the lawns which swept down to the large-leaved
lime trees at the end of the garden. It was very still.
She heard the post come through the letterbox but

she resisted the urge to get up and open it. She stayed at the kitchen table and picked up another file.

At half past nine she made a cup of coffee and took it up to Francis. He was still asleep, sprawled across the bed. She kissed his warm cheek with its dusting of early morning beard and placed the coffee gently beside him.

'Good morning,' she said.

He stirred and grunted.

'I love you,' she said. She waited for him to say something but he rolled over and pulled the duvet around him. She was sure she was not imagining it but the last few days he had seemed distracted. And distant. It was probably nothing. It was probably just InterTrust. And James. But what if it wasn't? What if he was getting bored with her? Or she had pushed him too far on Wednesday night?

'Good morning,' she said again. 'I love you.'

Francis breathed deeply but said nothing. Rachel went downstairs and opened up another file.

Then, at ten o'clock, he came downstairs in a jogging suit. 'I'm just going for a run,' he said.

'I love you,' she said.

'I love you,' he said.

Rachel returned happily to her files.

At eleven o'clock, she started on the stock. She had never done much cooking, but now she wanted to. She wanted to cook for Francis. Peel and chop the carrots. And peel and chop the potatoes. And skin the onion. And chuck in the chicken. There. Chicken soup. With added saw palmetto and pumpkin seeds.

Cooking wasn't so difficult. And so back to the Ramsden files while the soup bubbled nutritiously, satisfyingly, generatively on the stove.

Francis came back from his run and had a shower. 'How was it?' she called as she heard him come in. 'I love you.'

She turned down the chicken stock and turned on the laptop again. Francis came into the kitchen, fresh from the shower and carrying the newspaper. He trod softly, careful not to disturb her. He took some milk out of the fridge and poured it.

She turned to look at him and smiled. He looked so fine, his hair still damp and tousled from the shower. And she loved being with him. She had not been irritated by the surprise in her mother's face when she introduced them. She loved it. She had hated the way her mother had always found something nice to say about her boyfriends in the past. 'Richard is so pleasant,' she said, when she clearly meant 'plain'. 'Robert seems so intelligent,' she said, when she obviously meant 'spotty'. 'Martin is very considerate,' she said, when she plainly meant 'dull'. 'Patrick seems like a decent man,' she said, when she undoubtedly meant 'plain, spotty and dull, but you are lucky to get anyone'.

But when she met Francis, her mother said, 'How nice to meet you,' and adjusted her hair. 'How long have you known him?' she asked Rachel afterwards, meaning, 'This won't last long.' But it had. Five years. And they were married. And she loved him. And his gentle assurance. And his serious, handsome face. And his tenderness towards her. Rachel loved Francis.

'That smells nice,' he said. And he took the paper into the living room.

Rachel loved their routines at the weekend and the comforting sense of them being together. It never felt like that during the week when they were both driven by a rhythm of meetings and lunches and commuting. At the weekends, they were a unit.

She looked at the pile of files for the Ramsden case. This lawyers' labyrinth was important, even for Rother & Fenwick. If she did well, her card would be marked. Partnership.

The rich, nourishing smell of the simmering stock now filled the kitchen. Birds sang in the garden, lush green in the high summer. Francis sat next door in the living room, reading the paper. She could hear the occasional rustle of the pages. It was all so nearly there. Francis; the partnership. She could see the visiting cards: Rachel Carroll, Partner, Rother & Fenwick. And the baby. Their baby. Why could she not get pregnant?

She could see their baby so clearly. Every day she could see him so clearly: the perfect miniature hands, the soft, unblemished skin. She could smell the fresh milk on him.

Rother & Fenwick had once sent her on a creative visualisation course. World-class footballers used it, apparently, to keep on top, and nothing less than that would do for Rother & Fenwick's world-class lawyers. 'If you can imagine it, you can achieve it,' they told her. 'See that ball bulging the back of the net,' they said. 'Focus your mind until what you want to achieve

317

becomes the focus of your reality,' they told her. 'Create the image of what you want to achieve. Focus on it until it becomes reality.'

It didn't work. Every day she created an image of the baby, a perfect, darling baby, and she focused on it until there was no other reality in her brain, no Rother & Fenwick, no Ramsden case, no Surrey villa, not even any Francis. And she focused on it until she had nothing but positive attitude bulging in her brain. But nothing happened. She was not pregnant.

She picked up another file from the table. Positive attitude.

'I love you,' she called to Francis in the living room.

'I love you too,' he called back.

forty-five

sunday 7.50 a.m.

Roger sensed something was wrong the instant he woke up that Sunday. He had woken before the alarm, every nerve alert, and he could not account for it. Everything seemed as it always was. The house was quiet and Maggie breathed deeply beside him. It was still and nothing moved in the street outside. It was eerily still. But then it always was, this early on a Sunday morning. He strained to hear anything unusual. Nothing moved. Maggie shifted in her sleep. Three streets away, a car started up and moved off. Then there was silence again.

A vein throbbed in his temple. Unease spread through him. Something was wrong. Somewhere in the house, something creaked and Roger tensed. He listened intently. Nothing stirred. No follow-up creaking. He waited but there was nothing.

He got up very carefully, trying not to disturb his gently slumbering wife. He went into the bathroom and put on his dressing gown. The silk slid comfortingly over his pyjamas. He opened the mirrored medicine cabinet, catching sight of his face as he did so, intent, serious, as if he was glimpsing someone else.

At the back of it, his fingers felt for a button flush with the wall and pressed it. The catch released and he opened a door to reveal a small, deep safe, recessed into the wall. There was some jewellery in a small grey leather box, thirty thousand pounds in fifty-pound notes in four foolscap envelopes, and four passports in false names. Roger believed in taking precautions. It was a risk keeping it all here, but then, as he always said to himself, if they got as far as this, the game was up anyway.

And there was a sleek Walther P99. Roger never took a gun anywhere with him. Stupid people carried guns around, he thought. He had no time for it. He felt sorry for those who thought it would help them. He was always careful never to place himself in situations where one might be needed. Prevention not cure, Roger liked to say to himself.

But at home it was a different matter. Where his family was concerned, it was different. You could never be too careful at home. You could never be sure that someone would not come after you there, no matter how careful you were. And you could not avoid being at home. And you had to take every possible precaution where your family was concerned.

Roger took the gun out and put it in the pocket of the dressing gown, keeping his hand on it. He shut the safe and then the mirrored cabinet. He tried to avoid catching a glimpse of himself. He moved carefully and softly back into the bedroom. Maggie was still sleeping. He stopped and listened.

There was nothing. He could hear nothing but he

could not rid himself of the unease. Over the years, Roger had relied on his instincts. He trusted them. And his instinct now was that something was wrong.

The house creaked again. Roger's right hand tensed around the gun in his dressing-gown pocket but he did not take it out. He moved quickly and silently to the door of the bedroom. With his left hand, he carefully turned the handle and eased the door open. He stopped and listened. Nothing. Still nothing.

He went out on the landing and again he stopped and listened. Now he was listening for something on the roof. It was very difficult to control movement on a roof. If someone was there they would have to make a sound sooner or later. Nothing. No-one was on the roof.

He moved quietly into Samantha's empty room. She was away, staying with a friend. Her room faced onto the street and the curtains were drawn. Delicately he moved them a fraction apart and looked out. The street was deserted. No-one about, no strange cars parked anywhere in the street. It was just as it always was.

Roger was beginning to feel less agitated now. His methodical checking was calming him down. Its purposefulness soothed him. If something was wrong, he was going to find it. Nothing was going to catch him by surprise.

He went into Natalie's room which looked down on the garden. She rolled over in her sleep as he opened the door. The curtains were half open so he moved carefully, keeping close to the walls. From one side of the window, he looked out at the garden. He was proud of it. It had cost him twenty thousand pounds – cash to friends of friends – to get a new lawn laid, design and build the fishpond and stock it with the carp that kept dying, install the fountain – a classically naked woman spouting out of her mouth – and create the paved area by the house with the built-in barbecue.

It was not particularly large, no garden was in this street, but Roger liked it. He liked to sit out on a Sunday, with his girls and Maggie, having a barbecue while the fountain gently splashed in the background. Maggie did the preparation, he did the cooking. Nothing elaborate but it was nice. He liked being among his family in his garden on a Sunday. It was what he worked for.

He flexed his hand around the gun in his pocket. From this height he could see into the neighbours' gardens as well. Nothing moved. Whatever it was, it was not in the garden. He went back onto the landing. He could not get rid of the feeling that something was seriously wrong.

He decided to go downstairs. He moved with the same wary deliberation, carefully stopping every other step to listen with imperturbable concentration. Only when he was certain that nothing was moving did he go down another two steps.

The house was still. At the bottom of the steps he stopped again. The thick carpet would deaden foot-steps. He would have to listen for the other indistinct sounds of human beings on the move. He would have to pick up the almost imperceptible clues to the presence of another, the slightest warming of the air by their body temperature, the merest whisper of breath being exhaled, the sound of their thinking, the smell of their fear. Roger thought no-one would break into a house, his house, without at least contemplating the prospect of it going wrong, perhaps badly wrong. They would have to give something away. He shifted the gun in his pocket.

He went into the lounge. All the windows were intact. Nobody had got in that way. Keeping his finger round the trigger and angling the gun so it pointed out away from him in his pocket, he moved swiftly round the room, casting a rapid eye behind each piece of furniture in turn, the chairs, the sofa – all covered in pink leather – his black leather lounger, checking methodically.

Nothing. He went into the kitchen. Nothing. He went into the dining room and stood there, listening. The house was silent, still.

Then he heard it. There was no doubt, no straining to work out whether it really was something or just an overheated imagination suggesting it was something. He heard it. He definitely heard it. Someone was coming up the front path.

In two seconds, Roger was by the front door, the gun out of his pocket. He waited, every nerve in his body electrically alert. The footsteps were coming closer. Whoever it was, they were making no attempt to conceal their approach. Cocky bastards, Roger thought, and he eased off the safety catch.

The footsteps stopped by the door. Roger felt the first twinge of panic. They were obviously extremely confident. Were they just stupid or did they know something? Perhaps they were coming in from the back as well? He tensed.

There was silence for a moment. Roger waited. Then there was a noise outside the front door. He trained the gun at the door at head height so as to be able to take them straight out.

The letterbox was poked open and through it came the Sunday papers. The footsteps retreated down the path and were gone. Everything was silent once more.

Relief surged through his body. He put the gun slowly back in his pocket and for the first time in ten minutes took his hand off it. He felt drained. He picked up the papers off the mat and went into the kitchen.

He put the papers on the table and sat down. Perhaps his instincts were getting rusty, he thought. Perhaps he needed a holiday. Perhaps he should take off for Hawaii in six months and not wait the full year. All that over the paperboy. He ran his hands through his hair. He still could not shake off this feeling that something was wrong, but the house was still, nothing was moving, early sunlight was beginning to dapple the garden, the papers sat on the table. A typical Sunday. He needed a cup of tea.

He didn't feel like waiting till Maggie got up. He boiled the kettle and then stood waiting by the breakfast bar while the tea brewed to the strength he liked.

He took the cup to the table and sat down. He took his first sip. The tea was hot and strong and sweet.

He needed this. He picked up the *News of the World* and read the sports news. This is why he bought it. Not much happening.

He picked up the *Observer* and skimmed the front page. He took another sip of tea. Lovely. He turned to the business news. BMW rescue plan for Rover. More arguments about the Millennium Bug. He had read somewhere that thousands of small business were going to go bust because they had not got their computers ready for the Millennium. Not his. Not University Books. None of the real business was on the computer.

He turned back to the main paper and glanced at pages two and three, and turned the page. It was there on page five. Not a huge story, but big enough. His early morning instinct had not been mistaken. There was something wrong. Very wrong.

forty-six

monday 7.45 a.m.

They came for him the next day. Roger's office block
had a small underground car park. As he got out of
his car on Monday morning, the two cousins appeared
beside him. He had last seen them in the basement
with Jason.

'Hello, Roger,' said the older one. 'George would
like a word.'

Roger had been expecting it. The Crasks would not
have appreciated the article in the *Observer*.

'It's the car at the end of the row,' said the younger
one. 'The BMW. Get in the back. It's open. Lie down
and put the rug over you.'

It couldn't be a hit, Roger thought. Not like this.

He locked his car and walked down to the BMW.
He was not sure what the point was but there was no
point in not doing it. The cousins stayed where they
were. He could feel them watching him. He got into
the back seat and put the rug there over him, as he
had been told. He couldn't see the point but he had
been told to do it, so he did it. He waited.

Although experience and common sense told him
he was only going for a chat, he still felt nervous. You

never knew with the Crasks. They could have decided he was too much of an embarrassment. But then again the newspaper piece on its own couldn't have persuaded them of that. Not yet. They could have decided to hurt him a bit to encourage him to be more careful but they couldn't have thought he needed encouraging about this. But you never knew with the Crasks. And George was strange. Roger always found him so. You never knew with George.

The car was warm and it was stifling under the blanket, but Roger did not move. After a few minutes, someone got into the car and started the engine. It could have been the cousins. It could have been someone different.

The car moved off. The air-conditioning started and Roger began to feel more comfortable. They seemed to be moving through traffic because the car kept stopping and starting. Inside the car, it was silent. No-one spoke. Roger could not work out how long the journey was taking and he did not try. He waited to see George, huddled under the rug in the back.

Eventually, the car stopped. 'We're here,' someone said. 'Get out.' Roger sat up, emerging from the rug. He placed it on the seat and got out. The driver was already standing by the door. A very tall, thin man with a long nose and shaving cuts, he stood there, unsmiling, waiting for him. Roger had never seen him before.

'In here,' the man said.

They were in a busy shopping street. Roger did not recognise it. It could have been anywhere in London.

The car had parked outside a narrow doorway over which there was a brown awning with a gold fringe. It was sandwiched between a betting shop and a rundown Costcutters minimart.

The door had a brass plate set into it at head height. 'Private Club' it said. 'Members Only'.

The door led straight into a cell-like lobby with another door. Cameras were set into the ceiling. The tall, thin man pressed a buzzer and spoke into a grille beside it. 'It's us,' he said. There was a buzz and he pushed the door open. 'In here,' he said.

There was another lobby with a cloakroom off it, and a full-length security screening device which looked as if it had been removed from an airport. Roger walked through it. There was no choice. In front of him, there was another door.

'In here,' said the tall man.

They were in a thickly carpeted large room with no windows and warm lighting. The club was for gambling. There were tables covered in green baize, a roulette wheel and security cameras everywhere. At the back of the room was a bar. There was nothing on the walls. It was clearly not intended for the casual, speculative punter.

'In here,' said the tall, thin man, and pressed against a blank expanse of wall. A concealed door opened and led through to another smaller, windowless room. A man in thick glasses was sitting at a table covered in tidy piles of banknotes. He was counting them. At another table, watching him, was George Crask.

'Hello, Roger,' he said. 'Good of you to c-come.'

He spoke with a slight stutter. Roger knew that it was a sign of agitation. He was always very careful when he heard it.

'Hello, George,' Roger said. 'Good to see you again.' The man counting the banknotes got up and left the room with the tall, thin man. Roger was alone with George Crask. A newspaper lay on the table in front of him. Roger supposed it was the *Observer*.

'You've seen the p-paper?'

Roger nodded. This was not the moment for him to say anything.

'I'm not very happy. None of us are very happy,' said George Crask. He was the oldest brother, nearly fifty. He was the shortest of them and plump. His round face was jowly with good living and his eyes twinkled from general contentment with his lot. He looked like a television conjurer from the 1950s. He ran the operation. The other brothers did the physical work and they decided the big things together – they were a close family, the Crasks – but George ran it.

The Crasks operated a cold-eyed business. That was down to George, even though he never did the work personally. Everybody knew that. Roger had not met him very often. He had much more to do with the other two brothers. You only saw George when it was serious. When he first started working with the Crasks, it was George he saw first. It was George with whom he conducted the negotiations and did the deal. They had got on well then. The negotiations had been swift and efficient. They saw business the same way.

But Roger knew it was also George who decided when to take out competition, and how and when to expand, and how and when to act to protect their position. It was the unpredictable savagery of those decisions that made the Crasks so respected. And Roger knew that it was George who managed the business to keep the police away.

'This is not a good story for us, Roger,' George said sadly. He looked at the newspaper: '"University in grip of drug ring",' he quoted. '"Students spending up to five hundred pounds a week on cocaine . . . organised crime . . . overdose, prostitution" and so on and on. "We take these allegations very seriously, said a spokesperson . . . we are calling in the police".' George Crask shook his head sorrowfully. '"Calling in the police",' he repeated. He stared at Roger, straight in the eye. 'What happened, Roger? Who did this?'

Despite himself, Roger felt he was being accused and asked to deny his culpability. But he knew how important this first answer would be. The truth could be fatal. If he simply said he did not have a clue who had done this or how they had found out all the information, and if he swore it was nothing to do with him, this would be true but it might turn out to be a lethal candour. It might assert his innocence but it would also demonstrate his incompetence, revealing to George Crask that he was not in control. And that was all George Crask cared about. Someone not in control was dangerous. And George Crask did not believe in leaving danger alone to breed more danger.

'I have a good idea,' Roger said with meaning and menace. Without opening himself up to further interrogation, he hoped that would be sufficient to reassure George Crask. If he felt their operation was compromised by Roger, he would just remove Roger. Roger knew that.

'I hope so, Roger. I do hope so,' said George Crask mildly. 'And I hope you know how to deal with it?'

Roger nodded, more assured now. He had got through the most dangerous part of the interview. George had clearly been reassured that he was in control.

'I expect you to be careful about this, Roger.' George Crask's tone was suddenly icy. 'This is a national newspaper, not some pimply kid straight out of c-college trying to make a name for themselves on some local free-sheet. These aren't some t-toerags no-one cares about. These are important people's k-kids. Look at them.' He gestured scornfully at the paper. 'You can't treat them the same way.' He sounded regretful, although Roger could not tell if that was only for his benefit. 'The p-police will be crawling all over the place.' He stared at Roger intently. 'I don't want any more attention, Roger.'

Roger understood. This was now the dangerous part of the interview.

'This has got to be dealt with – but very c-c-carefully. I know you understand that. But however you do it, Roger, get a grip.'

Roger nodded. He was not sure he could speak at that moment.

'Do you need any help?' George Crask asked in a benevolent tone. Roger could feel his heart tightening. Now this really was the dangerous part of the interview. George Crask might be genuine and trying to help. Or he might be testing Roger. If he took the help, the Crasks could learn how little he actually knew about what was going on and might come to the conclusion that he was not sufficiently in control to be allowed to continue. And if he didn't take the Crasks' help, the situation could continue to fall apart. Disastrously. It was a conundrum. It all depended on how genuine George Crask was being with the offer. And you never knew with the Crasks.

'I'm all right, George,' he said.

'I hope so,' George said coldly. 'This is bad news, Roger. It has got to be stopped. Now.'

Roger nodded. 'I know.' He did know. He knew he had a serious problem. George Crask had just made it clear how serious. 'I'll deal with it, George,' he said.

George Crask looked at him. 'I know you'll t-t-try, Roger,' he said. He kept looking at him as if he was trying to make up his mind about something. 'We've done good business together over the last few years. We've understood each other. I would hate anything to interfere with that, Roger. Now, Dave will take you back.'

George Crask did not get up or shake hands. Sometimes he did. Sometimes he didn't. You never knew with the Crasks.

forty-seven

monday 10.30 a.m.
'Why didn't you pay him?'

'You weren't there. You don't know how awful he was.' Virginia sat in Francis's office, a coquettish mix of defiant and contrite. She ran her hand through her hair. 'And when it came to it, I didn't see why we should pay it. I turned up intending to pay him, honestly, Francis, but he was so obstreperous. And charging interest – six thousand pounds, just because I paid him on Friday instead of a Tuesday. It's just testosterone. Why should we give in to it?'

Francis sighed. 'Because it's very dangerous not to.'

'Don't sigh at me. He thinks he can jerk us around any way he wants. Well, he can't. It takes me a year of hard labour to get that much money and then I have to pay tax on it. Do you think he does?'

Francis felt the collar of his shirt tight against his neck. Virginia could be such hard work, but he had noticed her use of the collective pronoun.

'That's not the point,' he said mildly. 'There is no point sitting in judgement. As you so often tell me. We have a choice, as you have pointed out. We can pay him. Or we can not pay him. We agreed that we should pay him. And move on. I don't like paying this man more money any more than you do. But I'd rather pay him and hope this really will be the end than not pay him and have him turn up whenever he feels like threatening me.'

'Do you really think it is so simple? You can just say goodbye? It will all just go away?'

Francis recognised the process. Having adopted a position instinctively, Virginia would then dig in, deploying every conceivable argument to entrench herself.

'Virginia, please. I'll transfer the extra money immediately. Please just pay him.'

'I don't think we should. We should draw a line in the sand.'

'I don't want to draw a line in the sand. I want to pay him. It's my money. I am giving it to you. Please pay him.'

'I do not want to see this man again. I told him to fuck off when he asked for more money and I meant it. He can just fuck off.'

'Virginia, please, just pay him.'

'I don't want to pay him. I told him to fuck off. I meant it.'

'Virginia, please. This is just testosterone. Please don't decide what you are going to do on the basis of the fact that you told him to fuck off.'

'I'm not.'

'Virginia, please. I am asking you. All you have to do is give it all to him. Please? We agreed you would do it. This is difficult for me. This is all you have to do. Please?'

'What do you think will happen if I do? He'll just come back for more. Wouldn't you? If you lucked out with an easy touch like us? What would you do if you hit the spot with a couple of pathetic creatures, with more money than sense – at least, you have – who are so terrified that all you have to do is cough and spit and up comes another six thousand pounds? It takes me nearly three months to earn that. Before tax. So why wouldn't he just come back for more? And more? And more again? So before you railroad me like this why don't you just think what would happen if we just pay up?'

'Why don't you think what will happen if we don't pay up? Just think about that.' Francis was cross. Virginia could see that.

'I have thought about it.'

'Virginia, please.'

'You keep saying that. Please what?'

'This is not a game, Virginia. This is dangerous now. I know what it is like to be beaten up and I do not want to go through that again. Or worse.'

She looked at him.

'Let's get this behind us,' he said. 'Just pay him and it's over.'

'I'm not so sure,' she said. But she thought of how that horrible little man must have felt when he read the newspapers yesterday. She had done for him and it had been so easy. One phone call to that helpful friend of Alex and thirty six hours later, there it was.

Page five in the *Observer*. And it still felt so good that she thought she might now be able to relent on Francis.

'Look, Virginia, the longer we delay the more dangerous it becomes. We don't know what these people will do. The only good thing is that James is now out of harm's way.'

She looked away. 'I'll do what's needed,' she said.

Joanne knocked on the door. 'There's a call from Jonathan Miles,' she said.

'I had better take this,' Francis said. 'But please, Virginia,' he said before he picked up the phone 'Let's get this over. Just pay him and finish it.' Virginia was getting up to go but he did not want her to leave yet. They had to finish this off. 'Virginia, please. Wait a minute. I will just take this call. It won't take long.' Jonathan Miles never took long.

'No, Francis. I won't wait. You take all the time you need. Don't worry about me. I'll do what's needed.'

As he turned to pick up the phone, Francis watched her sweep out. 'I'll call you later,' he said to her retreating back.

At least James was safely out of the way.

forty-eight

monday 11.30 a.m.

The cigar was not working. Roger had smoked it down to the band and placed it carefully in the Carrara marble ashtray and it had smouldered its way out, and still nothing occurred to him. It did not make sense. Why would anyone do this? Who could benefit from putting all this in the newspapers?

The whole point of the business was to keep it away from heat, yet here was someone deliberately turning it up. Deliberately. Why would anyone do that? If they wanted to take it over, then why would they try to do that by destroying it first? To Roger's way of thinking, it did not make sense. He could understand it if someone had tried to kill him, but why kill the business?

He had been turning it over and over in his mind for the last twenty-four hours but no answers emerged. Nothing had worked, none of his comforting routines. This morning he had got up and shaved as usual, looking at himself in the smoked mirror, muddy-blond Rogers echoing through the chocolate marble bathroom. Nothing. His breakfast had been on the table as usual, with the silver coffee-pot, the toast, the bacon and perfectly poached egg. Still nothing. The view from his office window, the cars crawling by outside in the summer fug, the air-conditioning soothing him, the cigar, the second cigar. Nothing. Nothing. And still nothing. Why would anyone do this to him?

He got up and stood by the window. He had to do something. He knew that. Nothing was not an option. George Crask had made that clear. He had to get a grip, otherwise the Crasks would cut him loose. And Roger knew there was not much he could do if they really decided he was more trouble than he was worth. He reckoned they would not want to create more heat than necessary. But you never knew what they might do if the situation got out of hand. Further out of hand. You never knew with the Crasks.

And, quite apart from the Crasks, doing nothing would make him look weak. Pathetic. Have his business attacked like this and do nothing? Not possible. As soon as he looked weak, that little prick Chris would be all over him. Nothing was not possible. He had get this dealt with. He knew what to do. But he did not know who to do it to. That was the problem.

Roger stared out of the window. Why would anyone do this? It did not make sense. He tilted back in the big leather chair. It had cost him fifteen hundred pounds. No-one else knew that. Even those few people who came to his office would not have guessed it cost that much. It just looked like another big leather chair. They could not see the special hydraulic suspension or feel the softness of the leather. But Roger knew.

He felt it. You have earned this, it said to him. You deserve it.

Roger sighed. Twenty-four hours later he was no further forward than he had been when he first saw George Crask looking at page five in the *Observer*. And he knew he needed to get further forward soon. He needed to get a grip. But he knew nothing. So perhaps he should start by getting to know something. First things first. One step at a time. The Long March had started with a single step. But where should he start?

Roger felt something beginning to flow now, at last. He took another Romeo y Julieta out from the humidor on his desk. That had been a big step forward when he bought the humidor. They were essential to keep the cigars in tip-top condition. You could not really appreciate a cigar fully unless it had been kept in tip-top condition. In a humidor. He puffed reflectively on the cigar.

The simplest place to start was at the beginning. To Roger's way of thinking. And to Mao Zedong's way of thinking. Roger drew again on the cigar and looked out of the window at the cars crawling by. The place to start was with the newspaper. That fucking piece in the newspaper. And the place to start there was with the little prick who had written it. Or, more precisely, with the little prick who had given that little prick of a reporter the information to write it. That was where to start. And who could that have been?

Roger stared out of the window. When you thought about it, there were lots of people who could have supplied the information. There was no point in trying to guess. You had to know. You had to find out for certain who had given up the information. How to do that?

Roger placed the cigar carefully in the ashtray. It was beginning to make him feel sick. It was his third today. There must be some way he could find out who had supplied the information. Out of weakness, strength. That was what they said. Mao Zedong probably said it. He probably said most things in that Little Red Book of his.

Out of weakness, strength. What was his weakness? He did not know who the fuck was doing this to him. That was a weakness to start with.

Roger picked up the cigar butt and rolled it between his fingers. On the Long March, Mao Zedong would have had worse days than this. Regularly. Sleeping in ditches, seeing his comrades picked off day after day by the forces of Generalissimo Chiang Kai-Shek armed with state-of-the-art anti-Mao weapons, not to mention murderous, thieving peasants. He probably ate insects and drank rice-water from the paddy fields and he never relaxed. If something was bad, he probably still asked if it could get worse. That was how he got to become Chairman of the Peoples' Republic and abolish mosquitoes and sparrows from China.

What else?

Roger knew someone was trying to do him in. That was also a weakness but relatively unimportant. It was inevitable that, from time to time, someone would try to do him in. If they could.

What else?

No. That was it. If they could. Yes. Got it. They were able to do him in. That was a very important second weakness. Someone trying to do him in would not matter, if they could not actually do him in. But this little prick, whoever it was, had found a way. It was clever going to the *Observer*. Roger acknowledged that. The little prick, whoever it was, had found a weakness. No doubt about that.

Light flooded into the dark corners of his brain. His weakness came from his strength. His strong point had always been his market. These stuck-up little pricks in college. Who always paid up or could be easily persuaded to pay up because they did not want the publicity. And that was because they were important. And because they were important college students, it was a story for the *Observer*. How often would they run a story like this about Moss Side?

That was where he was vulnerable, but – and this was Roger's inspiration – from his weakness came strength. Because these stuck-up little pricks in college were important, two things followed.

First, some of his clients were connected. That was what happened when you went to college like these little pricks. You got connected. And some of them would be connected with the media. And one of them would connect him into some little prick or other who would know who had done this to him.

And then, secondly, because they had something to lose, it would not be very difficult to persuade them to give him the name. Out of weakness, strength. Yin and yang. Mao would have understood. Chairman Mao would have been proud of him.

Roger stood up. Got it. That little prick, whoever he was, might have thought he was clever using Roger's strength as a weakness. But he had not reckoned on Roger using that weakness as a strength. Fuck you, you little prick.

Now all he had to do was get to work. It was eleven forty-five. He made a phone call. He pointed out some salient facts. At half past twelve he was standing in the piazza at Canary Wharf talking to a tall young man with wavy black hair in a cream suit and beige shirt and primrose tie. Five minutes later he was on his own again and talking on his mobile phone. At a quarter past one, a slight young woman with short, straw-coloured hair and protruding eyes approached where he sat looking at the water. She did not stay long, but as she left, Roger made another call on his mobile phone. And then another one.

At six o'clock he was waiting outside a terraced house in a narrow street near the British Museum. Tourists brushed past him as he looked into the window of a shop selling antique music-scores. At half past six he was still there. He was still looking at expensive parchment in the window. No-one took any notice of him, a dapper blond in a silver-grey suit and a cream shirt and a soft grey tie.

At a quarter to seven, a stocky, bullet-headed young man with small rectangular steel glasses, in a rumpled suit and an open-necked shirt without a tie, came out of the terraced house. He started down the street without noticing Roger. Then he did. He couldn't not notice him as Roger was beside him and imperceptibly edging him against the tall walls of the narrow street. Within three steps he had been forced to stop. He appeared to be disconcerted about this but Roger did not raise his voice.

A column of Japanese tourists walked around them, stepping politely off the pavement into the road apparently without noticing them. Roger and the young man continued their conversation. An elderly couple brushed irritably past them. The young man looked agitated and shifty. The expression on Roger's face did not change. They talked some more. The young man was not happy. They talked further.

Finally, at seven o'clock, Roger took a small leather-bound notebook from a pocket inside his suit and wrote something in it. He said something to the young man and walked back towards the British Museum. The young man did not move for a moment. He took a deep breath and pulled off his glasses. He tugged his shirt out of his trousers and polished his glasses with it. He then walked off in the opposite direction from Roger.

Roger bought an ice-cream from a van outside the British Museum as the traffic crawled past in the evening heat. From weakness, strength. Now he knew what he had needed to know. The question was what to do about it now. He took a slurp of his rich vanilla ice-cream. It was delicious.

He was getting his grip back. And he could see how to show that to the Crasks. And to that little prick

Chris. As Mao Zedong had said: power grows out of the barrel of a gun. And now, with that in mind, an example must be made. As Edmund Burke said: example is the school of mankind and they will learn at no other. He had read that in a spectacularly ill-selling Spanish language textbook on eighteenth-century British politics from Bolivar University in Bogota.

The next question was who should be the example? Those responsible must now take the consequences of their actions. But where did responsibility lie? He now knew who had put the story in the papers, but was that the extent of responsibility? And what was the best way of getting all the messages across? He needed to send two messages: one to the Crasks and the other to that little prick.

Roger put the remnants of the cornet and the ice-cream in his mouth. It had been delicious.

What about using that boy lawyer to send the message? He had created the problem in the first place. He was responsible. Making an example of him would show the Crasks he had taken a grip on things again. And because he was Chris's connection, it would also drive the same message home to that prick. So maybe he should start with the little pimple who owed him thirty thousand pounds? And interest. He knew where he lived. And where he worked.

Roger started to walk with his measured, regular pace. He had taken the new first step on his Long March. And he was now moving firmly forwards.

forty-nine

tuesday 8.00 a.m.

Prendergast, Markby and Matthews was deserted. Not even Miranda Evans was hunched over her terminal, chewing her fingernails through another brief. The cleaners had gone, leaving the open-plan offices preternaturally calm, the new plastic-bags in the waste-paper bins poised for the daily dumping of screwed-up drafts and Mars Bar wrappers. The computers in the partners' offices waited silently to come alive under the sensitive tutelage of a hundred middle-aged fingers caressing fees out of thin air.

The silence was expectant. These offices knew what was about to happen. This was the still noiselessness before the air-conditioning was switched on at eight thirty. And then the arrival of lawyers.

But now, before any of that, into this mute calm, came first of all the workers, and, for the first time ever, James Carroll.

Who should have been in Paris or Rome, shagging his way through his father's fifteen hundred pounds. Or in Amsterdam smoking himself into a stupor. Who should have been somewhere away from all this until his mum and dad had sorted it all out. But who now came first of all the workers into the offices of Prendergast, Markby and Matthews, carrying an untidy bundle of papers on which he had been working all last night.

James Carroll had a meeting with Raymond Chivers. And he could not let a client down.

He put the papers down on the desk in his office and went to turn on the coffee machine. He just had time to go through the papers once more before Raymond Chivers arrived. And he had an idea he wanted to test out.

Half an hour later, Miranda Evans walked in.

'Hello,' she said. 'You're early.'

'Yes,' he replied, scrolling intently through the case report up on his screen.

'Busy?' she asked.

'Yes,' he said, without looking up.

'Oh.' She sat down and turned on her computer.

At nine o'clock, Katie rang. 'Your client's here.' There was no amusement in her voice this morning.

'I didn't see you come in,' she said as he came out into the reception area.

'Yes, well,' James said, 'that's because I was in before you.'

'So you should be,' she said. 'You get paid more than me.'

'That's because I am worth more.'

Katie laughed. 'I am sure it helps you to believe that,' she said. 'He's in Barnet.'

James could smell him as he walked through the door. A stale odour clung around Raymond Chivers, barely masked by a heavy, spicy aftershave. He was sitting at the conference table leafing through his papers.

'Good morning,' James said.

'Good morning, James,' Raymond Chivers replied, without looking up. 'I'll just be a minute. I am trying to find my notes.'

James sat down opposite him. 'Can I get you a coffee?' he asked.

'No, no. I'll just be a minute.' Like a densely furred forest animal snuffling among the roots for insects, Raymond Chivers foraged through his papers.

'I took some notes,' he said, almost to himself. 'I know they are here somewhere.'

James watched him. Even at this early hour, his skin had a waxy sheen of sweat.

'Here. Here it is.' Raymond Chivers pulled out a sheet of paper covered in handwriting. 'I went round my parents' friends and asked them what they remembered. And it was what you might call a fruitful exercise.'

A self-satisfied smile curved his plump lips. It was a rare moment of calm surfacing from the nervy, fidgeting agitation in which Raymond Chivers lived his days. 'I think the most promising is Auntie Freda. She's not actually an aunt but she lived next door and she was a great friend of Mum's. She will swear an affidavit that Mum wanted the money to come to me. And she would have been appalled if she had known Dad was going to leave it all to that woman.'

James discreetly opened his file and glanced at the top page while he nodded as Raymond Chivers spoke.

'That's very helpful,' he said encouragingly. 'But I am afraid it may not do the trick on its own. We really need to show an express agreement between your mum and dad not to revoke the wills.'

Raymond Chivers's face flushed with ill temper. 'What do you mean?' he said. 'I spent a lot of time getting this together.'

'It's very helpful,' James said quickly. 'But a court won't necessarily find it conclusive.' As he spoke, he heard echoes of Evans in his words. He had obviously absorbed more in those interminable meetings than he had realised. 'But there's enough here to make a case plausible. Perhaps what we should be thinking about is opening negotiations.'

He had been thinking about this over the last three days. How to find a commercial way to deal with this. His father had said that to him when he first joined Prendergast's. 'Always remember this when you advise your clients,' Francis had said, forgetting James was the lowliest of solicitors and was hardly going to be allowed anywhere near advising clients. 'They will want the best. But your job is to get them to accept the best they can get. Take a commercial approach. The best is the enemy of the good.'

'If you were prepared to do a deal with your dad's second wife, this would be helpful in persuading her to settle. What do you think of trying to do a deal?'

Raymond Chivers was silent. James could see his professional experience wrestling with his emotions.

'Yes,' he said eventually. 'I suppose you are right. It's not the money. It's the principle. And I suppose it's right she should have something. Why don't you open discussions with her lawyer.'

'How much would you be prepared to accept?' James asked.

'Go and see what they offer and then we'll start talking.' The professional was now in control of Raymond Chivers.

'I'll get right on to it,' James said. This would be his first negotiation. And Raymond Chivers had not even suggested that Evans should do it. 'Let's see what they start off with.' He had heard Evans say that too.

'Thank you, James,' Raymond Chivers said, and held out his hand.

As he walked back to his office, James thought about how he would open the negotiation. 'My client has asked me,' he would start. And then, after protracted discussions, he would deliver for Raymond Chivers more money than he could ever have realistically hoped to get.

James felt the glow of achievement he usually felt when he thought up a new documentary series. He was getting to be seriously good at this.

And then it came to him.

This could be the way out of his problem. Negotiation. At which he was proving himself so adept. Doing a deal. Not the wild solution his mother was proposing. Which was illegal. And, as his father had pointed out, that meant trouble. No, that was not the way. Negotiation was the answer. And he could do it himself. And get himself out of trouble.

fifty

tuesday 10.30 a.m.

It had needed to be somewhere busy enough to allow him to slip away unnoticed but not somewhere so busy people would get in his way. Roger had only been halfway through his first cigar when he sorted it out.

He had never liked getting too close to brand maintenance. But this time he wanted to do it himself. And he had given a lot of thought to the method. He had considered carefully the merits of cutting the brake cable. It had much to recommend it. It was impossible to trace – if you were careful – but it was also unreliable. It could just end up as a parking accident, one car scraping another, just another episode of life in the city. He would keep that one for another time.

For this one, when it came down to it, Roger had concluded, there was no substitute for a drive-by shooting. With a twist. It had been a satisfying morning's work sorting out all the details. Fulfilling. And now he was ready, observing, waiting for the moment.

Virginia and Julie stood and watched the young

girls shopping in St Christopher's Place, as up and down they walked, laughing, gorgeous in the sunshine.

Julie said: 'The way I see it there's not much point in men any more.'

Virginia remembered the time she had bloomed like these young women. Those years had just slipped away without her noticing. And now here she was, a mother fighting for her baby, among all these golden girls, even younger than James, in their prime before heartache and childbirth and heartbreak and regret. And drifting among them, linking past and future, a faint autumnal scent of time passing. 'They have got their uses,' she said.

'What?' Julie said. 'Money? We can work. Babies? We can clone them. And even if we can't, we only need the sperm. Why do we have to take the man as well?'

'If only it were so simple,' Virginia said. Why had she given in to Francis? When she walked out of his office, she was not going to. She was going to make that horrible little man sweat. The *Observer* article must be causing him real grief and with any luck the police would already be after him. And there must be other ways she could tighten the screws on him.

But then, as she waited for a bus outside, she suddenly felt exhausted. Why did she always resist everything Francis said? Even when he was obviously right? It was obviously best to pay off the man and get James out of this mess. He was her baby and he needed her to protect him. And standing in the grimy, humid street outside Silvergate House, Virginia realised that that was what she now had to do. Francis was right. She would make the pay-off. And she should just about be able to fit it into her lunch hour.

'They keep us warm at night,' she said to Julie. 'Sometimes.'

Two girls floated by, carrying large red carrier-bags, one small and dark in a white shift with huge almond eyes, the other with a tousled mane of honey-coloured hair, in a pair of beige suede trousers. She was smoking as she walked.

'Convince me,' Julie said.

Sweet these girls may be, but it was the sweetness of decay, Virginia thought. Eighteen was a selfish, muddled age, hormones jumbling that strange, unsettling sense of power over men and a yearning for love. She had not been happy then. She was glad she had asked Julie to keep her company. Even though he could not possibly know what she had done to him, she still felt deeply uneasy about seeing that horrible little man again after last Friday in Paddington.

'You can't, can you?' Julie said. 'You're really just a sentimental old bitch.'

Roger was poised. This was the moment when thought became act. Thought without action was a fog of unrealised dreams. Nothing. Action without thought was the twitch of a muscle, a spasm in space which left no mark. Meaningless. Poised between the ethereal and the animal, Roger was ready, focusing his energies into one point to punch on through.

He had a silk balaclava tucked under his chin and

his baseball cap, with its long, broad peak, shadowed his face, and his collar was folded up. He was as anonymous as it was possible to be without drawing attention to himself. When it was time, he would pull up the balaclava and no-one would be able to make out anything about him at all. In the meantime, no-one noticed him, a slight figure in a baggy linen jacket, with his hands thrust into the deep pockets, sitting slouched in a chair outside a coffee house.

As he watched his target through the strolling crowds, he kept his hand on the Walther. It had never been used. It was clean. It was fitting that this was its first time. It was Roger's first time too. Man and machine were fused in history and purpose.

Virginia basked in the mid-morning warmth, leaning against a bollard. While Julie developed her thesis about the redundancy of men, Virginia closed her eyes and tilted her face to the urban sun. The money was in her bag. Surrender was indigestible but this would be it. The last time.

Roger smiled to himself. The edgy blonde thought she was clever, setting him up once already and thinking now she could do it again. He felt the Walther in his pocket. She did not know he knew it was her. It was always a mistake to come sniffing back over the same ground. She should have left it alone.

She should not have rung him. It was her voice that had sealed it. That condescending, demanding edge. No wonder the banker had dumped her.

'I'll give you the money,' she had said. 'Where do you want to collect it?'

He was astonished to hear that voice again. He had assumed she would hide away. And did she really think he would believe her that she was going to pay him the money? After giving him up to the papers? She must think he was really stupid.

Then he had remembered she could not know he knew it had been her. How could she possibly know that he knew? And then he had realised how convenient she had made it. Instead of having to seek her out, she had come to him. How much easier it was going to be now.

And so her call had finally persuaded him that the example was to be made of Virginia. That boy lawyer had had a lucky escape.

Virginia looked at her watch. She had been early and now the ghastly little man was late. She adjusted her position on the bollard.

'And who would miss all that shoving and grinding?' Julie said.

'It's not always like that.' Virginia smiled drowsily in the sunshine.

'No,' Julie said. 'Not always. But often.'

This was the moment. Roger could feel the forces gathering in him, flowing together. She must have thought he was an idiot to try to set him up again. He stared at her stretching in the sun. There was an animal litheness in her which stirred him briefly. He

354

watched her. There was a tiny blonde woman talking to her. She had not stopped talking all the time Roger had been watching them, moving her hands around. Chat, chat, chat.

What was she there for? Was she a photographer? Or a decoy, with a photographer perched at the end of a long lens at one of the windows overlooking the street. No matter. They would not get much of a picture of him from above. Not with his cap on. And it would be so quick she would not get in the way.

In one continuing movement, he got up from the chair and pulled the balaclava up over his face and strode forward towards Virginia, through the crowds, seven, eight, nine paces and then he pulled the Walther out of his pocket and pointed it directly at Virginia.

As he did so, Julie made an emphatic gesture with her hand. And it knocked Roger as he straightened his arm.

'Whoops, sorry,' Julie said, turning round. The gun went off into the air with a puttering sigh. No-one noticed. An upper window looking down on the street cracked. People went on strolling up and down the street.

Roger disappeared.

'Sorry,' Julie said again, just as a scream came from the office on the upper floor overlooking the street. 'What was that?' Julie said. People now stopped and looked up. No-one appeared at the window. Virginia opened her eyes and looked up. Then a man opened the window carefully and looked out. He saw a small group of people looking up at him while around them continued to swirl the flow of shoppers and beauty. He did not see Roger. Roger had gone.

As soon as the gun had gone off, Roger put it back in his pocket and walked round the next corner. He wanted to fire it again. He wanted to fire the next shot at the little blonde, at close range. At that moment, he wanted her to suffer even more than Virginia. But he knew this would have to be a pleasure deferred. Even as he rounded the corner, he realised that the tiny woman with the bobbed blonde hair had had the luckiest day of her life and she did not even realise it. And she never would. He would never catch up with her. And Virginia would now have to wait for another day.

Roger pulled the balaclava back down under his chin and walked quickly on to Oxford Street and mingled with the seething throng of shoppers. He held on tightly to the Walther in his pocket. He would need it again.

He felt his heart pounding through his chest but no-one paid him any attention.

It had been a good plan. The walk-by shooting. A twist on the classic drive-by. It had been the right location. The police could stop cars and search them and the occupants, but there was no way that they could stop every shopper within a half-mile radius of Oxford Street, and Roger had reckoned he could get at least half a mile away from St Christopher's Place, walking steadily, without drawing attention to himself, by the time the police turned up.

It would have worked if it had not been for the bad luck of that midget blonde. Sometimes the dice rolled against you. But she had just used up all the good luck that was due to her for the rest of her life. And so had Virginia. And neither of them even realised it.

Virginia was still sitting on her bollard. But now she felt she needed its support. Two facts danced round in her mind. One: that a shot had been fired. The police were now swarming all over St Christopher's Place. Shortly after the man's face had appeared at the window, she heard sirens, and soon three vans had arrived one after the other, disgorging police who busily, efficiently started logging people's names and began laboriously taking statements.

Fact two was that the dapper little blond never turned up. At least, not before the shot was fired. Virginia felt sick. A connection between the two facts was swimming up to the surface of her mind. She was shaken and she was not yet quite sure why. Then she got it. He had turned up. He had fired the shot. At her. He had tried to kill her but missed and hit the upper window.

Virginia had never believed in coincidence but now she believed in luck. This was obviously her lucky day. Obviously she had just used up her summer's quota of good luck. She waited on her bollard for the police to get round to her. She felt sweaty now. Perhaps she had even used up her quota of good luck for the rest of her life. Why else would he have made all the arrangements so carefully and meticulously – he was such a careful and meticulous little man – and then not turned up? And then this shot was fired. It was too much of a coincidence.

But why would he want to kill her? He could not possibly have worked out that she had given him up to the *Observer*. How could he? She was going to pay him the money and that would have been an end to it. That was all he had wanted, wasn't it? The money? But still he had tried to kill her. Why?

Whatever the reason, he had tried to kill her. And missed. But he was still out there, waiting to try again. There could not be any other conclusion.

Virginia felt sick.

fifty-one

tuesday 2.15 p.m.

Roger was still seething. He took an envelope from his inside breast pocket and slid it across the coffee table to Davey Boswell. 'It's all in there,' he said.

Names and addresses. And ten thousand pounds. It was expensive. Top end of the market. But Davey was reliable. And available. He had come straight over when Roger had rung, giving Roger just enough time to stop off at the bank to take the cash out of his safe-deposit box before going on to the hotel. He couldn't waste any more time on this. If he was to stay cred-ible, he had to get a grip on the situation, and now. George Crask had made that clear. That edgy blonde would have to be dealt with before she did any more damage. Who knew where she would stop? He had not been mentioned in the article. Nor had the Crasks. But who knew whether this was the end of it? Perhaps she had more to give up? He could not take the risk. She had to be dealt with. He had tried himself but it had not worked. Bad luck. It would have saved him five grand if it had worked, but there it was, bad luck, and he could not waste any more time on it. Davey would have to do it.

And he still had not been paid his thirty grand, thirty-six grand with interest. The banker had been warned. Roger could not spend any more time on that either. If he was to stay credible, Davey would have to do him too. That would show that little tangerine prick Chris how to run a business and stay credible.

The blonde had to be done, no question about that, but Roger was still considering doing the boy lawyer instead of the banker. There was no point in doing both. It would be a waste of money as the message would be clear enough with one. Settle your debts or get done. Why pay Davey an extra five grand when you did not need to? Doing the boy would have advantages. It fitted the punishment more precisely to the crime as it was the boy who had taken the Scotty and not paid for it. And whacking the boy might just give the banker one last shove into paying up, so Roger could end up with his thirty grand after all. And the boy would be more persuasive to the banker than the ex-wife. Roger couldn't see any reason why the banker would be concerned about her.

But, on the other hand, when the police investigated it, linking Roger to the boy would be easier for them. The police would have to be inspired to link the banker back to Roger. Everyone hated bankers. It could be anyone. And even if they suspected anything, what could they prove? It would be much easier to prove a connection to the boy lawyer. Doing him would be riskier. Was it worth it to give the banker one last shove into paying up?

All these decisions.

He would rather have used the Crasks for the banker but it was all a bit too soon after Jason. And that fucking blonde had really damaged him with George Crask. No question about that. She was Roger's business now. No question. So, all things considered, Davey would have to do it all. And it would cost Roger ten grand but that was the ups and downs of business life.

It was getting complicated. No question about that. Other people were fucking him up. It never ceased to exasperate Roger how other people could never be relied upon to do the rational, sensible thing. They would always do the thing that fucked him up.

But he could handle it. Managing other people's determination to fuck him up was how he earned his money. He was good at this business of management. Dealing with it was his ticket to Honolulu. That was what those little pricks could not understand. This is how you did the business. Analyse. Decide. Act. ADA, as Roger liked to think of it. That was probably how they taught it at Harvard Business School. ADA. Fucking ADA.

He had analysed it. He had decided. And now Davey would act. It was expensive but Davey was worth it. The clean slate was worth it. Clearing the decks for Hawaii was worth it.

'How much, man?' Davey asked.

The beautiful waitress returned with Davey's green tea and Roger waited while she poured it for him into a white porcelain cup.

'Ten grand,' Roger said.

'Cool, man.' Davey sipped his tea. Roger watched his expression. It was blank. He must have known what the job entailed. He had his rate, he knew Roger knew the rate, and there was only one thing that paid him ten grand without any further explanation.

'Be careful,' Roger added. 'People will come looking for them.'

'It's cool, man.'

Roger was forty-two grand down on this – twelve grand in total to Davey and the thirty grand the banker and that lollipop lawyer son of his owed him. Forty-eight grand with the interest. The time had come to draw a line.

'Any deadline?' Davey asked.

'As soon as possible,' Roger replied. 'But be careful. Don't just do it. Do it right. Better right than quick.'

He knew he did not really need to say this to Davey. Davey had learnt how to be careful. Davey pulverised teeth and flushed them away. Davey had a Black & Decker sander to file off the fingerprints. Davey knew a farmer in Norfolk who let Davey feed the pigs. Davey was obsessively thorough. Davey had done it all for Roger before – three times – and no-one had even come round asking. Those three had gone and never been found. Roger knew he could rely on Davey and that is why he paid him his price. No haggling or delay. They trusted each other.

And this was not going to be the most difficult job Davey had ever done. It was going to be an easy ten grand.

Fuck it. Why was he agonising over who should get

whacked? For ten grand why couldn't Davey do all three?

'These two shouldn't be any problem,' Roger said. 'They won't be expecting it.'

'That's cool, man.'

Roger looked at him. He could see nothing behind the inscrutably affable eyes. 'There's another one as well,' he said carefully. 'He shouldn't be a problem either.'

'Cool.'

'What about throwing it in?'

'You mean for the same money?'

'Yes.'

'Same location?'

Roger considered his answer and then decided there was no point in spinning it. 'Probably not,' he said.

'Then that's another five grand, man.'

'Come on, man,' Roger said. 'This is the easiest ten grand you'll ever make.'

'I've got my rates, man,' Davey said. 'And there's travel time. And expenses.'

'Cut me some slack,' Roger said. 'Three for two. Why not?'

'Your choice, man,' Davey said, implacable. 'Ten grand for two. Fifteen grand for three.'

Fuck it. Why not? When he was sitting on his verandah at Kaanapali, five grand more or less would be irrelevant. And why get into unnecessary grief with Davey? He might as well get it all sorted out now. 'I haven't got it here,' he said. 'But I'll pay you the balance on confirmation. OK?'

'That's cool.'

Roger took out his Mont Blanc rollerball pen and wrote a name and address on the back of one of the hotel napkins. He handed it to Davey. 'That's the third one.'

'Do you want to know when?' Davey asked.

'Not on the phone. We'll meet here in five days. That should give you long enough.'

'Any complications?'

Roger shook his head. Davey put the envelope in his pocket.

'Yeah. Five days should do it, man. See you here on Sunday.'

Roger watched him as he loped off with another ten thousand pounds of his money. And five grand more to come. He needed Davey to clear the decks for a clean exit. Blonde cleared away. Banker and boy lawyer cleared away. That little prick Chris put back in his box. Problems sorted. Squeeze the last few hundred grand from University Books and then he'd be away. Another twelve months and he was gone, him and Maggie, gone American Airlines to Honolulu.

fifty-two

Rachel was back in the marble-floored, chrome and smoked-glass lavatory at the end of corridor, with her handbag and its contents, including the small, accurate, sensitive and cheap pregnancy test. This was now a daily event.

There was someone in one of the cubicles. She washed her hands carefully. They were taking a long time. She washed her hands again.

'Hello, Rachel.' It was Penny Warrender. Everywhere she turned nowadays there seemed to be a partner, a potential spy.

'Hello, Penny.'

'Are you well?'

What did she mean by that? Had Brendan been talking to her? 'I'm fine,' Rachel said. 'How are you?'

'Fine, fine,' Penny said. 'How are you getting along with the Ramsden case?'

Brendan had been talking to her. 'Fine, I think,' Rachel said. 'Yes. Fine.'

'Good, good,' Penny said. 'Good luck.' And at last Rachel was alone.

She opened her handbag and took it out, the small,

accurate, sensitive and cheap test. Be there human chorionic gonadotrophin. Be there two pink lines. Be there little baby in me.

She counted to sixty. Come on. Come on, please come on. Two lines. Two pink lines. Yes. Please. Yes. Thank you. Wait. She counted to a hundred. Nothing changed. Still two pink lines. What did the leaflet say? She rummaged in her bag with her free hand. Yes. Two pink lines in the window indicates a strong possibility that you are pregnant. Yes. Yes. I am pregnant. There is a strong possibility that I am pregnant. Yes, I am. Yes. Thank you. Yes. Yes. Oh thank you.

Francis was going to be so thrilled. How could he ever lose interest in her now she was carrying his baby? She went back to her office to ring him. Yes, there is a strong possibility that I am pregnant. A strong possibility. But hold on. Only a possibility. Not a certainty. Perhaps it's a mistake. It may be a small and sensitive test but it is also cheap. Maybe it is not always accurate? She sat down in her office and looked out at the side of the building. She should not ring Francis until it was certain. It could be a bad mistake to get him all wound up when it might not even be true.

She got out her Rother & Fenwick personal digital assistant and tapped away with the stylus until she found the number she was looking for. It would be cruel to get his hopes up only to dash them again.

She made an appointment for the clinic. She would get it confirmed and then she would tell Francis. She would make him happy. This pregnancy would make him happy. It was new life. A symbol of starting again. This baby would make him happy. She would make him happy. Those two pink lines had changed their lives for ever.

Rachel felt like crying but she could not be sure that someone might not walk in, and no-one cried at Rother & Fenwick, not even in their own office, not even with happiness.

fifty-three

tuesday 3.30 p.m.

Roger was in his office, looking again at the details of the condo in Kaanapali, when Maggie rang. It looked good, straight out on the ocean, a verandah soothed by soft Pacific breezes and he could buy another smaller one in the same development for the girls to come out to visit.

It was a bit different from Spain. Better than Spain. It was further to go and that distance was one of the beauties of it. He was hardly likely to run into any of those little pricks that had been fucking up his life the last ten years. Down on the Costa del Sol you wouldn't be able to avoid them. Living there, visiting there. You would be pottering round the golf course or doing some light shopping in the supermarket, stocking up on the Baileys and Black Label and suddenly there they would be and you would have to socialise, have a drink, even a round of golf. They wouldn't be so quick to drop in on you in Honolulu. That was the thing about the Pacific. It was not the Med. You did not just bump into people in the Pacific.

The phone rang. 'University Books,' he said.

Maggie was crying. 'It was in the post, Roger. It was in the post.'

'Calm down,' he said. 'What's happened?'

'It was in the second post, Roger.'

'What was?'

He could hear her whimpering on the other end of the line. 'Maggie,' he said. 'Stop crying. Stop. Crying. Maggie. I cannot understand what you are saying. Stop crying. Stop. Stop it. Stop crying. Maggie. Stop crying.'

She was not listening.

'Maggie,' he said. 'Unless you stop crying I am going to put the phone down. How can I help you if you won't tell me what's happened? Maggie. Maggie, I will put the phone down until you stop crying. Maggie. I am going to count to three and then I will put the phone down. I can't help you unless you tell me what's happened. Maggie. One. Two . . .' Roger put the phone down.

The Kaanapali brochure lay on the desk. He looked out of the window. The phone rang again. She was calmer now.

'I'm sorry, Roger,' she said. 'I'm sorry. It came in the post. I was just opening the letters and there it was. It was so horrible, Roger.'

Roger breathed deeply. 'What was, Maggie? What was?'

'It was in a Jiffy bag.'

'Maggie, please just tell me what.'

'The finger.'

'Finger? What finger?'

'A finger. A man's finger. A real middle finger.'

'What do you mean, a finger?' But he was getting it now. It was all going very fast now. 'What did it look like?'

Down the line, he could hear her trying to control the crying.

'It was a finger, just one finger. On a hand. With no other finger. Just a black middle finger. With cotton wool at the bottom. It was all covered in blood.' He could hear her starting to cry again.

Now the message was clear. Someone was flipping him the finger.

But why? And like that? And why was it a black finger?

Black? That was it. Davey's story about the Yardies, the Crasks' connection. Done in with an MP5K. And Davey had said there had been an MP5K in that little prick's wardrobe. Got it. It was war. Chris had done the Jamaicans. The Crasks thought Chris worked for him. The Crasks wanted him to know what was coming to him because of what that little prick had done.

War.

Fuck.

'Maggie, listen to me. Stop crying. Listen to me. Now. Go to the safe in the bathroom, you know where it is?'

'Yes.'

'The combination is your birthday backwards, in it there's thirty grand . . .'

'What do you mean . . . ?'

'What do you mean "what do I mean"? Thirty thousand pounds . . .'

'No,' she said. She had stopped crying now. 'No, I mean what do you mean my birthday backwards?'

Roger took a deep breath. 'I mean, take the year you were born – 1960 – reverse it – 0619 – fuck, I mean 0691– then take the month of April – 04 – reverse it – 40 – and then take the date and reverse it, and you've got 06, whatever, you know – fuck it, Maggie, you do it, get some paper and work it out. But, Maggie, get a move on. There's thirty grand in four envelopes and four passports. Take them and get out of the house as quickly as possible. Take the car, get the girls and go to Heathrow, and do not stop and then get on the first flight you can, and I mean the first flight, do not hang about, and go to that hotel we went to last summer. Remember?'

'Yes,' she said. The urgency in his voice had now got through to her.

'Maggie, go now. I will contact you later. But go now and do not stop or answer the phone or anything else. Especially do not answer the phone. I will contact you later.'

'Roger,' she said. 'I love you.'

'I love you too,' he said. 'It's just a precaution. I will sort it out. I always do, don't I? But better to be safe. Tell the girls there's nothing to worry about. Just an extra holiday.'

'Ring me soon.'

'I will. Just go.'

They probably would not go after Maggie and the

girls. They never usually touched the family. But better to be safe. You never knew with the Crasks.

He better get going too. They would not wait long after the message. They might not wait at all. They could be outside now. Roger looked round the office. What did he need to take with him? Money. Fuck. He did not have any money.

He picked up the phone and punched the redial. He listened to the phone ringing in his house. Pick it up, Maggie. Please pick it up. Please. Just this once don't do what you're told. Please pick up the phone. Just this once, ignore me. Please pick up the phone. But it went on ringing and ringing until the answerphone cut in. He put the phone down and rang again. And still it rang and rang. She was gone, along with his thirty grand.

He was fucked. He could not use his credit cards because the Crasks had a contact who traced where they were being used. He might as well wear a bell. If he used his cards, they would find him in six hours. And they would be watching his bank so he could not get to his safe-deposit box.

He needed to get out before the Crasks found him. He needed money for that. And he did not have any money. He needed to get the Crasks off him and he needed money for that. And he did not have any money. And he needed to stay somewhere safe while he found a way of getting the Crasks off him. And he needed money for that. And he did not have any money.

Actually, he did have some money. He pulled out

his wallet. Five hundred quid in fifties. Always there. Five hundred quid. Something. But not enough. Not nearly enough.

Roger realised he had been standing staring at the wall while he held the phone waiting for Maggie to answer and the thoughts whirled round. Why was he hanging around here? They could be outside now. He needed to get out. That was what he needed to do first. Now. Get out.

He started walking down the stairs to the car park. That was a bad idea. They could be waiting to do him there. Or they could have rigged the car to blow as soon as he started it. He would get a bus. They would not want to whack him on the A40. No-one got whacked on the A40. That was one benefit of the traffic jams. They could not whack him and get away and there would be hundreds of witnesses. Waiting for a bus outside the office was probably as safe as anywhere.

He would go on the bus and when he was certain no-one was following him he would get off at the nearest Tube station and go somewhere. Where? Where? Where would he be safe from the Crasks for a couple of days while he got it together?

It was another muggy day and Roger could feel the sweat beginning to stain his shirt as he waited for the bus. Although he had worked out that waiting at the bus stop was as safe as anywhere else, it did not feel like that. Any driver and any passenger in any car that crawled by could be the one that had got the Crasks' commission. Any one of them. And every so often the traffic started to move more freely, ten miles an hour, twenty miles an hour, easily enough to take him out, move on and disappear. Any one of them could be the one. And he was a sitting target, standing, sweating by the bus stop. On his own.

Finally, a bus crept into view. Roger put his hand out and it stopped. As he got on, he saw he would have to pay the driver. It had been a very long time since Roger had taken a bus.

He put his hand in his pocket and there was nothing there. He took out his wallet and gave the driver a fifty-pound note.

'No change?'

'No.'

'Sorry, mate, I can't change that.' The driver looked straight ahead as he spoke. 'You'll have to get off.'

'What do you mean?' Roger asked. 'I'm paying the fare. You got no change, that's your problem.'

'If you want to take that attitude, you'll get off anyway.'

'It's not my attitude that's the problem, it's yours.'

'Off my bus.'

'Fuck you.'

'This bus is not going anywhere until you get off. Now get off my bus.'

Roger considered killing him but he was like that midget blonde, he would never know how lucky he was. Roger could not kill him. Not today.

'Take the fifty quid, keep the fucking change and go,' he said.

'Get off my bus.'

Roger could see the handful of other passengers looking at him. A couple of ladies at the back were obviously talking about him. Outside, the traffic was crawling past and every minute mattered. What was wrong with this man?

'Take the fifty quid and keep the change,' he said. 'I am not going to tell you again. Get off my bus.'

'Oi, mate, you heard what the man said, get off the fucking bus, we can't wait here all day,' a burly middle-aged man in jeans and a dusty T-shirt called to Roger. He looked like some sort of builder. He looked like he was in the mood for a fight.

Roger put his hand through the opening and grabbed the driver's shirt, bending down and turning his body so no-one else in the bus could see.

'Listen: take the fifty pounds and keep the fucking change,' he hissed. 'Do you understand? That's forty-nine pounds pure fucking profit. Yours. To keep. Now keep it and move this fucking bus. Because if you don't, I will fucking kill you. That's your choice. Forty-nine pounds, yours to keep, and move this fucking bus. Or death. You choose. Forty-nine pounds. Or death. You choose. Now.'

Although he was lying, he obviously convinced the driver because he said, 'OK, OK,' and took the fifty pounds and flicked the indicator to show that he was going to pull out.

'Fucking nutter,' Roger heard him muttering as he walked to the back of the bus. The builder clapped sarcastically as he passed. Clap, clap, clap. Spoiling for it, but not today, Roger thought. It's your lucky day too. Recently there had been too many lucky days for people like that.

On the back seat he could feel the sweat clammy around his neck. He looked round the bus. Two old ladies. The builder. A couple of girls in a green school-uniform. None of them from the Crasks. And anyway, how would anyone know he was going to get the bus and which bus he was going to get? They would have had to have got on the stop before, and how could they have known? It was not anyone on the bus.

Roger looked at the cars outside the window. None of them seemed to be following the bus. He wiped the sweat off his brow.

The bus stopped. No-one got on and no-one got off. The bus pulled out and continued its stately progress down the A40. Roger looked to his left and his right and behind him but he did not notice any of the cars slowing down and waiting till the bus moved off again.

At the next stop the builder lumbered off and a young man got on. Slight, wearing a white long-sleeved T-shirt loose over his jeans. He paid the driver and moved inside. Roger watched him. He sat halfway down the bus and looked out of the window. He was listening to a personal stereo. It could be a mobile phone giving him instructions from the tracking car.

Roger watched him and darted glances out of the window to see if he recognised any of the cars. They all looked the same, blurring into one another. He stared at the back of the young man who was rocking gently in his seat. Surely not, surely the Crasks would not use someone like that? But you never knew with the Crasks.

At the next stop the young man got off. No-one got on. Roger could feel the sweat drying. It did not look as if they had got on to him yet.

At the next stop, Roger looked out and saw Hanger Lane Tube station. This was it. He sat in his seat until the bus had stopped and then rushed for the door. No-one followed him. On the road, the traffic kept moving. He walked briskly into the station and paused by the ticket machine. No-one came after him. He went to the ticket window and offered another of his fifty-pound notes. No arguments. The woman just took it and gave him his change. He looked around. There was no-one in the station at all. He went down to the platform. He was alone. He walked up and down but no-one appeared. An eastbound Central Line train arrived and he got on to it. He was not being followed. Now what?

He sat down. An old woman sat opposite him staring into space, two bulging plastic carrier-bags at her feet. Two Muslim girls, their heads covered, read mathematical textbooks, annotating the margins. There was no-one else in the carriage.

Now what?

He had to get the Crasks off him. That fucking little prick Chris. He was dead. He was a walking corpse.

But first Roger had to get the Crasks to back off him. He remembered the zest with which Phil Crask had described how Ramirez was still alive when he was buried in concrete. The Crasks had to be convinced to back off him.

Roger had a sudden premonition of Maggie sitting alone on the verandah overlooking the beach at Kaanapali, watching the Pacific Ocean break upon the sand.

And then worse. He saw her sitting there on a reclining chair with an Hawaiian beach boy serving her Baileys and macadamia nuts on a sterling silver tray.

And how else would he be serving her?

Roger had to get the Crasks to back off.

They thought Chris was working for him when he did the Jamaicans. He could tell them the truth but they would not believe him. He would say that, wouldn't he? He needed to think. Think. He needed a cigar. He had left them all in the office. He should have thought about stuffing a few in his pocket when he left. He hadn't thought. And he couldn't go back until this was sorted. Right now, he really needed a cigar.

How could he persuade the Crasks? Money. He did not have any but that was obviously the answer. It usually was. Money to make up for the inconvenience of losing their connection.

And he would also whack Chris. That should keep them happy.

If those two things made him more credible with the Crasks, they might back off doing him. They still might not believe him but he would have shown willing to put things right, and as long as the Crasks were not out of pocket then business could probably go on as before. They were businessmen and they would not want unnecessary grief.

It would cost him – what? A hundred grand? It could be that painful but it would have to be paid. That was the painful bit but it would sweetened by the pleasure of whacking Chris. That little prick had just stepped over the line and he would not be stepping back this time.

The Tube was hot and Roger could feel himself beginning to sweat again. He fingered the coins in his pocket. It was useful to have them. He had not realised how useful change was.

The problem was that he would not be able to whack Chris until he got some money. And he could not do that until he had got the Crasks off his back. And he could not even approach the Crasks to do a deal without putting some serious money on the table. And he did not have any money. Where could he get it?

Maggie had his thirty grand and he had no way of contacting her now until she had left the country. Thirty grand. He knew who had thirty grand – and more. That edgy blonde and that stiff-arsed banker. They owed him. Thirty grand. Fuck. He had just sent Davey to kill them. If that deranged hippie whacked them, that was his last chance gone. And he would whack them, there was no doubt about that. Davey was implacable. He would whack them. The only question was when.

But there was a plan for action. At least he now

had a plan. Roger wiped the sweat off his brow with his fingers. Find Davey. Stop him killing the banker and the blonde. It didn't matter about the boy lawyer. Get the money out of the banker and the blonde, use it as a down payment to the Crasks – thirty grand was serious – to get them off him, whack Chris, get the rest of the money out of the Swiss account. Pay off the Crasks. And then back to business.

He would have to shift a lot of stuff to pay for this. Another year at least. Fuck. That fucking little prick. Fuck him. He was a walking corpse. It had all been going so well. A week ago, two hours ago even, who would have thought he would end up here, running for his life, on the Tube, sweating into his shirt, so far from Hawaii, and so near to Shepherd's Bush.

fifty-four

Wimbledon. Jonathan Miles was a genius. Francis saw it as soon as he spoke.

'You need to bring it all together, Francis. Crystallise the possibilities. Close the deals.'

And he was right. He did.

'An event at Wimbledon could do it. Get them all in the same room. Get a buzz going. Make them feel they want to be part of it. Then you can close the deals.'

And he was right. He could.

Francis could visualise it so clearly. The food, the champagne, white linen on the tables, crisp cotton on the lithe young bodies at the peak of their physical prowess, the relaxed chat, shared moments leading to shared destinies. It was the image of what he wanted to achieve. There would be his investors. And there to celebrate the moment would be Rachel. This would justify her pride in him. As soon as Jonathan Miles had suggested it, Francis could see it. And there too would be James, his son. Why not? To see what he had made of himself. And Virginia? Why not? Past and present and future all there in one room at the same time. Why not? Francis could see it all clearly now. If only his father had been alive to see it.

This would be the event that symbolised Francis's fresh start. And this would be the place to do it. As Mandy Shaw said, 'Wimbledon is unique.' She was round within twenty-four hours of Jonathan suggesting it. 'A good little company, making a real name for themselves in corporate hospitality,' he had said. And round had come Mandy Shaw, in a little black suit, to prove it.

She arrived with a handful of brochures, setting out the sumptuous packages on offer, the coffee and Danish pastries on arrival, the champagne and canapés beforehand, the four-course lunch, sample menus luscious with smoked-salmon roulades, and trios of chicken and medallions of beef, summer puddings and Chardonnay, and traditional English teas, with, of course, strawberries and cream, reserved car-parking, official souvenir programmes, auto-graphed and plain, and Centre Court tickets. Corporate hospitality at its finest.

'Of course, as you know, Mr Carroll,' Mandy Shaw said, 'corporate hospitality can be an invaluable marketing tool, but only if it works.' She smiled at him. White teeth, tanned skin, blonde hair, long nose, practised smile. 'There is nothing worse than some-thing which does not quite work. A successful event sends all the right messages. But an unsuccessful one is a disaster.'

She smiled at him again. 'We go over everything for you. Everything. We make sure yours is one of the successful events. Microsoft, Schroders, Marks & Spencer, all satisfied clients. Nothing is too much trouble for your guests. If I could just take you through the brochure.'

And she did. The food, the drink, the parking. And Francis thought this was genius. He could get them all there. The image was right. The atmosphere was right. And Francis, with his family, past and present, around him, would crystallise the possibilities there. He would close the deals. He would do it.

'How much will it cost?' he asked.

'We will create a package to fit your budget. We have found this is one of the most cost-effective marketing tools. One of the most cost-effective.' She repeated it for emphasis and smiled at him again.

'Can you give me some rough idea of how much it will cost?'

'We will tailor the event for you. This is not a one-size-fits-all service. This will be tailor-made. For you.' She smiled. And then just to make sure he got the point, she said it again. 'We will tailor the event for you. And the price.'

And again she smiled. She had obviously been trained never to give a price until the possibilities had been crystallised and the deals closed.

'Approximately?' he asked again.

'You tell us what you want and we will make sure the price is right. You won't be unhappy with the price. None of our clients are.'

Francis gave up. He took the brochure. 'Who's going to win?' he asked.

'Exactly,' she said. 'That's why it is such a great event. You never know. There's always seeds getting knocked out – and you can be there, with your clients, watching the drama unfold before you.' She seemed genuinely excited by the prospect. 'It's not like any other sport. You never know who is going to win until they've won.'

Francis looked at her.

She chuckled. 'I know. It sounds daft but think about it. In football, a team goes three-nil up in the eightieth minute, you know it's all over. There's no point watching the last ten minutes. Look at cricket: if you have to score three hundred runs in three hours with ten wickets left, you know it's a draw. There's no point watching the last three hours. But tennis, you can be two sets down, five-love down, and then you fight back. You win seven games in a row. Then you win a tie-break and you are into the fifth set. And then it can go either way. And you never know who's going to win until they have won, until it's over.' Francis recognised a performance which had been polished and honed on many similar pitches. 'That is why tennis is as much a game of will as a game of skill. How often have you seen someone two sets, five-love up and then they choke? They see the victory ceremony too clearly. And then they choke. And it is the player who has the grip and the will who wins in the end. That's why tennis is so exciting. And that is why this is going to be an event you will never forget.'

She knew she had hooked him.

'I don't want to pressurise you,' she said, 'but this is very late in the day to be doing this. It's next week. The only reason we might be able to help you is that there have been a couple of cancellations. Cash-flow issues, you know. So if you do want to go ahead, I will need to know in the next forty-eight hours.' She smiled at him again.

'I will draw up the guest list today and get back to you tomorrow,' he said. And he would tell Rachel later. And ring Virginia. Inviting her was the civilised thing to do. And James. Jonathan Miles was right. This would be the decisive moment for InterTrust, the moment when all its possibilities crystallised. It was a defining moment and it was right that everyone who had been important in his life should be there.

fifty-five

Would Davey do the banker first? Or the edgy blonde? It did not matter about the boy lawyer, but which of those two would he do first?

Roger sat in the hotel room on the eighteenth floor staring out over the villas of Notting Hill towards the streaming traffic on the Westway, trying to think how Davey would think. Who would he do first?

Roger knew he needed to move fast. His money would not last long and the Crasks would catch up with him soon. He reckoned he had to get to Davey in the next twenty-four hours. And then get the thirty grand out of the banker within another twenty-four hours. After that the Crasks would be catching up with him.

Would Davey do bankers before blondes or women before men? Roger needed a cigar. How would Davey work it out? It was hard trying to guess how someone would think when their brains had been flattened by psychotropic pharmaceuticals.

Roger stared out of the window. What would the bombed-out hippie do?

He knew what the Crasks would do. They would

386

kill him. If they found him before he got the thirty grand to them, they would kill him. But he could not get the money until he got to the banker. And first he had to get to Davey to stop him killing him. There again, that woman probably still had the money she had run off with. That fucking dirty blonde. He could get it off her instead. But again, he had to get to Davey before he whacked her. But where was Davey? Where was he?

Roger thought. Nothing occurred. He stared out of the window and nothing occurred. The traffic flowed unceasingly across the Westway. Between it and him, Notting Hill sat comfortably in the afternoon. Behind the windows giving blankly onto the world, the wealthy and the fashionable drank tea and did drugs and had sex after lunch. But nothing occurred to Roger. Where was Davey? What was he going to do first?

Why wouldn't that fucking hippie use a mobile phone? Somehow Davey had got it into his addled little mind that mobile phones fried his brain cells. How would he notice the difference? But he was immovable. Roger knew. Roger had tried. And now the psychopathic little hippie was uncontactable.

Over to his left, an oily sun came out from behind the lowering clouds. Roger looked at his watch. He had been staring out of the window for two hours. He did not have two hours to waste like this. He had to get going. But where?

Roger got up from the chair and looked in the mirror on the wall. He had to stop trying to get into the vacant spaces of Davey's mind and start getting back in control. He had to get a grip.

Logically, there were only two options. They could be done at work. Or at home. Doing the banker in the middle of the City of London would be very risky. Too many people about. And Davey had become more careful about taking risks. The teacher was on holiday, so work was not an option for her either. So Davey would do them at their homes. That was the inescapable conclusion for any professional. And, whatever else he was, Davey was a professional.

But who first? Which home should Roger stake out to intercept Davey? If he picked the wrong one, it might all be too late and the Crasks would catch up with him before he got the money.

Nothing suggested itself. He needed a cigar. He should have taken a handful when he left the office.

Roger sat back down on the chair and stared out of the window. The sun had gone back behind the clouds. On the Westway the traffic streamed east and west. Down in Notting Hill there was tea and drugs and sex. Up in the hotel-room minibar, there was Coca-Cola, a miniature of Vladivar vodka and peanuts. But there were no cigars. No cigars when he needed one so badly. And it was not only cigars he lacked. He needed money badly. His life depended on it.

Who would Davey do first? He had to decide. Who? Roger felt paralysed by indecision. It did not matter when the boy lawyer got whacked but he had to decide whether it would be the blonde or the banker first. The blonde? The banker? He decided. It was the banker. Any professional would have come to the same conclusion. The banker at home. That was it. Davey would go first to Surrey.

fifty-six

tuesday 6.05 p.m.

James sat by the river and sipped his tonic water. The terrace was crowded but he had arrived early to make sure he got a table. This was going to be an important conversation. James thought about how he was going to sort out his problem. He now had the solution and he was going to do it for himself. James wished he had thought of it before he had talked to his mother last week.

Waiters in crisp white shirts and elegant long black aprons scurried between the tables clearing empty glasses and taking new orders. Just outside the bar area, on the flagstones that flanked the walkway along the river, a pretty girl with short black hair played the saxophone and beside her a young Chinese man stood on his head and juggled three brass balls with his feet. Up and down the banked stone that separated the bar area from the walkway swooped a man in a Grateful Dead T-shirt on a skateboard. Elegantly, the forty-something with long hair tied into a ponytail swooped up and down.

James watched him vacantly as he worked out what he was going to say. The hippie looked quite old to be skateboarding.

'What's all this about then?' Sushila said as she came up to the table. She was wearing a cream suit today and her hair rested on the collar. Her shirt was tucked tightly into her skirt and James could not help noticing how her breasts strained against the silk.

'Oh, hi, Sushila,' he said. 'What do you want to drink?'

'White wine,' she said. 'But come on, James, what is this? We can drink wine at the flat.'

One of the scurrying waiters stopped at their table.

'White wine please,' James said. 'And another tonic water.'

Sushila sat down. 'Look at that old guy go,' she said as the ponytailed hippie swooped up the banked paving and then did a heel-flip on the way down.

'Cool,' James said. The hippie seemed to think he was still nineteen. It must be hard letting go when you got old. 'Letting Go' would be a good title for a documentary series. That skater in the Grateful Dead T-shirt couldn't be much younger than his mum. All her generation seemed to find it hard to grow up. Her idea for dealing with Chris was like the fantasy of a teenage boy. Could she actually be going backwards in time, like regressing? It was weird how things changed. She had always looked after him. Now he was going to have to look out for her.

Sushila looked at him. 'Well?' she said. 'What do you want?'

'I want to know how you are.' James smiled his crooked, self-deprecatory grin that women always liked.

'You want a shag.'

'What sort of way is that to refer to something so beautiful?'

'That's not how I remember it,' she said, but smiling.

'It's weird how things change.'

The waiter put the white wine and tonic water on the table without looking at them and tucked a small sheet of paper under the wineglass. 'Pay at the till,' he told them.

The ponytailed man in the Grateful Dead T-shirt swooped near them and executed an impressive frontside nosegrind.

'Yes, it is,' Sushila said. 'Once we were an item. And now we're not. Now, not, James.' There was a dusting of freckles on her nose. She was hard work but lovely.

He could not let Mum go ahead with that crazy plan. Dad was right. You couldn't do things like that. He would have to sort it out himself.

'I just thought you might like to spend some of my dad's money with me,' he said. 'I told you he's given me fifteen hundred quid to have a holiday.'

'Come on, James. We went through all this on Friday.'

The ageing hippie with the ponytail did a hard-flip, followed rapidly by a salad-grind. He was so close that he seemed to be putting on a show just for them.

He would negotiate a deal with Chris to pay back the thirty grand bit by bit. He'd be bound to get a promotion soon the way things were going with Raymond Chivers and he couldn't see any good reason why Chris would not agree to repayment by instalment.

'Hard work but lovely,' he said. 'That's what you are.'

'Yes, James.'

'For old times' sake?'

'James,' she said. 'Don't ruin it. I am enjoying my wine.'

He would go and see his mum and tell her. It was time he got a grip on these things for himself. And got her out of that weird scheme of hers.

'You know you'd love it,' he said.

'Another white wine, please,' she said to the waiter.

And, elegantly on his skateboard, the hippie with the ponytail in the Grateful Dead T-shirt swooped up and down.

fifty-seven

tuesday 6.45 p.m.
The streets outside Silvergate House were swarming with people. The scurrying crowds never stopped. Couriers nipping in and out. Self-important suits getting in and out of taxis. Limousines disgorging big-money suits and swallowing them up again. Executive assistants with urgent briefcases. Harassed rumpled suits lugging laptop computers.

Davey liked his coffee. He had a cappuccino while he sat watching the street outside Silvergate House. People were good. Lots of people were better. He could just do him and walk away. By the time anyone noticed, he would be gone, swallowed up by the crowds.

That was it. Do him as he came through the door. Walk up to him, pull the trigger and move on round the corner. There was an alleyway ten yards down which continued on to join the street the other side of the block. He could park a motorbike there, muddy unreadable plates. Walk up to him, pull the trigger, phutt, phutt, keep moving, round the corner, into the alleyway, on the bike and away. He would be gone before anyone had realised the guy was dead.

Davey sipped his coffee. Sorted. He would do it tomorrow morning. When these people would still be wrapped up in their own little worlds, while they were getting going slowly and fogged with sleep, he would come among them and do it. And then, with one less financial titan to keep the money churning out, he would zip away through rush-hour traffic before they woke up to what had happened. Five grand for that and then another ten grand for the woman and the lawyer. He would work out how to do them after he had done this.

Then he saw a patrol car go up the street. Then another one. And then in the next ten minutes two more. Suddenly the forces of the state seemed to be everywhere. Up and down the street they went, protecting global capitalism.

The balance tilted. Now there were too many people. Too much fuzz. What if one of these noddy cars was passing when he did the banker? Now Davey did not like the feel of this. You had to trust what you felt and this felt bad. He could not do him here. Too many people, too much fuzz. He would never get away.

Davey sighed. It had looked so good. He considered doing it inside. Going up in the lift, walking into the guy's office, doing him and going straight out again. But that had risks too. The guy might not be in his office. So he would have to walk around trying to find him. And that might mean he had to do other suits as well, like, if they got in the way. And then the lift might not come quickly when he was on his way out. That would mean he might have to do, like, the receptionist and anyone waiting in any waiting area. It could all get messy. And Davey had learnt that mess was not cool. Davey did not do mess.

Davey got another coffee, even though he had now come to the conclusion he was not going to do anything here. He contemplated his options. And then as he drained the coffee-mug he was enlightened. He realised exactly where he should do it. When he thought about it, it was obvious, any professional would come to the same conclusion. And, whatever else he was, Davey was a professional. He had better get going. It was obvious when you thought about it. He knew exactly where to start.

fifty-eight

wednesday 9.15 a.m.
Blood, opaque red blood, is the transporter of oxygen and nutrients and the disposer of waste, evolved from the sea-water out of which human life began to clamber four hundred million years ago. Blood is the vehicle of life and it was everywhere she looked.

Blood gets its distinctive red colour from haemoglobin, a complex protein, which transports oxygen to the tissues. Haemoglobin helped mammals climb the evolutionary ladder – reptilian blood has less of it than mammalian blood and can therefore carry less oxygen and that is why reptiles are not able to sustain swift, dextrous activity in the same way mammals can. And blood, the home of haemoglobin, that vehicle of evolutionary change, was everywhere. Bright red blood everywhere.

The average adult has around sixty millilitres of blood for every kilogram of body weight. So she must have had, on an average day, around three and a half litres of blood, and it looked as if most of it was rapidly departing. She could see the blood everywhere. Red oozing across the floor, running down the walls, and red seeping through her clothes. Everything was red.

Red. The colour of blood and life. And death.

Or so it seemed to Rachel.

The bleeding started just after she got to work. She felt the stickiness on her thigh and touched it. Blood. It was her time of the month but the test had been so clear she had not used a tampon. She had quite deliberately not used a tampon. For the next nine months she would not be using tampons. So today, to symbolise her new life, she had deliberately not used one even though the alarm on her Rother & Fenwick personal digital assistant had gone off alerting her to the fact that it was that time of the month. And now she was bleeding. How could this be?

Her appointment at the clinic was at ten fifteen. She had thought she could just slip away for forty-five minutes without anyone noticing. It would be really bad luck if anyone noticed that. It would not take very long even if they kept her waiting. She had only wanted a professional to confirm it. The test had been so clear. And yet now she was bleeding. How could this be?

The minutes dragged by. She saw the blood everywhere. She kept touching her thigh to see if more had seeped out. She had put a tampon in now but still she kept touching herself. She knew that slipping out without telling anyone might cause problems with Brendan Simpson but how could she ask for time off for yet another doctor's appointment when, after all, he had asked her three times if there was anything wrong? And she really needed to talk to someone.

★

At ten twenty-five, the doctor in the clinic was sympathetic but definite. 'It sometimes happens,' she said. 'You must try not to feel too bad about it. The test might have been defective but it is just as likely to have been the very early loss of the pregnancy. It is quite natural and it happens more often than you might think.'

Rachel stared at her, this decent, hard-pressed, middle-aged woman in a white coat in a small cubicle in this rundown clinic trying to comfort someone she had never met before and would probably never see again.

Yes. No. No. Yes. No. No. No. Rachel gave the answers automatically as the doctor went dutifully through her list of questions. No. No. No.

'Come back in a week and I'll have another look at you then.' The doctor smiled sympathetically at Rachel. 'I know how disappointing this must be. To get your hopes up and then have them dashed like this. But there is absolutely no reason why you should not get pregnant again. Really, this happens much more often than you might think.'

But this is happening to me. And now. And I can't bear it. 'Thank you,' Rachel said.

Back in her office, she stared out of the window at the side of the building. Blood everywhere. She could feel it over and over again, that slowly dawning horror as she had felt that curious stickiness and realised what it was.

On her desk sat the files of the Ramsden case.

Rother & Fenwick needed a result on the Ramsden case and Rachel was required to help get it. But the files sat unopened today while Rachel saw blood.

At eleven thirty she realised she had done nothing all morning. She might as well not be here. And she could not face it any longer, being in this humming, industrious office, with its hundreds of bright, busy lawyers getting and earning, clocking up the hours at three hundred pounds an hour, while she sat there not being pregnant. She had not even had time to tell Francis that she was pregnant before she wasn't any more.

She could not stay here any longer. She had to go home. She felt sick. She was sick. She was going home. She told her secretary. She would explain it to Brendan Simpson some other time if she had to. Right now, Brendan Simpson no longer seemed that important. She was going home.

fifty-nine

wednesday 11.45 a.m.
Roger had arrived at ten thirty and parked on a grass
verge opposite the entrance to the house. It was
another dull, overcast day. He walked through the
gates and up to the house and rang the bell. No answer.
He rang again. As he had thought, there was no-one
home. It was just a week since he had last been here
to give the banker a chance. It would have been better
for everyone if he had taken it.

He stepped back from the door and looked at the
front of the house. Just what he would have expected.
Windows with leaded lights. Decorative security. An
ostentatious alarm box above the front door. No video
cameras, anyway. To the left-hand side was a detached
double garage. Roger looked round. The neighbouring
houses were all some distance away – that was what
you got for your money in Surrey – and the front
garden was not overlooked. He walked up to the
garage and turned the handle. It opened. He would
not have expected that. But he turned it back and did
not open it more fully. Down the side of the garage,
he could see the back garden.

He went back to the car. He had hired the Renault

Clio in Kingston. It was all he could afford and he felt uneasy about even this modest expense. But he had no choice. He could not just stand in the road for hours and hours. He would be conspicuous to every passing car. He needed the Clio.

He tilted the seat back as far as he could and lay back. He put his hand in his pocket and felt the Stanley knife. He had got that in Kingston, along with the bottle of bleach. They would not be much use against a P99 or an MP5K, but if he caught up with them first and had surprise on his side they would be better than nothing. Throw the bleach in their faces and hope to get some in the eyes and then in close with the Stanley knife, hunting for an artery. The Crasks would probably never let him get that close, and if they did catch up with him before he got the money then the game was probably up anyway. But the knife and the bleach were better than nothing.

Plus, Roger thought, he might have to find a way of persuading the banker to part with the thirty thousand. He was just assuming that because he had given it up once – and it was only that fucking blonde who had fucked it up when she ran away – then he would give it up again. But he might not. He had been difficult enough the last time they had met in this garden. So he might need some persuading. And the Stanley knife and the bleach might contribute persuasive arguments.

Yes, Roger thought, as he lay back in the Renault Clio, they could well be persuasive. He could use them, or suggest that he could use them, on the wife while the banker went and got the thirty grand. Probably more persuasive than using them on the banker himself. Yes, thought Roger, they could well be useful. He settled down in the seat. But it could be hours before anything happened. He needed to be ready. Calm. Relaxed, but ready to spring into action the second he was required. Nothing to do now except be calm and relaxed and ready. He turned the radio on.

'Boom, boom, boom, boom,' went the Vengaboys. Roger turned the radio off.

Nothing to do but sit and wait for someone to turn up. He closed his eyes.

sixty

wednesday 12.15 p.m.

Buddha said that a tamed mind brings happiness. Davey knew that. Buddha said even the gods admire one whose senses are controlled. Davey got that. He was cool. He knew what he had to do. He was going to have to do them at home.

He drove the van through South London thinking through what he had to do. He was careful as he drove, stopping at every red light and not going again until they were green. He gave way at every pedestrian crossing. He indicated every time he turned left or right. Before he set off, he checked his brake lights. No police officer or traffic warden was going to be given any excuse to stop him today. That would not be helpful. He had to get there and do the first one. Then do the other one. And then tell Roger. And that was it. Sorted.

He waited patiently as an old lady hobbled across a pedestrian crossing. The lights turned green but Davey did not hoot his horn or drum his fingers on the wheel. He waited patiently and smiled benignly at her. Behind Davey a car sounded its horn. Poop-poop-poop. But no Mr Toad was going to upset Davey today. He smiled at the old lady as she continued her halting progress across the road. He knew what he had to do and how to do it. He had reached the state of *samadhi*, untroubled by passion or the torments of the ego. Buddha said that rain makes its way into a badly roofed house as passion makes its way into an unreflecting mind. Davey was united with a higher reality. He was focused, and nothing, not even the traffic of South London, was going to disturb him.

He had the MP5K underneath the tools in the tool-bag in the back of the van. He had the canister concealed within a can of paint. A scent of geranium and lime-flowers filled the car. He was cool.

The old lady finally reached the other side of the road. Davey smiled peacefully at her. Anyone catching sight of him might have thought he was stoned. But he wasn't. He was focused. He had reached *samadhi*.

Davey arrived. Home. He parked the van opposite the block of flats. He would do the blonde first, then the banker. Yin and yang. Five grand, ten grand. Sorted. First he would kill Virginia.

sixty-one

But Virginia was not at home. Virginia was with George Crask. She had to get this sorted out before it ruined her summer holiday.

George Crask looked at Virginia. His eyes twinkled encouragingly but he said nothing and waited for her to continue speaking.

'This situation is not helping anyone, Mr Crask,' she said.

'George, George. P-please call me George,' he said.

He sat behind his desk in the windowless room, his plump hands clasped together on the blotter. Virginia sat opposite him on a black-leather swivel chair. To one side of the desk sat the two silent, muscle-bound cousins. On the other side sat Chris, looking as if he usually sat at George Crask's right hand. He said nothing and his face was expressionless. But he had winked at Virginia when she came in. Male energy simmered in the gloom. From somewhere a scent of geranium and lime-flowers lingered on the air.

'It would be better for everyone if we could settle it,' Virginia said. 'George,' she added. She did not seem daunted by the men in front of her. George Crask, flanked by the three stony young men, said nothing. But his eyes still twinkled. That was the thing about the Crasks, people said, you never knew with them. Virginia seemed oblivious to everything except what she was saying.

'I will pay him the thirty thousand pounds. No arguments. The full amount. That's not nothing. Thirty thousand pounds. That's a lot of money for something that wasn't my son's fault in the first place. And I will pay the interest, although I think he's got a nerve asking for it. That's another six thousand pounds. That makes thirty-six thousand pounds. Do you know how long it takes me to earn that?'

George Crask twinkled at her. 'But you don't earn it, do you, my dear?' he said. The cousins watched her unblinkingly. 'You don't earn it. You are a l-lucky young woman. You do not have to earn it. Now, m-m-many of Roger's customers do have to earn it – they have to earn every penny of what they owe – and they run into real trouble when they make a mistake like this. But you are lucky. You are very l-lucky because you have got a rich husband.'

'Ex-husband,' Virginia said. 'And father to our son.'

George Crask said nothing. He looked steadily at Virginia and twinkled.

'I am paying thirty-six thousand pounds – that is a lot of money – that is what he asked – thirty-six thousand pounds ought to be enough for anyone. So why does he want to kill me?'

George Crask looked at her. He did not twinkle now. 'There was a story in the p-papers. About d-drugs in universities. Do you know anything about that?'

Chris stared at her. But what was past was past. Virginia was focused on being positive and what should happen now. Not on what was past.

'Let's assume he succeeds in killing me next time, what then?' Virginia said. 'Do you really think that will put an end to the problems? It will make them worse, that's what it will do.'

'You see, stories in the p-papers can be very upsetting,' George Crask continued as if Virginia had not spoken. 'It makes people very c-c-c-cross.'

The four men were concentrating intensely on Virginia. She treated their attention with the same indifference that she treated all male attentiveness. She was used to men looking at her.

'What good would it do, Mr Crask, killing me?' Virginia asked. 'Do you think that would make the police more or less interested in what that man is doing?'

George Crask looked at her. 'George. P-please call me George,' he said. 'Who said anything about killing you?' The twinkle had returned.

'I know that man is trying to kill me. He just missed me in St Christopher's Place. And I know, I just know, it was him. He is trying to kill me. And you know that too. George.'

The cousins looked stonily at her. Chris was expressionless.

'I am sorry, my dear, I don't know anything about this. You could always go to the p-police if you are worried.' The cousins and Chris all smiled dutifully at this sally. 'But you would have to give them some evidence. Otherwise they will think you have lost it. They will think you are imagining things. P-Paranoid. They will give you some P-Prozac and then the men in white coats will come to take you away.' His eyes were twinkling. 'So you will need to give them some evidence. Have you got any evidence?'

'Thank about it,' Virginia persisted. 'What would happen if he got me next time? What then? Bad for me. But also quite bad for you. Does the problem go away or does it get worse? Think about it.' She looked at him. 'George,' she added.

'I admire you for trying, my dear.' The conjurer was at his most avuncular now. 'I do, really. But you talk as if all this has something to do with me. I am sorry to hear about your problems but what do you expect me to do about it? This man you are talking about – he is nothing to do with me.'

At this, Virginia looked sharply at Chris. He stared blankly back at her. George Crask watched this silent exchange. He smiled at her, eyes still twinkling.

'Of course, I am interested in what goes on. I like everything to be in good order. Chris knows that. So you don't need to look at him like that, my d-dear. You are not in the wrong place. He was right to escort you here. Good order is important. Chris understands that. And you need to understand that.'

Virginia could not see whether he was still twinkling as he said that because he had taken off his glasses and was gently massaging the inside corners of his eyes between the forefinger and thumb of his right hand. An imperceptible tightening of the expression on the face of the cousins suggested that he might have stopped twinkling as he said this. But you never knew with the Crasks.

'You need to understand that,' he repeated. 'This story in the p-p-paper was not helpful. It did not c-contribute to good order at all.' He put his glasses back on and looked at her. There was no twinkle in his eyes. 'You need to understand that.'

'Whatever has happened has happened.' Virginia ploughed on oblivious. She needed to get him to understand this. 'We can't make it un-happen. We must focus on what should happen now. What's the point of staring at a problem instead of looking for the answer?'

All four men looked at her incredulously. The cousins shifted in their chairs. Chris stared at her. She obviously did not understand what George Crask had been telling her. He took off his glasses and began massaging the corners of his eyes again. 'You need to understand the problem,' he said wearily. 'You really do.'

'I understand it,' Virginia said impatiently. 'I have said I understand that it is a problem. That is why I did it. I wanted to cause this man a problem.'

George Crask put his glasses back on again and looked at her. He could not remember meeting anyone like her.

'But it's done. Now I am giving in. I will pay that bloody little man his money. And his interest. I give in. I will pay him the thirty-six thousand pounds. But what is the point if he is just going to go on and on trying to kill me?'

'But you see, my d-dear, from his point of view, how can he be really certain the past is really past? There he is, trying to run his business, not doing any harm to anyone. And suddenly there it is – all over the papers. Full of mistakes, the media getting it wrong, as usual. But that is not good for his business. It is a distraction. Now, how does he know, this mutual friend, that these distractions are really not going to happen again?'

'Because I say so,' Virginia said shortly. 'I keep saying so. I keep saying we should look to the future, not the past.'

'You say so,' George Crask said ruminatively. 'You do say so, do you?'

The cousins watched him attentively. One of them cracked his knuckles. There was a silence as George Crask looked at Virginia. She stared back at him.

'Sometimes there is no easy way. There's problems this way, and problems that way. So you can't avoid problems. So sometimes the only option is to take the way where there are fewer problems. And stories in the papers are a big problem. A very big problem.' George Crask was speaking almost to himself as he said this.

'I want it finished with so I can get back to my life,' Virginia said.

'So you can get back to your life?' repeated George Crask pensively, laying a careful emphasis on the last word.

Then he smiled. No-one was sure why.

'Thank you, my d-dear,' he said. 'We will consider everything you have said. I will consider it very carefully. Steve will show you out.'

One of the cousins stood up. Virginia stood up. George Crask got up and shook her hand. Sometimes he did. Sometimes he didn't. You never knew with the Crasks.

sixty-two

wednesday 12.35 p.m.

Every journey has a beginning, but when it's a journey in the BMW 3-Series Convertible it could be the beginning of a whole new experience. The brochure said that. Roger had picked it up in the car-hire office to pass the time while he waited. You will feel the power of the six-cylinder engine and find yourself taking turnings that might otherwise have been over-looked. And suddenly you're somewhere you've never been before. That's what the brochure said a BMW 3-Series Convertible could do for you.

And suddenly there was one, a BMW 3-Series Convertible, slowing down as it passed Roger and turning into the house he was watching. One moment he was reading about it. Then he must have nodded off for a moment and the next moment there was one in real life. How weird was that? And in it, he could see clearly as it slowed down to turn into the driveway, was the banker's wife. Roger remembered her from that evening a week ago when she had come out of the house to see who was talking to her husband.

He watched it as it pulled into the driveway. He had not expected anyone to come back to the house so soon. There was no sign of anyone else. No sign of Davey. No sign of the Crasks or anyone they might have sent. No-one except the banker's wife. What now? Did her arrival make any difference? She wasn't a threat to him. She didn't alter the original equation: avoid the Crasks, intercept Davey, get thirty grand, pay off the Crasks.

But what about the car, though? 1999 registration. It was probably worth thirty grand on its own. It could be very helpful. The brochure was right: you find your-self taking turnings that might otherwise have been overlooked. But he would need the papers to sell it on. He needed to get the wife to sign the car over to him. That should not take long. Roger felt for the Stanley knife in his pocket. Still there. Then he reached into the back seat and got hold of the bleach. Prepared. Ready.

He got out of the car and walked across the road. It was still and very quiet. Nothing passed. In the distance a dog barked, that was all. Nothing else. It should not take very long to persuade her to sign over the papers.

He looked round. No-one anywhere. He started to walk up the drive.

sixty-three

wednesday 12.40 p.m.

Rachel slammed the front door, went to the bathroom
and changed her tampon. She threw the old bloody
one in the bin. It was not fair. She loved Francis so
much. She wanted his baby so much. And it just
seemed that whatever she did, it was not going to
happen. She walked downstairs, telling herself not to
be so melodramatic, that if she got pregnant once, she
could get pregnant again, that it was all going to be
all right. But it was still so unfair. She had been pregnant this morning. And now she wasn't. She felt like
crying. She supposed she would carry on and get over
it. But just at the moment, she did not feel like that.

She walked through the house with these thoughts
tumbling round in her head. She knew she should be
at work now. She knew these absences were not going
to help her get made a partner in September. She
could see the Ramsden files sitting unopened on her
desk at this very moment. She deserved to be made
a partner. And she so wanted to be carrying Francis's
baby. But she was not. She had been. And now she
was not.

As she thought, she wandered, stomping through

the rooms that should have had children romping through them. Bedrooms, kitchen, living room. She stared out of the window at the front garden. Nothing went by in the street outside. There was a Renault Clio parked there that had not moved since she came home. No sign of anyone. Dead. Rachel was fed-up.

She wandered off again into the kitchen. She looked out at the lawn spreading away to the large-leaved lime trees at the end of the garden. She took off her shoes and walked out.

The grass felt fresh and damp under her bare feet. There was a faint scent of roses on the humid air. She squeezed her toes into the loamy soil. It felt soft and moist, and pushed the thoughts roaring round in her head back down into ambient noise. It was very still. She stood in the middle of the lawn and let it all wash over her – the scents of grass and roses, the warm air of the afternoon and the deathly quiet of the Surrey suburbs.

Calmed, she wondered what she should do now. She looked at her watch. It was probably too late to go back into work. Suddenly she felt lonely. She wanted to talk to someone. She wanted to talk to Francis. She turned and walked back towards the house.

sixty-four

wednesday 12.45 p.m.

Roger had the bleach in his hand, with the top off the bottle, and felt the Stanley knife in his pocket. He did not expect the wife to need much persuasion to hand over the papers. He would go through the garage and then in the back door. Bleach was nasty stuff. A splash on the hand to start with. That should be sufficient. He probably would not need to get to the face or do any serious cutting with the Stanley knife. Terrify her enough so she would not call the police. And then off down the A3 in the BMW. Get the thirty grand for it and he would be set. Back on course again.

'Hello, Mr Oates.' Roger stopped. His eyes had not yet got used to the gloom of the garage but he knew it was a gun sticking into his back. And he could smell the geranium and lime-flowers again. 'You come in the front. We come in the back. Neat, isn't it. Yin and yang, Mr Oates. Back and front. East and west.' It was that fucking little prick. What was he doing here?

Roger looked straight ahead. Through a small, dusty window, he could see the garden.

'Drop the bottle.'

Roger could feel the gun prodding him. He dropped

the bleach. He could hear the liquid glugging out over the floor.

'Tie him up, Jason.'

What the fuck were they doing here? His hands were wrenched behind him and someone – Jason? – lashed them together with some sort of twine. It hurt. Someone kicked his ankle, hard, and he fell over. It really hurt.

'Lock the door,' Chris said. Roger heard a bolt being slammed to.

'You stupid little pricks, what do you think you are doing?' he spluttered furiously. They had hurt him. As his eyes acclimatised to the murky gloom, Roger focused on two winking dots of light. Two sparkling points on either side of Jason's face. Two large diamond studs in Jason's ears.

'Who's stupid?' Jason asked, and then immediately repeated the question. 'Who's stupid?' And then he kicked Roger hard in the stomach.

Roger curled up. The pain made him gasp out loud. He felt as if he was going to vomit. The fucking little prick.

'Who's stupid now?' Jason asked again, and then kicked him again in the stomach.

'Don't waste any effort on him,' said Chris.

'You're dead,' Jason said to Roger.

'No, you're dead, you little fuckers,' Roger spluttered furiously. 'The Crasks have put the word out on you.'

'What are you talking about, Mr Oates?' Chris asked.

'They know you killed the Yardies in Harlesden. You are dead.'

'Of course they know. They told me to do it.' Chris smiled down at Roger.

'Who's stupid now?' Jason asked again and kicked his kneecap. Hard.

It was all moving very slowly for Roger. It sounded horribly true. But if the Crasks had whacked the Yardies and got Chris to do it for them, who had sent the finger to Maggie? That fucking little prick. Chris and Jason were after him. They were actually trying to whack him.

'I told you, Mr Oates. You people have had your day. You're finished.'

'Yeah,' Jason said and kicked him hard again in the kneecap, the diamonds sparkling crazily in his ears as he grunted with the effort of hurting Roger.

'See, Mr Oates, it's like that Golden Bough.'

Roger looked up at Chris. He was mad. Off his fucking head. Through the pain, the smell of geraniums and lime seemed to be getting stronger.

'In the olden days, Mr Oates, there was this sacred tree. And there was a priest who kept guard. And the priest was also the king. But you could only get to be the priest and the king if you got to kill the old priest and king.'

The little prick had not been meant to read the books. University Books was only a front. He was not actually meant to read them.

'So it's like the young take over from the old,' Chris continued. 'The old king has to give way to the new

419

king, the young king. That's the story of the Golden Bough. I told you, Mr Oates. Your lot have had their day.'

'What are you talking to him for?' Jason mumbled. 'Let's just whack him. That's what you said.'

'He needs to understand, Jason. For his education.'

'What's the point? We're going to whack him,' Jason persisted. He was a tenacious little prick. 'Hear that?' he asked Roger and kicked him again in the kneecap. 'Hear that? You're going to be whacked. Whacked. What do you think about that?' He kicked him again. Roger could not stop himself. He whimpered. It hurt.

'Can't take it?' Jason kicked him again. And again. 'It's different being on the other end of it, isn't it?' He kicked him again for emphasis. 'Isn't it? It was different when you was nailing me, wasn't it? Well now I am nailing you.' And Jason kicked Roger again. 'Come on,' he said to Chris. 'Let's do it.'

Chris picked up a long, thin butcher's knife that he had obviously placed on the garage workbench earlier. 'Yes,' he said, 'we will do it, but in a moment. First Mr Oates needs to make his peace with the world.'

Roger kicked out with his feet. Chris deftly stepped away and Roger connected with air.

'No point, Mr Oates,' he said. 'You are just wasting your last moments. Try to be at peace with yourself. Death comes to all of us in the end. And when it comes we should embrace it. The Romans valued the idea of a good death. People today don't understand that. They don't understand how important it is to make a Good Death. I think they should. I think we

420

should rediscover the importance of the Good Death. Don't you agree, Mr Oates? You should try to make sure you have a Good Death. You really should.'

Chris held the knife up to the light and turned it in his hand, admiring the way the light glinted off it. 'You must try to be at peace, Mr Oates. You must not blame yourself for this. You were never going to be able to get away from us.'

'What the fuck are you talking about, you little prick?'

'I told you – you have had your day,' Chris said. 'You're over. Shit businesses never last. And yours is a shit business. Time for new blood. You were getting careless. Bad debts are bad business, Mr Oates. Everyone knows that. And all that bad publicity in the newspapers. That was very careless. Very bad for business. Everyone knows that. Everyone could see it was time for new blood.'

So that was it. Of course. It had been that fucking little prick. He had found out it was the blonde that had grassed him up to the papers, but he had not thought to ask how she had known all the details. He had just assumed it had come from her dealings with Roger. But, of course, she could not have worked it all out from that. He should have thought more carefully about who stood to benefit from the crime.

The little prick was right. Roger was getting careless. Never assume anything. Always ask the next question. There is always a next question. The little prick had grassed him up to the blonde who had grassed him up to the papers. Of course. The little prick had grassed him up to persuade the Crasks he was getting careless, over the hill. Got it. But too late.

'What the fuck are you talking about, you little prick? How did you get to me here?' Roger could still not work this bit of it out and he could not help asking.

'Your wife told us.' Chris smiled down at him. 'Jason and I had a very enjoyable time interrogating her. And your daughters. Very enjoyable.'

'You are dead. You two are fucking dead. You never found them. You just guessed. You guessed. You just guessed.'

His ribs ached. His kneecaps ached. They were both very slowly dead. How could they have guessed? They were too thick to guess. But they could not have got Maggie and the girls. How could they have found them? Unless they were following them? Perhaps they had been staking out the house? But he was sure they did not know where he lived. No-one knew where he lived. The Crasks could find out, but why would they? This was nothing to do with the Crasks. This was to do with these two fucking little pricks thinking they could run his business better than him.

Fuck them. How could they have found him? How could they have worked it out? How could they have found Maggie and the girls? And anyway, Maggie did not know where he was going. He never told her anything. How could they have found him?

Perhaps it was not him they were after? Perhaps they were just after the thirty grand, just like him? After all, it had been Chris's deal originally. Perhaps they were actually here to get the banker. For the same reason as him. And it was just a coincidence. An unlucky fluke.

'You came to find the banker, didn't you?'

'You will never know, Mr Oates, will you? Your last thoughts will be doubts, wondering what the truth is. Of course, everybody dies wondering that. But you will be worrying about something specific. Did we come here for something else and just bump into you and think we could kill two birds with one stone? You and thirty grand.' Chris smiled at him. 'Or were we after you all along and we got to you through your lovely wife and your gorgeous daughters,' he said. 'Equally possible, equally very possible. Did we get it out of your wife and daughters? Enjoyably? Shall I describe to you how we might have got it out of your wife? And then your daughters, while your wife watched? Shall I put you out of your misery and satisfy your curiosity and tell you, Mr Oates?'

'Stop fucking about,' said Jason implacably. 'Just whack him.'

Chris turned the knife back and forth so it picked up light refracted through the small garage window.

'I will, Jason, I will. But in time. All in good time. First we need to satisfy Mr Oates's curiosity. And even before that we need to put the gag in. Put the gag in, Jason.'

The blade glinted as he turned it back and forth.

sixty-five

wednesday 12.50 p.m.

Francis would make her feel better. The more she thought about it the more she wanted to speak to him. She went back into the kitchen. The tiles were cool and hard under her feet after the damp grass. She dialled his office. 'Hello, Joanne,' she said. 'Is Francis there?'

'No,' Joanne said. 'Isn't he with you?'

There was a brief silence while they both digested this. 'No he isn't,' said Rachel eventually. 'Isn't he there?'

'I'm sure he's meant to be with you,' Joanne said. 'Hold on a moment, I'll just check in the diary.' Rachel could hear the keyboard clicks and taps as Joanne went into the diary on the computer. 'Got it. Yes, here it is. "Half past one: Mrs Carroll".'

Rachel said nothing. She did not have any meeting scheduled with Francis for half past one. Or at any other time today.

'Hello, are you there?' called Joanne.

'Are you sure?' asked Rachel.

'Yes, absolutely,' Joanne said. 'He is always very careful now about putting things in the diary.' She dropped her voice confidentially. 'There was a bit of a slip-up the other day. He was out somewhere and it wasn't in the diary and Jonathan Miles could not get hold of him. And he does not want that to happen again.' Her voice grew solemn. 'This is such an important few weeks for InterTrust. He was absolutely clear about putting everything in the diary. There it is. "One thirty: Mrs Carroll: Home." I'm sure he'll be with you soon. He's probably just held up in traffic.'

Except that he wasn't. Except that Rachel had no appointment with Francis today. Not now. Not ever.

'Thank you, Joanne,' she said.

Francis had gone to see her. *That* Mrs Carroll. Not *this* Mrs Carroll. Not the *current* Mrs Carroll. *That* Mrs Carroll. The *ex* Mrs Carroll. *Her*. And why was he going to see *her* without saying anything?

It was insupportable. On top of everything else, this. Betrayal. What did he think he was doing? Rachel's listless gloom was giving way to incandescent fury. Rapidly. It was almost with relief that she realised how enraged she was. At last she had a legitimate focus for her anger about how unfair it all was. This really was unfair. Today of all days.

She needed him to know this. Now. She dialled his mobile phone, ferociously punching in the numbers. And got the infuriating automated message on his voicemail.

'"One thirty: Mrs Carroll: Home." I'm sure he'll be with you soon.' That's what Joanne had said. Well, she would be with him soon. At home. Virginia's home.

Battersea. That flat. She was going to go there. Now.

She pulled on her shoes and opened the front door. Keys. She had forgotten the keys. Where had she put them down? They were not on the hall table. In the living room? No. Kitchen? No. In the study? There was her bag. In the bag were her keys. Got the keys. Got the bag. Out of the door and off to Battersea. How could he have done this? Today of all days? It was all so unfair.

Rachel got to the garage door and turned the handle and pushed. Nothing happened. She turned the handle again and pushed again. Still nothing happened. What was wrong with this door? She tried again, and still nothing. She gave it a kick. It hurt. The door rattled but nothing moved. She kicked it again. Why was everything going wrong today? Everything. The door had been perfectly all right when she came home fifteen minutes ago. What was wrong with it? She gave it another kick. Nothing.

She stared at the door. What was she going to do now? She could go round the back and see if she could get the door open from the inside. But why did everything have to be so difficult? She could feel the rage boiling up inside her. Then she stopped. Perhaps this was a warning sign. Perhaps she should not drive when she was this cross. She was not really in control. After all, she had been so distracted she had not been able to remember where she put her keys. Perhaps she would not be safe driving a car. Rachel stopped and thought.

Better she did not drive. It would be safer. She would get a taxi to the station and get a train into

Clapham Junction and get a cab from there. It could even be quicker. And it would certainly be safer. She was not in the mood to drive. Rachel gave the door a final bad-tempered kick and walked back to the front door and let herself in. She picked up the phone in the hall and dialled the local taxi-firm.

sixty-six

Chris stopped when he heard the handle move. He looked at the door. Jason looked at the door. Roger lay on the floor and did not move. The door shook as the handle was rattled again, more vigorously this time. Chris looked at Jason and then he looked back at Roger.

Then the door was kicked. 'Out the back,' Chris whispered to Jason.

'What do you mean?' Jason whispered back.

'Out now,' Chris hissed. 'We can't stay here.'

'What about him?' Jason whispered furiously. 'We haven't finished with him.'

'We've got to go.'

'Why?' Jason demanded. 'We haven't finished with him yet.' In the dim light, the studs in his ears – big, artificial diamonds – twinkled and shone.

'Keep your voice down.' The door was kicked again. 'We can't be caught here with him.'

'Why not?' said Jason. 'We haven't finished with him.'

'Shut up, you thick prick. What if it's the police?'

'Why should it be the police?'

428

'How the fuck should I know?'

Roger lay on the floor without moving while Chris and Jason bickered in distraught whispers.

'What if it's not the police? What if it's just that woman? We could whack her. And then finish him.'

The door rattled as it was kicked again.

'Can't risk it. I'm off.' Chris fumbled open a case that was lying on the workbench and put the knife inside. 'You do what you like. I'll wait in the car for two minutes, and then you're on your own.' He opened the back door and looked out. Left. Right. And then he bolted.

Jason looked after him and then back at Roger. The door was rattled again. Jason looked at it. Then he gave a little hop by way of a run-up and kicked Roger as hard as he could. Then, reluctantly, he set off after Chris.

Suddenly it was quiet. Nothing moved anywhere. Roger shifted on the ground. Everything hurt. His back and his knees and his stomach where Jason had kicked him. He felt sick. He wanted to lie there until he felt better. Until next week. But he knew he could not wait. They might change their minds and come back for him. Who would have guessed that the little prick would panic like that? But Jason had wanted to finish the job and they might still return. He had to get moving.

He shuffled himself into a sitting position and propped himself up against the wall. It hurt, but he had to keep going. They could be back at any moment. He wriggled his bottom between his pinioned arms and then jiggled and squirmed his legs through so his arms were in front of him. It was agonising.

They had not searched him and the Stanley knife was still in his jacket pocket. He shuffled it out and bent down and slid the blade out with his mouth. The pain ripped through him, but he had to keep going.

Roger placed the knife between his teeth and placed the blade on the twine that bound his wrists together. He began rocking his head back and forth in little jerky movements. Everything hurt, but he had to keep going. They could be back at any moment.

Then he got through the first strand. It was working. Back and forth. The nerve-endings in his knees were jangling, his back and his stomach were raw with pain and his head hurt. But he had to keep going. They could be back at any moment. Another strand went and then another and then he was free. He wanted to curl up and sleep, but he could not stop. He stood up awkwardly and carefully and stumbled over to the door at the front of the garage. He slid back the bolt. Carefully, very carefully, he opened the garage door. No-one there. He stepped out into the front garden. No sign of anyone there. He had to keep going.

In the house, Rachel's head was beginning to throb. She went upstairs to take an aspirin. She looked out of the window to see if she could see the taxi coming. No sign of it. Outside in the street, a slight man in a rumpled grey suit was hobbling down the street towards the Renault Clio. She watched him get in and drive away.

sixty-seven

wednesday 1.45 p.m.

Virginia looked out at the park through the net
curtains that still pleased her after all these years. They
were not nylon, as a casual observer might assume,
but antique Lille lace patterned with fine swirling floral
designs, which she had bought in a shop near the
Grand Place in Brussels shortly after the divorce.
Francis's departure had shocked her – she had never
expected him to leave and then not return – and she
had needed to indulge herself.

She loved what they represented to her – the
screening of private passions that took place behind
the drab facades of dull streets. Virginia was uncon-
cerned about the grand movements of money and
politics. She could barely distinguish one Prime
Minister from another. But she had always been fasci-
nated by the infinite variety of human passion and
sensual experience, lived, in tiny, perfect pulses,
behind the curtains that hid them from the gaze of
the crowd outside.

Through the window she saw fine summer rain
falling again.

Francis sat in the taxi and looked out at the familiar

431

streets. For years, they had been part of his life. Then they had become part of his history, existing only in recollection. Now, over the last few weeks, they had returned to the foreground, memories newly infused with quick urgency. The streets he had walked with James and shopped with Virginia were today resonant with recent visits. The past could never be rerun. He knew that. Time moved only forwards but from a past that can be denied no more than it can be revisited.

The last week had reminded him how turbulent his life with Virginia had been. She had a genius for disturbance. But at least now she had finally paid up; the problem with James was over. He supposed there would be something else at some point in the future. He was resigned to that. But for now, all was calm. This was what life with Virginia was like. Up and down. Nothing was ever easy. Or dull.

Francis could hide it from himself no longer. He was excited. He knew it as soon as he recognised the guilt that surged through him when he put down the phone. He had never intended to invite himself round. He had just meant to invite her to the Wimbledon event. But somehow it just happened and the conversation kept going round and round in his head. It had seemed clearer and clearer that he could not just leave things dangling as they were with Virginia. Now it was all sorted out, there had to be some closure, some resolution. He should see her just once more in the flat to seal it properly. It had all worked out in the end. It was the civilised way to do it. Why should he not see his ex-wife?

Apart from anything else, he owed her the admission that she had been right about James. He should have been different. He knew that now and he wanted to tell her so. She had been right. That was the decent thing to do – to admit you had been wrong. He would get it all sorted out now so there was nothing left unresolved between them by the time of the Wimbledon event. It was all reasonable and nothing to which Rachel could object – except for that eye-opening surge of guilt.

He had not thought what exactly he was going to say to Virginia. He did not want to interrogate this part of the future too closely. He just knew he wanted to see her again.

Davey sat in the back of his van and pulled on the cyclist's lycra one-piece-suit in fluorescent lime and yellow. The cycling helmet was a size too large so it shadowed his face. A pollution mask completed the outfit. He had tried it out from every angle in the mirror. From every angle, he was unrecognisable. Davey was pleased with his outfit. Much less obvious than a biker's leathers with a crash-helmet. So predictable. He liked this creative variation. It was different, freaky even. And it would work.

This way, he thought, anyone noticing him would only remember the fluorescent lime and yellow, even if they could make out his face – and he was confident that the helmet and the mask would prevent them doing that anyway. They would only be able to see his eyes. And what would that tell anyone about anything?

From the back windows of the van he could see the front door to the blonde's block of flats. He was almost ready.

The taxi drew up. And Francis got out. As he leant through the window to pay he heard steps coming up fast behind him. That was strange, he thought. He had not noticed anyone in the street as he got out.

'Keep the change,' he said.

The steps were now very close behind him.

Then he felt a hand on his buttocks.

'Hello, Frankie,' Julie said. 'What are you doing here?'

'I have come to talk to Virginia about James. What are you doing here?'

'I've come to do the cleaning.'

'Well please could you go away and do it some other time.'

'Not for you to say, Frankie. I work for Virginia. And she asked me to come now.'

'I'm sure she did not.' What was it with this woman?

'And I'm sure she did.'

She could not have done. How could she have done when she knew he was coming over?

'Don't mind me, Frankie. I'll just clean around you.'

Francis stared at her. Why did she hate him so much? What had he ever done to her?

Davey watched from the van as the banker and this little blonde chick talked outside the block of flats. She was waving her hands around. She looked like a lively little chick. It made it all more complicated. Were they going to go in or not? Was he going to have to do all three?

'Are you quite sure Virginia asked you to come over now?' Francis said. How could he resolve things with Virginia with this woman dusting around his feet?

'Ask her.'

'I will. Wait here.'

'No, I won't wait here. Let's go up together and ask her.'

She was going to ruin everything.

'No. I will ask her on the entryphone.'

'Let's both ask her on the entryphone.'

Davey watched as the tall banker and the foxy little blonde chick walked up to the door together. Who was she?

Francis pressed the bell. 'Virginia,' he said. 'It's Francis.'

'And me,' Julie said.

'Virginia, did you really ask her to come and clean now?' Francis asked.

'Tell him, Virginia,' Julie said.

There was a pause and then Virginia's voice came crackling distorted out of the speaker. 'I am really sorry, Julie. I forgot you were coming over. Would you mind coming back tomorrow?'

'Sure,' Julie said and then she looked at Francis. 'See, I told you she asked me to come over now.'

'Goodbye.' Francis pushed the door open as Virginia pressed the buzzer.

Davey watched the banker go inside as the little blonde walked off down the street. That was one less but it was still complicated. He had not expected anyone to be there apart from the target.

'Come in.' As Virginia spoke, Francis realised he did not know what to say. He felt seventeen again. 'Are you coming in or not?'

Virginia never changed. He walked past her into the flat.

'You know that little bastard tried to kill me,' she said as she followed him.

'What do you mean?' He had not imagined their conversation would start like this.

Virginia explained what had happened in St Christopher's Place.

'Are you sure you're not imagining it?' he asked.

'Someone fired a shot. He was meant to meet me there. What else could it have been?'

'Did you pay him the money?'

'Francis, listen. I went there to pay him. Don't be so suspicious. I did what we agreed. I did what you asked me to do. I arranged to meet him to pay the money. And his fucking interest. And then the little bastard tries to kill me.'

'Virginia, calm down. You can't be sure.'

'What do you mean, I can't be sure? Of course I am sure. I was there. You weren't. Someone fired a shot and of course it was him and of course he was trying to kill me.' She started to cry. 'What can I do?' she said. 'I've been off sick since yesterday afternoon.

How could I go into school when he's trying to kill me? How could I risk exposing the children to that?'

Francis could not ever remember her crying.

'Ginny, please.' Before he knew it he had taken her into his arms. 'Ginny, please.'

Two of them at the same time made it more difficult, but not impossible. That was why he always had a fall-back plan. Davey wondered if he could use the MP5K on both of them. But he was a realist and he knew it would increase the chances of failure. He was confident he could do one. But two? At the same time? He had stopped taking unnecessary risks. That was why he had the gas.

The one small container had cost him fifteen hundred pounds. This was the real thing. From Russia. It would easily take out everyone in her flat and the pollution mask would give him time to get away. He had been through it all with the jovial Russian. It had cost him five hundred pounds to get the introduction. This was an expensive business. But he would still make a good profit from Roger's ten grand and it would only be this one time.

The sealed canister, no bigger than a jar of honey, sat on the floor of the van beside the front wheel of the bicycle. He picked up. The key arrangement looked primitive to him. He had heard bad things about Russian kit. Such as it did not work. The raw materials were good but the packaging was Soviet. He could be in trouble if it did not work. It would be his first choice but he would take the MP5K in the clutch-bag just in case.

'What am I going to do now?' Virginia sobbed. 'Francis, that little bastard is trying to kill me.'

He stroked her hair. How could he not comfort her when she was crying?

Davey picked up the canister and looked out of the van windows to see if he could get across to the entrance safely. He would wait a few minutes to check the coast was clear and then it would be time to move. In the fluorescent lime and yellow and the helmet, he was like a lethal insect.

sixty-eight

wednesday 1.50 p.m.
They parked in the underground car park and took the lift to his office. When there was no reply, one of the cousins took a leather pouch from his pocket and started trying the lock with different keys. Eventually, he managed to jiggle his way through the chambers of the lock and open the door.

They looked quickly round the office. There was a neat stack of invoices on Roger's desk. Otherwise there was no sign of anyone working there. On the coffee table in the small reception area were laid out a selection of textbooks – Elementary Chemistry from a university in Brazil, a Polish treatise on the nineteenth-century origins of sociology and a translation of *The Aeneid* into Finnish. Roger was not there. It was impossible to say whether he had just left or if he had not been there for days.

They locked the door behind them when they left. Sitting in their parked car, one of the cousins spoke into his mobile phone. Then he punched in another number and waited. Nothing. He redialled it and waited again. He then spoke briefly, obviously leaving a message on a voicemail. Meanwhile, his cousin took out an *A–Z* from the glove compartment and started hurriedly leafing through it. The BMW accelerated out of the car park and joined the queue of cars on the A40.

Davey had watched the flat for fifteen minutes. No-one else had gone in through the main entrance. It was time. He crossed the road and looked at the entry-phone. None of the flats had names on them, only numbers. He knew she lived in Flat Twelve. He pressed the bell for Flat Seventeen. No reply. Then he tried Flat Twenty-three. No reply. He was trying numbers where he guessed they would not be able to look out of their window and see him. And far enough away from Flat Twelve so they could not check what he was about to say.

He adjusted the helmet. He was getting warm inside the one-piece suit. He pulled the zip down his chest to let in some air. He pressed the bell for Flat Twenty-seven. No reply. And then Flat Eighteen. An old lady answered.

'I am sorry to disturb you,' Davey said, using his softest and most middle-class voice. He had dealt with enough lawyers and professionals to know how they sounded and there was no trace of hippie now. He was a professional man. 'I am very sorry to disturb you,' he purred into the entryphone. 'It's just that I have a present for Mrs Carroll in Flat Twelve and there doesn't appear to be anyone home. So I should be terribly grateful if I could just leave it inside the door for her.'

What could be more reassuring than that?

'Yes,' said the electronic voice of the old lady, but nothing happened. The buzzer remained silent.

Patiently, Davey repeated his request. 'I'm sorry, but I have a present for Mrs Carroll in Flat Twelve and there doesn't appear to be anyone home. So I should be terribly grateful if I could just leave it inside the door for her.'

'Yes, I know that,' said the old lady. 'I heard you the first time. I said "yes" the first time.'

Davey wondered if she was senile. He had had an aunt who kept repeating things.

The BMW was stuck in traffic at Shepherd's Bush. 'I told you we should have stayed on the Westway,' one cousin said. The other said nothing but stared at the motionless cars ahead. He drummed his fingers on the steering wheel.

'There does not appear to be anyone home at Flat Twelve.' Davey spoke the words increasingly slowly and loudly.

'What do you want me to do about it? And there's no need to shout,' said the old lady in Flat Eighteen.

Davey thought of *kundalini* and made his voice into honey. 'I'd be terribly grateful if you could just push the buzzer to let me in.'

'Why didn't you say that was what you wanted?' said the old lady. 'My son told me never to do that.'

Davey summoned up the calm of Buddha under the Bodhi Tree. 'I understand,' he said. 'If you were my mother I would tell you never to answer the door to strangers as well. But I would be so grateful if you could just let me through the main door. I won't need to bother you at all. There is no question of you opening your own door to me. Just the main door.'

There was silence. The old lady was obviously thinking about it.

'If you could just press the buzzer for the main door, I should be so grateful,' Davey said.

The BMW had finally escaped from Shepherd's Bush. The cousins were on Battersea Bridge, weaving in and out of the traffic with practised spurts of acceleration. The cousin in the passenger seat looked straight ahead and kept his hand resting lightly on his pocket. It always comforted him to feel the Beretta there.

'You see, it's Mrs Carroll's birthday,' Davey said, taking a chance. 'She will be so disappointed if she does not get this present.'

The old lady was obviously still thinking.

'What did you say your name was?' she asked.

'I am an old friend of hers,' he said, trying to think of a plausible alias. He never used his name if he could avoid it. Prison had made him careful about personal details.

'That is as may be, but what is your name?' the old lady insisted. Davey could not decide if she was very shrewd or just on the edge of going daft.

'Dave,' he said, giving up.

'Dave what?' the voice said.

'Dave Watney,' he said desperately.

'Dave Watney?'

'Yes. Dave Watney.'

There was another silence. Please, Davey thought. *Please.*

'Mr Watney? Are you there, Mr Watney?'

'Yes, I'm here.'

'What is the present?'

Why couldn't she have been senile?

'It's some lovely flowers,' he said. 'Really lovely.'

There was a further silence. And then the buzzer sounded.

'Leave them on the table in the hall, Mr Watney,' the voice said. 'And then get out.'

'I've made her day,' thought Davey as he pushed open the door. 'And now she is going to make mine.'

The BMW pulled up outside the block of flats just as the slight figure in fluorescent lime and yellow was going through the front door.

sixty-nine

wednesday 2.00 p.m.

As Davey pushed the door open, a woman came up fast behind him. He could feel her impatience jostling at his back. As the door swung shut, she brushed past him. Then she stopped. Davey stood beside her as they both looked at the wooden board dominating the hallway. Davey heard the dark-haired woman's breath hard beside him. She ignored him. She wouldn't remember him. She was scrutinising the board. Checking. As if she wanted to be absolutely sure. Flat Twelve. First floor.

The woman turned and pressed the button for the lift. And pressed it again. She was agitated and impatient. Davey looked for the stairs. Never get caught in a lift. At the end of the hallway there were a pair of swing doors. The stairs would be somewhere beyond them. He went through the doors and, yes, there in front of him were the stairs. He loped up them. He had the MP5K in the bag, and the canister too. When he got to the flat he would put the bag down and take out the gun and the gas. He was ready. He was cool.

Up the stairs, round the bend, up another flight and round another bend, and there were the swing doors with the sign in gold paint on a brown board: 'First Floor'. That's where he wanted to be. He went through the swing doors.

In the lift, Rachel looked at herself in the mirror. She pursed her lips to smooth the lipstick over them. Her mouth had always been one of her best features. This was weird. It did not feel as if it should be happening. She had started the day pregnant. Now she wasn't. Now, instead, she was pursuing her husband in the middle of the afternoon to the flat of his ex-wife. In Battersea. Through a hallway populated with stringy couriers in iridescent wetsuits.

Rachel pushed the hair off her face. She was pretty. Everyone said so. Even her mother. Especially her mother. She was not like Virginia – or what Francis said Virginia was like. She had never been a magnet for men like that. But Rachel was pretty – a bit like a rounded Winona Ryder, in her view.

And she was married to Francis. That was incontestable, not a point of view or true only in a certain light with a certain expression on her face. It was a fact. And she made him happy. Another fact. She knew it. In her heart, she knew for a fact she made him happy in a way Virginia never did. And never could.

Her eyes did not really need mascara. They had always been a good feature of hers, with smudged shadows of sleep permanently underlining their deep, dark pools. She looked good in black. Rachel adjusted the suit in the mirror. This is where they had lived. Francis and Virginia. They had raised James here.

The lift stopped at the first floor and she got out.

As she turned the corner she saw the courier in the fluorescent suit approaching from the opposite direction. There it was. Flat Twelve. In plain sanserif numerals on the door. She stood outside it. This was where Francis had come home every day, fumbling in his pockets for his keys. This was where an infant James used to run out to meet him, calling 'Daddy, Daddy, Daddy'. This was where Virginia still lived.

Davey saw her as she approached the door. Past Flat Ten. Past Flat Eleven. And stopped outside Flat Twelve. Too much. Bad karma. He was ready for two. Gun. Gas. Ready. But three? Too many. No way, man. Later.

Rachel rang Virginia's bell.

seventy

wednesday 2.05 p.m.

Francis stroked her hair. Once this had been the most natural thing in the world. How had it come to feel so strange? And illicit?

In the still, guilty flat, the bell rang. Virginia spoke into the answerphone.

'It's Rachel,' she said.

Francis sat on the sofa. He heard Virginia open the door and he heard Rachel say, 'Is Francis here?' And then she walked into the living room.

Francis got up as she came into the room.

At first, it seemed natural for him to be there. She had been thinking so much about him and Virginia all the way to the flat that she was not surprised to see him. Him and Virginia. The two people she had been thinking about. Then she remembered that he had no reason to be there. No acceptable reason.

'Why are you here?' she asked. And then, before he had a chance to speak. 'No, don't tell me. I don't want you to lie to me. Not any more.'

'Rachel,' he said.

'Don't speak. Don't lie to me. Not any more.'

'She has come to fight me for you, Francis,' Virginia said drily. 'Why don't we all sit down.'

'I did not come here to fight you, you patronising cow,' said Rachel.

'Rachel,' Francis began, 'it's not what you think. That man is trying to kill her.' He forgot he had only discovered that when he arrived. It seemed so natural he should be here. 'She needs help.'

'As usual,' Rachel said.

'Who would like some coffee?' Virginia asked.

Rachel looked at Francis looking at Virginia. She realised now why she had felt she was losing control. She was.

Despite everything, Francis was being sucked back to Virginia. She had sensed it. Now she knew it. And there was nothing she could do. She had tried so hard to be a good wife and make his life secure and peaceful again. She had tried everything. And she had failed. It had all meant nothing beside the lazy, poisonous allure of Virginia. She did not need to do anything. She was irresistible. Rachel was helpless. How could he have done this to her?

Francis looked at Rachel. There was so much he should say. And explain. He said nothing. He was ashamed of the irritation he had felt when Rachel walked in. She was his wife. And he felt guilty about being found here, even though nothing had happened. Perhaps nothing would ever have happened. But Virginia was not his wife. Rachel was. He should have told her. Why hadn't he?

Francis felt uncomfortably that he was learning

something. Was it that he should not have married Rachel? Had he just been searching for comfort on the rebound? Rachel never stopped trying to make their life together into her fantasy of a marriage. And she never made him feel like Virginia. She never brought him alive like that.

Virginia looked at Francis looking at Rachel. He was the one. She knew that now. Beyond doubt.

Through her long quest to take hold of every fugitive moment, he had always been there, the prize she had sought and never found again. Now, she realised with cold despair what she had lost. She knew he loved her as she loved him. That had always been true. It would always be true. But now he had gone somewhere she could no longer reach him. He had been too hurt. He would not take the risk of loving like that again. He needed someone who was not her. Not someone to go on exploring. He needed someone to adore him and make her life his home.

Virginia could not regret her choices. Plans always disintegrate so what was the point of them? How can appetite ever be satisfied but in the present? And for all the chaos, there had been moments sublime and transcendent. How could she have exchanged them? But now she knew, finally, what she had lost.

Sweet dreams, Virginia thought. Sweet dreams.

The doorbell went. 'It's me, Mum,' James called through the door. 'Open up. I need to talk to you.'

Virginia went to open the door. James followed her back into the living room. 'Oh,' he said. 'Hi, Dad. Hi, Rachel.'

'I thought I told you to leave London,' Francis said.

Rachel stared furiously at him, silently, a basilisk.

'Can I talk to you, Mum?' James turned to Virginia.

'Yes, James,' Virginia said.

James shifted and glanced at Francis and Rachel. 'Alone,' he said. 'I need to talk to you alone.'

'Not now, James,' Virginia said. 'I'll call you later.'

'It's sort of urgent,' James persisted.

Francis stared at the floor. Rachel glared at James.

'Not now, James,' Virginia repeated. 'I will call you later.'

'But Mum,' James intoned, 'it is really urgent.' She was still treating him like a child. He had to make her understand he had found the answer. 'You mustn't do anything until you have spoken to me.'

'No, James,' Virginia promised. 'I won't.'

'I'm not joking, Mum,' he said. 'It's serious. You know that thing we were talking about, don't do anything about that until you've spoken to me.'

'No, James,' she said again. 'I promise I won't.' Then she realised what he was talking about. Why had he come round to talk about it now? 'Is there a problem?' she asked.

'I've got the answer. A better one,' James said. 'I need to talk to you about it.'

Now Virginia understood. Of course. No-one had told James what had happened over the last three days. He must think she was still planning to hire that hit-man. God knows what wheeze the lovely boy had come up with now.

'It's OK, darling,' she said. 'Everything is OK now.'

He looked at her doubtfully.

'Really,' she insisted. She could see he wanted to believe her.

'James,' Rachel interrupted, 'shouldn't you be at work?'

'No, it's fine,' he said. 'It's my lunch hour. And anyway, I have been in at eight o'clock the last two mornings. I am entitled to some personal time.'

'James,' Rachel said. 'We are having a private conversation here.'

James looked at her. 'Oh,' he said. 'OK.'

'I will call you later, darling,' Virginia said. 'Really, everything is fine.'

'I suppose I'd better get back then. But don't forget to call me, Mum.'

'No, James, I won't. You can let yourself out.'

They heard the door close behind him.

Francis looked at Rachel.

He looked at Virginia.

Then he knew.

seventy-one

wednesday 2.05 p.m.

Roger was not happy. His back ached, his knees hurt and he could feel the bruises coming through on his stomach. He had been kicked raw. Driving the little car had been an agony. He only had two hundred and twenty pounds left, he had not found Davey or the banker or the blonde with the thirty grand. And everything hurt. He had achieved nothing and everything really hurt.

And the Crasks might still be closing in on him. They might not be. But you never knew with the Crasks and you could not take the risk. If the Crasks had had those Yardies whacked then they would not blame him for it and he was away clean. But that depended on whether those little pricks had been telling the truth. And anyway, you never knew with the Crasks. He could not risk it. Not until he knew for certain. They might have been persuaded by those little pricks that he was more trouble than he was worth. And anyway, whatever the Crasks intended for him, those little pricks were certainly coming after him to kill him.

And the suit did not fit.

Roger was not happy.

There was no doubt about it: the suit did not fit. He was in Bond Street, in a shop he had often patronised with an assistant telling him the suit looked lovely when it was quite obvious that it did not fit. Roger was really not happy. The material was quality, not the best but acceptable, fine grey wool with a thin white line. The cut was adequately trim but the suit did not fit. Roger could see it in the mirror. The assistant was telling him how good it looked while Roger could see, actually see, it did not fit. The shoulders were too long and the sleeves revealed too much cuff. Roger was not happy. And his head hurt.

But he needed a new suit. Those little pricks had ruined the one he was wearing.

Roger was even prepared to use a credit card to acquire a new suit and take the risk the Crasks would trace him. He reckoned if he only used it this once there was a good chance that getting a fix on him in Bond Street might not get them very far. He would be gone by the time they arrived and as long as he did not use it again he ought to be able to get away with it for another twenty-four hours at least. And if he had not sorted this out by then, the game would be up anyway.

Roger looked in the mirror. It hurt to see himself like this. But he could not spend any more time on it.

'I'll wear it,' he said. 'Put the old one in a bag.' He gave his credit card to the lying assistant. He sat in a leather armchair while the card was run through the electronic till. What was he going to do now?

He did not dare to go back to Surrey for the BMW or wait for the banker to get home. Even though he was ready now for those little pricks and they would not creep up on him again like that, they might still be waiting there for him and that could get in the way. He could not afford anyone else getting in his way and delaying him. He had to get this sorted out. Now.

He could head for the blonde but there was no guarantee that she would have the money. That only really left one option. And one big problem. Davey. He could still ruin everything unless Roger got to him in time. But where was Davey? He had not gone to Surrey. So where was he?

The shop assistant presented Roger with his credit card and a pristine bag with his battered old suit in it. 'It's a great choice, sir,' he said. 'But you can always bring it back if you are not comfortable with it.'

Roger limped back to the car. Stupid prick. The suit was not a great choice. It did not fit. And he was not happy. And he could not bring it back if he was not comfortable in it as he had nothing else to wear.

The words of the shop assistant went round and round in his head. Bring it back if he was not comfortable in it? There was a reason why the words were going round and round in his head. An idea was germinating. And then. He got it. A refund.

He had given Davey ten grand for the two jobs. If he could find Davey he might be able to get it back. That would be a start. It would cut out the aggravation of getting the thirty grand out of the banker in the next twenty-four hours. Ten grand would be a start. It might buy a few days. It might even buy enough space from the Crasks to get him unharmed to the safe-deposit box so he could pay off the Crasks in full. Ten grand would be a good start. If he could persuade Davey to refund him. If. If he could find Davey.

If. If. If.

Where was Davey? More than ever, this was the key question. Where was he? There was really only one place left for Roger to go.

seventy-two

wednesday 2.10 p.m.

In Battersea, Rachel looked at Virginia. How had her life ended up here, at the mercy of this woman? Five years ago, Rachel had never heard of Virginia.

Virginia looked at Rachel. Why is she looking at me like that? She is married to him.

Francis looked at Virginia and he looked at Rachel. And he knew. Finally, he knew.

The doorbell went again.

'It's a French farce,' Virginia said. She went into the hall to answer it. Before she could get to the door, a voice called out in the hallway. It was so loud that even Francis and Rachel could hear it in the living room.

'*Roger*,' it called sternly in a strong South London accent. '*Roger.*'

A mobile phone rang. It belonged to Francis.

'Sorry,' Francis and Rachel heard Virginia open the door and say. 'There's no-one called Roger here.' Everyone else is here, Virginia thought. But not him. Then she recognised the two burly men in suits at her door. She had seen them before. She had seen them standing stolidly behind George Crask in his office.

It got through to her then. The little mad drummer was called Roger. He would be.

'He's not here,' she said.

'He's not been here,' she said.

'Why do you think he's here?' she said.

'Can't you phone him?' she said.

They looked at her impassively. The one on the left buttoned up his jacket. 'Not here?' the other one asked.

'No,' she replied. 'Why can't you phone him?'

'He doesn't answer the phone,' the other one said.

'We don't know where he is,' the other one said.

'We thought he was here,' the other one said.

'He's not,' she said.

She could hear Francis on his mobile phone in the other room. 'I can't hear you,' he was shouting. 'Hold on, I'm going to move into another room to see if I can get better reception there. Hold on. No, no. Hold on.'

'What do you want him for?' she asked. She wanted to know if George Crask had agreed to pull Roger off her. But she did not want to push her luck. She really wanted to ask if they were going to kill him but she did not know how to phrase the question.

'OK,' one of them said.

'We'd better go,' the other one said.

'Tell us if you see him,' the other one said and they swaggered off down the corridor.

'Where do I call you?' she called at their broad, departing backs. But they had turned the corner and were gone.

Virginia closed the door and went back into the living room.

457

'I have got to go,' Francis said, 'I think we've done the deal.'

Rachel and Virginia looked at him. What was this man thinking about?

'I think we've got the money,' he said. He was glowing. The two women stared at him. Where was this man's head? Had he forgotten what they were talking about? What was happening between them? How could it just vanish from his head? Just like that?

'That was Jonathan. Jonathan Miles,' he said. 'He has got five million lined up. And we can go on the back of that.'

He looked at Rachel.

He looked at Virginia.

He had not forgotten what was going on before the doorbell rang and before his mobile phone rang. But this had elbowed its way in. He knew something important had happened. He knew something significant was taking place in his life and in the lives of the two women who were staring at him. But he could not ignore this. This was it.

'This is the moment we've been waiting for,' he said. 'I have got to crystallise it. I have got to get back to the office. I am sorry.'

He wanted to add that he would talk about it all later. But he sensed that might break the dam of their incredulous resentment at his leaving.

It might make it a bit more difficult but they could wait. Jonathan said this deal would not wait. Francis had lost five million when he was in Spain, or almost certainly, Jonathan had said. He could not afford to blow it twice. Jonathan would not trust him again. And that could be the end of InterTrust. This moment could not wait, Jonathan had said.

He had to get back to the office. He would talk to Virginia and Rachel later. He would make it right. But now, right now, he had to go.

'Sorry,' he said as he headed for the front door. The two women stared after him.

seventy-three

wednesday 5.30 p.m.

Silvergate House glistened in the afternoon sunshine.
The polished marble shone and the burnished metal
round the door reflected the flowing crowds and the
traffic inching past. It was a mighty testament to the
dominion of money. It was a beating heart of capitalism, circulating the attendants on wealth and
fortune, pumping them in and out and out and in. In
came the couriers, shouldering their way through the
revolving doors and pausing inside to remove their
crash helmets. Out came the secretaries in black suits
with short skirts exchanging confidences on their way
home. In went the lawyers and accountants carrying
laptops and files for late meetings. And out went the
systems managers and analysts hastening for their
trains. Silvergate House was a City temple to the fat
profusion of capital. In it squatted old-money firms
of lawyers and new financial entrepreneurs, bulging
accountants and obscure consultants on obese
commissions from ponderous agencies of the state.
Home to all this, Silvergate House sat majestically in
the late-afternoon sunshine.

And opposite it, in an air-conditioned coffee house

sat Roger Oates, watching and waiting for his moment. This was where the trails must come to meet. It was the banker's nest where he came each day to weave and spin his money. It was where Davey must come to do the job Roger had commissioned him to do. There were no other options. Roger was now clear about this. If he sat here long enough, everyone he needed to find must come here, threading their way through the scurrying crowds. And from his perch at the bar that ran along the window, his mug of expensive caffeine and froth in front of him, Roger would see them. And act.

Behind him, Roger heard someone come into the coffee shop. He turned round. It was a short, dark-haired girl who collected a tall carton of coffee and left again. Outside Silvergate House there was no sign of Davey. Nor of the banker. Then he saw, from the back, a man with grey hair in a ponytail. He peered through the plate-glass. The man stood out from the rest of the crowd by the aimless way he ambled through the pressing throng. Roger heard someone else come in behind him. But he could not turn away unless he lost the man who might be Davey. Then the man turned to cross the road away from Silvergate House. And he saw that it was not Davey.

But it was the cousins sent by the Crasks who came into the coffee shop while he was searching the crowds for Davey. They stood either side of Roger as he sat at the bar. Roger did not move. He was aware there was no-one else there apart from the coffee-maker who was stooped behind the counter.

'Hello, Roger,' one of the cousins said.

'We've been looking for you,' the other one said.

'We looked everywhere,' the other one said, 'until Mickey thought you might come here.'

Roger was not sure what the point of this conversation was but there was no point not listening. He did not have any choice.

'You've put us to a lot of trouble,' the other one said.

Roger was beginning to get a bad feeling about this. Why couldn't everyone just leave him alone to get on with his business.

He had gone to Surrey to collect thirty grand the banker owed him and stop Davey killing him. And what was wrong with that? Collecting debts and preventing murder. But could he just get on and do it? No. Up turn those two little pricks and try to kill him.

And did it discourage him from doing his duty, collecting debts and preventing murder? No, it did not. Dutifully, diligently, up he came to the City of London to collect the thirty grand the banker owed him and stop Davey killing him. What could be wrong with that?

But here were these two. Why?

He turned to look at the cousin on the right and as he did so he put his hand in his pocket, hoping they would not notice, and slid open the blade on the Stanley knife.

'Take your hand out of your pocket,' said the other one. 'Please, Roger.'

The door opened again behind them.

Roger turned this time to look, hoping the cousins would turn too so he could slip his hand back in his pocket. Three young men came in, laughing. Not as big as the cousins but there were three of them. Roger launched himself off the stool towards the door, barging through the young men. He felt one of them stumble and heard an angry shout but he had somehow wriggled through and he was out in the street. He could hear, behind him, more shouting. The cousins appeared to be running into obstacles as they tried to follow him. Roger darted across the road between the traffic crawling forward. Someone sounded their horn but he was now outside Silvergate House.

He must keep moving. He ran round the corner. Everything hurt. His ankle was aching and his calf muscles throbbed. He wanted to run as fast as he could but his body would not do what he told it. It all hurt too much. He could feel himself hobbling and limping as the fear drove him on through the crowds muttering and exclaiming as he thumped into them and shoved them out of the way.

He could not go on much longer. He had to get a taxi. Or a bus. He looked up and down the road. No buses in either direction. A taxi stopped in traffic beside him. Empty.

'Liverpool Street,' he called through the window to the driver and stepped out into the road to open the door.

The driver shook his head. 'I'm going home.'

What was wrong with these people? Roger tried the door. Once he was in he could make the driver take him. The door was locked.

'Get off my cab,' the driver yelled at him.

'Fifty quid to take me to Liverpool Street,' he called to the driver.

'Fuck off,' the driver said and crawled away as the traffic lurched forward.

Roger stepped hurriedly back on the kerb and started running again. He could not run any faster. His ankle really hurt. Round another corner and straight on. He did not know where he was, but he had to keep moving. Everything hurt. No buses anywhere. Taxis passed him, carrying chattering bankers and lawyers. How badly did they need a taxi compared to him? It was not just. What was so wrong with collecting debts and preventing murder? But there were no empty taxis. There were no buses.

He passed a narrow alleyway and instinctively ducked into it. It ran between two tall Victorian buildings and curved away. He turned the corner. And faced the impenetrable back of a towering glass-and-steel building. At some point, the alley had been plugged to allow this block to be put up. The alley went nowhere.

Roger stopped and leant against the wall. His heart was pounding. He was stuffed. He could not do anything now. He was run out. Maybe they had lost him in the crowd. But, whether or not that had happened, he could not do anything about it now.

He could feel he was getting his breath back. Maybe

he had lost them for long enough to duck in here undetected. They would be trying to find him but, in the end, they might reckon he had given them the slip and give up. He could shelter in here for ten minutes, then go back towards the street and, linger in the opening of the alleyway until he saw an empty taxi crawling by. Then all he had to do was nip out, get in and he would be away. That was it. He leant back against the wall and looked at his watch. Another five minutes should do it.

They came round the corner together and stopped when they saw him.

'Hello, Roger,' one of the cousins said. And smiled.

'You shouldn't have made us look so hard for you,' the other one said. And he smiled too.

'George wanted us to give you this,' the other one said.

seventy-four

The early evening sun glinted on the great plate-glass windows of the office blocks opposite. Francis looked out at his view and reflected on the last hour. One of the very best hours of his life. He had an ineluctable sense of destiny moving. After so much time spent rushing around, with no apparent results, after meeting after meeting ending inconclusively, after days passing when he could pin nothing down and say something had happened, had definitely, unmistakably happened, there came a day like today. Jonathan Miles was right. Crystallise. That was the word. It was a day when everything crystallised. Things happened. Events.

The grey humidity and drizzle of the afternoon had burned away into a glorious summer evening. And, high above, a silver plane soared across the liquid blue sky.

When he'd got back to the office from Battersea, Jonathan was already there, sitting in his office with a bottle of Krug in front of him. 'Congratulations,' he'd said. 'Three million congratulations to be precise. I've got a firm pledge from Jones & Oliver for a three and six zeros.'

Francis knew he should take this in his stride. The first three million. The foundation. This was what he had worked so hard for, all the planning and meetings and worrying had all been for this. It should not be a surprise nor anything more than a day's work. How often had he done deals for twenty times that amount? But then he was working for someone else. Then he was part of a team of fifteen others. This was different. This was his. His own. All his own work. And he could not help smiling. He could not stop smiling.

'And that's not all,' Jonathan Miles continued. 'I was talking to Matt this morning, about something else, and I think Lloyd is going to come in for two.' Francis could not stop smiling. Five million. That was it. He was away. InterTrust was on the road.

'We could do the deals at Wimbledon next week,' Jonathan said. 'You should be able to get the paperwork together by then. It will form part of the legend. When we go for the second tranche of funding and the flotation in a year it will be part of the InterTrust legend. It will be where InterTrust was born. At Wimbledon. The year of Sampras and Hingis.'

Francis could not stop smiling. Crystallise. That was the word.

'Congratulations, Francis,' Jonathan had said again as he left, on his way to the next deal. 'I'll be honest. There were moments when I had my doubts. But you have done it. Congratulations. Now go for it.'

The champagne had left him with a pleasant glow. He knew he should make a list of everything he now had to do. A new list, for everything had changed an hour ago. But, for once, he thought, the list could wait. He would allow himself this indulgence of just sitting here, looking out of the window and letting these happy thoughts wash over him.

He looked out at his four-hundred-pounds-a-day view and considered the future. All those in InterTrust on three month contracts could now have them extended to twelve months. That would be a good feeling: telling them that their faith had been rewarded.

Then the next twelve months building to the flotation. That was really the big step forward. How much of his stake would he sell? Ten per cent? That would be around a million. Possibly north of a million. Possibly nicely north. It would do. He had done it.

Even the knowledge that soon he was going to have to talk to Rachel and Virginia could not dampen his mood. He knew how cross they would be. And they would be justified. He knew that. He knew he should not have left like that. But he had no choice. He could not have let his chance go again.

Francis felt every knot of tension in his body had been smoothed away and he was gliding on spun silk. And even the thought of having to explain himself to Rachel and Virginia did not make him feel less utterly wonderful. Even the knowledge that he did not know what to say to them did not make him feel less incredibly perfect.

The plane was now just a silver dot in the sky. In

the corner of his room, the flat-screen monitor blinked its colour-coded commentary. No red this afternoon. The markets were having a good day. Today it was blue. Everything was blue: bright, gorgeous blue.

He watched the plane disappear, leaving puffs of golden trail behind. And aching, tender melancholy crept in behind the euphoria, inevitable companion to the realised dream, a wistful yearning for the promise yet to be redeemed.

His mobile phone rang. He let it ring. He wanted to bask in this moment alone, undisturbed. Jonathan Miles could wait. Joanne could wait. So could Lawrence. And so could Marion. They could all wait. This was his time.

What now? Things had changed. The stress he had felt about InterTrust, all those tangled anxieties over the funding, the pressure from all those nagging questions about whether he could do it, all that had dissolved in Jonathan Miles's champagne. All that had changed.

And he was in love again. As he sat and looked out of his window in the mellow golden evening, Francis realised the inescapable truth. He was in love again. That numinous feeling was not just a satisfying nostalgia for the days when the future of InterTrust was an uncertain struggle. It was the heady awakening of love and love returned. He was in love again. Things had changed.

Perhaps he had never really fallen out of love? Perhaps it was only now that he felt able to admit that to himself? She loved him. He knew that now. He had seen it this afternoon. Felt it. She had always loved him. As she always said. He knew that now. This afternoon he could believe that it was possible to go back and take the other path through the woods. There were second chances.

seventy-five

Marion and Alison were interrogating Joanne. They had seen Jonathan Miles come in carrying a dark-maroon paper bag with a bottle of champagne poking out of it. Then they had seen Francis return exhilarated and disappear into his office where Jonathan Miles was waiting for him. And he had not come out since. Jonathan Miles had left an hour ago and Francis was still in his office. And they wanted to know what was going on.

'Come on,' Alison said. 'You must know.'

Joanne smiled complicitly. 'All I know is that I have never seen him so happy.'

'You think he's got the money?' Marion asked.

'How would I know?' said Joanne. 'But it looks like it, doesn't it? What else would make him so happy? Have you ever seen him smile like that?'

'Think of what that means for our options,' said Alison. 'What do you reckon: a hundred million?'

'For your options?' Joanne asked incredulously.

'No,' said Alison, 'for the company. That would mean I was worth fifty thousand. So what do you think? Has he got the money?' Her eyes were shining.

Davey picked her out as soon as he walked in. Foxy lady. Great hair. Good skin. Nice eyes. He liked that.

He had to come here. He could not wait around the blonde's flat any more. Not once he had seen those two dudes come in. Something was going down. He did not know what but he knew he had better split. There was too much noise around that flat. The blonde, the banker, that dark-haired woman who had come in with him and then those two Arnies in suits. Time to split. And that left only the office as the place. It had to be the office. The banker would come back there at some point so he had better go and look it out.

They stopped talking as he walked in. Alison looked at him vacantly, her mind still full of fifty thousand pounds. Marion was mildly curious about this middle-aged hippie with a claret-and-gold-streaked ponytail, an Armani suit and sunglasses.

Davey reckoned the hair-dye and the sunglasses would distract them enough. He would not be around long enough for them to identify him once he had washed the colouring out and thrown away the shades.

Joanne was instantly professional, ready to greet him and make him feel at home. In the last three months they had been visited by several potential investors who looked like Davey. According to Jonathan Miles, new money from rock music and the media was one of the best sources of finance for ventures like InterTrust. They understood creative risk, according to Jonathan, these many-millioned middle-aged hippies. Yeah, right, you only had to look at their hair to know that, thought Marion, remembering his words.

'Hey,' Davey said, smiling, crinkling his eyes. Chicks liked that.

'Hello,' Joanne said. Marion smiled at him professionally but said nothing. Alison was still away with her fifty thousand pounds.

'Can I help you?' Joanne asked.

'Is Francis around?'

'He's in a meeting. Can I help?'

'No,' said Davey. 'I'm cool,' said Davey. 'I can wait.'

It was a shame. Three good-looking chicks like this. He might have chanced it if he had gone straight in to Francis. But waiting around and talking to them? It was too much of a risk. Even with the claret-and-gold streaks in his hair and even with the shades. He would have to do them too. It didn't look as if anyone else was around. The MP5K was in the black leather case he had under his arm.

'Is he expecting you?' Joanne asked.

'Yeah,' Davey said. 'He is.'

What name shall I say?'

'Dave,' he said. 'Dave Watney.' He had grown to like it.

He sat down on one of the leather chairs in the waiting area and regarded the three women with an amiable smile. 'Nice weather,' he commented. There was a brief silence.

Joanne smiled at him professionally. 'Yes it is,' she said. 'It has really turned out lovely. It was so miserable this afternoon.' You never knew. And you had to be nice to the millionaire hippie investors.

'I'd better get back to work,' said Marion.

'Yes,' added Alison. 'Me too.'

Maybe it would be OK. They had not been around too long after all. Once he had washed the streaks out and ditched the shades, identification would not be very reliable. They could live.

Joanne, on the other hand, was dutifully engaging him in conversation. 'This is such a great place to work,' she said, enthusiastically.

'Cool,' Davey and smiled affably at her. Silence.

Joanne tried again. 'What time was Mr Carroll expecting you?'

'Round about now,' he said. 'It's cool. I can wait.'

It was a shame. She was a nice chick. Nice teeth.

seventy-six

wednesday 5.50 p.m.

Roger leant back against the wall of the alleyway. His heart was still thudding against his chest. The cousins had disappeared after handing him the letter.

He could see George Crask – or someone – had written his name in ink on the envelope.

'Roger,' he read. That was all. 'Roger'. Underlined with a stroke of the pen. He could not remember ever receiving a letter from George Crask. Usually someone just told you what he wanted. But this time, according to the cousins, he had written it himself. In ink.

He opened the envelope. The alley was quiet and still. No-one passed. Why should they? It was a dead-end. Only Roger had not known that. His heart was beginning to calm down, but he still could not under-stand why George Crask had written him a letter when he had thought he wanted to kill him.

There was a sheet of stiff, laid paper inside the envelope. On it, in immaculate cursive handwriting, George Crask had written: 'Dear Roger. Lay off the blonde. George.'

Why had he written this? Lay off the blonde? Roger

did not know. And anyway, how had George known it was the blonde? Roger had never said anything about who it was. He had been very careful. So how had George known? And why had George written it to him – and in ink? Roger did not know that either. He just did not understand. You really never knew with the Crasks.

But there it was. He had to lay off the blonde. That was OK. He knew he had to do that anyway. He had been trying to stop Davey killing her so he could get the money to pay off the Crasks. Now he had to stop Davey killing her because George Crask had told him to lay off her. For some reason unfathomable to him. But there it was. Something new. Something different. Progress. Change. The facts of modern life. But one thing remained constant. He had to haul Davey off killing the blonde.

High overhead, in the square of blue sky framed by the tall buildings, a plane passed, glinting silver in the sun.

And he supposed he might as well stop Davey killing the banker as well. That would give him one last chance to get the money. Thirty grand was thirty grand, after all.

His heart finally stopped thudding. He was off the hook. If George had wanted him whacked, he would not have given him the letter. The cousins would have done him five minutes ago. No. Hold on. That was not right, necessarily. Roger's brain was in gear now. For some reason he did not understand, George did not want the blonde whacked. And George would guess that if Roger was going to whack the blonde he would have got someone else to do it. So if George whacked Roger before he called off the whack on the blonde, the blonde might still get whacked.

It was so quiet in the little alleyway that Roger could hear the distant roar of the plane receding away over Essex. And then he could hear his heart beating again. Perhaps George was just going to wait until he had called off the whack on the blonde. And then he was going to whack him. Then. After all, those little pricks had clearly poisoned the Crasks against him. All that stuff in the papers. The Crasks might still think it was time for new blood. Maybe he was not safe yet. Roger could feel his heart beginning to race again.

But then George had written him this letter. Would he have done that if he was going to whack him? You never knew with the Crasks. The balance of probabilities was that he was probably all right. At least for now. As long as he could find Davey in time.

He straightened up. Where was Davey? He hoped he was not in Surrey. He could not go back there just yet in case those two little pricks were still hanging around. He would deal with them, but when he was ready. Which was not now. Now he had to get to Davey.

A shaft of sunlight, reflected off an office block, cut across the alleyway, refracting soft, golden light into the city canyon.

Where was Davey? He would not do it in the office. No professional would do that. Too risky.

So he would do him somewhere outside – between the office and Surrey. But where? Maybe Davey would do the blonde first? Then do the banker later once he had left the office. Yes. That would be it. That was the professional way to do it. Blonde first. Then banker. Ladies before men. Blondes before bankers.

So he had to get to Battersea where the blonde lived. What could he lose by going there first? The banker would be safe in his office for another hour at least. He could go to Battersea, haul Davey off and move on. And even if he did not get to Davey there, he could still get back in time to track the banker as he left the office and intercept Davey if he made his move then. That was it. That was the answer. The professional answer. Battersea. The answer to everything.

Roger began to feel better. It had been a bad twenty-four hours, but he was getting back into control. This happened when you did things professionally. Analyse. Decide. Act. ADA. Like they taught at Harvard Business School. ADA. Fucking ADA. And get back in control.

Roger straightened his tie and tightened the knot. He could feel his calf muscles stiffening and the sweat drying on his skin. Time to move. It shouldn't take more than half an hour to get to Battersea even at this time of day. Everything hurt but he was feeling better. He was back there. In the zone.

And now he was back on the street. Where was the best place to get a cab? Probably round the corner, where the banker's office was. Roger started to wade his way through the hurrying crowds. And then something occurred to him. If he was going there anyway, why didn't he just pop in and see the banker and remind him about his debt? It couldn't hurt. That would be an efficient use of time. Pop in. Remind him about the importance of paying your debts. Go off to Battersea. Get hold of Davey. Get his refund. Go back to the banker. Collect the thirty grand. Pay off the Crasks. Or not. And that would be that. Oh, and whack those two little pricks. And then off to Hawaii. He was back. In the zone.

Where was it? Left here. Now where? Left again. Yes. There it was. Silvergate House, sitting grand and prosperous in the mellow evening sun.

Roger patted down his tie and went through the door. There was a little fountain splashing in a corner and large subtropical trees. A very tall, very fat man in a dark-navy security uniform sat behind the reception desk. Roger pulled out his mobile phone and pretended to talk on it as he stopped and watched. No sign of Davey. Would the guard stop him going up to the banker's office? Would he insist on ringing up to see if he had an appointment? How did it work here? If he tried to blag his way through it could cause a security alert. And how would that help him get to Davey?

A courier came through the doors, brushed past Roger and went up to the reception desk, removing his helmet as he walked. The fat man pointed to the lifts. That was all right then. Roger put his mobile phone away and marched purposefully over to the lifts and got in with the courier. No-one called after him. He looked at the list of buttons. No names beside them. He pressed the top button. He would just have to get out at every floor and look.

He found it on the nineteenth floor. He had been careful in case the security guard was monitoring the lifts. He had got out of the lift on the top floor, looked around, then gone down the stairs, looked around, then back into the lift and down, out, looked around, then down the stairs, looked around and then, down, down, down, floor by floor, by lift and stairs until he found it. On the nineteenth floor.

A discreet brass plate by the door said 'InterTrust'. Roger tried the door. It opened. He saw a reception area with walls the golden yellow of cream-crust, framing monitors showing market prices. On some of the screens, Roger saw images of waves and water-falls. What was all that about?

Across the rich, soft carpet, behind a low reception desk, sat a good-looking blonde woman entering data on a keyboard. Roger could see the black screen in front of her flickering in response. There was a man with claret and gold streaks in his hair and sunglasses sitting in one of the black leather chairs to the side of the desk.

The receptionist looked up and saw him. 'Can I help you?' Joanne said.

Then Roger saw it was Davey sitting in that black leather chair.

'I am with my colleague here,' Roger replied.

Davey smiled his lazy smile at him. 'Hey, man,' he said.

So he was a big-money investor, Joanne thought. The millionaire hippie and now his financial advisor come to join him. More good news for Francis.

'Please take a seat. Mr Carroll will be with you shortly.' Joanne smiled at them. She did not want to disturb Francis right away. If he had made this appointment himself she was sure he would be out shortly. But there was obviously something important going on and she did not like to intrude. She would give it another five minutes before she went to remind him. Joanne continued to type away happily.

'Change of plan,' Roger muttered as he sat down beside Davey.

'Cool, man,' said Davey. 'What's up?'

'Change of plan. You don't do him. You don't do anyone.'

'Cool, man,' Davey said. 'Let's split then.' He got up.

Roger followed. 'Sorry,' he said to Joanne. 'We've got to go now.'

'I'm sure he won't be long,' Joanne said. 'Please wait. I will just go and see how long it will be.' And she got up from her desk.

'It's cool,' said Davey.

'Don't worry,' said Roger at the same time. 'I'll be back.'

'Are you sure?' asked Joanne.

'I'm sure,' said Roger.

'Sure,' said Davey added and he smiled at her.

'Well, if you're sure,' Joanne said uncertainly. 'I will tell him you called, Mr Watney.' She smiled back at Davey 'And that you waited for him.'

'Cool,' Davey said as they went out the door.

'I'll be back,' Roger said.

Roger looked at Davey as they waited for the lift. He did not seem to have understood. 'The deal's off,' he told him. 'Change of plan.'

'Yeah, you said,' Davey said. 'That's cool.'

'Have you got the ten grand with you?' Roger asked.

'What do you mean?' Davey said.

'The ten grand,' Roger said.

'What do you mean, man?'

'The ten grand I gave you for the job,' Roger explained patiently. Sometimes he was never quite sure exactly how many cells the drugs had destroyed in Davey's brain.

'Yes, I've got it,' Davey said. 'Why?' His tone never wavered from its amiable low mumble but Roger had begun to sense there might be a problem here.

'You have not done the job. No whack, no jack.'

'No, man. That is not how it works. You ask me to help you. You change your mind. I get paid just the same. It's my time, man. My trouble, man.' It looked as if Davey might be difficult about this. But Roger needed cash.

'Cool, man,' Roger said. He knew he had to be careful now. Even the Crasks were careful around Davey. Even the Crasks never knew quite where they were with someone who was so obviously out of his skull. 'You're right,' he agreed. 'Of course you get paid, man.'

'Of course,' Davey said. They stared at each other. 'Just half.'

'No, man.'

They continued to stare at each other. The lift arrived. The doors opened with a low ting. Roger and Davey did not move. The lift doors closed again.

'There's got to be some difference between doing the job and not doing the job.'

'Your choice, man. You asked me to help you out. That's ten grand. You want me to do them, I do them. You change your mind, I don't do them. That's down to you. But the ten grand is mine.'

They stared at each other some more. There was a problem here. Roger felt his heart starting up again. There was definitely a problem here.

The door to the InterTrust office opened. Joanne looked out. 'Oh good,' she said. 'I'm so glad you are still here. Mr Carroll is free now.'

Roger looked at her, his mind still full of Davey. Davey stared at Roger. It was not clear whether this was because his mind was still full of Roger or because his bombed-out brain cells were just slow to adjust to the appearance of Joanne.

Ten grand. Thirty grand. Roger weighed it up. He looked at Joanne. He looked at Davey. He thought about the banker. He continued looking at Davey who stared back at him with that unwaveringly amiable stare. Ten grand. Thirty grand. Roger weighed it up. It was a tricky calculation. Banker with thirty grand?

Or bombed-out psychopath with ten grand and an MP5K in his briefcase? Thirty grand won.

'OK. It's yours. Cool?' He spoke softly to Davey so Joanne could not hear.

'Always,' Davey said and pressed the lift button again.

'I'll be right with you,' Roger said to Joanne.

'I'll tell Mr Carroll,' she said, disappearing back into the office.

'Are we cool, man?' Roger asked. 'It's yours.'

'We're cool,' Davey replied, and got into the lift.

Roger stared at his back, the claret-and-gold-streaked pigtail hanging over the black Armani jacket. The doors closed behind Davey. Roger could hear the lift purring as it carried Davey, and Roger's ten thousand pounds, down to the ground floor. He had to get the thirty grand from the banker now. It had turned out to be just as well he had come here first. Given Davey's attitude. Inspired. Roger slid the blade open on the Stanley knife in his pocket. That ought to be enough.

'Where's your colleague?' Joanne asked as Roger went back in.

'He had to go,' Roger said, 'but I'm here to see Mr Carroll.'

'I'll show you to his office,' Joanne said, smiling nicely at him.

'Hello, Mr Carroll,' Roger said as he walked in.

Francis stared at him. What was he doing here?

'You owe me thirty thousand pounds.'

Hadn't Virginia paid him? Francis's mood was scrambling. He remembered she had said he had tried to kill her. He remembered asking her if she had paid him. He could not remember what she had replied. He wanted to get rid of this now. He needed to get this threatening little man out of his office. Now.

Roger tightened his grip round the Stanley knife. He was tired of fucking around with these people.

'Wait a minute,' Francis said, and picked up the phone and rang Virginia. 'Did you pay him?' he said. 'The man for James. He's in my office now.'

Roger watched him as Francis listened to the person on the other end of the phone. Roger did not relax his grip on the Stanley knife.

'I know. I know. I am really sorry,' Francis was saying. 'I am really, really sorry.'

Roger felt the impatience rising up inside him.

'But did you pay him?' Francis persisted. 'I know,' he said. 'I am sorry. Have you still got the money?' There was a short pause. 'Can you get in a taxi and bring it over here now?' he asked.

Better, Roger thought. In the zone. He relaxed his grip on the Stanley knife.

'I know,' Francis was saying. 'I am sorry. But we can talk about it when I see you. It would be better to do it face to face. Not on the phone. Can you get in a taxi and bring it over here now?' he repeated. 'Please,' he said.

'Please Virginia.' There was another pause. Roger waited. 'Thank you,' Francis said and put down the phone.

He looked up at Roger, who had begun to smile.

'Tough bitch, isn't she?' Roger said.

Francis stared at him. He could not find the words for this ghastly little man.

'She'll be here with the thirty thousand pounds within an hour. And then you can go. As you said.'

Roger was still smiling. It was not worth the hassle about the interest. The thirty grand would do. And it would be here inside the hour. He had not expected it to be so easy. Not after the day he had had. Right now, the thirty grand would do. Then he could do a deal with the Crasks, sort out those two little pricks, get Maggie and the girls home and then make the arrangements for Hawaii. He was certainly ready for it now. 'I'll wait outside,' he said.

Francis looked at Roger's back as he went out. It was not a perfect end to the day but at least he was about to get rid of this problem. And he did need to see Virginia. And then Rachel.

Francis felt the pieces settling into position, all the tangled stories flowing into one.

Roger shut the door politely behind him.

For years, Francis thought, his life had been in sections. His marriage with Rachel, his stalling career, his feelings about Virginia, his commitment to InterTrust, his relationship with James. None of it hung together. In every section of his life he was a different man. He could see that now. And now, for the first time since the divorce, he was becoming one again. He was becoming whole. InterTrust was now safely on the way, riding the crest of the dotcom revolution. In an hour James's problem would have been paid off and gone. And good had come out of that. He felt he had made a new start with James. His son.

And now he needed to talk to Virginia.

And then he'd go home and talk to Rachel.

seventy-seven

wednesday 6.15 p.m.

She was going to kill him. There was now no doubt in her mind. She was going to kill him. With her bare hands. She loved him, and now she was going to kill him. She had always loved him. Unlike Virginia. She had always shown him she loved him. Unlike Virginia. How could he now do this to her? With Virginia? She was going to kill him.

Why had he ever asked her to marry him if he was still in love with Virginia? Why had he ever let her believe that they could have a life together? But then again, the way he touched her, the way she sometimes caught him looking at her, what was that but love? But how could he behave like that and then still be in love with Virginia? How could he do this to her? She was going to kill him.

Rachel could feel her nose beginning to run again. She fished the sodden handkerchief out of her handbag as the taxi wove through the ungenerous streets of South London. A mother struggled to lug a buggy up the narrow front steps to her flat. A gang of schoolchildren meandered home, eating ice-creams. An old lady waited patiently while her dog soiled the pavement. And in among this afternoon life, Rachel knew she was going to kill Francis.

When he had bolted, she had frozen, not knowing what to do. She realised everything had changed. She had seen it in his eyes. She had begun to realise it when Joanne had told her about the appointment. She had got used to it as she travelled to Virginia's flat. And when she had seen them together, she knew it. She just knew it. How could he have done this to her? And how could he have left her like that, with Virginia?

She had started to follow him out of the door before she thought how pathetic she must look. Then she turned round to see Virginia also staring after Francis and she thought she could not cope with being left alone with her. What would she say to her? She had frozen. How could he have just bolted like that?

She could not go. But neither could she stay. Not after Francis had gone. So then, without a word, she brushed past the two burly men talking in the hallway and marched out into the street.

For hours she had walked in Battersea Park in the grey, humid afternoon, up and down the paths, over to the pagoda and back, thinking of Francis.

And as she walked she grew more and more angry. She would have given up everything for him. For them. She had probably already given up her career for him. How could she hope to become a partner now after she had taken all this time off? To try to become pregnant. For him. For them. For their life together. She should be at work now, dealing with the Ramsden files. Yet once again she was not there because once again she was tangled up in Francis's life.

Mothers and nannies pushed babies in buggies across the park and held the perfect miniature hands of tiny children taking their first tottering steps. She should have known better. How could she have given up everything for a man who was not prepared to give up anything for her. Who was still in love with his first wife. How could she?

And how could he have just walked out like that? The unfairness settled in her soul like grit at the bottom of a riverbed. Why should he just get away with it? This extraordinary selfishness?

As a tongue seeks an aching tooth, she could not stop returning to that Judas image of him in the flat as he looked at Virginia. She had always loved that fond gaze on his handsome face, with the fine lines around his eyes where he smiled. Now that image was smashed, to be replaced for always by that memory of how he looked this afternoon, in that flat in Battersea. She was going to kill him.

She walked onto the street. There was a taxi. She stopped it and got in. She knew what she was going to do.

'Silvergate House,' she said to the driver. 'In the City.'

Twenty minutes later she marched in, past the very tall, fat security guard, past the gently plashing fountain, under the subtropical trees and into the lift. She pressed the button. Nineteen. And as the doors closed, she pressed it again. And again as the lift began its ascent. How could he do this to her?

Hot with anger, she felt the tears starting to her eyes again. The lift doors opened and she got out. And stopped. She could not walk into InterTrust like this. She took her handkerchief out of her bag and blew her nose again. Then she took out a small mirror and looked at her eyes. A mess. She could not go in like that, but all the washrooms were in the InterTrust offices. She pressed the lift button. When she got in, she pressed the button for it to stop at every floor. Rachel looked in the mirror and started to mop away the running mascara. Then she began to repair her face. The lift reached the ground floor. She pressed the button for it to stop again on every floor on its way back to the nineteenth.

By the time she finally got out again at the InterTrust offices, there was only a slight redness round the eyes to indicate she had been crying. She was now presentable. She marched into the offices. Joanne was still sitting at her desk, typing.

There was a slender man in a light-grey suit sitting with his legs neatly crossed in one of the black leather chairs, looking into the middle distance. He took no notice of Rachel. She took no notice of him.

'Hello, Joanne,' Rachel said.

'Oh, hello, Mrs Carroll,' Joanne said, looking up and smiling at her. 'Shall I tell him you're here?'

'No, thank you, Joanne,' Rachel said. 'I will go straight in.' And kill him.

*

Francis was sitting in his chair, looking out of the window. He swivelled round as he heard the door open.

'How could you do it?' Rachel said. And started to cry.

'Rachel,' he said, getting up. 'What is it?'

'Don't do that,' she exploded between her tears. 'Don't pretend you don't know. It's always been the same. Virginia this. Virginia that. You should never have left her. You should never have married me. You should never have let me marry you.'

'Rachel. Please,' he said. 'Please. Sit down. Please.' He put his arm round her. He hated to see her cry.

'Get your hands off me. How long have you been sleeping with her?'

'Rachel, please. I have not been sleeping with her.'

'Don't give me that. I saw. You know I saw. What were you doing there? In her flat? In the middle of the afternoon? Without telling me? Well? Well? You can't answer that, can you?' She started crying again and then sat down to wipe her eyes.

'Rachel. Please. Let me explain. I know how difficult this is for you. There is no easy way to explain it. But please believe me, I have not been sleeping with Virginia. Please, Rachel. This is very difficult for everyone.'

'What are you talking about, Francis? Difficult for who? Difficult for who, exactly?' She leaned forward in the chair in her fury. 'What is so difficult for you? I love you, Francis. I have done everything I know how to show you how much I love you, Francis. And what do I get? You know I would have done anything for you, Francis. Anything. I have tried so hard to have your baby. Not a baby, Francis. Your baby. Why? Because I love you. This is not fair, Francis. It is not right.'

Her face flared with anger. Francis could not tear his eyes away. Her rage was magnificent. And she was right. It was not fair.

His mobile phone rang. Francis looked at Rachel. The tears rolled down her face. The phone continued to ring. He remembered it had rung earlier and he had ignored it then.

'Rachel, I am sorry,' he said. 'I had better answer it.'

'Yes, why don't you,' she said.

'Philippe?' He looked at Rachel who stared back at him, her face glistening from the tears. She continued to stare at him in a cold fury.

'Yes, Philippe. Yes. No, I can't talk now. No, I am busy tomorrow. I will call you. Goodbye.' Francis put the phone back in his pocket.

'Do you have any idea of what I have given up for you, Francis? You know how much I want to be a partner. And what do you think it has done for my chances to spend all that time at the doctor trying to have your baby? How could you do this to me?'

She was right. How could he? He did not know how this could have happened. The evening sun softened the room with a mellow glow. It burnished her dark hair.

'I love you, Francis,' she said. 'I really love you.

Unlike your first wife, I don't sleep with other men. How could you do this to me?'

'Rachel. Please believe me. I have not been sleeping with her.'

'Don't give me that, Francis. Do not give me that. Why were you there? In the middle of the afternoon? Without telling me? At least don't lie to me.' She blew her nose furiously. 'Do you have any idea how much I love you, Francis? Do you? Do you have any idea of how much I wanted your baby? It was not just going to that horrible Doctor Gray, you know.' She looked at him. 'You just don't know what I have done for you. For us. I am on the most repulsive diet you can imagine. You don't know because I never told you. I did not want to bother you with it. But I can tell you it is disgusting. But I do it because I love you and I want to have your baby. Your baby, Francis. While you are off shagging her, I am swigging red clover and black cohosh. I swig. You shag. That's it. That's the difference between us. Is that right? Is that fair?'

Francis had never realised. She was magnificent. But she was also, clearly, a little bit mad. What was all this about clover and cohosh? What was cohosh?

'You have no idea the trouble I went to for you. You know that omelette you liked so much on Saturday. Well, that was full of pulverised palmetto to enlarge your prostate to pep up your pathetic sperm, and crushed pumpkin seeds to get them moving better. Yes, Francis, look surprised. It is a surprise, isn't it? You thought it tasted a bit different, didn't you? Well it was different. It was to make you give me a baby.'

Pumpkin seeds sounded harmless enough. But what was palmetto? Then he saw Rachel begin to cry again.

'How could you do this to me? If you still loved her, why did you ever marry me? It would have been far better if I had never met you. If I had never loved you.'

She stopped. Everything in the room was still. Suddenly silent, Rachel looked at him. Francis was frozen. She looked as if she was going to start crying again, but then she started to speak again, more slowly, measured, composed.

'No, that's not true,' she said. 'It is not true. It would not have been better. I am glad you married me. I love you. I loved you from the moment I saw you. I still love you. I am glad I met you. No-one else could ever have made me feel the way you make me feel. I don't care what you have done. I don't care what you do. I love you. How could I ever be sorry about that. I was wrong. It would not have been better if I had never met you. It would have been worse. Far worse.'

As she spoke, Francis knew she was right. In this moment, everything made sense in a way that nothing in his life had ever made sense before. She loved him. Precious enough. But, miraculously, he loved her too. At last, he understood. That passion, that crazy intensity which burst through that precise lawyer's demeanour was a rage for their life together and he could no more live without it than he could do without the blood in his veins.

At last, he understood. It could not be Virginia. Not now, not ever again. She had always followed her heart and it had led her on a thrilling, intoxicating journey which had passed through him and now was heading back his way. But it could never be for him again.

Rachel was different. For her, he was not part of any journey. She was not travelling anywhere. Her heart knew it had enough to do where it was, pumping her feelings and his feelings through their marriage. He was not a destination to be reached or left. She had no choice but to stay where she was. He was her purpose.

This realisation flowed through him in one exquisite second. And in it, at last, he understood that his need for Virginia had been an intoxication. And pride and hurt had imprisoned him in it. Those moments in the flat in Battersea this afternoon had not opened a new chapter of romance rediscovered, love found again and returned. He had been wrong. Instead, they had redeemed his past and set him free. And, by some crazy, snaking chain of accident and coincidence, he had found this out. If Jones & Oliver had not decided today about the three million, if Jonathan Miles had not called him when he did, if Rachel had not followed him here, he might never have realised this.

But now he knew he had passed through the veils of illusion and found a new truth. Rachel.

'I know,' he said. And he did. 'I am glad too.'

The door opened.

Joanne came in. And stopped. And coughed.

And said, 'Mrs Carroll is here.'

And Virginia walked in. And stopped. And said, 'Hello, Francis.' And looked at Rachel. What was she doing here? she thought. 'Hello, Rachel,' she said.

Rachel stared at her. What was *she* doing here? she thought. 'Hello,' she said.

Francis knew this was the moment. He must not get it wrong again. 'Have you got the money?' he said to Virginia.

Virginia reached into her bag and handed over a thick brown foolscap envelope to Francis. 'It's all in there. You can count it if you want. If you don't, I'm sure that horrible little man outside will.'

'I trust you,' Francis replied. 'I will now finally get rid of this. Hold on.' And he left the room.

Virginia and Rachel stared after him.

Again? she thought.

Again? she thought.

In the reception area, Roger took the envelope. He let the smile fade from his face as he opened it. Without taking the money out, he counted it. Joanne typed discreetly in the background. Tap, tap, tap, went her fingers. Flick, flick, flick, went his fingers. Thirty grand. It would do.

'OK,' Roger said. 'That's it. A pleasure doing business with you, Mr Carroll. Goodbye. And this is goodbye. I told you: pay me and I go. I said it. And I meant it. You paid me. And I am going. Goodbye.' He pressed the button for the lift and the doors opened immediately. He stepped in and faced the wall, pressing another button to his left-hand side.

Francis stared at Roger's back as the doors closed

behind him. This was the end. He believed him. He could hear the lift purring as it carried Roger, and his thirty thousand pounds, down to the ground floor.

'Goodbye,' said Francis. 'Goodbye.' And he went back into his office.

'That's the end of that,' he said.

He knew Virginia and Rachel were staring at him. It was the moment. He must get it right.

'Thank you for coming so quickly,' Francis said to Virginia. 'I think we have finally sorted James out. I don't think he'll be doing that again.'

She looked at him, a long stare, and then she smiled. A quiet, reflective smile. She understood. It was all too late. It really was all too late.

'Yes,' she said. 'I think he may have grown up now. At last.' She looked at him. And then she looked at Rachel sitting in her chair, still, looking at her lap, waiting. She said: 'I'd better get going.' She smiled again at Francis. The same quiet smile. 'Sweet dreams, Francis,' she said. And then Virginia left. Lawrence was talking to Joanne in the reception area as she went out. He needed a haircut and a new shirt but he was quite good-looking, Virginia thought as she got into the lift.

'We'd better go home now,' Francis said to Rachel.

seventy-eight

DEATH CRASH ON LONDON ROAD

A Bromley man was killed on Thursday night when his BMW hit a tree on the London Road. Krishnan Singh, 19, of Limes Avenue, died when his car left the road and hit a tree. A witness, Percy Jones, who was walking his dog and saw the crash, said, 'Cars always stop at the junction with Meadow Lane. But the BMW just kept going until it hit the tree. It was like the brakes didn't work. There was a terrible mess, blood and glass everywhere.'

Kent Gazette 2 February 2000

'DOOR SLAMS SHUT ON DOTCOM FUNDING'

'The door is now firmly shut on most dotcom floats and on the market for second round fund-raising. With access to capital drying up it will

not be long before other Net stocks follow
boo.com and call in receivers.'

Sunday Times 21 May 2000

CARROLL

To Rachel and Francis: a daughter, Amy
Rebecca, 8 lb 3 oz.

The Times 27 May 2000

MR VK SINGH AND
MRS VIRGINIA CARROLL

The engagement is announced between
Virendra, oldest son of Mr and Mrs Sunil Singh
of London and Mrs Virginia Carroll of Battersea.

The Times 28 June 2000

ROTARIANS KARAOKE

Kaanapali Rotarians held a charity karaoke
luncheon in aid of the Meals on Wheels program

last Tuesday. First prize was awarded to Kent Matthews for his rendition of 'Always on My Mind'. Second prize went to Maggie Oates for her duet with Bobbie Kapua, 'It Takes Two'.

Honolulu Star-Bulletin 21 July 2000

INJECTIONS OF REALITY

Anaesthetists give other people bad dreams. What about their own? A 35 mm exploration of ambiguity on the time-space axis by first time film-maker James Carroll.

Hull International Film Festival Programme
October 2000

THE VENGABOYS

The last single by the Vengaboys, 'Forever As One', was released on 12 February 2001. It peaked at number 28 in the charts.